2004

A BRAND-NEW YEAR—
A PROMISING NEW START

Enter Sydney Omarr's star-studded world of accurate day-by-day predictions for every aspect of your life. With expert readings and forecasts, you can chart a course to romance, adventure, good health, or career opportunities while gaining valuable insight into yourself and others. Offering a daily outlook for 18 full months, this fascinating guide shows you:

- The important dates in your life
- What to expect from an astrological reading
- How the stars can help you stay healthy and fit
- Your lucky lottery numbers
  And more!

Let this expert's sound advice guide you through a year of heavenly possibilities—for today and for every day of 2004!

SYDNEY OMARR'S® DAY-BY-DAY
ASTROLOGICAL GUIDE FOR

ARIES—March 21–April 19
TAURUS—April 20–May 20
GEMINI—May 21–June 20
CANCER—June 21–July 22
LEO—July 23–August 22
VIRGO—August 23–September 22
LIBRA—September 23–October 22
SCORPIO—October 23–November 21
SAGITTARIUS—November 22–December 21
CAPRICORN—December 22–January 19
AQUARIUS—January 20–February 18
PISCES—February 19–March 20

IN 2004

SYDNEY OMARR'S®

DAY-BY-DAY ASTROLOGICAL GUIDE FOR

LEO

JULY 23–AUGUST 22

2004

With Carol Tonsing

A SIGNET BOOK

SIGNET
Published by New American Library, a division of
Penguin Group (USA) Inc., 375 Hudson Street,
New York, New York 10014, U.S.A.
Penguin Books Ltd, 80 Strand,
London WC2R 0RL, England
Penguin Books Australia Ltd, 250 Camberwell Road,
Camberwell, Victoria 3124, Australia
Penguin Books Canada Ltd, 10 Alcorn Avenue,
Toronto, Ontario, Canada M4V 3B2
Penguin Books (N.Z.) Ltd, Cnr Rosedale and Airborne Roads,
Albany, Auckland 1310, New Zealand

Penguin Books Ltd, Registered Offices:
80 Strand, London WC2R 0RL, England

First published by Signet, an imprint of New American Library,
a division of Penguin Group (USA) Inc.

First Printing, June 2003
10 9 8 7 6 5 4 3 2 1

PUBLISHER'S NOTE
While the author has made every effort to provide accurate telephone numbers
and Internet addresses at the time of publication, neither the publisher nor the
author assumes any responsibility for errors, or for changes that occur after
publication.

CONTENTS

INTRODUCTION

Leap Year and What It Means

It's Leap Year 2004! What better time to ask how February 29 came to be associated with women "popping the question" to their sweethearts?

As one legend goes, it all started in Ireland. Beloved St. Bridget complained to St. Patrick that women had to wait for a man to propose. In response, St. Patrick solved the problem by declaring that women could propose to men on the day of February 29, a day outside the domain of normal customs.

For hundreds of years, February 29 has been a window of opportunity for lovelorn lasses. In the thirteenth century Scotland passed a law that allowed women to propose on this day, and if a man declined he had to pay a fine. In twentieth-century America cartoonist Al Capp invented Sadie Hawkins Day, a day when women were allowed to trap their man by any means at hand—no doubt inspired by former Leap Year traditions.

It is a romantic custom that a man should ask for a woman's hand in marriage, going down on bended knee. (And writers of books like *The Rules* would agree.) Today, though, it's accepted practice for a woman to ask a man out on dates, lure him into bed, and even pop the question herself—never mind waiting for Leap Year.

How does astrology say a man would react? An Aries would admire her courage. A Leo would be flattered. A Cancer might want her to meet Mother first.

To celebrate Leap Year 2004, we've included some helpful astrological tips for seducing every sign. Just knowing the other person's sun sign can give you many clues to how to make your relationship a happy one. You can troubleshoot problems in advance and, if they crop up, find a way to make them work for you. This autumn, as Jupiter moves into Libra, the marriage sign, is a great time to fall in love and march down the aisle.

There are other challenges ahead in 2004. What about the possibility of changing careers? And how about coping with a midlife crisis? In this book we'll deal in many ways with the question of timing. There are the potentially difficult times, which also present positive challenges, there are the times with potential for delays and misunderstandings, and there are the best times to take risks.

For those who would like to know more about astrology, there is basic information to start you on your astrological journey. Then you can put your whole astrological portrait together by looking up the other planets in your horoscope.

Anyone with access to the Internet has a world of astrological connections available. We'll show you the best astrology Web sites, where you can find wonderful free information. And if you're interested in connecting with other astrologers, we provide an extensive resource list of contacts and organizations as well as computer program recommendations for fun or serious study.

Bring astrology into your life every day with Sydney Omarr's astonishingly accurate day-by-day forecasts for eighteen months ahead. Let this book become your astrological partner and companion, ready to enhance every aspect of your life. Here's wishing you love, happiness, health, and success in Leap Year 2004!

CHAPTER 1

What's New in 2004?

The Dance of Uranus and Neptune

Last year, the slow-moving planet Uranus moved into
Pisces. Uranus will remain in Pisces until 2011. Whenever
a slow-moving planet changes signs, there is a deep influence on the collective atmosphere. The Uranus transit
through Pisces also creates a new dynamic with planet
Neptune, which is continuing its slow transit through
Aquarius.

Planets Uranus and Neptune are doing a kind of astrological dance, called a "mutual reception." In this mutual
reception Uranus is in Pisces, the sign ruled by Neptune,
while Neptune is in Aquarius, the sign ruled by Uranus.
Mutual reception is generally considered beneficial, as
the two planets support each other. When this seven-
year dance of Uranus and Neptune is over, it is very
likely that the world will be in a very different condition
politically and socially.

Uranus in Pisces

Uranus, known as the "Great Awakener," tends to cause
both upheaval and innovation in the sign it transits. During previous episodes of Uranus in Pisces, great religions
and spiritual movements have come into being, most recently Mormonism and Christian Fundamentalism.

In its most positive mode, Pisces promotes imagination
and creativity, the art of illusion in theater and film, the

3

inspiration of great artists. A water sign, Pisces is naturally associated with all things liquid—oceans, oil, alcohol—and with those creatures that live in water—fish, the fishing industry, fish habitats. Pisces also rules the underdog, the enslaved, and the disenfranchised, whose status has been illuminated in previous Uranus in Pisces periods.

The last time Uranus was in Pisces was early in the twentieth century from 1919 to 1927, during the "roaring 20s." Prohibition of alcohol (Pisces-ruled) began in 1920, causing secret bootleg industries and speakeasy clubs where racy dancing and upbeat music signaled the "Jazz Age." A unique American music evolved, with great musicians like Louis Armstrong and George Gershwin. It was a time of innovation in the Pisces fields of film and theater, which extended to the electronic inventions of radio and television. In literature, the "Lost Generation" of American writers began publishing. Socially, the underdog triumphed. Women finally won the right to vote in 1920. Gandhi began the peaceful noncooperation movement against the British in India. Yet the underworld also thrived, such as the Mafia's secret "Cosa Nostra" and the precursor of the IRA in Ireland.

The nineteenth-century period of Uranus in Pisces, from 1836 to 1843, a time of widespread Pisces and Aquarius issues, might also give us a preview of what to expect. At that time, as the Victorian Era began, there were rumblings of women's rights. Victoria Woodhull, who would later be the first female to run for U.S. President, was born. The issue of slavery was coming to a head. The slave ship *Amistad* mutinied and ran aground on Long Island, New York, in 1839. A legal battle ensued that went to the Supreme Court, where former President John Quincy Adams argued for the rebel slaves' freedom and won. The saga of the *Amistad* has inspired books, an opera, and a major film. The Cherokee "Trail of Tears" march to Oklahoma was another dramatic and sorrowful episode. Baseball was invented. Financier J. P. Morgan and John D. Rockefeller, founder of Standard Oil, were born. Many great artists and composers, such as Cézanne, Monet, Renoir, Winslow Homer, and Tchaikovsky, were born. The Cunard Line celebrated its first Atlantic crossing. There were great inventions in photography, such as the stereoscope and the daguerreotype. The Opium Wars erupted in China. Wars between the Afghans and the British resulted in the British being driven from Afghanistan. In America, Mexicans defeated 182 Texans at the Alamo.

These moments from history could give us clues about what to expect in the current Uranus in Pisces transit. Perhaps the first woman president of the United States will be elected, and the emancipation of women in Arab countries will proceed.

· Pisces rules the prenatal phase of life, which is related to regenerative medicine. The controversy over embryonic stem cell research should continue to be debated.

Petroleum issues, both in the oil-producing countries and offshore oil drilling, will come to a head. Uranus in Pisces suggests that development of new hydroelectric sources may provide the power we need to continue our current power-thirsty lifestyle.

Just as we saw in the previous eras, there should continue to be a flourishing of the arts. We are seeing many new artistic forms developing now, such as computer-created actors and special effects. The sky's the limit on this influence.

Those who have problems with Uranus are those who resist change, so the key is to embrace the future. Those born in early Pisces, February 20 to 26, are most likely to have Uranus changes in their lives this year. Go with the flow!

Neptune in Aquarius

Neptune is a planet of imagination and creativity, but also of deception and illusion. In recent years there have been dramatic scams and scandals, especially in the high-tech area associated with Aquarius.

Neptune is associated with hospitals, which are acquiring cutting-edge technology. The atmosphere of many hospitals is already changing from the intimidating and sterile environment of the past to that of a health-promoting spa. Here alternative therapies such as massage, diet counseling, and aromatherapy are available, which tells of the Neptune and Pisces trend. New procedures in plastic surgery, also a Neptune glamour field, and antiaging therapies should restore the illusion of youth.

Those born February 1 to 5 will feel the foggy influence of Neptune this year.

Pluto in Sagittarius: Religious Intensity Continues

The slow-moving planet Pluto is our guide to life-changing, long-term trends. In Sagittarius until 2008, Pluto is emphasizing everything associated with this sign to prepare us philosophically and spiritually for things to come. Those born from December 11 to 14 will be feeling the force of Pluto this year.

Perhaps the most pervasive sign of Pluto in Sagittarius over the past few years has been globalization in all its forms. We are re-forming boundaries, creating new forms of travel. A space station may soon be one of the brightest objects in the sky.

In true Sagittarius fashion, Pluto will shift our emphasis away from acquiring wealth to a quest for the meaning of it all, as upward strivers discover that money and power are not enough and religious extremists assert themselves. Sagittarius is the sign of linking everything together. Therefore, the trend will be to find ways to interconnect on a spiritual, philosophical, and intellectual level.

The spiritual emphasis of Pluto in Sagittarius has already filtered down to our home lives. Home altars and private sanctuaries are becoming a part of our personal environment.

Pluto in Sagittarius has expanded the experience of religion into other areas of our lives. For example, vast church complexes are now being built, which combine religious activities with sports centers, health clubs, malls, and theme parks. Look for an expansion in religious education and religious book publishing as well.

Sagittarius are known for their love of animals, especially horses. Horse racing has become popular again, thanks to charismatic horses like War Emblem. America has never been more pet-happy. Look for extremes related to animal welfare, such as vegetarianism, which will become even more popular and widespread as a lifestyle. As habitats are destroyed, the care, feeding, and control of wild animals will become a larger issue, especially where there are deer, bears, and coyotes in the backyard.

The Sagittarius love of the outdoors combined with Pluto's power has already promoted extreme sports, especially those that require strong legs, like rock climbing, trekking, or snowboarding. Rugged, sporty all-terrain vehicles continue to be popular. Expect the trend toward more adventurous travel as well as fitness or sports-oriented vacations to accelerate. Exotic hiking trips to unexplored territories, mountain-climbing expeditions, spa vacations, and sports-associated resorts are part of this trend.

Publishing, which is associated with Sagittarius, has been transformed by the Internet, with an enormous variety of books available. Internet publishing is coming of age and should continue to develop under Pluto in Sagittarius. It is fascinating that the on-line bookstore Amazon.com took the Sagittarius-influenced name of the fierce female tribe of archer-warriors. There should continue to be more inspirational books, aimed at those who are interested in spirituality outside of traditional religions.

Jupiter: Who's Lucky in 2004?

Good fortune, expansion, and big money opportunities are associated with the movement of Jupiter, the planet that embodies the principle of expansion. Jupiter has a twelve-year cycle, staying in each sign for approximately one year.

When Jupiter enters a sign, the fields associated with that sign usually provide excellent opportunities. Areas of speculation associated with the sign Jupiter is passing through will have the hottest market potential—the ones that currently arouse excitement and enthusiasm.

Those born under Virgo and Libra, the signs through which Jupiter is moving in 2004, should have many opportunities during the year.

However, the key is to keep your feet on the ground. The flip side of Jupiter is that there are no limits. You can expand off the planet under a Jupiter transit, which is why the planet is often called the "Gateway to Heaven." If something is going to burst (such as an artery) or overextend or go over the top in some way, it could happen under a supposedly "lucky" Jupiter transit—so be aware. A current Jupiter-favored celebrity is embroiled in a devastating scandal because of a foolish slipup. Don't let it happen to you!

Those born under Pisces and Aries may find their best opportunities working with partners this year, as Jupiter will be transiting their seventh house of relationships.

Saturn in Cancer

Saturn gives us the rewards we work for. But first we must put in the time, be focused and disciplined. There are no shortcuts with Saturn.

Saturn is currently transiting the sign of Cancer, which has special significance for Americans. The United States is a Cancer country, born July 4, 1776, and President

George W. Bush was born under Cancer (July 7, 1946). So this country is likely to experience the restrictive influence of Saturn, but also the rewards and maturity that come after being tested.

Other Cancer areas under Saturn's influence will be: domesticity, the home and homeland, the food supply, digestion, motherhood, milk, dairy products, hotels, restaurants, boating, cruise ships, waterways, water-related industries, crabs, seafowl, the tides, the moon.

CHAPTER 2

Timing Secrets of the Stars: How to Pick the Best Time to Make Your Big Moves

Have you ever wondered if there was a lucky time to plan big events, schedule meetings and medical appointments, even change your hairstyle? Maybe you could benefit by timing an event to happen on an astrologically auspicious day.

For instance, when mischievous Mercury creates havoc with communications, you'll back up your vital computer files, read between the lines of contracts, and put off closing that deal until you have double-checked all the information. When Venus passes through your sign, you're the romantic flavor of the month. That's when your sex appeal is hottest. Get a knockout new outfit or hairstyle, then ask someone you'd like to know better to dinner. Venus timing can also help you charm clients with a stunning sales pitch or make an offer they won't refuse.

Coordinating your schedule with the stars couldn't be easier, thanks to this book! In this chapter you will learn how to find your best times as well as which times to avoid. You will also learn how to read the moods of the moon and make them work for you. Use the information and tables in this chapter and in chapter 4 on the planets, and also use the moon sign listings in your daily forecasts.

Here are the happenings to note on your agenda:

- Dates of your sun sign (high-energy period)
- The month previous to your sun sign (low-energy period)
- Dates of planets in your sign this year
- Full and new moons (Pay special attention when these fall in your sun sign!)
- Eclipses
- Moon in your sun sign every month, as well as moon in the opposite sign (listed in daily forecast)
- Mercury retrogrades
- Other retrograde periods

Your Birthday Starts Your Solar Cycle

You should feel a new surge of vitality as the powerful sun enters your sign. This is the time when predominant energies are most favorable to you. So go for it! Start new projects, make your big moves (especially when the new moon is in your sign, doubling your charisma). You'll get the recognition you deserve now, when everyone is attuned to your sun sign. Look in the tables in this book to see if other planets will also be passing through your sun sign at this time. Venus (love, beauty), Mars (energy, drive), and Mercury (communication, mental sharpness) reinforce the sun and give an extra boost to your life in the areas they affect. Venus will rev up your social and love life, making you seem especially attractive. Mars amplifies your energy and drive. Mercury fuels your brainpower and helps you communicate. Jupiter signals an especially lucky period of expansion.

There are two "down" times related to the sun. During the month before your birthday period, when you are winding up your annual cycle, you could be feeling especially vulnerable and depleted. So at that time get extra rest, watch your diet, and take it easy. Don't overstress yourself. Use this time to gear up for a big "push" when the sun enters your sign.

Another "down" time is when the sun is in a sign opposite your sun sign (six months from your birthday). That's when the prevailing energies are very different from yours. You may feel at odds with the world. You'll have to work harder for recognition because people are not on your wavelength. However, this could be a good time to work on a team, in cooperation with others, or behind the scenes.

Make the Moon Your Daily Planner

The moon is a powerful tool to divine the mood of the moment. You can work with the moon in two ways. Plan by the *sign* the moon is in; plan by the *phase* of the moon. The sign will tell you the kind of activities that suit the moon's mood. The phase will tell you the best time to start or finish a certain activity.

Working with the phases of the moon is as easy as looking up at the night sky. During the new moon, when both the sun and moon are in the same sign, begin new ventures—especially activities that are favored by that sign. Then you'll utilize the powerful energies pulling you in the same direction. You'll be focused outward, toward action, and in a doing mode. Postpone breaking off, terminating, deliberating, or reflecting—activities that require introspection and passive work. These are better suited to a later moon phase.

Get your project under way during the first quarter. Then go public at the full moon, a time of high intensity, when feelings come out into the open. This is your time to shine—to express yourself. Be aware, however, that because pressures are being released, other people will also be letting off steam. Since confrontations are possible, take advantage of this time either to air grievances or to avoid arguments. Traditionally, astrologers often advise against surgery at this time, which could produce heavier bleeding.

About three days after the full moon comes the disseminating phase, a time when the energy of the cycle begins to wind down. From the last quarter of the moon to the next new moon, it's a time to cut off unproductive relationships, do serious thinking, and focus on inward-directed activities.

You'll feel some new and full moons more strongly than others, especially those new moons that fall in your sun sign and full moons in your opposite sign. Because that full moon happens at your low-energy time of year, it is likely to be an especially stressful time in a relationship, when any hidden problems or unexpressed emotions could surface.

Full and New Moons in 2004

All dates are calculated for Eastern Standard Time and Eastern Daylight Time.

Full Moon—January 7 in Cancer
New Moon—January 21 in Aquarius

Full Moon—February 6 in Leo
New Moon—February 20 in Pisces

Full Moon—March 6 in Virgo
New Moon—March 20 in Aries

Full Moon—April 5 in Libra
New Moon—April 19 in Aries

Full Moon—May 4 in Scorpio
New Moon—May 18 in Taurus

Full Moon—June 3 in Sagittarius
New Moon—June 17 in Gemini

Full Moon—July 2 in Capricorn
New Moon—July 17 in Cancer
Full Moon—July 31 in Aquarius

13

New Moon—August 15 in Leo
Full Moon—August 29 in Pisces

New Moon—September 14 in Scorpio
Full Moon—September 28 in Aries

New Moon—October 13 in Libra
Full Moon—October 27 in Taurus

New Moon—November 12 in Scorpio
Full Moon—November 26 in Gemini

New Moon—December 11 in Sagittarius
Full Moon—December 26 in Cancer

Moon Sign Timing

To forecast the daily emotional "weather," to determine your monthly high and low days, or to synchronize your activities with the cycles of the moon, take note of the moon's sign under your daily forecast at the end of the book. Here are some of the activities favored and the moods you are likely to encounter under each moon sign.

Moon in Aries

Get moving! The new moon in Aries is an ideal time to start new projects. Everyone is pushy, raring to go, rather impatient, and short-tempered. Leave details and follow-up for later. Competitive sports or martial arts are great ways to let off steam. Quiet types could use some assertiveness, but it's a great day for dynamos. Be careful not to step on too many toes.

Moon in Taurus

It's time to lay the foundations for success. Do solid, methodical tasks like follow-through or backup work.

Make investments, buy real estate, do appraisals, do some hard bargaining. Attend to your property. Get out in the country or spend some time in your garden. Enjoy creature comforts, music, a good dinner, sensual love-making. Forget starting a diet—this is a day when you'll feel self-indulgent.

Moon in Gemini

Talk means action today. Telephone, write letters, fax! Make new contacts, stay in touch with steady customers. You can juggle lots of tasks today. It's a great time for mental activity of any kind. Don't try to pin people down—they, too, are feeling restless. Keep it light. Flirtations and socializing are good. Watch gossip—and don't give away secrets.

Moon in Cancer

This is a moody, sensitive, emotional time. People respond to personal attention, to mothering. Stay at home, have a family dinner, call your mother. Nostalgia, memories, and psychic powers are heightened. You'll want to hang on to people and things (don't clean out your closets now). You could have shrewd insights into what others really need and want. Pay attention to dreams, intuition, and gut reactions.

Moon in Leo

Everybody is in a much more confident, warm, generous mood. It's a good day to ask for a raise, show what you can do, dress like a star. People will respond to flattery, enjoy a bit of drama and theater. You may be extravagant, treat yourself royally, and show off a bit—don't break the bank! Be careful you don't promise more than you can deliver.

Moon in Virgo

Do practical down-to-earth chores. Review your budget, make repairs, be an efficiency expert. Not a day to ask for a raise. Tend to personal care and maintenance. Have a health checkup, go on a diet, buy vitamins or health food. Make your home spotless. Take care of details and piled-up chores. Reorganize your work and life so they run more smoothly and efficiently. Save money. Be prepared for others to be in a critical, faultfinding mood.

Moon in Libra

Attend to legal matters. Negotiate contracts. Arbitrate. Do things with your favorite partner. Socialize. Be romantic. Buy a special gift, a beautiful object. Decorate yourself or your surroundings. Buy new clothes. Throw a party. Have an elegant, romantic evening. Smooth over any ruffled feathers. Avoid confrontations. Stick to civilized discussions.

Moon in Scorpio

This is a day to do things with passion. You'll have excellent concentration and focus. Try not to get too intense emotionally. Avoid sharp exchanges with loved ones. Others may tend to go to extremes, get jealous, overreact. Great for troubleshooting, problem solving, research, scientific work—and making love. Pay attention to those psychic vibes.

Moon in Sagittarius

A great time for travel, philosophical discussions, setting long-range career goals. Work out, do sports, buy athletic equipment. Others will be feeling upbeat, exuberant, and adventurous. Risk taking is favored. You may feel like taking a gamble, betting on the horses, visiting a local casino, buying a lottery ticket. Teaching, writing, and spiritual activities also get the green light. Relax outdoors. Take care of animals.

Moon in Capricorn

You can accomplish a lot now, so get on the ball! Attend to business. Issues concerning your basic responsibilities, duties, family, and elderly parents could crop up. You'll be expected to deliver on promises. Weed out the deadwood from your life. Get a dental checkup. Not a good day for gambling or taking risks.

Moon in Aquarius

A great day for doing things with groups—clubs, meetings, outings, politics, parties. Campaign for your candidate. Work for a worthy cause. Deal with larger issues that affect humanity—the environment and metaphysical questions. Buy a computer or electronic gadget. Watch TV. Wear something outrageous. Try something you've never done before. Present an original idea. Don't stick to a rigid schedule—go with the flow. Take a class in meditation, mind control, yoga.

Moon in Pisces

This can be a very creative day, so let your imagination work overtime. Film, theater, music, ballet could inspire you. Spend some time alone, resting and reflecting, reading or writing poetry. Daydreams can also be profitable. Help those less fortunate. Lend a listening ear to someone who may be feeling blue. Don't overindulge in self-pity or escapism, however. People are especially vulnerable to substance abuse now. Turn your thoughts to romance and someone special.

How to Handle Eclipses

One of the most amazing phenomena, which many of us take for granted, is the spatial relationship between the sun and moon. How many of us have ever noticed or marveled that, relative to our viewpoint here on earth, both the largest source of energy (the sun) and the smallest (the moon) appear to be almost exactly the same size? Or wondered what would happen if the moon's orbit became closer to earth or farther away?

This fascinating relationship is most evident to us at the time of the solar eclipse, when the moon is directly aligned with the sun and so nearly covers it that scientists use the moment of eclipse to study solar flares. The darkening of the sun has been used in history and mythology to indicate dire happenings ahead. In some parts of the world, people hide in their homes during the darkening of the sun. When the two most powerful forces in astrology—the sun and moon—are lined up, we're sure to feel the effects both in world events and in our personal lives. Both solar and lunar eclipses are times when our natural rhythms are changed, depending on where the eclipse falls in your horoscope. If the eclipse falls on or close to your birthday, you're going to have important changes in your life, perhaps a turning point.

Lunar Eclipses

Lunar eclipse: A momentary "turnoff" that could help us turn our lives around.

A lunar eclipse happens during a full moon when the earth moves exactly between the sun and moon, breaking their natural monthly opposition. Normally, the earth is not on a level plane; otherwise, eclipses would occur every month. During a lunar eclipse, the earth "short-circuits" the connection between the sun and moon. The effect on us can be either confusion or clarity. Our subconscious lunar energies, which normally respond to the rhythmic cycle of opposing sun and moon, are momentarily turned off. This could cause a bewildering disorientation that intensifies our insecurities. On the other hand, this moment of clarity might give us insights that could help change destructive emotional patterns such as addictions.

Solar Eclipses

Solar eclipse: Deep feelings come to the surface.

The solar eclipse occurs during the new moon. This time, the moon blocks the sun's energies as it passes exactly between the sun and the earth. In astrological interpretation, the moon darkens the objective, conscious force, represented by the sun, allowing subconscious lunar forces, which activate our deepest emotions, to dominate. Emotional truths can be revealed or emotions can run wild, as our solar objectivity is cut off. If your sign is affected, you may find yourself beginning a period of work on a deep inner level. And you may have psychic experiences or deep feelings that come to the surface.

You'll start feeling the energies of an upcoming eclipse a few days after the previous new or full moon. The energy continues to intensify until the actual eclipse, then disperses for three or four days. So plan ahead at least a week or more before an eclipse, then allow several days afterward for the natural rhythms to return. Try not to make major moves during this period. (It's not a great time to get married, change jobs, or buy a home, for instance.)

Eclipses in 2004

There are four eclipses this year.

    New Moon and Solar Eclipse—April 19 in Aries
    Full Moon and Lunar Eclipse—May 4 in Scorpio
    New Moon and Solar Eclipse—October 13 in Libra
    Full Moon and Lunar Eclipse—October 27 in Taurus

Retrogrades: When the Planets Seem to Backstep

All the planets, except for the sun and moon, have times when they appear to move backward—or retrograde—as it seems from our point of view on earth. At these times, planets do not work as they normally do. So it's best to "take a break" from that planet's energies in our life and to do some work on an inner level.

Mercury Retrograde: The Key Is in "Re"

Mercury goes retrograde most often, and its effects can be especially irritating. When it reaches a short distance ahead of the sun several times a year, it seems to move backward from our point of view. Astrologers often compare retrograde motion to the optical illusion that occurs when we ride on a train that passes another train traveling at a different speed—the second train appears to be moving in reverse.

What this means to you is that the Mercury-ruled areas of your life—analytical thought processes, communications, scheduling—are subject to all kinds of confusion. Be prepared. Communications equipment can break down. Schedules may be changed on short notice. People are late for appointments or don't show up at all. Traffic is terrible. Major purchases malfunction, don't work out, or get delivered in the wrong color. Letters don't arrive or are delivered to the wrong address. Employees will make errors that have to be corrected later. Contracts don't work out or must be renegotiated.

Since most of us can't put our lives on "hold" during Mercury retrogrades, we should learn to tame the trickster and make it work for us. The key is in the prefix *re-*. This is the time to go back over things in your life, *re*flect on what you've done during the previous months. Now you can get deeper insights, spot errors you've missed. So take time to *re*view and *re*evaluate what has happened. *Re*st and *re*ward yourself—it's a good time to take a vacation, especially if you *re*visit a favorite place. *Re*organize your work and finish up projects that are backed up. Clean out your desk and closets. Throw away what you can't *re*cycle. If you must sign contracts or agreements, do so with a contingency clause that lets you *re*evaluate the terms later.

Postpone major purchases or commitments for the time being. Don't get married (unless you're *re*marrying the same person). Try not to *re*ly on other people keeping appointments, contracts, or agreements to the letter; have several alternatives. Double-check and *re*ad between the lines. Don't buy anything connected with communications or transportation (if you must, be sure to cover yourself).

Mercury retrograding through your sun sign will intensify its effect on your life.

If Mercury was retrograde when you were born, you may be one of the lucky people who don't suffer the frustrations of this period. If so, your mind probably works in a very intuitive, insightful way.

The sign in which Mercury is retrograding can give you an idea of what's in store—as well as the sun signs that will be especially challenged.

MERCURY RETROGRADES IN 2004

Mercury has four retrograde periods this year.

December 17, 2003 to January 6, 2004 from Scorpio to Sagittarius
April 6 to April 30 from Taurus to Aries
August 9 to September 2 from Virgo to Leo
November 30 to December 20 in Sagittarius

Venus Retrograde: Relationship Alert!

Retrograding Venus can cause your relationships to take a backward step, or it can make you extravagant and impractical. Shopping till you drop and buying what you cannot afford are trip-ups at this time. It's *not* a good time to redecorate—you'll hate the color of the walls later. Postpone getting a new hairstyle. Try not to fall in love either. But if you wish to make amends in an already troubled relationship, make peaceful overtures at this time.

VENUS RETROGRADES IN 2004

Venus has one retrograde period this year: May 17 to June 29 in Gemini.

Mars Moves: When to Step on the Gas

Mars shows how and when to get where you want to go. Timing your moves with Mars on your side can give you a big push. On the other hand, pushing Mars the wrong way can guarantee that you'll run into frustrations in every corner. Your best times to forge ahead are during the weeks when Mars is traveling through your sun sign or your Mars sign (look these up at the end of chapter 4 on the planets). Also consider times when Mars is in a compatible sign (fire with air signs, or earth with water signs). You'll be sure to have planetary power on your side.

MARS RETROGRADES IN 2004

There is no Mars retrograde period in 2004.

When Other Planets Retrograde

The slower-moving planets stay retrograde for months at a time (Jupiter, Saturn, Neptune, Uranus, and Pluto).

When Saturn is retrograde, it's an uphill battle with self-discipline. You may not be in the mood for work. You may feel more like hanging out at the beach than getting things done.

Neptune retrograde promotes a dreamy escapism from

reality, when you may feel you're in a fog (Pisces will feel this, especially).

Uranus retrograde may mean setbacks in areas where there have been sudden changes, when you may be forced to regroup or reevaluate the situation.

Pluto retrograde is a time to work on establishing proportion and balance in areas where there have been recent dramatic transformations.

When the planets move forward again, there's a shift in the atmosphere. Activities connected with each planet start moving ahead, plans that were stalled get rolling. Make a special note of those days on your calendar and proceed accordingly.

OTHER RETROGRADES IN 2004

The five slower-moving planets all go retrograde in 2004.

Jupiter retrogrades from January 3 to May 4 in Virgo.

Saturn retrogrades from October 25, 2003 to March 7, 2004 in Cancer, then turns retrograde again on November 8, also in Cancer, for the duration of the year.

Uranus retrogrades from June 10 to November 11 in Pisces.

Neptune retrogrades from May 17 to October 24 in Aquarius.

Pluto retrogrades from March 24 to August 30 in Sagittarius.

CHAPTER 3

Introduction to Astrology

The basic principles of astrology are easy to learn. Once you know the basics, you can penetrate beyond the realm of your sun sign into the deeper areas of this fascinating subject, which combines science, art, spirituality, and psychology. You'll find the more you know, the more you'll want to know. So let's get started.

Signs and Constellations: What's the Difference?

First, let's get our "sign language" straight because, for most readers, that's the starting point of astrology.

Signs are actually a type of celestial real estate, located on the *zodiac,* an imaginary 360-degree belt circling the earth. This belt is divided into twelve equal 30-degree portions, and these are the signs. There's confusion about the difference between the *signs* and the *constellations* of the zodiac. Constellations are patterns of stars that originally marked the twelve divisions, like signposts. Though a sign is named after the constellation that once marked the same area, the constellations are no longer in the same place relative to the earth they were centuries ago. Over hundreds of years, the earth's orbit has shifted, so that from our point of view here on earth the constellations moved. However, the signs remain in place. Most Western astrologers use the twelve-equal-part division of the zodiac. However, there are some methods of astrology that do still use the constellations instead of the signs.

Most people think of themselves in terms of their *sun sign*. A sun sign refers to the sign the sun is orbiting through at a given moment (from our point of view here on earth). For instance "I'm an Aries" means that the sun was passing through Aries when that person was born. However, there are nine other planets (plus asteroids, fixed stars, and sensitive points) that also form our total astrological personality, and some or many of these will be located in other signs. No one is completely "Aries," with all their astrological components in one sign! (Please note that, in astrology, the sun and moon are usually referred to as "planets," though of course they're not.)

As mentioned before, the sun signs are areas on the zodiac. They do not *do* anything (planets are the doers). However, they are associated with many things, depending on their location.

Why Is a Sign Defined a Certain Way?

What makes Aries the sign of go-getters, Taurus savvy with money, Gemini talk a blue streak, and Sagittarius footloose? Definitions of the signs are not accidental. They are derived from different combinations of four concepts: a sign's *element, quality (modality,* or the way it operates), polarity, and *place (order)* in the zodiac lineup.

Take the element of fire: it's hot, passionate. Then add the active cardinal mode. Give it a jolt of positive energy, and place it first in line. And doesn't that sound like the active, me-first, driving, hotheaded, energetic Aries?

Then take the element of earth: it's practical, sensual, where things grow. Add the fixed, stable mode. Give it energy that reacts to its surroundings, that settles in. Put it after Aries. Now you've got a good idea of how sensual, earthy Taurus operates.

Another way to grasp the idea is to pretend you're doing a magical puzzle based on the numbers that can divide into twelve (the number of signs): 4, 3, and 2. There are four "building blocks" or elements, three ways a sign operates (qualities), and two polarities. These alternate in turn around the zodiac, with a different combination coming up for each sign.

The Four Elements

First, consider the four elements that describe the physical concept of the sign. Is it *fiery* (dynamic), *earthy* (practical), *airy* (mental), *watery* (emotional)? Therefore, there are three zodiac signs of each of the four elements: *fire* (Aries, Leo, Sagittarius); *earth* (Taurus, Virgo, Capricorn); *air* (Gemini, Libra, Aquarius); *water* (Cancer, Scorpio, Pisces). These are the same elements that make up our planet: earth, air, fire, and water. But astrology uses the elements as *symbols* that link our body and psyche to the rhythms of the planets.

Fire signs spread warmth and enthusiasm. They are able to fire up or motivate others. They have hot tempers. These are people who make ideas catch fire and spring into existence. Earth signs are the builders of the zodiac who follow through after the initiative of fire signs to make things happen. These people are solid, practical realists who enjoy material things and sensual pleasures. They are interested in ideas that can be used to achieve concrete results. Air signs are mental people, great communicators. Following the consolidating earth signs, they'll reach out to inspire others through the use of words, social contacts, discussion, and debate. Water signs complete each four-sign series adding the ingredients of emotion, compassion, and imagination. Water sign people are nonverbal communicators who attune themselves to their surroundings and react through the medium of feelings.

The Three Qualities

The second consideration when defining a sign is how it will operate. Will it take the initiative, or move slowly and deliberately, or adapt easily? It's *quality* (or modality) will tell. There are three qualities and four signs of each quality: cardinal, fixed, and mutable.

Cardinal signs are the start-up signs that begin each season (Aries, Cancer, Libra, Capricorn). These people love to be active, involved in projects. They are usually on the fast track to success, impatient to get things under way. *Fixed signs* (Taurus, Leo, Scorpio, Aquarius) move steadily, always in control. They happen in the middle of a season, after the initial character of the season is established. Fixed signs are naturally more centered. They tend to move more deliberately, do things more slowly but thoroughly. They govern parts of your horoscope where you take root and integrate your experiences. *Mutable signs* (Gemini, Virgo, Sagittarius, Pisces) embody the principle of distribution. These are the signs that break up the cycle, then prepare the way for a change by distributing the energy to the next group. Mutables are flexible, adaptable, communicative. They can move in many directions easily, darting around obstacles.

The Two Polarities

In addition to an element and a quality, each sign has a *polarity,* either a positive or a negative electrical charge that generates energy around the zodiac, like a giant battery. Polarity refers to opposites, which you could also define as masculine/feminine, yin/yang, active/reactive. Alternating around the zodiac, the six fire and air signs are positive, active, masculine, and yang in polarity. These signs are open, expanding outward. The six earth and water signs are reactive, negative, and yin in polarity. They are nurturing and receptive, which allows the energy to develop and take shape. All positive energy would be like a car without brakes. All negative energy would be like a stalled vehicle, going nowhere. Both polarities are needed in balanced proportion.

The Order of the Signs: Their Place

Finally we must consider the *order* of the signs—that is the *place* each sign occupies in the zodiac. This consideration is vital to the balance of the zodiac and the transmission of energy throughout the zodiac. Each sign is quite different from its neighbors on either side. Yet each seems to grow out of its predecessor like links in a chain. And each transmits a synthesis of energy gathered along the chain to the following sign—beginning with the fiery, active, positive, cardinal sign of Aries and ending with the watery, mutable, reactive Pisces.

The table shows how the signs shape up according to the four characteristics discussed.

How the Signs Add Up

Sign	Element	Quality	Polarity	Place
Aries	fire	cardinal	masculine	first
Taurus	earth	fixed	feminine	second
Gemini	air	mutable	masculine	third
Cancer	water	cardinal	feminine	fourth
Leo	fire	fixed	masculine	fifth
Virgo	earth	mutable	feminine	sixth
Libra	air	cardinal	masculine	seventh
Scorpio	water	fixed	feminine	eighth
Sagittarius	fire	mutable	masculine	ninth
Capricorn	earth	cardinal	feminine	tenth
Aquarius	air	fixed	masculine	eleventh
Pisces	water	mutable	feminine	twelfth

The Houses and the Horoscope Chart

A horoscope chart is a map of the heavens at a given moment in time. It looks somewhat like a wheel divided with twelve spokes. In between each of the "spokes" is a section called a *house.*

Each house deals with a different area of life and is influenced by a special sign and a planet. In addition, the house is governed by the sign passing over the spoke (or cusp of the house) at that particular moment. For example, the first house is naturally associated with Aries and Mars. However, if Capricorn was the sign passing over the house cusp at the time the chart was cast, that house would have a Capricorn influence as well.

The houses start at the left center spoke (the number 9 position if you were reading a clock) and are read *counterclockwise* around the chart.

Astrologers look at the houses to tell in what area of a subject's life an event is happening or about to happen in the subject's career, finances, health, or other area designated by the house.

The First House: Home of Aries and Mars

The sign passing over the first house at the time of your birth is known as your *ascendant,* or *rising sign.* The first house is the house of "firsts"—the first impression you make, how you initiate matters, the image you choose to project. This is where you advertise yourself, where you project your personality. Planets that fall here will intensify the way you come across to others. Often the first house will project an entirely different type of personality than the sun sign. For instance, a Capricorn with Leo in the first house will come across as much more flamboyant than the average Capricorn.

The Second House: Home of Taurus and Venus

This house is where you experience the material world—what you value. Here are your attitudes about money, possessions, finances, whatever belongs to you, and what you own, as well as your earning and spending capacity. On a deeper level, this house reveals your sense of self-worth, the inner values that draw wealth in various forms.

The Third House: Home of Gemini and Mercury

This house describes how you communicate with others, how you reach out to others nearby, and how you interact with the immediate environment. It shows how your thinking process works and the way you express your thoughts. Are you articulate or tongue-tied? Can you think on your feet? This house also shows your first relationships, your experiences with brothers and sisters, and how you deal with people close to you such as your neighbors or pals. It's where you take short trips, write letters, or use the telephone. It shows how your mind works in terms of left-brain logical and analytical functions.

The Fourth House: Home of Cancer and the Moon

The fourth house shows the foundation of life, the psychological underpinnings. At the bottom of the chart, this house shows how you are nurtured and made to feel secure—your roots! It shows your early home environment and the circumstances at the end of your life (your final "home") as well as the place you call home now. Astrologers look here for information about the parental nurturers in your life.

The Fifth House: Home of Leo and the Sun

The fifth house is where the creative potential develops. Here you express yourself and procreate in the sense that children are outgrowths of your creative ability. But this house most represents your inner childlike self who delights in play. If your inner security has been established by the time you reach this house, you are now free to have fun, romance, and love affairs and to give of yourself. This is also the place astrologers look for playful love affairs, flirtations, and brief romantic encounters (rather than long-term commitments).

The Sixth House: Home of Virgo and Mercury

The sixth house has been called the "repair and maintenance" department. This house shows how you take care of your body and organize yourself to perform efficiently in the world. Here is where you get things done, where you look after others, and fulfill service duties such as taking care of pets. Here is what you do to survive on a day-to-day basis. The sixth house demands order in your life; otherwise there would be chaos. This house is your "job" (as opposed to your career, which is the domain of the tenth house), your diet, and your health and fitness regimens.

The Seventh House: Home of Libra and Venus

This house shows your attitude toward partners and those with whom you enter commitments, contracts, or agreements. Here is the way you relate to others, as well as your close, intimate, one-on-one relationships (including open enemies—those you "face off" with). Open hostilities, lawsuits, divorces, and marriages happen here. If the first house represents the "I," the seventh or opposite house is the "not-I"—the complementary partner you attract by the way you come across. If you are having trouble with partnerships, consider what you are attracting by the energies of your first and seventh house.

The Eighth House: Home of Scorpio and Pluto (also Mars)

The eighth house refers to how you merge with something or someone, and how you handle power and control. This is one of the most mysterious and powerful houses, where your energy transforms itself from "I" to "we." As you give up power and control by uniting with something or someone, two kinds of energies merge and become something greater, leading to a regeneration of the self on a higher level. Here are your attitudes toward sex, shared resources, taxes (what you share with the government). Because this house involves what belongs to others, you face issues of control and power struggles, or undergo a deep psychological transformation as you bond with another. Here you transcend yourself with dreams, drugs, and occult or psychic experiences that reflect the collective unconscious.

The Ninth House: Home of Sagittarius and Jupiter

The ninth house shows your search for wisdom and higher knowledge—your belief system. As the third house represents the "lower mind," its opposite on the wheel, the ninth house, is the "higher mind"—the abstract, intuitive, spiritual mind that asks "big" questions like "Why are we here?" After the third house has explored what was close at hand, the ninth stretches out to broaden you mentally with higher education and travel. Here you stretch spiritually with religious activity. Since you are concerned with how everything is related, you tend to push boundaries, take risks. Here is where you express your ideas in a book or thesis, where you pontificate, philosophize, or preach.

The Tenth House: Home of Capricorn and Saturn

The tenth house is associated with your public life and high-profile activities. Located directly overhead at the "high noon" position on the horoscope wheel, this is the most "visible" house in the chart, the one where the world sees you. It deals with your career (but not your routine "job") and your reputation. Here is where you go public, take on responsibilities (as opposed to the fourth house, where you stay home). This will affect the career you choose and your "public relations." This house is also associated with your father figure or the main authority figure in your life.

The Eleventh House: Home of Aquarius and Uranus

The eleventh house is where you extend yourself to a group, a goal, or a belief system. This house is where you define what you really want, the kinds of friends you have, your political affiliations, and the kind of groups you identify with as an equal. Here is where you become concerned with "what other people think" or where you rebel against social conventions. Here is where you could become a socially conscious humanitarian or a partygoing social butterfly. It's where you look to others to stimulate you and discover your kinship to the rest of humanity. The sign on this house can help you understand what you gain and lose from friendships.

The Twelfth House: Home of Pisces and Neptune

The twelfth house is where the boundaries between yourself and others become blurred, and you become selfless. Old-fashioned astrologers used to put a rather negative spin on this house, calling it the "house of self-undoing." When we "undo ourselves," we surrender control, boundaries, limits, and rules. But instead of being self-undoing, the twelfth house can be a place of great creativity and talent. It is the place where you can tap into the collective unconscious, where your imagination is limitless.

In your trip around the zodiac, you've gone from the "I" of self-assertion in the first house to the final house symbolizing the dissolution that happens before rebirth. It's where accumulated experiences are processed in the unconscious.

Spiritually oriented astrologers look to this house for evidence of past lives and karma. Places where we go for solitude or to do spiritual or reparatory work such as retreats, religious institutions, and hospitals belong to the twelfth house. Here is also where we withdraw from society voluntarily or involuntarily, put to prison because of antisocial activity. Selfless giving through charitable acts is part of this house, as is helpless receiving or dependence on charity.

In your daily life, the twelfth house reveals your deepest intimacies, your best-kept secrets, especially those you hide from yourself and keep repressed deep in the unconscious. It is where we surrender a sense of a separate self to a deep feeling of wholeness, such as selfless service in religion or any activity that involves merging with the greater whole. Many sports stars have important planets in the twelfth house that enable them to lay in the "zone," finding an inner, almost mystical, strength that transcends their limits.

Who's Home in Your Houses?

Houses are stronger or weaker depending on how many planets are inhabiting them. If there are many planets in a given house, it follows that the activities of that house will be especially important in your life. If the planet that rules the house is also located there, this also adds power to the house.

In the next chapter we will visit the planets.

CHAPTER 4

Know Your Planets

When you know a person's sun sign, you already know some very useful generic qualities about that person. But when you know the placement of all ten planets, that person becomes an astrological individual with a unique horoscope. Therefore, you have a much more accurate profile of the person. And, with the full planetary picture of the horoscope, you'll be much more capable of predicting how that individual will act in a given situation.

Your horoscope includes nine other planets besides the sun—the moon is regarded as a "planet," too. Each planet represents a basic force in life. The planets are the actors of the horoscope chart. The sign and house where the planet is located in the chart represents how and where this force will manifest.

The importance of a planet in your horoscope depends on its position. A planet that's close to your rising sign will be highlighted in your chart. If two or more planets are grouped together in one sign, they usually operate like a team, playing off each other rather than expressing their energy singularly. A planet that stands alone, away from the others, is usually outstanding and often calls the shots.

Each planet has two signs where it is especially at home. These are called its *dignities*. The most favorable place for a planet is in the sign or signs it rules; the next best place is in a sign where it is *exalted,* or especially harmonious. On the other hand, there are places in the horoscope where a planet has to work harder to play its role. These places are called the planets *detriment* and *fall*. The sign opposite a planet's rulership, which embodies the opposite area of life, is its *detriment*. The sign opposite its exaltation is its *fall*. Though these terms may suggest unfortunate circumstances for the planet, that is not always true. In fact, a planet that is debilitated can actually be more complete because it must stretch itself to meet the challenges of living in a more difficult sign. Like world leaders who've had to struggle for greatness, this planet may actually develop great strength and character.

Here's a list of the best places for each planet to be. Note that, as new planets were discovered, they replaced the traditional rulers of signs which best complemented their energies.

ARIES—Mars
TAURUS—Venus, in its most sensual form
GEMINI—Mercury, in its communicative role
CANCER—the moon
LEO—the sun
VIRGO—also Mercury, this time in its more critical capacity
LIBRA—also Venus, in its more aesthetic, judgmental form
SCORPIO—Pluto, replacing Mars, the sign's original ruler
SAGITTARIUS—Jupiter
CAPRICORN—Saturn
AQUARIUS—Uranus, replacing Saturn, its original ruler
PISCES—Neptune, replacing Jupiter, its original ruler

A person who has many planets in exalted signs is lucky indeed, for here is where the planet can accomplish the most and be its most influential and creative.

SUN—exalted in Aries, where its energy creates action
MOON—exalted in Taurus, where instincts and reactions operate on a highly creative level
MERCURY—exalted in Aquarius, where it can reach analytical heights

VENUS—exalted in Pisces, a sign whose sensitivity encourages love and creativity

MARS—exalted in Capricorn, a sign that puts energy to work productively

JUPITER—exalted in Cancer, where it encourages nurturing and growth

SATURN—at home in Libra, where it steadies the scales of justice and promotes balanced, responsible judgment

URANUS—powerful in Scorpio, where it promotes transformation

NEPTUNE—especially favored in Cancer, where it gains the security to transcend to a higher state

PLUTO—exalted in Pisces, where it dissolves the old cycle to make way for transition to the new

The Sun Is Always First to Consider

Your sun sign is the part of you that shines brightest. Since the sun is always the first consideration, it is important to treat it as the star of the show. It is your conscious ego. It is always center stage, even when sharing a house or a sign with several other planets. This is why sun sign astrology works for so many people. In chart interpretations, the sun can also play the parental role.

The sun rules the sign of Leo, gaining strength through the pride, dignity, and confidence of this fixed, fiery personality. It is exalted in "me-first" Aries. In its detriment, Aquarius, the sun ego is strengthened through group participation and social consciousness rather than through self-centeredness. Note how many Aquarius people are involved in politics, social work, public life, and follow the demands of their sun sign to be spokesperson for a group. In its fall, Libra, the sun needs the strength of a partner—an "other"—to enhance balance and self-expression.

Like your sun sign, each of the other nine planet's personalities is colored by the sign it is passing through at the time. For example, Mercury, the planet that rules the way you communicate, will express itself in a dynamic, headstrong Aries way if it is passing through the sign of Aries when you were born. You would communicate in a much different way if it is passing through the slower, more patient sign of Taurus. And so on through the list.

Here's a rundown of the planets and how they behave in every sign.

The Moon Expresses Your Inner Feelings

The moon can teach you about the inner side of yourself, your needs and secrets, as well as those of others. It is your most personal planet—the receptive, reflective, female, nurturing side of you. And it reflects who you were nurtured by—the "mother" or mother figure in your chart. In a man's chart, the moon position also describes his female, receptive, emotional side as well as the woman in his life who will have the deepest effect. (Venus reveals the kind of woman who attracts him physically.)

The sign the moon was passing through at your birth reflects your instinctive emotional nature, what appeals to you subconsciously. Since accurate moon tables are too extensive for this book, check through these descriptions to find the moon sign that feels most familiar. Or, better yet, have your chart calculated by a computer service to get your accurate moon placement.

The moon rules maternal Cancer and is exalted in Taurus—both comforting, home-loving signs where the natural emotional energies of the moon are easily and productively expressed. But when the moon is in the opposite signs—in its Capricorn detriment and its Scorpio fall—it leaves the comfortable nest and deals with emotional issues of power and achievement in the outside world. Those of you with the moon in these signs will find your emotional role more challenging in life.

Moon in Aries

You are an idealistic, impetuous person who falls in and out of love easily. This moon placement makes you both independent and ardent. You love a challenge, but could cool once your quarry is captured. You should cultivate patience and tolerance. Otherwise, you might gravitate toward those who treat you rough, just for the sake of challenge and excitement.

Moon in Taurus

You are a sentimental soul who is very fond of the good life. You gravitate toward solid, secure relationships. You like displays of affection and creature comforts—all the tangible trappings of a cozy, safe, calm atmosphere. You are sensual and steady emotionally, but very stubborn and determined. You can't be pushed and tend to dislike changes. You should make an effort to broaden your horizons and to take a risk sometimes.

Moon in Gemini

You crave mental stimulation and variety in life, which you usually get through an ever-varied social life or the excitement of flirtation, or multiple professional involvements—or all of these. You may marry more than once and have a rather chaotic emotional life due to your difficulty with commitment and settling down. Be sure to find a partner who is as outgoing as you are. You will have to learn at some point to focus your energies because you tend to be somewhat fragmented—to do two things at once, to have two homes, even to have two lovers. If you can find a creative way to express your many-faceted nature, you'll be ahead of the game.

Moon in Cancer

This is the most powerful lunar position. It is sure to make a deep imprint on your character. Your needs are very much associated with your reaction to the needs of others. You are very sensitive and self-protective, though some of you may mask this with a hard shell. This placement also gives an excellent memory, keen intuition, and an uncanny ability to perceive the needs of others. All of the lunar phases will affect you, especially full moons and eclipses, so you would do well to mark them on your calendar. Because you're happiest at home, you may work at home or turn your office into a second home where you can nurture and comfort people. (You may tend to "mother the world.") With natural psychic and intuitive ability, you might be drawn to occult work in some way. Or you may get professionally involved with providing food and shelter to others.

Moon in Leo

This warm, passionate moon takes everything to heart. You are attracted to all that is noble, generous, and aristocratic in life (and may be a bit of a snob). You have an innate ability to take command emotionally, but you do need strong support, loyalty, and loud applause from those you love. You are possessive of your loved ones and your turf, and will roar if anyone threatens to take over your territory.

Moon in Virgo

You are rather cool until you decide if others measure up. But once someone or something meets your ideal standards, you hold up your end of the arrangement perfectly. You may, in fact, drive yourself too hard to attain some notion of perfection. Try to be a bit easier on yourself and others. Don't always act the censor! You love to be the teacher. You are drawn to situations where you can change others for the better, but sometimes you must learn to accept others for what they are. Enjoy what you have!

Moon in Libra

A partnership-oriented moon, you may find it difficult to be alone or to do things alone. After you have learned emotional balance by leaning on yourself first, you can have excellent relationships. It is best for you to avoid extremes, which set your scales swinging and can make your love life precarious. You thrive in a rather conservative, traditional, romantic relationship where you receive attention and flattery—but not possessiveness—from your partner. You'll be your most charming in an elegant, harmonious atmosphere.

Moon in Scorpio

This is a moon that enjoys and responds to intense, passionate feelings. You may go to extremes and have a very dramatic emotional life, full of ardor, suspicion, jealousy, and obsession. It would be much healthier to channel your need for power and control into meaningful work. This is a good position for anyone in the fields of medicine, police work, research, the occult, psychoanalysis, or intuitive work, because life-and-death situations don't faze you. However, you do take personal disappointments very hard.

Moon in Sagittarius

You take life's ups and downs with good humor and the proverbial grain of salt. You'll love 'em and leave 'em, taking off on a great adventure at a moment's notice. "Born free" could be your slogan. Attracted by the exotic, you have wanderlust mentally and physically. You may be too much in search of new mental and spiritual stimulation to ever settle down.

41

Moon in Capricorn

Are you ever accused of being too cool and calculating? You have an earthy side, but you take prestige and position very seriously. Your strong drive to succeed extends to your romantic life where you will be devoted to improving your lifestyle and rising to the top. A structured situation where you can advance methodically makes you feel wonderfully secure. You may be attracted to someone older or very much younger or from a different social world. It may be difficult to look at the lighter side of emotional relationships. Though this moon is placed in the sign of its detriment, the good news is that you tend to be very dutiful and responsible to those you care for.

Moon in Aquarius

You are a people collector with many friends of all backgrounds. You are happiest surrounded by people and may feel uneasy when left alone. Though you usually stay friends with lovers, intense emotions and demanding one-on-one relationships turn you off. You don't like anything to be too rigid or scheduled. Though tolerant and understanding, you can be emotionally unpredictable and may opt for an unconventional love life. With plenty of space, you will be able to sustain relationships with liberal, freedom-loving types.

Moon in Pisces

You are very responsive and empathic to others, especially if they have problems or are the underdog. (Be on guard against attracting too many people with sob stories!) You'll be happiest if you can express your creative imagination in the arts or in the spiritual or healing professions. Because you may tend to escape in fantasies or overreact to the moods of others, you need an emotional anchor to help you keep a firm foothold in reality. Steer clear of too much escapism (especially in alcohol) or reclusiveness. Places near water soothe your moods. Working in a field that gives you emotional variety will also help you be productive.

The Personal Planets: Mercury, Venus, and Mars

These planets work in your immediate personal life.

Mercury affects how you communicate and how your mental processes work. Are you a quick study who grasps information rapidly? Or do you learn more slowly and thoroughly? How is your concentration? Can you express yourself easily? Are you a good writer? All these questions can be answered by your Mercury placement.

Venus shows what you react to. What turns you on? What appeals to you aesthetically? Are you charming to others? Are you attractive to look at? Your taste, your refinement, your sense of balance and proportion are all Venus-ruled.

Mars is your outgoing energy, your drive and ambition. Do you reach out for new adventures? Are you assertive? Are you motivated? Self-confident? Hot-tempered? How you channel your energy and drive is revealed by your Mars placement.

Mercury Is the Mental Planet

Since Mercury never travels far from the sun, read Mercury in your sun sign, then the sign preceding and following it. Then decide which reflects the way your mind works.

Mercury in Aries

Your mind is very active and assertive. You never hesitate to say what you think, never shy away from a battle.

43

In fact, you may relish a verbal confrontation. Tact is not your strong point, so you may have to learn not to trip over your tongue.

Mercury in Taurus

Though you may be a slow learner, you have good concentration and mental stamina. You want to make your ideas really happen. You'll attack a problem methodically and consider every angle thoroughly, never jumping to conclusions. You'll stick with a subject until you master it.

Mercury in Gemini

You are a wonderful communicator with great facility for expressing yourself both verbally and in writing. You love gathering all kinds of information. You probably finish other people's sentences, and express yourself with eloquent hand gestures. You can talk to anybody anytime . . . and probably have phone and e-mail bills to prove it. You read anything from sci-fi to Shakespeare, and might need an extra room just for your book collection. Though you learn fast, you may lack focus and discipline. Watch a tendency to jump from subject to subject.

Mercury in Cancer

You rely on intuition more than logic. Your mental processes are usually colored by your emotions, so you may seem shy or hesitant to voice your opinions. However, this placement gives you the advantage of great imagination and empathy in the way you communicate with others.

Mercury in Leo

You are enthusiastic and very dramatic in the way you express yourself. You like to hold the attention of groups, and could be a great public speaker. Your mind thinks big, so you prefer to deal with the overall picture rather than with the details.

Mercury in Virgo

This is one of the best places for Mercury. It should give you critical ability, attention to details, and thorough analysis. Your mind focuses on the practical side of things. This type of thinking is very well suited to being a teacher or editor.

Mercury in Libra

You're either a born diplomat who smooths over ruffled feathers or a talented debater. Many lawyers have this placement. However, since you're forever weighing the pros and cons of a situation, you may vacillate when making decisions.

Mercury in Scorpio

This is an investigative mind that stops at nothing to get the answers. You may have a sarcastic, stinging wit or a gift for the cutting remark. There's always a grain of truth to your verbal sallies, thanks to your penetrating insight.

Mercury in Sagittarius

You are a supersalesman with a tendency to expound. Though you are very broad-minded, you can be dogmatic when it comes to telling others what's good for them. You won't hesitate to tell the truth as you see it, so watch a tendency toward tactlessness. On the plus side, you have a great sense of humor. This position of Mercury is often considered by astrologers to be at a disadvantage because Sagittarius opposes Gemini, the sign Mercury rules, and squares off with Virgo, another

Mercury-ruled sign. What often happens is that Mercury in Sagittarius oversteps its bounds and loses sight of the facts in a situation. Do a reality check before making promises you may not be able to deliver.

Mercury in Capricorn

This placement endows good mental discipline. You have a love of learning and a very orderly approach to your subjects. You will patiently plod through the facts and figures until you have mastered the tasks. You grasp structured situations easily, but may be short on creativity.

Mercury in Aquarius

An independent, original thinker, you'll have more cutting-edge ideas than the average person. You will be quick to check out any unusual opportunities. Your opinions are so well-researched and grounded that once your mind is made up, it is difficult to change.

Mercury in Pisces

You have the psychic and intuitive mind of a natural poet. Learn to make use of your creative imagination. You may think in terms of helping others, but check a tendency to be vague and forgetful of details.

Venus Relates

Venus tells how you relate to others and to your environment. It shows where you receive pleasure, what you love to do. Find your Venus placement from the charts at the end of this chapter (pages 78–85) by looking for the year of your birth in the left-hand column. Then follow the line of that year across the page until you reach the time period of your birthday. The sign heading that column will be your Venus. If you were born on a day when Venus was changing signs, check the signs preceding or following that day to determine if that sign feels more like your Venus nature.

Venus in Aries

You can't stand to be bored, confined, or ordered around. But a good challenge, maybe even a rousing row, turns you on. Confess—don't you pick a fight now and then just to get someone stirred up? You're attracted by the chase, not the catch, which could cause some problems in your love life if the object of your affection becomes too attainable. You like to wear red, and you can spot a trend before anyone else.

Venus in Taurus

All your senses work in high gear. You love to be surrounded by glorious tastes, smells, textures, sounds, and visuals. Austerity is not for you! Neither is being rushed. You like time to enjoy your pleasures. Soothing surroundings with plenty of creature comforts are your cup of tea. You like to feel secure in your nest, with no sudden jolts or surprises. You like familiar objects—in fact, you may hate to let anything or anyone go.

Venus in Gemini

You are a lively, sparkling personality who thrives in a situation that affords a constant variety and a frequent change of scenery. A varied social life is important to you, with plenty of stimulation and a chance to engage in some light flirtation. Commitment may be difficult, because playing the field is so much fun.

Venus in Cancer

An atmosphere where you feel protected, coddled, and mothered is best for you. You love to be surrounded by children in a cozy, homelike situation. You are attracted to those who are tender and nurturing, who make you feel secure and well provided for. You may be quite secretive about your emotional life, or attracted to clandestine relationships.

Venus in Leo

First-class attention in large doses turns you on, and so does the glitter of real gold and the flash of mirrors. You like to feel like a star at all times, surrounded by your admiring audience. The side effect is that you may be attracted to flatterers and tinsel, while the real gold requires some digging.

Venus in Virgo

Everything neatly in its place? On the surface, you are attracted to an atmosphere where everything is in perfect order, but underneath are some basic, earthy urges. You are attracted to those who appeal to your need to teach, to be of service, or to play out a Pygmalion fantasy. You are at your best when you are busy doing something useful.

Venus in Libra

Elegance and harmony are your key words. You can't abide an atmosphere of contention. Your taste tends toward the classic, with light harmonies of color—nothing clashing, trendy, or outrageous. You love doing things with a partner, and should be careful to pick one who is decisive but patient enough to let you weigh the pros and cons. And steer clear of argumentative types!

Venus in Scorpio

Hidden mysteries intrigue you. In fact, anything that is too open and aboveboard is a bit of a bore. You surely have a stack of whodunits by the bed, along with an erotic magazine or two. You like to solve puzzles, and may also be fascinated with the occult, crime, or scientific research. Intense, all-or-nothing situations add spice to your life, and you love to ferret out the secrets of others. But you could get burned by your flair for living dangerously. The color black, spicy food, dark wood furniture, and heady perfume all get you in the right mood.

Venus in Sagittarius

If you are not actually a world traveler, your surroundings are sure to reflect your love of faraway places. You like a casual outdoor atmosphere and a dog or two to pet. There should be plenty of room for athletic equipment and suitcases. You're attracted to kindred souls who love to travel and who share your freedom-loving philosophy of life. Athletics and spiritual or New Age pursuits could be other interests.

Venus in Capricorn

No fly-by-night relationships for you! You want substance in life, and you are attracted to whatever will help you get where you are going. Status objects turn you on. And so do those who have a serious, responsible, businesslike approach as well as those who remind you of a beloved parent. It is characteristic of this placement to be attracted to someone of a different generation. Antiques, traditional clothing, and dignified behavior are becoming to you.

Venus in Aquarius

This Venus wants to make friends, to be "cool." You like to be in a group, particularly one pushing a worthy cause. You feel quite at home surrounded by people, and could even court fame. Yet all the while you remain detached from any intense commitment. Original ideas and unpredictable people fascinate you. You don't like everything to be planned out in advance, preferring spontaneity and delightful surprises.

Venus in Pisces

This Venus loves to give of yourself, and you find plenty of takers. Stray animals and people appeal to your heart and your pocketbook, but be careful to look at their motives realistically once in a while. You are extremely vulnerable to sob stories of all kinds. Fantasy, the arts (especially film, dance, and theater), and psychic or spiritual activities also speak to you.

Mars Creates Action

Mars is the mover and shaker in your life. It shows how you pursue your goals, whether you have energy to burn or proceed in a slow, steady pace. It will also show how you get angry. Do you explode or do a slow burn or hold everything inside, then get revenge later?

To find your Mars, turn to the charts on pages 86–94. Then find your birth year in the left-hand column and trace the line across horizontally until you come to the column headed by the month of your birth. There you will find an abbreviation of your Mars sign. If the description of your Mars sign doesn't ring true, read the description of the sign preceding and following it. You may have been born on a day when Mars was changing signs, in which case your Mars might be in the adjacent sign.

Mars in Aries

In the sign it rules, Mars shows its brilliant fiery nature. You have an explosive temper and can be quite impatient. On the other hand, you have tremendous courage, energy, and drive. You'll let nothing stand in your way as you race to be first! Obstacles are met head-on and broken through by force. However, those that require patience and persistence can have you exploding in rage. You're a great starter, but not necessarily around for the finish.

Mars in Taurus

Slow, steady, concentrated energy gives you staying power to last until the finish line. You have great stamina, and you never give up. Your tactic is to wear away obstacles with your persistence. Often you come out a winner because you've had the patience to hang in there. When angered, you do a slow burn.

Mars in Gemini

You can't sit still for long. This Mars craves variety. You often have two or more things going on at once—it's all an amusing game to you. Your life can get very complicated, but that only adds spice and stimulation. What drives you into a nervous, hyper state? Boredom, sameness, routine, and confinement. You can do wonderful things with your hands, and you have a way with words.

Mars in Cancer

You rarely attack head-on. Instead, you'll keep things to yourself, make plans in secret, and always cover your actions. This might be interpreted by some as manipulative, but you are only being self-protective. You get furious when anyone knows too much about you. But you do like to know all about others. Your mothering and feeding instincts can be put to good use if you work in the food, hotel, or child-care businesses. You may have to overcome your fragile sense of security, which

51

prompts you not to take risks and to get physically upset when criticized. Don't take things so personally!

Mars in Leo

You have a very dominant personality that takes center stage. Modesty is not one of your traits, nor is taking a backseat. You prefer giving the orders, and have been known to make a dramatic scene if they are not obeyed. Properly used, this Mars confers leadership ability, endurance, and courage.

Mars in Virgo

You are the faultfinder of the zodiac. You notice every detail. Mistakes of any kind make you very nervous. You may worry, even if everything is going smoothly. You may not express your anger directly, but you sure can nag. You have definite likes and dislikes, and you are sure you can do the job better than anyone else. You are certainly more industrious and detail-oriented than other signs. Your Mars energy is often most positively expressed in some kind of teaching role.

Mars in Libra

This Mars will have a passion for beauty, justice, and art. Generally, you will avoid confrontations at all costs. You prefer to spend your energy finding diplomatic solutions or weighing pros and cons. Your other techniques are passive aggression or exercising your well-known charm to get people to do what you want.

Mars in Scorpio

This is a powerful placement, so intense that it demands careful channeling into worthwhile activities. Otherwise, you could become obsessed with your sexuality or might use your need for power and control to manipulate others. You are strong-willed, shrewd, and very private about your affairs, and you'll usually have a secret agenda behind your actions. Your great stamina, focus, and discipline would be excellent assets for careers in the military or medical fields, especially research or surgery. When angry, you don't get mad—you get even!

Mars in Sagittarius

This expansive Mars often propels people into sales, travel, athletics, or philosophy. Your energies function well when you are on the move. You have a hot temper, and are inclined to say what you think before you consider the consequences. You shoot for high goals—and talk endlessly about them—but you may be weak on groundwork. This Mars needs a solid foundation. Watch a tendency to take unnecessary risks.

Mars in Capricorn

This is an ambitious Mars with an excellent sense of timing. You have an eye for those who can be of use to you, and you may dismiss people ruthlessly when you're angry. But you drive yourself hard and deliver full value. This is a good placement for an executive. You'll aim for status and a high material position in life, and you'll keep climbing despite the odds. A great Mars to have!

Mars in Aquarius

This is the most rebellious Mars. You seem to have a drive to assert yourself against the status quo. You may enjoy provoking people, shocking them out of traditional views. Or this placement could express itself in an offbeat sex life. Somehow you often find yourself in unconventional situations. You enjoy being a leader of an active group, which pursues forward-looking studies, politics, or goals.

Mars in Pisces

This Mars is a good actor who knows just how to appeal to the sympathies of others. You create and project wonderful fantasies, or you use your sensitive antennae to crusade for those less fortunate. You get what you want through creating a veil of illusion and glamour. This is a good Mars for someone in the creative and imaginative fields—a dancer, performer, photographer, actor. Many famous film stars have this placement. Watch a tendency to manipulate by making others feel sorry for you.

Jupiter Is the Optimist

Jupiter is the planet in your horoscope that makes you want *more.* This big, bright, swirling mass of gases is associated with abundance, prosperity, and the kind of windfall you get without too much hard work. You're optimistic under Jupiter's influence, when anything seems possible. You'll travel, expand your mind with higher education, and publish to share your knowledge widely. On the other hand, Jupiter's influence is neither discriminating nor disciplined. It represents the principle of growth without judgment. Therefore, if not kept in check, it could result in extravagance, weight gain, laziness, and carelessness.

Be sure to look up your Jupiter in the tables in this book. When the current position of Jupiter is favorable, you may get that lucky break. This is a great time to try new things, take risks, travel, or get more education. Opportunities seem to open up easily, so take advantage of them.

Once a year, Jupiter changes signs. That means you are due for an expansive time every twelve years, when Jupiter travels through your sun sign. You'll also have "up" periods every four years, when Jupiter is in the same element as your sun sign.

Jupiter in Aries

You are the soul of enthusiasm and optimism. Your luck-iest times are when you are getting started on an exciting project or selling an idea that you really believe in. You may have to watch a tendency to be arrogant with those who do not share your enthusiasm. You follow your impulses, often ignoring budget or other commonsense limitations. To produce real, solid benefits, you'll need patience and follow-through wherever this Jupiter falls in your horoscope.

Jupiter in Taurus

You'll spend on beautiful material things, especially those that come from nature—items made of rare woods, natural fabrics, or precious gems, for instance. You can't have too much comfort or too many sensual pleasures. Watch a tendency to overindulge in good food, or to overpamper yourself with nothing but the best. Spartan living is not for you! You may be especially lucky in matters of real estate.

Jupiter in Gemini

You are the great talker of the zodiac, and you may be a great writer, too. But restlessness could be your weak point. You jump around, talk too much, and could be a jack-of-all-trades. Keeping a secret is especially difficult, so you'll also have to watch a tendency to spill the beans. Since you love to be at the center of a beehive of activity, you'll have a vibrant social life. Your best opportunities will come through your talent for language—speaking, writing, communicating, and selling.

Jupiter in Cancer

You are luckiest in situations where you can find emotional closeness or deal with basic security needs such as food, nurturing, or shelter. You may be a great collector. Or you may simply love to accumulate things—you are the one who stashes things away for a rainy day. You probably have a very good memory and love children. In fact, you may have many children to care for. The food, hotel, child-care, and shipping businesses hold good opportunities for you.

Jupiter in Leo

You are a natural showman who loves to live in a larger-than-life way. Yours is a personality full of color that always finds its way into the limelight. You can't have too much attention or applause. Showbiz is a natural place for you, and so is any area where you can play to a crowd. Exercising your flair for drama, your natural playfulness, and your romantic nature brings you good fortune. But watch a tendency to be overly extravagant or to monopolize center stage.

Jupiter in Virgo

You actually love those minute details others find boring. To you, they make all the difference between the perfect and the ordinary. You are the fine craftsman who spots every flaw. You expand your awareness by finding the most efficient methods and by being of service to others. Many of you will be drawn to medical or teaching fields. You'll also have luck in publishing, crafts, nutrition, and service professions. Watch out for a tendency to overwork.

Jupiter in Libra

This is an other-directed Jupiter that develops best with a partner. The stimulation of others helps you grow. You are also most comfortable in harmonious, beautiful situations, and you work well with artistic people. You have a great sense of fair play and an ability to evaluate the pros and cons of a situation. You usually prefer to play the role of diplomat rather than adversary.

Jupiter in Scorpio

You love the feeling of power and control, of taking things to their limit. You can't resist a mystery. Your shrewd, penetrating mind sees right through to the heart of most situations and people. You have luck in work that provides for solutions to matters of life and death. You may be drawn to undercover work, behind-the-scenes intrigue, psychotherapy, the occult, and sex-related ventures. Your challenge will be to develop a sense of moderation and tolerance for other beliefs. This Jupiter can be fanatical. You may have luck in handling other people's money—insurance, taxes, and inheritance can bring you a windfall.

Jupiter in Sagittarius

Independent, outgoing, and idealistic, you'll shoot for the stars. This Jupiter compels you to travel far and wide, both physically and mentally, via higher education. You may have luck while traveling in an exotic place. You also have luck with outdoor ventures, exercise, and animals, particularly horses. Since you tend to be very open about your opinions, watch a tendency to be tactless and to exaggerate. Instead, use your wonderful sense of humor to make your point.

Jupiter in Capricorn

Jupiter is much more restrained in Capricorn, the sign of rules and authority. Here, Jupiter can make you overwork and heighten any ambition or sense of duty you may have. You'll expand in areas that advance your position, putting you farther up the social or corporate ladder. You are lucky working within the establishment in a very structured situation where you can show off your ability to organize and reap rewards for your hard work.

Jupiter in Aquarius

This is another freedom-loving Jupiter, with great tolerance and originality. You are at your best when you are working for a humanitarian cause and in the company of many supporters. This is a good Jupiter for a political career. You'll relate to all kinds of people on all social levels. You have an abundance of original ideas, but you are best off away from routine and any situation that imposes rigid rules. You need mental stimulation!

Jupiter in Pisces

You are a giver whose feelings and pocketbook are easily touched by others, so choose your companions with care. You could be the original sucker for a hard-luck story. Better find a worthy hospital or a charity that will appreciate your selfless support. You have a great creative imagination. You may attract good fortune in fields related to oil, perfume, pharmaceuticals, petroleum, dance, footwear, and alcohol. But beware of overindulgence in alcohol—focus on a creative outlet instead.

Saturn Puts on the Brakes

Jupiter speeds you up with *lucky breaks,* then along comes Saturn to slow you down with the *disciplinary brakes.* Saturn has unfairly been called a malefic planet, one of the bad guys of the zodiac. On the contrary, Saturn is one of our best friends, the kind who tells you what you need to hear even if it's not good news. Under a Saturn transit, we grow up, take responsibility for our lives, and emerge from whatever test this planet has in store as far wiser, more capable, and mature human beings. It is when we are under pressure that we grow stronger.

When Saturn hits a critical point in your horoscope, you can count on an experience that will make you slow up, pull back, and reexamine your life. It is a call to eliminate what is not working and to shape up. By the end of its twenty-eight-year trip around the zodiac, Saturn will have tested you in all areas of your life. The major tests happen in seven-year cycles, when Saturn passes over the *angles* of your chart—your rising sign, midheaven, descendant, and nadir. This is when the real life-changing experiences happen. But you are also in for a testing period whenever Saturn passes a *planet* in your chart or stresses that planet from a distance. Therefore, it is useful to check your planetary positions with the timetable of Saturn to prepare in advance, or at least to brace yourself.

When Saturn returns to its location at the time of your birth, at approximately age twenty-eight, you'll have your first Saturn return. At this time, a person usually takes stock or settles down to find his or her mission in life and assumes full adult duties and responsibilities.

Another way Saturn helps us is to reveal the karmic lessons from previous lives and to give us the chance to overcome them. So look at Saturn's challenges as much-needed opportunities for self-improvement. Under a Jupiter influence, you'll have more fun. But Saturn gives you solid, long-lasting results.

Look up your natal Saturn in the tables in this book for clues on where you need work.

Saturn in Aries

Saturn here puts the brakes on Aries natural drive and enthusiasm. There is often an angry side to this placement. You don't let anyone push you around, and you know what's best for yourself. Following orders is not your strong point, and neither is diplomacy. You tend to be quick to go on the offensive in relationships, attacking first, before anyone attacks you. Because no one quite lives up to your standards, you often wind up doing everything yourself. You'll have to learn to cooperate and tone down self-centeredness. Both Pat Buchanan and Saddam Hussein have this Saturn.

Saturn in Taurus

A big issue is getting control of the cash flow. There will be lean periods that can be frightening, but you have the patience and endurance to stick them out and the methodical drive to prosper in the end. Learn to take a philosophical attitude, like Ben Franklin who also had this placement and who said, "A penny saved is a penny earned."

Saturn in Gemini

You are a serious student of life, but you may have difficulty communicating or sharing your knowledge. You may be shy, speak slowly, or have fears about communicating, like Eleanor Roosevelt. You dwell in the realms of science, theory, or abstract analysis—even when you are dealing with the emotions, like Sigmund Freud who also had this placement.

Saturn in Cancer

Your tests come with establishing a secure emotional base. In doing so, you may have to deal with some very basic fears centering on your early home environment. Most of your Saturn tests will have emotional roots in those early childhood experiences. You may have difficulty remaining objective in terms of what you try to achieve. So it will be especially important for you to deal with negative feelings such as guilt, paranoia, jealousy, resentment, and suspicion. Galileo and Michelangelo also navigated these murky waters.

Saturn in Leo

This is an authoritarian Saturn—a strict, demanding parent who may deny the pleasure principle in your zeal to see that rules are followed. Though you may feel guilty about taking the spotlight, you are very ambitious and loyal. You have to watch a tendency toward rigidity, also toward overwork and holding back affection. Joseph Kennedy and Billy Graham share this placement.

Saturn in Virgo

This is a cautious, exacting Saturn. You are intensely hard on yourself. Most of all, you give yourself the roughest time with your constant worries about every little detail, often making yourself sick. You may have difficulties setting priorities and getting the job done. Your tests will come in learning tolerance and understanding of others. Charles de Gaulle, Mae West, and Nathaniel Hawthorne had this meticulous Saturn.

Saturn in Libra

Saturn is exalted here, which makes this planet an ally. You may choose very serious, older partners in life, perhaps stemming from a fear of dependency. You need to learn to stand solidly on your own before you commit to another. You are extremely cautious as you deliberate every involvement—with good reason. It is best that you find an occupation that makes good use of your sense of duty and honor. Steer clear of fly-by-night situations. Both Khrushchev and Mao Tse-tung had this placement.

Saturn in Scorpio

You have great staying power. This Saturn tests you in situations involving the control of others. You may feel drawn to some kind of intrigue or undercover work, like J. Edgar Hoover. Or there may be an air of mystery surrounding your life and death, like Marilyn Monroe and Robert Kennedy who both had this placement. There are lessons to be learned from your sexual involvements. Often sex is used for manipulation or is somehow out of the ordinary. The Roman emperor Caligula and the transvestite Christine Jorgensen are extreme cases.

Saturn in Sagittarius

Your challenges and lessons will come from tests of your spiritual and philosophical values, as happened to Martin Luther King and Gandhi. You are high-minded and sincere with this reflective, moral placement. Uncompromising in your ethical standards, you could become a benevolent despot.

Saturn in Capricorn

With the help of Saturn at maximum strength, your judgment will improve with age. And like Spencer Tracy's screen image, you'll be the gray-haired hero with a strong sense of responsibility. You advance in life slowly but steadily, always with a strong hand at the helm and an eye for the advantageous situation. Like Pat Robertson, you're likely to stand for conservative values. Negatively, you may be a loner, prone to periods of melancholy.

Saturn in Aquarius

Your tests come from relationships with groups. Do you care too much about what others think? Do you feel like an outsider, like Greta Garbo? You may fear being different from others and therefore slight your own unique, forward-looking gifts. Or like Lord Byron and Howard Hughes, you may take the opposite tack and rebel in the extreme. You can apply discipline to accomplish great humanitarian goals, as Albert Schweitzer did.

Saturn in Pisces

Your fear of the unknown and the irrational may lead you to the safety and protection of an institution. You may go on the run like Jesse James, who had this placement, to avoid looking too deeply inside. Or you might go in the opposite, more positive direction and develop a disciplined psychoanalytic approach, which puts you more in control of your feelings. Some of you will take refuge in work with hospitals, charities, or religious institutions. Queen Victoria, who had this placement, symbolized an era when institutions of all kinds were sustained. Discipline applied to artistic work, especially poetry and dance, or to spiritual work, such as yoga or meditation, might be helpful.

How Uranus, Neptune, and Pluto Influence Your Generation

These three planets remain in signs such a long time that a whole generation bears the imprint of the sign. Mass movements, great sweeping changes, fads that characterize a generation, even the issues of the conflicts and wars of the time are influenced by these "outer three" planets. When one of these distant planets changes signs, there is a definite shift in the atmosphere, the feeling of the end of an era.

Since these planets are so far away from the sun—too distant to be seen by the naked eye—they pick up signals from the universe at large. These planetary receivers literally link the sun with distant energies, and then perform a similar function in your horoscope by linking your central character with intuitive, spiritual, transformative forces from the cosmos. Each planet has a special domain, and will reflect this in the area of your chart where it falls.

Uranus: The Great Awakener

There is nothing ordinary about this quirky green planet that seems to be traveling on its side, surrounded by a swarm of moons. Is it any wonder that astrologers assigned it to Aquarius, the most eccentric and gregarious sign? Uranus seems to wend its way around the sun, marching to its own tune.

Significantly, Uranus follows Saturn, the planet of limitations and structures. Often we get caught up in the structures we have created to give ourselves a sense of security. However, if we lose contact with our spiritual roots, then Uranus is likely to jolt us out of our comfortable rut and wake us up.

Uranus energy is electrical, happening in sudden flashes. It is not influenced by karma or past events, nor does it regard tradition, sex, or sentiment. The Uranus key words are surprise and awakening. Suddenly, there's that flash of inspiration, that bright idea, that totally new approach to revolutionize whatever scheme you were undertaking. A Uranus event takes you by surprise; it happens from out of the blue, for better or for worse. The Uranus place in your life is where you awaken and become your own person, leaving the structures of Saturn behind. And it is probably the most unconventional place in your chart.

Look up the sign of Uranus at the time of your birth and see where you follow your own tune.

Uranus in Aries

Birth Dates:
  March 31, 1927–November 4, 1927
  January 13, 1928–June 6, 1934
  October 10, 1934–March 28, 1935

Your generation is original, creative, pioneering. It developed the computer, the airplane, and the cyclotron. You let nothing hold you back from exploring the unknown, and you have a powerful mixture of fire and electricity behind you. Women of your generation were among the first to be liberated. You were the unforgettable stylesetters. You have a surprise in store for everyone. Like Yoko Ono, Grace Kelly, and Jacqueline Onassis, your life may be jolted by sudden and violent changes.

Uranus in Taurus

Birth Dates:
   June 6, 1934–October 10, 1934
   March 28, 1935–August 7, 1941
   October 5, 1941–May 15, 1942

The great territorial shake of World War II began during your generation. You are independent, probably self-employed or would like to be. You have original ideas about making money, and you brace yourself for sudden changes of fortune. This Uranus can cause shakeups, particularly in finances, but it can also make you a born entrepreneur.

Uranus in Gemini

Birth Dates:
   August 7, 1941–October 5, 1941
   May 15, 1942–August 30, 1948
   November 12, 1948–June 10, 1949

You were the first children to be influenced by television. Now, in your adult years, your generation stocks up on answering machines, cell phones, computers, and fax machines—any new way you can communicate. You have an inquiring mind, but your interests may be rather short-lived. This Uranus can be easily fragmented if there is no structure and focus.

Uranus in Cancer

Birth Dates:
   August 30, 1948–November 12, 1948
   June 10, 1949–August 24, 1955
   January 28, 1956–June 10, 1956

This generation came at a time when divorce was becoming commonplace, so your home image is unconventional. You may have an unusual relationship with your parents; you may have come from a broken home or an unconventional one. You'll have unorthodox ideas about parenting, intimacy, food, and shelter. You may also be interested in dreams, psychic phenomena, and memory work.

Uranus in Leo

Birth Dates:
   August 24, 1955–January 28, 1956
   June 10, 1956–November 1, 1961
   January 10, 1962–August 10, 1962

This generation understood how to use electronic media. Many of your group are now leaders in the high-tech industries, and you also understand how to use the new media to promote yourself. Like Isadora Duncan, you may have a very eccentric kind of charisma and a life that is sparked by unusual love affairs. Your children, too, may have traits that are out of the ordinary. Where this planet falls in your chart, you'll have a love of freedom, be a bit of an egomaniac, and show the full force of your personality in a unique way, like tennis great Martina Navratilova.

Uranus in Virgo

Birth Dates:
   November 1, 1961–January 10, 1962

August 10, 1962–September 28, 1968
May 20, 1969–June 24, 1969

You'll have highly individual work methods. Many of you will be finding newer, more practical ways to use computers. Like Einstein, who had this placement, you'll break the rules brilliantly. Your generation came at a time of student rebellions, the civil rights movement, and the general acceptance of health foods. Chances are, you're concerned about pollution and cleaning up the environment. You may also be involved with nontraditional healing methods. Heavyweight champ Mike Tyson has this placement.

Uranus in Libra

Birth Dates:
    September 28, 1968–May 20, 1969
    June 24, 1969–November 21, 1974
    May 1, 1975–September 8, 1975

Your generation will be always changing partners. Born during the era of women's liberation, you may have come from a broken home and have no clear image of what a marriage entails. There will be many sudden splits and experiments before you settle down. Your generation will be much involved in legal and political reforms and in changing artistic and fashion looks.

Uranus in Scorpio

Birth Dates:
    November 21, 1974–May 1, 1975
    September 8, 1975–February 17, 1981
    March 20, 1981–November 16, 1981

Interest in transformation, meditation, and life after death signaled the beginning of New Age consciousness. Your generation recognizes no boundaries, no limits, and no external controls. You'll have new attitudes toward death and dying, psychic phenomena, and the occult. Like Mae West and Casanova, you'll shock 'em sexually, too.

Uranus in Sagittarius

Birth Dates:
    February 17, 1981–March 20, 1981
    November 16, 1981–February 15, 1988
    May 27, 1988–December 2, 1988

Could this generation be the first to travel in outer space? An earlier generation with this placement included Charles Lindbergh and a time when the first zeppelins and the Wright Brothers were conquering the skies. Uranus here forecasts great discoveries, mind expansion, and long-distance travel. Like Galileo and Martin Luther, those born in these years will generate new theories about the cosmos and mankind's relation to it.

Uranus in Capricorn

Birth Dates:
    December 20, 1904–January 30, 1912
    September 4, 1912–November 12, 1912
    February 15, 1988–May 27, 1988
    December 2, 1988–April 1, 1995
    June 9, 1995–January 12, 1996

This generation, now growing up, will challenge traditions with the help of electronic gadgets. In these years, we got organized with the help of technology put to practical use. The Internet was born following the great economic boom of the 1990s. Great leaders, who were movers and shakers of history, like Julius Caesar and Henry VIII, were born under this placement.

Uranus in Aquarius

Birth Dates:
  January 30, 1912–September 4, 1912
  November 12, 1912–April 1, 1919
  August 16, 1919–January 22, 1920
  April 1, 1995–June 9, 1995
  January 12, 1996–March 10, 2003
  September 15, 2003–December 30, 2003

The last generation with this placement produced great innovative minds such as Leonard Bernstein and Orson Welles. The next will become another radical breakthrough generation, much concerned with global issues that involve all humanity. Already this is a time of high-tech experimentation on every level, when home computers are becoming as ubiquitous as television. It is also a time of globalization, of surprise attacks (9/11), and of "wake-up" calls, as underdeveloped countries demand attention.

Uranus in Pisces

Birth Dates:
  April 1, 1919–August 16, 1919
  January 22, 1920–March 31, 1927
  November 4, 1927–January 12, 1928
  March 10, 2003–September 15, 2003
  December 20, 2003–May 28, 2010

Uranus moved into Pisces last year, ushering in a new generation that will surely spark new intuitions, innovations, and creativity in the arts as well as in the sciences. In the past century, Uranus in Pisces focused attention on the rise of such electronic entertainment as radio and the cinema as well as on the secretiveness of Prohibition. This produced a generation of idealists exemplified by Judy Garland's theme, "Somewhere Over the Rainbow." Uranus in Pisces hints at stealth activities, at hospital and prison reform, at high-tech drugs and medical experiments.

Neptune Takes You Beyond Reality

Neptune is often called the planet of dissolution. It is the "dissolver" of reality. It is often maligned as the planet of illusions, drugs, and alcohol where you escape the real world. Under Neptune's influence, you see what you want to see. But Neptune also encourages you to create, to let your imagination run free. Neptune embodies the energy of glamour, subtlety, mystery, and mysticism. It governs anything that takes you beyond the mundane world, including out-of-body experiences.

Neptune acts to break through and transcend your ordinary perceptions to take you to another level of reality where you experience either confusion or ecstasy. Neptune's force can pull you off course, but only if you allow this to happen. Those who use Neptune wisely can translate their daydreams into poetry, theater, design, or inspired moves in the business world, avoiding the tricky "con artist" side of this planet.

Find your Neptune listed below.

Neptune in Cancer

Birth Dates:
    July 19, 1901–December 25, 1901
    May 21, 1902–September 23, 1914
    December 14, 1914–July 19, 1915
    March 19, 1916–May 2, 1916

Dreams of the homeland, idealistic patriotism, and glamorization of the nurturing assets of women characterized this time. You who were born here have unusual psychic ability and deep insights into basic needs of others.

Neptune in Leo

Birth Dates:
    September 23, 1914–December 14, 1914
    July 19, 1915–March 19, 1916
    May 2, 1916–September 21, 1928
    February 19, 1929–July 24, 1929

Neptune in Leo brought us the glamour and high living of the 1920s and the big spenders of that time. The Neptune temptations of gambling, seduction, theater, and lavish entertaining distracted from the realities of the age. Those born in that generation also made great advances in the arts.

Neptune in Virgo

Birth Dates:
    September 21, 1928–February 19, 1929
    July 24, 1929–October 3, 1942
    April 17, 1943–August 2, 1943

Neptune in Virgo encompassed the 1930s, the Great Depression, and the beginning of World War II, when a new order was born. There was a time of facing "what doesn't work." Many were unemployed and found solace at the movies, watching the great Virgo star Greta Garbo or the escapist dance films of Busby Berkeley. New public services were born. Those with Neptune in Virgo later spread the gospel of health and fitness. This generation's devotion to spending hours at the office inspired the term "workaholic."

Neptune in Libra

Birth Dates:
    October 3, 1942–April 17, 1943
    August 2, 1943–December 24, 1955
    March 12, 1956–October 19, 1956
    June 15, 1957–August 6, 1957

This was the time of World War II and the postwar period, when the world regained balance and returned to relative stability. Neptune in Libra was the romantic generation who would later be concerned with relating. As this generation matured, there was a new trend toward marriage and commitment. Racial and sexual equality became important issues, as they redesigned traditional roles to suit modern times.

Neptune in Scorpio

Birth Dates:
    December 24, 1955–March 12, 1956
    October 19, 1956–June 15, 1957
    August 6, 1957–January 4, 1970
    May 3, 1970–November 6, 1970

Neptune in Scorpio brought in a generation that would become interested in transformative power. Born in an era that glamorized sex, drugs, rock and roll, and Eastern religion, they matured in a more sobering time of AIDS, cocaine abuse, and New Age spirituality. As they evolve, they will become active in healing the planet from the results of the abuse of power.

Neptune in Sagittarius

Birth Dates:
    January 4, 1970–May 3, 1970
    November 6, 1970–January 19, 1984
    June 23, 1984–November 21, 1984

Neptune in Sagittarius was the time when space and astronaut travel became a reality. The Neptune influence glamorized new approaches to mysticism, religion, and mind expansion. This generation will take a new approach to spiritual life, with emphasis on visions, mysticism, and clairvoyance.

Neptune in Capricorn

Birth Dates:
   January 19, 1984–June 23, 1984
   November 21, 1984–January 29, 1998

Neptune in Capricorn brought a time when delusions about material power were glamorized in the mid-1980s and 1990s. There was a boom in the stock market, and the Internet era spawned young tycoons who later lost it all. It was also a time when the psychic and occult worlds spawned a new category of business enterprise, and sold services on television.

Neptune in Aquarius

Birth Dates:
   January 29, 1998–April 4, 2111

This should continue to be a time of breakthroughs. Here the creative influence of Neptune reaches a universal audience. This is a time of dissolving barriers, of globalization—when we truly become one world.

Pluto: The Power Planet

Pluto is a mysterious little planet with a strange elliptical orbit that occasionally runs inside the orbit of its neighbor Neptune. Because of its eccentric path, the length of time Pluto stays in any given sign can vary from thirteen to thirty-two years. It covered only seven signs in the last century. Though it is a tiny planet, its influence is great. When Pluto zaps a strategic point in your horoscope, your life changes dramatically.

This little planet is the power behind the scenes. It affects you at deep levels of consciousness, causing events to come to the surface that will transform you and your generation. Nothing escapes, or is sacred, with this probing planet. Its purpose is to wipe out the past so something new can happen. The Pluto place in your horoscope is where you have invisible power (Mars governs the visible power)—where you can transform, heal, and affect the unconscious needs of the masses. Pluto tells lots about how your generation projects power, what makes it seem "cool" to others. And when Pluto changes signs, there's a whole new concept of what's "cool."

Pluto in Gemini

Birth Dates:
  Late 1800s–May 28, 1914

This was a time of mass suggestion and breakthroughs in communications, a time when many brilliant writers such as Ernest Hemingway and F. Scott Fitzgerald were born. Henry Miller, D. H. Lawrence, and James Joyce scandalized society by using explicit sexual images and language in their literature. "Muckraking" journalists exposed corruption. Pluto-ruled Scorpio President Theodore Roosevelt said, "Speak softly, but carry a big stick." This generation had an intense need to communicate and made major breakthroughs in knowledge. A compulsive restlessness and a thirst for a variety of experiences characterized many of this generation.

Pluto in Cancer

Birth Dates:
  May 26, 1914–June 14, 1939

Dictators and mass media arose to wield emotional power over the masses. Women's rights was a popular issue. Deep sentimental feelings, acquisitiveness, and possessiveness characterized these times and people. Most of the great stars of the Hollywood era that embodied the American image were born during this period:

Grace Kelly, Esther Williams, Frank Sinatra, Lana Turner, to name a few.

Pluto in Leo

Birth Dates:
  June 14, 1939–August 19, 1957

The performing arts played on the emotions of the masses. Mick Jagger, John Lennon, and rock and roll were born at this time. So were "baby boomers" like Bill and Hillary Clinton. Those born here tend to be self-centered, powerful, and boisterous. This generation does its own thing, for better or for worse.

Pluto in Virgo

Birth Dates:
  August 19, 1957–October 5, 1971
  April 17, 1972–July 30, 1972

This is the "yuppie" generation that sparked a mass movement toward fitness, health, and career. It is a much more sober, serious, driven generation than the fun-loving Pluto in Leo. During this time, machines were invented to process detail work efficiently. Inventions took a practical turn with answering machines, fax machines, car phones, and home office equipment—all making the workplace far more efficient.

Pluto in Libra

Birth Dates:
  October 5, 1971–April 17, 1972
  July 30, 1972–November 5, 1983
  May 18, 1984–August 27, 1984

A mellower generation, people born at this time are concerned with partnerships, working together, and finding diplomatic solutions to problems. Marriage is important to this generation, and they will redefine it by combining traditional values with equal partnership. This was a time of women's liberation, gay rights, ERA, and legal battles over abortion, all of which transformed our ideas about relationships.

Pluto in Scorpio

Birth Dates:
   November 5, 1983–May 18, 1984
   August 27, 1984–January 17, 1995

Pluto was in the sign it rules for a comparatively short period of time. In 1989, it was at its perihelion, or closest point to the sun and earth. We have all felt the transforming power somewhere in our lives. This was a time of record achievements, destructive sexually transmitted diseases, nuclear power controversies, and explosive political issues. Pluto destroys in order to create new understanding—the phoenix rising from the ashes—which should be some consolation for those of you who felt Pluto's force before 1995. Sexual shockers were par for the course during these intense years when black clothing, transvestites, body piercing, tattoos, and sexually explicit advertising pushed the boundaries of good taste.

Pluto in Sagittarius

Birth Dates:
   January 17, 1995–April 20, 1995
   November 10, 1995–January 27, 2008

During our current Pluto transit, we are being pushed to expand our horizons, to find deeper spiritual meaning in life. Pluto's opposition with Saturn in 2001 brought an enormous conflict between traditional societies and the forces of change. It signals a time when religious convictions will exert more power in our political life as well.

Since Sagittarius is the sign that rules travel, there's a good possibility that Pluto, the planet of extremes, will make space travel a reality for some of us. Already, we are seeing wealthy adventurers paying for the privilege of travel on space shuttles. Discovery of life-forms on other planets could transform our ideas about where we came from.

New dimensions in electronic publishing, concern with animal rights and the environment, and an increasing emphasis on extreme forms of religion are other signs of these times. Look for charismatic religious leaders to arise now. We'll also be developing far-reaching philosophies designed to elevate our lives with a new sense of purpose.

VENUS SIGNS 1901–2004

	Aries	Taurus	Gemini	Cancer	Leo	Virgo
1901	3/29–4/22	4/22–5/17	5/17–6/10	6/10–7/5	7/5–7/29	7/29–8/23
1902	5/7–6/3	6/3–6/30	6/30–7/25	7/25–8/19	8/19–9/13	9/13–10/7
1903	2/28–3/24	3/24–4/18	4/18–5/13	5/13–6/9	6/9–7/7	7/7–8/17
						9/6–11/8
1904	3/13–5/7	5/7–6/1	6/1–6/25	6/25–7/19	7/19–8/13	8/13–9/6
1905	2/3–3/6	3/6–4/9	7/8–8/6	8/6–9/1	9/1–9/27	9/27–10/21
	4/9–5/28	5/28–7/8				
1906	3/1–4/7	4/7–5/2	5/2–5/26	5/26–6/20	6/20–7/16	7/16–8/11
1907	4/27–5/22	5/22–6/16	6/16–7/11	7/11–8/4	8/4–8/29	8/29–9/22
1908	2/14–3/10	3/10–4/5	4/5–5/5	5/5–9/8	9/8–10/8	10/8–11/3
1909	3/29–4/22	4/22–5/16	5/16–6/10	6/10–7/4	7/4–7/29	7/29–8/23
1910	5/7–6/3	6/4–6/29	6/30–7/24	7/25–8/18	8/19–9/12	9/13–10/6
1911	2/28–3/23	3/24–4/17	4/18–5/12	5/13–6/8	6/9–7/7	7/8–11/8
1912	4/13–5/6	5/7–5/31	6/1–6/24	6/24–7/18	7/19–8/12	8/13–9/5
1913	2/3–3/6	3/7–5/1	7/8–8/5	8/6–8/31	9/1–9/26	9/27–10/20
	5/2–5/30	5/31–7/7				
1914	3/14–4/6	4/7–5/1	5/2–5/25	5/26–6/19	6/20–7/15	7/16–8/10
1915	4/27–5/21	5/22–6/15	6/16–7/10	7/11–8/3	8/4–8/28	8/29–9/21
1916	2/14–3/9	3/10–4/5	4/6–5/5	5/6–9/8	9/9–10/7	10/8–11/2
1917	3/29–4/21	4/22–5/15	5/16–6/9	6/10–7/3	7/4–7/28	7/29–8/21
1918	5/7–6/2	6/3–6/28	6/29–7/24	7/25–8/18	8/19–9/11	9/12–10/5
1919	2/27–3/22	3/23–4/16	4/17–5/12	5/13–6/7	6/8–7/7	7/8–11/8
1920	4/12–5/6	5/7–5/30	5/31–6/23	6/24–7/18	7/19–8/11	8/12–9/4
1921	2/3–3/6	3/7–4/25	7/8–8/5	8/6–8/31	9/1–9/25	9/26–10/20
	4/26–6/1	6/2–7/7				
1922	3/13–4/6	4/7–4/30	5/1–5/25	5/26–6/19	6/20–7/14	7/15–8/9
1923	4/27–5/21	5/22–6/14	6/15–7/9	7/10–8/3	8/4–8/27	8/28–9/20
1924	2/13–3/8	3/9–4/4	4/5–5/5	5/6–9/8	9/9–10/7	10/8–11/12
1925	3/28–4/20	4/21–5/15	5/16–6/8	6/9–7/3	7/4–7/27	7/28–8/21

Libra	Scorpio	Sagittarius	Capricorn	Aquarius	Pisces
8/23–9/17	9/17–10/12	10/12–1/16	1/16–2/9	2/9–3/5	3/5–3/29
			11/7–12/5	12/5–1/11	
10/7–10/31	10/31–11/24	11/24–12/18	12/18–1/11	2/6–4/4	1/11–2/6
					4/4–5/7
8/17–9/6	12/9–1/5			1/11–2/4	2/4–2/28
11/8–12/9					
9/6–9/30	9/30–10/25		1/30–2/24	2/24–3/19	3/19–4/13
		10/25–11/18	11/18–12/13	12/13–1/7	
10/21–11/14	11/14–12/8	12/8–1/1/06			1/7–2/3
8/11–9/7	9/7–10/9	10/9–12/5	1/1–1/25	1/25–2/18	2/18–3/14
	12/15–12/25	12/25–2/6			
9/22–10/16	10/16–11/9	11/9–12/3	2/6–3/6	3/6–4/2	4/2–4/27
			12/3–12/27	12/27–1/20	
11/3–11/28	11/28–12/22	12/22–1/15			1/20–2/4
8/23–9/17	9/17–10/12	10/12–11/17	1/15–2/9	2/9–3/5	3/5–3/29
			11/17–12/5	12/5–1/15	
10/7–10/30	10/31–11/23	11/24–12/17	12/18–12/31	1/1–1/15	1/16–1/28
				1/29–4/4	4/5–5/6
11/19–12/8	12/9–12/31		1/1–1/10	1/1–1/12	2/3–2/27
9/6–9/30	1/1–1/4	1/5–1/29	1/30–2/23	2/24–3/18	3/19–4/12
	10/1–10/24	10/25–11/17	11/18–12/12	12/13–12/31	
10/21–11/13	11/14–12/7	12/8–12/31		1/1–1/6	1/7–2/2
8/11–9/6	9/7–10/9	10/10–12/5	1/1–1/24	1/25–2/17	2/18–3/13
	12/6–12/30	12/31			
9/22–10/15	10/16–11/8	1/1–2/6	2/7–3/6	3/7–4/1	4/2–4/26
		11/9–12/2	12/3–12/26	12/27–12/31	
11/3–11/27	11/28–12/21	12/22–12/31		1/1–1/19	1/20–2/13
8/22–9/16	9/17–10/11	1/1–1/14	1/15–2/7	2/8–3/4	3/5–3/28
		10/12–11/6	11/7–12/5	12/6–12/31	
10/6–10/29	10/30–11/22	11/23–12/16	12/17–12/31	1/1–4/5	4/6–5/6
11/9–12/8	12/9–12/31		1/1–1/9	1/10–2/2	2/3–2/26
9/5–9/30	1/1–1/3	1/4–1/28	1/29–2/22	2/23–3/18	3/19–4/11
	9/31–10/23	10/24–11/17	11/18–12/11	12/12–12/31	
10/21–11/13	11/14–12/7	12/8–12/31		1/1–1/6	1/7–2/2
8/10–9/6	9/7–10/10	10/11–11/28	1/1–1/24	1/25–2/16	2/17–3/12
	11/29–12/31				
9/21–10/14	1/1	1/2–2/6	2/7–3/5	3/6–3/31	4/1–4/26
	10/15–11/7	11/8–12/1	12/2–12/25	12/26–12/31	
11/13–11/26	11/27–12/21	12/22–12/31		1/1–1/19	1/20–2/12
8/22–9/15	9/16–10/11	1/1–1/14	1/15–2/7	2/8–3/3	3/4–3/27
		10/12–11/6	11/7–12/5	12/6–12/31	

VENUS SIGNS 1901–2004

	Aries	Taurus	Gemini	Cancer	Leo	Virgo
1926	5/7–6/2	6/3–6/28	6/29–7/23	7/24–8/17	8/18–9/11	9/12–10/5
1927	2/27–3/22	3/23–4/16	4/17–5/11	5/12–6/7	6/8–7/7	7/8–11/9
1928	4/12–5/5	5/6–5/29	5/30–6/23	6/24–7/17	7/18–8/11	8/12–9/4
1929	2/3–3/7 4/20–6/2	3/8–4/19 6/3–7/7	7/8–8/4	8/5–8/30	8/31–9/25	9/26–10/19
1930	3/13–4/5	4/6–4/30	5/1–5/24	5/25–6/18	6/19–7/14	7/15–8/9
1931	4/26–5/20	5/21–6/13	6/14–7/8	7/9–8/2	8/3–8/26	8/27–9/19
1932	2/12–3/8	3/9–4/3	4/4–5/5 7/13–7/27	5/6–7/12 7/28–9/8	9/9–10/6	10/7–11/1
1933	3/27–4/19	4/20–5/28	5/29–6/8	6/9–7/2	7/3–7/26	7/27–8/20
1934	5/6–6/1	6/2–6/27	6/28–7/22	7/23–8/16	8/17–9/10	9/11–10/4
1935	2/26–3/21	3/22–4/15	4/16–5/10	5/11–6/6	6/7–7/6	7/7–11/8
1936	4/11–5/4	5/5–5/28	5/29–6/22	6/23–7/16	7/17–8/10	8/11–9/4
1937	2/2–3/8 4/14–6/3	3/9–4/13 6/4–7/6	7/7–8/3	8/4–8/29	8/30–9/24	9/25–10/18
1938	3/12–4/4	4/5–4/28	4/29–5/23	5/24–6/18	6/19–7/13	7/14–8/8
1939	4/25–5/19	5/20–6/13	6/14–7/8	7/9–8/1	8/2–8/25	8/26–9/19
1940	2/12–3/7	3/8–4/3	4/4–5/5 7/5–7/31	5/6–7/4 8/1–9/8	9/9–10/5	10/6–10/31
1941	3/27–4/19	4/20–5/13	5/14–6/6	6/7–7/1	7/2–7/26	7/27–8/20
1942	5/6–6/1	6/2–6/26	6/27–7/22	7/23–8/16	8/17–9/9	9/10–10/3
1943	2/25–3/20	3/21–4/14	4/15–5/10	5/11–6/6	6/7–7/6	7/7–11/8
1944	4/10–5/3	5/4–5/28	5/29–6/21	6/22–7/16	7/17–8/9	8/10–9/2
1945	2/2–3/10 4/7–6/3	3/11–4/6 6/4–7/6	7/7–8/3	8/4–8/29	8/30–9/23	9/24–10/18
1946	3/11–4/4	4/5–4/28	4/29–5/23	5/24–6/17	6/18–7/12	7/13–8/8
1947	4/25–5/19	5/20–6/12	6/13–7/7	7/8–8/1	8/2–8/25	8/26–9/18
1948	2/11–3/7	3/8–4/3	4/4–5/5 6/29–8/2	5/7–6/28 8/3–9/7	9/8–10/5	10/6–10/31
1949	3/26–4/19	4/20–5/13	5/14–6/6	6/7–6/30	7/1–7/25	7/26–8/19
1950	5/5–5/31	6/1–6/26	6/27–7/21	7/22–8/15	8/16–9/9	9/10–10/3
1951	2/25–3/21	3/22–4/15	4/16–5/10	5/11–6/6	6/7–7/7	7/8–11/9

Libra	Scorpio	Sagittarius	Capricorn	Aquarius	Pisces
10/6–10/29	10/30–11/22	11/23–12/16	12/17–12/31	1/1–4/5	4/6–5/6
11/10–12/8	12/9–12/31	1/1–1/7	1/8	1/9–2/1	2/2–2/26
9/5–9/28	1/1–1/3	1/4–1/28	1/29–2/22	2/23–3/17	3/18–4/11
	9/29–10/23	10/24–11/16	11/17–12/11	12/12–12/31	
10/20–11/12	11/13–12/6	12/7–12/30	12/31	1/1–1/5	1/6–2/2
8/10–9/6	9/7–10/11	10/12–11/21	1/1–1/23	1/24–2/16	2/17–3/12
	11/22–12/31				
9/20–10/13	1/1–1/3	1/4–2/6	2/7–3/4	3/5–3/31	4/1–4/25
	10/14–11/6	11/7–11/30	12/1–12/24	12/25–12/31	
11/2–11/25	11/26–12/20	12/21–12/31		1/1–1/18	1/19–2/11
8/21–9/14	9/15–10/10	1/1–1/13	1/14–2/6	2/7–3/2	3/3–3/26
		10/11–11/5	11/6–12/4	12/5–12/31	
10/5–10/28	10/29–11/21	11/22–12/15	12/16–12/31	1/1–4/5	4/6–5/5
11/9–12/7	12/8–12/31		1/1–1/7	1/8–1/31	2/1–2/25
9/5–9/27	1/1–1/2	1/3–1/27	1/28–2/21	2/22–3/16	3/17–4/10
	9/28–10/22	10/23–11/15	11/16–12/10	12/11–12/31	
10/19–11/11	11/12–12/5	12/6–12/29	12/30–12/31	1/1–1/5	1/6–2/1
8/9–9/6	9/7–10/13	10/14–11/14	1/1–1/22	1/23–2/15	2/16–3/11
	11/15–12/31				
9/20–10/13	1/1–1/3	1/4–2/5	2/6–3/4	3/5–3/30	3/31–4/24
	10/14–11/6	11/7–11/30	12/1–12/24	12/25–12/31	
11/1–11/25	11/26–12/19	12/20–12/31		1/1–1/18	1/19–2/11
8/21–9/14	9/15–10/9	1/1–1/12	1/13–2/5	2/6–3/1	3/2–3/26
		10/10–11/5	11/6–12/4	12/5–12/31	
10/4–10/27	10/28–11/20	11/21–12/14	12/15–12/31	1/1–4/5	4/6–5/5
11/9–12/7	12/8–12/31		1/1–1/7	1/8–1/31	2/1–2/24
9/3–9/27	1/1–1/2	1/3–1/27	1/28–2/20	2/21–3/16	3/17–4/9
	9/28–10/21	10/22–11/15	11/16–12/10	12/11–12/31	
10/19–11/11	11/12–12/5	12/6–12/29	12/30–12/31	1/1–1/4	1/5–2/1
8/9–9/6	9/7–10/15	10/16–11/7	1/1–1/21	1/22–2/14	2/15–3/10
	11/8–12/31				
9/19–10/12	1/1–1/4	1/5–2/5	2/6–3/4	3/5–3/29	3/30–4/24
	10/13–11/5	11/6–11/29	11/30–12/23	12/24–12/31	
11/1–11/25	11/26–12/19	12/20–12/31		1/1–1/17	1/18–2/10
8/20–9/14	9/15–10/9	1/1–1/12	1/13–2/5	2/6–3/1	3/2–3/25
		10/10–11/5	11/6–12/5	12/6–12/31	
10/4–10/27	10/28–11/20	11/21–12/13	12/14–12/31	1/1–4/5	4/6–5/4
11/10–12/7	12/8–12/31		1/1–1/7	1/8–1/31	2/1–2/24

VENUS SIGNS 1901–2004

	Aries	Taurus	Gemini	Cancer	Leo	Virgo
1952	4/10–5/4	5/5–5/28	5/29–6/21	6/22–7/16	7/17–8/9	8/10–9/3
1953	2/2–3/3	3/4–3/31	7/8–8/3	8/4–8/29	8/30–9/24	9/25–10/18
	4/1–6/5	6/6–7/7				
1954	3/12–4/4	4/5–4/28	4/29–5/23	5/24–6/17	6/18–7/13	7/14–8/8
1955	4/25–5/19	5/20–6/13	6/14–7/7	7/8–8/1	8/2–8/25	8/26–9/18
1956	2/12–3/7	3/8–4/4	4/5–5/7	5/8–6/23	9/9–10/5	10/6–10/31
			6/24–8/4	8/5–9/8		
1957	3/26–4/19	4/20–5/13	5/14–6/6	6/7–7/1	7/2–7/26	7/27–8/19
1958	5/6–5/31	6/1–6/26	6/27–7/22	7/23–8/15	8/16–9/9	9/10–10/3
1959	2/25–3/20	3/21–4/14	4/15–5/10	5/11–6/6	6/7–7/8	7/9–9/20
					9/21–9/24	9/25–11/9
1960	4/10–5/3	5/4–5/28	5/29–6/21	6/22–7/15	7/16–8/9	8/10–9/2
1961	2/3–6/5	6/6–7/7	7/8–8/3	8/4–8/29	8/30–9/23	9/24–10/17
1962	3/11–4/3	4/4–4/28	4/29–5/22	5/23–6/17	6/18–7/12	7/13–8/8
1963	4/24–5/18	5/19–6/12	6/13–7/7	7/8–7/31	8/1–8/25	8/26–9/18
1964	2/11–3/7	3/8–4/4	4/5–5/9	5/10–6/17	9/9–10/5	10/6–10/31
			6/18–8/5	8/6–9/8		
1965	3/26–4/18	4/19–5/12	5/13–6/6	6/7–6/30	7/1–7/25	7/26–8/19
1966	5/6–6/31	6/1–6/26	6/27–7/21	7/22–8/15	8/16–9/8	9/9–10/2
1967	2/24–3/20	3/21–4/14	4/15–5/10	5/11–6/6	6/7–7/8	7/9–9/9
					9/10–10/1	10/2–11/9
1968	4/9–5/3	5/4–5/27	5/28–6/20	6/21–7/15	7/16–8/8	8/9–9/2
1969	2/3–6/6	6/7–7/6	7/7–8/3	8/4–8/28	8/29–9/22	9/23–10/17
1970	3/11–4/3	4/4–4/27	4/28–5/22	5/23–6/16	6/17–7/12	7/13–8/8
1971	4/24–5/18	5/19–6/12	6/13–7/6	7/7–7/31	8/1–8/24	8/25–9/17
1972	2/11–3/7	3/8–4/3	4/4–5/10	5/11–6/11		
			6/12–8/6	8/7–9/8	9/9–10/5	10/6–10/30
1973	3/25–4/18	4/18–5/12	5/13–6/5	6/6–6/29	7/1–7/25	7/26–8/19
1974	5/5–5/31	6/1–6/25	6/26–7/21	7/22–8/14	8/15–9/8	9/9–10/2
1975	2/24–3/20	3/21–4/13	4/14–5/9	5/10–6/6	6/7–7/9	7/10–9/2
					9/3–10/4	10/5–11/9

Libra	Scorpio	Sagittarius	Capricorn	Aquarius	Pisces
9/4–9/27	1/1–1/2	1/3–1/27	1/28–2/20	2/21–3/16	3/17–4/9
	9/28–10/21	10/22–11/15	11/16–12/10	12/11–12/31	
10/19–11/11	11/12–12/5	12/6–12/29	12/30–12/31	1/1–1/5	1/6–2/1
8/9–9/6	9/7–10/22	10/23–10/27	1/1–1/22	1/23–2/15	2/16–3/11
	10/28–12/31				
9/19–10/13	1/1–1/6	1/7–2/5	2/6–3/4	3/5–3/30	3/31–4/24
	10/14–11/5	11/6–11/30	12/1–12/24	12/25–12/31	
11/1–11/25	11/26–12/19	12/20–12/31		1/1–1/17	1/18–2/11
8/20–9/14	9/15–10/9	1/1–1/12	1/13–2/5	2/6–3/1	3/2–3/25
		10/10–11/5	11/6–12/6	12/7–12/31	
10/4–10/27	10/28–11/20	11/21–12/14	12/15–12/31	1/1–4/6	4/7–5/5
11/10–12/7	12/8–12/31		1/1–1/7	1/8–1/31	2/1–2/24
9/3–9/26	1/1–1/2	1/3–1/27	1/28–2/20	2/21–3/15	3/16–4/9
	9/27–10/21	10/22–11/15	11/16–12/10	12/11–12/31	
10/18–11/11	11/12–12/4	12/5–12/28	12/29–12/31	1/1–1/5	1/6–2/2
8/9–9/6	9/7–12/31		1/1–1/21	1/22–2/14	2/15–3/10
9/19–10/12	1/1–1/6	1/7–2/5	2/6–3/4	3/5–3/29	3/30–4/23
	10/13–11/5	11/6–11/29	11/30–12/23	12/24–12/31	
11/1–11/24	11/25–12/19	12/20–12/31		1/1–1/16	1/17–2/10
8/20–9/13	9/14–10/9	1/1–1/12	1/13–2/5	2/6–3/1	3/2–3/25
		10/10–11/5	11/6–12/7	12/8–12/31	
10/3–10/26	10/27–11/19	11/20–12/13	2/7–2/25	1/1–2/6	4/7–5/5
			12/14–12/31	2/26–4/6	
11/10–12/7	12/8–12/31		1/1–1/6	1/7–1/30	1/31–2/23
9/3–9/26	1/1	1/2–1/26	1/27–2/20	2/21–3/15	3/16–4/8
	9/27–10/21	10/22–11/14	11/15–12/9	12/10–12/31	
10/18–11/10	11/11–12/4	12/5–12/28	12/29–12/31	1/1–1/4	1/5–2/2
8/9–9/7	9/8–12/31		1/1–1/21	1/22–2/14	2/15–3/10
9/18–10/11	1/1–1/7	1/8–2/5	2/6–3/4	3/5–3/29	3/30–4/23
	10/12–11/5	11/6–11/29	11/30–12/23	12/24–12/31	
	11/25–12/18	12/19–12/31		1/1–1/16	1/17–2/10
10/31–11/24					
8/20–9/13	9/14–10/8	1/1–1/12	1/13–2/4	2/5–2/28	3/1–3/24
		10/9–11/5	11/6–12/7	12/8–12/31	
			1/30–2/28	1/1–1/29	
10/3–10/26	10/27–11/19	11/20–12/13	12/14–12/31	3/1–4/6	4/7–5/4
			1/1–1/6	1/7–1/30	1/31–2/23
11/10–12/7	12/8–12/31				

VENUS SIGNS 1901–2004

	Aries	Taurus	Gemini	Cancer	Leo	Virgo
1976	4/8–5/2	5/2–5/27	5/27—6/20	6/20–7/14	7/14–8/8	8/8–9/1
1977	2/2–6/6	6/6–7/6	7/6–8/2	8/2–8/28	8/28–9/22	9/22–10/17
1978	3/9–4/2	4/2–4/27	4/27–5/22	5/22–6/16	6/16–7/12	7/12–8/6
1979	4/23–5/18	5/18–6/11	6/11–7/6	7/6–7/30	7/30–8/24	8/24–9/17
1980	2/9–3/6	3/6–4/3	4/3–5/12 6/5–8/6	5/12–6/5 8/6–9/7	9/7–10/4	10/4–10/30
1981	3/24–4/17	4/17–5/11	5/11–6/5	6/5–6/29	6/29–7/24	7/24–8/18
1982	5/4–5/30	5/30–6/25	6/25–7/20	7/20–8/14	8/14–9/7	9/7–10/2
1983	2/22–3/19	3/19–4/13	4/13–5/9	5/9–6/6	6/6–7/10 8/27–10/5	7/10–8/27 10/5–11/9
1984	4/7–5/2	5/2–5/26	5/26–6/20	6/20–7/14	7/14–8/7	8/7–9/1
1985	2/2–6/6	6/7–7/6	7/6–8/2	8/2–8/28	8/28–9/22	9/22–10/16
1986	3/9–4/2	4/2–4/26	4/26–5/21	5/21–6/15	6/15–7/11	7/11–8/7
1987	4/22–5/17	5/17–6/11	6/11–7/5	7/5–7/30	7/30–8/23	8/23–9/16
1988	2/9–3/6	3/6–4/3	4/3–5/17 5/27–8/6	5/17–5/27 8/28–9/22	9/7–10/4 9/22–10/16	10/4–10/29
1989	3/23–4/16	4/16–5/11	5/11–6/4	6/4–6/29	6/29–7/24	7/24–8/18
1990	5/4–5/30	5/30–6/25	6/25–7/20	7/20–8/13	8/13–9/7	9/7–10/1
1991	2/22–3/18	3/18–4/13	4/13–5/9	5/9–6/6	6/6–7/11 8/21–10/6	7/11–8/21 10/6–11/9
1992	4/7–5/1	5/1–5/26	5/26–6/19	6/19–7/13	7/13–8/7	8/7–8/31
1993	2/2–6/6	6/6–7/6	7/6–8/1	8/1–8/27	8/27–9/21	9/21–10/16
1994	3/8–4/1	4/1–4/26	4/26–5/21	5/21–6/15	6/15–7/11	7/11–8/7
1995	4/22–5/16	5/16–6/10	6/10–7/5	7/5–7/29	7/29–8/23	8/23–9/16
1996	2/9–3/6	3/6–4/3	4/3–8/7	8/7–9/7	9/7–10/4	10/4–10/29
1997	3/23–4/16	4/16–5/10	5/10–6/4	6/4–6/28	6/28–7/23	7/23–8/17
1998	5/3–5/29	5/29–6/24	6/24–7/19	7/19–8/13	8/13–9/6	9/6–9/30
1999	2/21–3/18	3/18–4/12	4/12–5/8	5/8–6/5	6/5–7/12 8/15–10/7	7/12–8/15 10/7–11/9
2000	4/6–5/1	5/1–5/25	5/25–6/13	6/13–7/13	7/13–8/6	8/6–8/31
2001	2/2–6/6	6/6–7/5	7/5–8/1	8/1–8/26	8/26–9/20	9/20–10/15
2002	3/7–4/1	4/1–4/25	4/25–5/20	5/20–6/14	6/14–7/10	7/10–8/7
2003	4/21–5/16	5/16–6/9	6/9–7/4	7/4–7/29	7/29–8/22	8/22–9/15
2004	2/8–3/5	3/5–4/3	4/3–8/7	8/7–9/6	9/6–10/3	10/3–10/28

Libra	Scorpio	Sagittarius	Capricorn	Aquarius	Pisces
9/1–9/26	9/26–10/20	1/1–1/26	1/26–2/19	2/19–3/15	3/15–4/8
10/17-11/10	11/10-12/4	12/4-12/27	12/27-1/20/78		1/4-2/2
8/6–9/7	9/7–1/7			1/20–2/13	2/13–3/9
9/17–10/11	10/11–11/4	1/7–2/5	2/5–3/3	3/3–3/29	3/29–4/23
		11/4–11/28	11/28–12/22	12/22–1/16/80	
10/30–11/24	11/24–12/18	12/18–1/11/81			1/16–2/9
8/18–9/12	9/12–10/9	10/9–11/5	1/11–2/4	2/4–2/28	2/28–3/24
			11/5–12/8	12/8–1/23/82	
10/2–10/26	10/26–11/18	11/18–12/12	1/23–3/2	3/2–4/6	4/6–5/4
			12/12–1/5/83		
11/9–12/6	12/6–1/1/84			1/5–1/29	1/29–2/22
9/1–9/25	9/25–10/20	1/1–1/25	1/25–2/19	2/19–3/14	3/14–4/7
		10/20–11/13	11/13–12/9	12/10–1/4	
10/16–11/9	11/9–12/3	12/3–12/27	12/28–1/19		1/4–2/2
8/7–9/7	9/7–1/7			1/20–2/13	2/13–3/9
9/16–10/10	10/10–11/3	1/7–2/5	2/5–3/3	3/3–3/28	3/28–4/22
		11/3–11/28	11/28–12/22	12/22–1/15	
10/29–11/23	11/23–12/17	12/17–1/10			1/15–2/9
8/18–9/12	9/12–10/8	10/8–11/5	1/10–2/3	2/3–2/27	2/27–3/23
			11/5–12/10	12/10–1/16/90	
10/1–10/25	10/25–11/18	11/18–12/12	1/16–3/3	3/3–4/6	4/6–5/4
			12/12–1/5		
11/9–12/6	12/6–12/31	12/31–1/25/92		1/5–1/29	1/29–2/22
8/31–9/25	9/25–10/19	10/19–11/13	1/25–2/18	2/18–3/13	3/13–4/7
			11/13–12/8	12/8–1/3/93	
10/16–11/9	11/9–12/2	12/2–12/26	12/26–1/19		1/3–2/2
8/7–9/7	9/7–1/7			1/19–2/12	2/12–3/8
9/16–10/10	10/10–11/13	1/7–2/4	2/4–3/2	3/2–3/28	3/28–4/22
		11/3–11/27	11/27–12/21	12/21–1/15	
10/29–11/23	11/23–12/17	12/17–1/10/97			1/15–2/9
8/17–9/12	9/12–10/8	10/8–11/5	1/10–2/3	2/3–2/27	2/27–3/23
			11/5–12/12	12/12–1/9	
9/30–10/24	10/24–11/17	11/17–12/11	1/9–3/4	3/4–4/6	4/6–5/3
11/9–12/5	12/5–12/31	12/31–1/24		1/4–1/28	1/28–2/21
8/31–9/24	9/24–10/19	10/19–11/13	1/24–2/18	2/18–3/12	3/13–4/6
			11/13–12/8	12/8	
10/15–11/8	11/8–12/2	12/2–12/26	12/26/01–	12/8/00–1/3/01	1/3–2/2
			1/18/02		
8/7–9/7	9/7–1/7/03		12/26/01–1/18	1/18–2/11	2/11–3/7
9/15–10/9	10/9–11/2	1/7–2/4	2/4–3/2	3/2–3/27	3/27–4/21
		11/2–11/26	11/26–12/21	12/21–1/14/04	
10/28–11/22	11/22–12/16	12/16–1/9/05		1/1–1/14	1/14–2/8

How to Use the Mars, Jupiter, and Saturn Tables

Find the year of your birth on the left side of each column. The dates when the planet entered each sign are listed on the right side of each column. (Signs are abbreviated to three letters.) Your birthday should fall on or between each date listed, and your planetary placement should correspond to the earlier sign of that period.

MARS SIGNS 1901–2004

Year				Year			
1901	MAR	1	Leo	1905	JAN	13	Scp
	MAY	11	Vir		AUG	21	Sag
	JUL	13	Lib		OCT	8	Cap
	AUG	31	Scp		NOV	18	Aqu
	OCT	14	Sag		DEC	27	Pic
	NOV	24	Cap	1906	FEB	4	Ari
1902	JAN	1	Aqu		MAR	17	Tau
	FEB	8	Pic		APR	28	Gem
	MAR	19	Ari		JUN	11	Can
	APR	27	Tau		JUL	27	Leo
	JUN	7	Gem		SEP	12	Vir
	JUL	20	Can		OCT	30	Lib
	SEP	4	Leo		DEC	17	Scp
	OCT	23	Vir	1907	FEB	5	Sag
	DEC	20	Lib		APR	1	Cap
1903	APR	19	Vir		OCT	13	Aqu
	MAY	30	Lib		NOV	29	Pic
	AUG	6	Scp	1908	JAN	11	Ari
	SEP	22	Sag		FEB	23	Tau
	NOV	3	Cap		APR	7	Gem
	DEC	12	Aqu		MAY	22	Can
1904	JAN	19	Pic		JUL	8	Leo
	FEB	27	Ari		AUG	24	Vir
	APR	6	Tau		OCT	10	Lib
	MAY	18	Gem		NOV	25	Scp
	JUN	30	Can	1909	JAN	10	Sag
	AUG	15	Leo		FEB	24	Cap
	OCT	1	Vir		APR	9	Aqu
	NOV	20	Lib		MAY	25	Pic

86

	JUL	21	Ari		AUG	19	Can
	SEP	26	Pic		OCT	7	Leo
	NOV	20	Ari	1916	MAY	28	Vir
1910	JAN	23	Tau		JUL	23	Lib
	MAR	14	Gem		SEP	8	Scp
	MAY	1	Can		OCT	22	Sag
	JUN	19	Leo		DEC	1	Cap
	AUG	6	Vir	1917	JAN	9	Aqu
	SEP	22	Lib		FEB	16	Pic
	NOV	6	Scp		MAR	26	Ari
	DEC	20	Sag		MAY	4	Tau
1911	JAN	31	Cap		JUN	14	Gem
	MAR	14	Aqu		JUL	28	Can
	APR	23	Pic		SEP	12	Leo
	JUN	2	Ari		NOV	2	Vir
	JUL	15	Tau	1918	JAN	11	Lib
	SEP	5	Gem		FEB	25	Vir
	NOV	30	Tau		JUN	23	Lib
1912	JAN	30	Gem		AUG	17	Scp
	APR	5	Can		OCT	1	Sag
	MAY	28	Leo		NOV	11	Cap
	JUL	17	Vir		DEC	20	Aqu
	SEP	2	Lib	1919	JAN	27	Pic
	OCT	18	Scp		MAR	6	Ari
	NOV	30	Sag		APR	15	Tau
1913	JAN	10	Cap		MAY	26	Gem
	FEB	19	Aqu		JUL	8	Can
	MAR	30	Pic		AUG	23	Leo
	MAY	8	Ari		OCT	10	Vir
	JUN	17	Tau		NOV	30	Lib
	JUL	29	Gem	1920	JAN	31	Scp
	SEP	15	Can		APR	23	Lib
1914	MAY	1	Leo		JUL	10	Scp
	JUN	26	Vir		SEP	4	Sag
	AUG	14	Lib		OCT	18	Cap
	SEP	29	Scp		NOV	27	Aqu
	NOV	11	Sag	1921	JAN	5	Pic
	DEC	22	Cap		FEB	13	Ari
1915	JAN	30	Aqu		MAR	25	Tau
	MAR	9	Pic		MAY	6	Gem
	APR	16	Ari		JUN	18	Can
	MAY	26	Tau		AUG	3	Leo
	JUL	6	Gem		SEP	19	Vir

	NOV	6	Lib		APR	7	Pic
	DEC	26	Scp		MAY	16	Ari
1922	FEB	18	Sag		JUN	26	Tau
	SEP	13	Cap		AUG	9	Gem
	OCT	30	Aqu		OCT	3	Can
	DEC	11	Pic		DEC	20	Gem
1923	JAN	21	Ari	1929	MAR	10	Can
	MAR	4	Tau		MAY	13	Leo
	APR	16	Gem		JUL	4	Vir
	MAY	30	Can		AUG	21	Lib
	JUL	16	Leo		OCT	6	Scp
	SEP	1	Vir		NOV	18	Sag
	OCT	18	Lib		DEC	29	Cap
	DEC	4	Scp	1930	FEB	6	Aqu
1924	JAN	19	Sag		MAR	17	Pic
	MAR	6	Cap		APR	24	Ari
	APR	24	Aqu		JUN	3	Tau
	JUN	24	Pic		JUL	14	Gem
	AUG	24	Aqu		AUG	28	Can
	OCT	19	Pic		OCT	20	Leo
	DEC	19	Ari	1931	FEB	16	Can
1925	FEB	5	Tau		MAR	30	Leo
	MAR	24	Gem		JUN	10	Vir
	MAY	9	Can		AUG	1	Lib
	JUN	26	Leo		SEP	17	Scp
	AUG	12	Vir		OCT	30	Sag
	SEP	28	Lib		DEC	10	Cap
	NOV	13	Scp	1932	JAN	18	Aqu
	DEC	28	Sag		FEB	25	Pic
1926	FEB	9	Cap		APR	3	Ari
	MAR	23	Aqu		MAY	12	Tau
	MAY	3	Pic		JUN	22	Gem
	JUN	15	Ari		AUG	4	Can
	AUG	1	Tau		SEP	20	Leo
1927	FEB	22	Gem		NOV	13	Vir
	APR	17	Can	1933	JUL	6	Lib
	JUN	6	Leo		AUG	26	Scp
	JUL	25	Vir		OCT	9	Sag
	SEP	10	Lib		NOV	19	Cap
	OCT	26	Scp		DEC	28	Aqu
	DEC	8	Sag	1934	FEB	4	Pic
1928	JAN	19	Cap		MAR	14	Ari
	FEB	28	Aqu		APR	22	Tau

	JUN	2	Gem
	JUL	15	Can
	AUG	30	Leo
	OCT	18	Vir
	DEC	11	Lib
1935	JUL	29	Scp
	SEP	16	Sag
	OCT	28	Cap
	DEC	7	Aqu
1936	JAN	14	Pic
	FEB	22	Ari
	APR	1	Tau
	MAY	13	Gem
	JUN	25	Can
	AUG	10	Leo
	SEP	26	Vir
	NOV	14	Lib
1937	JAN	5	Scp
	MAR	13	Sag
	MAY	14	Scp
	AUG	8	Sag
	SEP	30	Cap
	NOV	11	Aqu
	DEC	21	Pic
1938	JAN	30	Ari
	MAR	12	Tau
	APR	23	Gem
	JUN	7	Can
	JUL	22	Leo
	SEP	7	Vir
	OCT	25	Lib
	DEC	11	Scp
1939	JAN	29	Sag
	MAR	21	Cap
	MAY	25	Aqu
	JUL	21	Cap
	SEP	24	Aqu
	NOV	19	Pic
1940	JAN	4	Ari
	FEB	17	Tau
	APR	1	Gem
	MAY	17	Can
	JUL	3	Leo

	AUG	19	Vir
	OCT	5	Lib
	NOV	20	Scp
1941	JAN	4	Sag
	FEB	17	Cap
	APR	2	Aqu
	MAY	16	Pic
	JUL	2	Ari
1942	JAN	11	Tau
	MAR	7	Gem
	APR	26	Can
	JUN	14	Leo
	AUG	1	Vir
	SEP	17	Lib
	NOV	1	Scp
	DEC	15	Sag
1943	JAN	26	Cap
	MAR	8	Aqu
	APR	17	Pic
	MAY	27	Ari
	JUL	7	Tau
	AUG	23	Gem
1944	MAR	28	Can
	MAY	22	Leo
	JUL	12	Vir
	AUG	29	Lib
	OCT	13	Scp
	NOV	25	Sag
1945	JAN	5	Cap
	FEB	14	Aqu
	MAR	25	Pic
	MAY	2	Ari
	JUN	11	Tau
	JUL	23	Gem
	SEP	7	Can
	NOV	11	Leo
	DEC	26	Can
1946	APR	22	Leo
	JUN	20	Vir
	AUG	9	Lib
	SEP	24	Scp
	NOV	6	Sag
	DEC	17	Cap

1947	JAN	25	Aqu		MAR	20	Tau
	MAR	4	Pic		MAY	1	Gem
	APR	11	Ari		JUN	14	Can
	MAY	21	Tau		JUL	29	Leo
	JUL	1	Gem		SEP	14	Vir
	AUG	13	Can		NOV	1	Lib
	OCT	1	Leo		DEC	20	Scp
	DEC	1	Vir	1954	FEB	9	Sag
1948	FEB	12	Leo		APR	12	Cap
	MAY	18	Vir		JUL	3	Sag
	JUL	17	Lib		AUG	24	Cap
	SEP	3	Scp		OCT	21	Aqu
	OCT	17	Sag		DEC	4	Pic
	NOV	26	Cap	1955	JAN	15	Ari
1949	JAN	4	Aqu		FEB	26	Tau
	FEB	11	Pic		APR	10	Gem
	MAR	21	Ari		MAY	26	Can
	APR	30	Tau		JUL	11	Leo
	JUN	10	Gem		AUG	27	Vir
	JUL	23	Can		OCT	13	Lib
	SEP	7	Leo		NOV	29	Scp
	OCT	27	Vir	1956	JAN	14	Sag
	DEC	26	Lib		FEB	28	Cap
1950	MAR	28	Vir		APR	14	Aqu
	JUN	11	Lib		JUN	3	Pic
	AUG	10	Scp		DEC	6	Ari
	SEP	25	Sag	1957	JAN	28	Tau
	NOV	6	Cap		MAR	17	Gem
	DEC	15	Aqu		MAY	4	Can
1951	JAN	22	Pic		JUN	21	Leo
	MAR	1	Ari		AUG	8	Vir
	APR	10	Tau		SEP	24	Lib
	MAY	21	Gem		NOV	8	Scp
	JUL	3	Can		DEC	23	Sag
	AUG	18	Leo	1958	FEB	3	Cap
	OCT	5	Vir		MAR	17	Aqu
	NOV	24	Lib		APR	27	Pic
1952	JAN	20	Scp		JUN	7	Ari
	AUG	27	Sag		JUL	21	Tau
	OCT	12	Cap		SEP	21	Gem
	NOV	21	Aqu		OCT	29	Tau
	DEC	30	Pic	1959	FEB	10	Gem
1953	FEB	8	Ari		APR	10	Can

	JUN	1	Leo		NOV	14	Cap
	JUL	20	Vir		DEC	23	Aqu
	SEP	5	Lib	1966	JAN	30	Pic
	OCT	21	Scp		MAR	9	Ari
	DEC	3	Sag		APR	17	Tau
1960	JAN	14	Cap		MAY	28	Gem
	FEB	23	Aqu		JUL	11	Can
	APR	2	Pic		AUG	25	Leo
	MAY	11	Ari		OCT	12	Vir
	JUN	20	Tau		DEC	4	Lib
	AUG	2	Gem	1967	FEB	12	Scp
	SEP	21	Can		MAR	31	Lib
1961	FEB	5	Gem		JUL	19	Scp
	FEB	7	Can		SEP	10	Sag
	MAY	6	Leo		OCT	23	Cap
	JUN	28	Vir		DEC	1	Aqu
	AUG	17	Lib	1968	JAN	9	Pic
	OCT	1	Scp		FEB	17	Ari
	NOV	13	Sag		MAR	27	Tau
	DEC	24	Cap		MAY	8	Gem
1962	FEB	1	Aqu		JUN	21	Can
	MAR	12	Pic		AUG	5	Leo
	APR	19	Ari		SEP	21	Vir
	MAY	28	Tau		NOV	9	Lib
	JUL	9	Gem		DEC	29	Scp
	AUG	22	Can	1969	FEB	25	Sag
	OCT	11	Leo		SEP	21	Cap
1963	JUN	3	Vir		NOV	4	Aqu
	JUL	27	Lib		DEC	15	Pic
	SEP	12	Scp	1970	JAN	24	Ari
	OCT	25	Sag		MAR	7	Tau
	DEC	5	Cap		APR	18	Gem
1964	JAN	13	Aqu		JUN	2	Can
	FEB	20	Pic		JUL	18	Leo
	MAR	29	Ari		SEP	3	Vir
	MAY	7	Tau		OCT	20	Lib
	JUN	17	Gem		DEC	6	Scp
	JUL	30	Can	1971	JAN	23	Sag
	SEP	15	Leo		MAR	12	Cap
	NOV	6	Vir		MAY	3	Aqu
1965	JUN	29	Lib		NOV	6	Pic
	AUG	20	Scp		DEC	26	Ari
	OCT	4	Sag	1972	FEB	10	Tau

	MAR	27	Gem	1978	JAN	26	Can
	MAY	12	Can		APR	10	Leo
	JUN	28	Leo		JUN	14	Vir
	AUG	15	Vir		AUG	4	Lib
	SEP	30	Lib		SEP	19	Scp
	NOV	15	Scp		NOV	2	Sag
	DEC	30	Sag		DEC	12	Cap
1973	FEB	12	Cap	1979	JAN	20	Aqu
	MAR	26	Aqu		FEB	27	Pic
	MAY	8	Pic		APR	7	Ari
	JUN	20	Ari		MAY	16	Tau
	AUG	12	Tau		JUN	26	Gem
	OCT	29	Ari		AUG	8	Can
	DEC	24	Tau		SEP	24	Leo
1974	FEB	27	Gem		NOV	19	Vir
	APR	20	Can	1980	MAR	11	Leo
	JUN	9	Leo		MAY	4	Vir
	JUL	27	Vir		JUL	10	Lib
	SEP	12	Lib		AUG	29	Scp
	OCT	28	Scp		OCT	12	Sag
	DEC	10	Sag		NOV	22	Cap
1975	JAN	21	Cap		DEC	30	Aqu
	MAR	3	Aqu	1981	FEB	6	Pic
	APR	11	Pic		MAR	17	Ari
	MAY	21	Ari		APR	25	Tau
	JUL	1	Tau		JUN	5	Gem
	AUG	14	Gem		JUL	18	Can
	OCT	17	Can		SEP	2	Leo
	NOV	25	Gem		OCT	21	Vir
1976	MAR	18	Can		DEC	16	Lib
	MAY	16	Leo	1982	AUG	3	Scp
	JUL	6	Vir		SEP	20	Sag
	AUG	24	Lib		OCT	31	Cap
	OCT	8	Scp		DEC	10	Aqu
	NOV	20	Sag	1983	JAN	17	Pic
1977	JAN	1	Cap		FEB	25	Ari
	FEB	9	Aqu		APR	5	Tau
	MAR	20	Pic		MAY	16	Gem
	APR	27	Ari		JUN	29	Can
	JUN	6	Tau		AUG	13	Leo
	JUL	17	Gem		SEP	30	Vir
	SEP	1	Can		NOV	18	Lib
	OCT	26	Leo	1984	JAN	11	Scp

	AUG	17	Sag		JUL	12	Tau
	OCT	5	Cap		AUG	31	Gem
	NOV	15	Aqu		DEC	14	Tau
	DEC	25	Pic	1991	JAN	21	Gem
1985	FEB	2	Ari		APR	3	Can
	MAR	15	Tau		MAY	26	Leo
	APR	26	Gem		JUL	15	Vir
	JUN	9	Can		SEP	1	Lib
	JUL	25	Leo		OCT	16	Scp
	SEP	10	Vir		NOV	29	Sag
	OCT	27	Lib	1992	JAN	9	Cap
	DEC	14	Scp		FEB	18	Aqu
1986	FEB	2	Sag		MAR	28	Pic
	MAR	28	Cap		MAY	5	Ari
	OCT	9	Aqu		JUN	14	Tau
	NOV	26	Pic		JUL	26	Gem
1987	JAN	8	Ari		SEP	12	Can
	FEB	20	Tau	1993	APR	27	Leo
	APR	5	Gem		JUN	23	Vir
	MAY	21	Can		AUG	12	Lib
	JUL	6	Leo		SEP	27	Scp
	AUG	22	Vir		NOV	9	Sag
	OCT	8	Lib		DEC	20	Cap
	NOV	24	Scp	1994	JAN	28	Aqu
1988	JAN	8	Sag		MAR	7	Pic
	FEB	22	Cap		APR	14	Ari
	APR	6	Aqu		MAY	23	Tau
	MAY	22	Pic		JUL	3	Gem
	JUL	13	Ari		AUG	16	Can
	OCT	23	Pic		OCT	4	Leo
	NOV	1	Ari		DEC	12	Vir
1989	JAN	19	Tau	1995	JAN	22	Leo
	MAR	11	Gem		MAY	25	Vir
	APR	29	Can		JUL	21	Lib
	JUN	16	Leo		SEP	7	Scp
	AUG	3	Vir		OCT	20	Sag
	SEP	19	Lib		NOV	30	Cap
	NOV	4	Scp	1996	JAN	8	Aqu
	DEC	18	Sag		FEB	15	Pic
1990	JAN	29	Cap		MAR	24	Ari
	MAR	11	Aqu		MAY	2	Tau
	APR	20	Pic		JUN	12	Gem
	MAY	31	Ari		JUL	25	Can

Year	Mon	Day	Sign	Year	Mon	Day	Sign
	SEP	9	Leo		SEP	17	Vir
	OCT	30	Vir		NOV	4	Lib
1997	JAN	3	Lib		DEC	23	Scp
	MAR	8	Vir	2001	FEB	14	Sag
	JUN	19	Lib		SEP	8	Cap
	AUG	14	Scp		OCT	27	Aqu
	SEP	28	Sag		DEC	8	Pic
	NOV	9	Cap	2002	JAN	18	Ari
	DEC	18	Aqu		MAR	1	Tau
1998	JAN	25	Pic		APR	13	Gem
	MAR	4	Ari		MAY	28	Can
	APR	13	Tau		JUL	13	Leo
	MAY	24	Gem		AUG	29	Vir
	JUL	6	Can		OCT	15	Lib
	AUG	20	Leo		DEC	1	Scp
	OCT	7	Vir	2003	JAN	17	Sag
	NOV	27	Lib		MAR	4	Cap
1999	JAN	26	Scp		APR	21	Aqu
	MAY	5	Lib		JUN	17	Pic
	JUL	5	Scp		DEC	16	Ari
	SEP	2	Sag	2004	FEB	3	Tau
	OCT	17	Cap		MAR	21	Gem
	NOV	26	Aqu		MAY	7	Can
2000	JAN	4	Pic		JUN	23	Leo
	FEB	12	Ari		AUG	10	Vir
	MAR	23	Tau		SEP	26	Lib
	MAY	3	Gem		NOV	11	Sep
	JUN	16	Can		DEC	25	Sag
	AUG	1	Leo				

JUPITER SIGNS 1901–2004

Year	Mon	Day	Sign	Year	Mon	Day	Sign
1901	JAN	19	Cap		JUL	30	Can
1902	FEB	6	Aqu	1907	AUG	18	Leo
1903	FEB	20	Pic	1908	SEP	12	Vir
1904	MAR	1	Ari	1909	OCT	11	Lib
	AUG	8	Tau	1910	NOV	11	Scp
	AUG	31	Ari	1911	DEC	10	Sag
1905	MAR	7	Tau	1913	JAN	2	Cap
	JUL	21	Gem	1914	JAN	21	Aqu
	DEC	4	Tau	1915	FEB	4	Pic
1906	MAR	9	Gem	1916	FEB	12	Ari

	JUN	26	Tau	1949	APR	12	Aqu
	OCT	26	Ari		JUN	27	Cap
1917	FEB	12	Tau		NOV	30	Aqu
	JUN	29	Gem	1950	APR	15	Pic
1918	JUL	13	Can		SEP	15	Aqu
1919	AUG	2	Leo		DEC	1	Pic
1920	AUG	27	Vir	1951	APR	21	Ari
1921	SEP	25	Lib	1952	APR	28	Tau
1922	OCT	26	Scp	1953	MAY	9	Gem
1923	NOV	24	Sag	1954	MAY	24	Can
1924	DEC	18	Cap	1955	JUN	13	Leo
1926	JAN	6	Aqu		NOV	17	Vir
1927	JAN	18	Pic	1956	JAN	18	Leo
	JUN	6	Ari		JUL	7	Vir
	SEP	11	Pic		DEC	13	Lib
1928	JAN	23	Ari	1957	FEB	19	Vir
	JUN	4	Tau		AUG	7	Lib
1929	JUN	12	Gem	1958	JAN	13	Scp
1930	JUN	26	Can		MAR	20	Lib
1931	JUL	17	Leo		SEP	7	Scp
1932	AUG	11	Vir	1959	FEB	10	Sag
1933	SEP	10	Lib		APR	24	Scp
1934	OCT	11	Scp		OCT	5	Sag
1935	NOV	9	Sag	1960	MAR	1	Cap
1936	DEC	2	Cap		JUN	10	Sag
1937	DEC	20	Aqu		OCT	26	Cap
1938	MAY	14	Pic	1961	MAR	15	Aqu
	JUL	30	Aqu		AUG	12	Cap
	DEC	29	Pic		NOV	4	Aqu
1939	MAY	11	Ari	1962	MAR	25	Pic
	OCT	30	Pic	1963	APR	4	Ari
	DEC	20	Ari	1964	APR	12	Tau
1940	MAY	16	Tau	1965	APR	22	Gem
1941	MAY	26	Gem		SEP	21	Can
1942	JUN	10	Can		NOV	17	Gem
1943	JUN	30	Leo	1966	MAY	5	Can
1944	JUL	26	Vir		SEP	27	Leo
1945	AUG	25	Lib	1967	JAN	16	Can
1946	SEP	25	Scp		MAY	23	Leo
1947	OCT	24	Sag		OCT	19	Vir
1948	NOV	15	Cap	1968	FEB	27	Leo

	JUN	15	Vir	1981	NOV	27	Scp
	NOV	15	Lib	1982	DEC	26	Sag
1969	MAR	30	Vir	1984	JAN	19	Cap
	JUL	15	Lib	1985	FEB	6	Aqu
	DEC	16	Scp	1986	FEB	20	Pic
1970	APR	30	Lib	1987	MAR	2	Ari
	AUG	15	Scp	1988	MAR	8	Tau
1971	JAN	14	Sag		JUL	22	Gem
	JUN	5	Scp		NOV	30	Tau
	SEP	11	Sag	1989	MAR	11	Gem
1972	FEB	6	Cap		JUL	30	Can
	JUL	24	Sag	1990	AUG	18	Leo
	SEP	25	Cap	1991	SEP	12	Vir
1973	FEB	23	Aqu	1992	OCT	10	Lib
1974	MAR	8	Pic	1993	NOV	10	Scp
1975	MAR	18	Ari	1994	DEC	9	Sag
1976	MAR	26	Tau	1996	JAN	3	Cap
	AUG	23	Gem	1997	JAN	21	Aqu
	OCT	16	Tau	1998	FEB	4	Pic
1977	APR	3	Gem	1999	FEB	13	Ari
	AUG	20	Can		JUN	28	Tau
	DEC	30	Gem		OCT	23	Ari
1978	APR	12	Can	2000	FEB	14	Tau
	SEP	5	Leo		JUN	30	Gem
1979	FEB	28	Can	2001	JUL	14	Can
	APR	20	Leo	2002	AUG	1	Leo
	SEP	29	Vir	2003	AUG	27	Vir
1980	OCT	27	Lib	2004	SEP	24	Lib

SATURN SIGNS 1903–2004

1903	JAN	19	Aqu	1912	JUL	7	Gem
1905	APR	13	Pic		NOV	30	Tau
	AUG	17	Aqu	1913	MAR	26	Gem
1906	JAN	8	Pic	1914	AUG	24	Can
1908	MAR	19	Ari		DEC	7	Gem
1910	MAY	17	Tau	1915	MAY	11	Can
	DEC	14	Ari	1916	OCT	17	Leo
1911	JAN	20	Tau		DEC	7	Can

1917	JUN	24	Leo		SEP	16	Aqu
1919	AUG	12	Vir		DEC	16	Pic
1921	OCT	7	Lib	1967	MAR	3	Ari
1923	DEC	20	Scp	1969	APR	29	Tau
1924	APR	6	Lib	1971	JUN	18	Gem
	SEP	13	Scp	1972	JAN	10	Tau
1926	DEC	2	Sag		FEB	21	Gem
1929	MAR	15	Cap	1973	AUG	1	Can
	MAY	5	Sag	1974	JAN	7	Gem
	NOV	30	Cap		APR	18	Can
1932	FEB	24	Aqu	1975	SEP	17	Leo
	AUG	13	Cap	1976	JAN	14	Can
	NOV	20	Aqu		JUN	5	Leo
1935	FEB	14	Pic	1977	NOV	17	Vir
1937	APR	25	Ari	1978	JAN	5	Leo
	OCT	18	Pic		JUL	26	Vir
1938	JAN	14	Ari	1980	SEP	21	Lib
1939	JUL	6	Tau	1982	NOV	29	Scp
	SEP	22	Ari	1983	MAY	6	Lib
1940	MAR	20	Tau		AUG	24	Scp
1942	MAY	8	Gem	1985	NOV	17	Sag
1944	JUN	20	Can	1988	FEB	13	Cap
1946	AUG	2	Leo		JUN	10	Sag
1948	SEP	19	Vir		NOV	12	Cap
1949	APR	3	Leo	1991	FEB	6	Aqu
	MAY	29	Vir	1993	MAY	21	Pic
1950	NOV	20	Lib		JUN	30	Aqu
1951	MAR	7	Vir	1994	JAN	28	Pic
	AUG	13	Lib	1996	APR	7	Ari
1953	OCT	22	Scp	1998	JUN	9	Tau
1956	JAN	12	Sag		OCT	25	Ari
	MAY	14	Scp	1999	MAR	1	Tau
	OCT	10	Sag	2000	AUG	10	Gem
1959	JAN	5	Cap		OCT	16	Tau
1962	JAN	3	Aqu	2001	APR	21	Gem
1964	MAR	24	Pic	2003	JUN	3	Can

CHAPTER 5

How to Read the Symbols on Your Chart

Looking at an astrology chart for the first time, you will see symbols that seem as mysterious as ancient runes and cave drawings. These symbols, called *glyphs*, are used by astrologers worldwide and by computer astrology programs. In order to understand a horoscope chart or to use one of the popular astrology programs on your PC, you must learn to read the glyphs.

Each glyph contains clues to the meaning of the signs and the planets. Since there are only twelve signs and ten planets (not counting a few asteroids and other space creatures some astrologers use), it's a lot easier than learning to read a foreign language.

Here's a code cracker for the glyphs, beginning with the glyphs for the planets. To those who already know their glyphs, don't just skim over the chapter. These familiar graphics have hidden meanings you will discover!

The Glyphs for the Planets

The glyphs for the planets are easy to learn. They're simple combinations of the most basic visual elements: the circle, the semicircle or arc, and the cross. However, each component of a glyph has a special meaning in relation to the other parts of the symbol.

The circle, which has no beginning or end, is one of the oldest symbols of spirit or spiritual forces. All of the early diagrams of the heavens—spiritual territory—are shown in circular form. The never-ending line of the circle is the perfect symbol for eternity. The semicircle or arc is an incomplete circle, symbolizing the receptive, finite soul, which contains spiritual potential in the curving line.

The vertical line of the cross symbolizes movement from heaven to earth. The horizontal line describes temporal movement, here and now, in time and space. Combined in a cross, the vertical and horizontal planes symbolize manifestation in the material world.

The Sun Glyph ☉

The sun is always shown by this powerful solar symbol, a circle with a point in the center. The center point is you, your spiritual center, and the symbol represents your infinite personality incarnating (the point) into the finite cycles of birth and death.

The sun has been represented by a circle or disk since ancient Egyptian times when the solar disk represented the Sun god, Ra. Some archaeologists believe the great stone circles found in England were centers of sun worship. This particular version of the symbol was brought into common use in the sixteenth century after German occultist and scholar Cornelius Agrippa (1486–1535) wrote a book called *Die Occulta Philosophia,* which became accepted as the authority in its field. Agrippa collected many medieval astrological and magical symbols in this book, which have been used by astrologers since then.

The Moon Glyph ☽

The moon glyph is the most recognizable symbol on a chart, a left-facing arc stylized into the crescent moon. As part of a circle, the arc symbolizes the potential fulfillment of the entire circle, the life force that is still incomplete. Therefore, it is the ideal representation of the reactive, receptive, emotional nature of the moon.

The Mercury Glyph ☿

Mercury contains all three elemental symbols: the crescent, the circle, and the cross in vertical order. This is the "Venus with a hat" glyph (compare with the symbol of Venus). With another stretch of the imagination, can't you see the winged cap of Mercury the messenger? Think of the upturned crescent as antennae that tune in and transmit messages from the sun, reminding you that Mercury is the way you communicate, the way your mind works. The upturned arc is receiving energy into the spirit or solar circle, which will later be translated into action on the material plane, symbolized by the cross. All the elements are equally sized because Mercury is neutral; it doesn't play favorites! This planet symbolizes objective, detached, unemotional thinking.

The Venus Glyph ♀

Here the relationship is between two components: the circle of spirit and the cross of matter. Spirit is elevated over matter, pulling it upward. Venus asks, "What is beautiful? What do you like best? What do you love to have done to you?" Consequently, Venus determines both your ideal of beauty and what feels good sensually. It governs your own allure and power to attract, as well as what attracts and pleases you.

The Mars Glyph ♂

In this glyph, the cross of matter is stylized into an arrowhead pointed up and outward, propelled by the circle of spirit. With a little imagination, you can visualize it as the shield and spear of Mars, the ancient god of war. You can deduce that Mars embodies your spiritual energy projected into the outer world. It's your assertiveness, your initiative, your aggressive drive, what you like to do to others, your temper. If you know someone's Mars, you know whether they'll blow up when angry or do a slow burn. Your task is to use your outgoing Mars energy wisely and well.

The Jupiter Glyph ♃

Jupiter is the basic cross of matter, with a large stylized crescent perched on the left side of the horizontal, temporal plane. You might think of the crescent as an open hand, because one meaning of Jupiter is "luck," what's handed to you. You don't have to work for what you get from Jupiter; it comes to you, if you're open to it.

The Jupiter glyph might also remind you of a jumbo jet plane, with a huge tail fin, about to take off. This is the planet of travel, mental and spiritual, of expanding your horizons via new ideas, new spiritual dimensions, and new places. Jupiter embodies the optimism and enthusiasm of the traveler about to embark on an exciting adventure.

The Saturn Glyph ♄

Flip Jupiter over, and you've got Saturn. This might not be immediately apparent because Saturn is usually stylized into an "h" form like the one shown here. The principle it expresses is the opposite of Jupiter's expansive tendencies. Saturn pulls you back to earth: the receptive arc is pushed down underneath the cross of matter. Before there are any rewards or expansion, the duties and obligations of the material world must be considered. Saturn says, "Stop, wait, finish your chores before you take off!"

Saturn's glyph also resembles the sickle of old "Father Time." Saturn was first known as Chronos, the Greek god of time, for time brings all matter to an end. When it was the most distant planet (before the discovery of Uranus), Saturn was believed to be the place where time stopped. After the soul departed from earth, it journeyed back to the outer reaches of the universe and finally stopped at Saturn, or at "the end of time."

The Uranus Glyph ♅

The glyph for Uranus is often stylized to form a capital "H" after Sir William Herschel who discovered the planet. But the more esoteric version curves the two pillars of the H into crescent antennae, or "ears," like satellite disks receiving signals from space. These are perched on the horizontal material line of the cross of matter and pushed from below by the circle of the spirit. To many sci-fi fans, Uranus looks like an orbiting satellite.

Uranus channels the highest energy of all, the white electrical light of the universal spiritual force that holds the cosmos together. This pure electrical energy is gathered from all over the universe. Because Uranus energy doesn't follow any ordinary celestial drumbeat, it can't be controlled or predicted (which is also true of those who are strongly influenced by this eccentric planet). In the symbol, this energy is manifested through the balance of polarities (the two opposite arms of the glyph) like the two polarized wires of a lightbulb.

The Neptune Glyph ♆

Neptune's glyph is usually stylized to look like a trident, the weapon of the Roman god Neptune. However, on a more esoteric level, it shows the large upturned crescent of the soul pierced through by the cross of matter. Neptune nails down, or materializes, soul energy, bringing impulses from the soul level into manifestation. That is why Neptune is associated with imagination or "imagining in," making an image of the soul. Neptune works through feeling, sensitivity, and mystical capacity to bring the divine into the earthly realm.

The Pluto Glyph ♇

Pluto is written two ways. One is a composite of the letters "PL," the first two letters of the word Pluto and coincidentally the initials of Percival Lowell, one of the planet's discoverers. The other, more esoteric symbol is a small circle above a large open crescent that surmounts the cross of matter. This depicts Pluto's power to regenerate. Imagine a new little spirit emerging from the sheltering cup of the soul. Pluto rules the forces of life and death. After this planet has passed a sensitive point in your chart, you are transformed, reborn in some way.

Sci-fi fans might visualize this glyph as a small satellite (the circle) being launched. It was shortly after Pluto's discovery that we learned how to harness the nuclear forces that made space exploration possible. Pluto rules the transformative power of atomic energy, which totally changed our lives and from which there is no turning back.

The Glyphs for the Signs

On an astrology chart, the glyph for the sign will appear after that of the planet. For example, when you see the moon glyph followed first by a number and then by another glyph representing the sign, this means that the moon was passing over a certain degree of that astrological sign at the time of the chart. On the dividing lines between the houses on your chart, you'll find the symbol for the sign that rules the house.

Because sun sign symbols do not contain the same basic geometric components of the planetary glyphs, we must look elsewhere for clues to their meanings. Many have been passed down from ancient Egyptian and Chaldean civilizations with few modifications. Others have been adapted over the centuries.

In deciphering many of the glyphs, you'll often find that the symbols reveal a dual nature of the sign, which is not always apparent in the usual sun sign descriptions. For instance, the Gemini glyph is similar to the Roman numeral for two, and reveals this sign's longing to discover a twin soul. The Cancer glyph may be interpreted as resembling either the nurturing breasts or the self-protective claws of a crab, both symbols associated with the contrasting qualities of this sign. Libra's glyph embodies the duality of the spirit balanced with material reality. The Sagittarius glyph shows that the aspirant must also carry along the earthly animal nature in his quest. The Capricorn sea goat is another symbol with dual emphasis. The goat climbs high, yet is always pulled back by the deep waters of the unconscious. Aquarius embodies the double waves of mental detachment, balanced by the desire for connection with others in a friendly way. Finally, the two fishes of Pisces, which are forever tied together, show the duality of the soul and the spirit that must be reconciled.

The Aries Glyph ♈

Since the symbol for Aries is the Ram, this glyph is obviously associated with a ram's horns, which characterize one aspect of the Aries personality—an aggressive, me-first, leaping-headfirst attitude. But the symbol can be interpreted in other ways as well. Some astrologers liken it to a fountain of energy, which Aries people also embody. The first sign of the zodiac bursts on the scene eagerly, ready to go. Another analogy is to the eyebrows and nose of the human head, which Aries rules, and the thinking power that is initiated by the brain.

One theory of this symbol links it to the Egyptian god Amun, represented by a ram in ancient times. As Amun-Ra, this god was believed to embody the creator of the universe, the leader of all the other gods. This relates easily to the position of Aries as the leader (or first sign) of the zodiac, which begins at the spring equinox, a time of the year when nature is renewed.

The Taurus Glyph ♉

This is another easy glyph to draw and identify. It takes little imagination to decipher the bull's head with long curving horns. Like its symbol the Bull, the archetypal Taurus is slow to anger but ferocious when provoked, as well as stubborn, steady, and sensual. Another association is the larynx (and thyroid) of the throat area (ruled by Taurus) and the eustachian tubes running up to the ears, which coincides with the relationship of Taurus to the voice, song, and music. Many famous singers, musicians, and composers have prominent Taurus influences.

Many ancient religions involved a bull as the central figure in fertility rites or initiations, usually symbolizing the victory of man over his animal nature. Another possible origin is in the sacred bull of Egypt, who embodied the incarnate form of Osiris, god of death and resurrection. In early Christian imagery, the Taurus Bull represented St. Luke.

The Gemini Glyph ♊

The standard glyph immediately calls to mind the Roman numeral for two (II) and the Twins symbol, as it is called, for Gemini. In almost all drawings and images used for this sign, the relationship between two persons is emphasized. Usually one twin will be touching the other, which signifies communication, human contact, the desire to share.

The top line of the Gemini glyph indicates mental communication, while the bottom line indicates shared physical space.

The most famous Gemini legend is that of the twin sons, Castor and Pollux, one of whom had a mortal father while the other was the son of Zeus, king of the gods. When it came time for the mortal twin to die, his grief-stricken brother pleaded with Zeus, who agreed to let them spend half the year on earth in mortal form and half in immortal life, with the gods on Mt. Olympus. This reflects a basic duality of humankind, which possesses an immortal soul yet is also subject to the limits of mortality.

The Cancer Glyph ♋

Two convenient images relate to the Cancer glyph. It is easiest to decode the curving claws of the Cancer symbol, the Crab. Like the crab, Cancer's element is water. This sensitive sign also has a hard protective shell to protect its tender interior. The crab must be wily to escape predators, scampering sideways and hiding under rocks. The crab also responds to the cycles of the moon, as do all shellfish. The other image is that of two female breasts, which Cancer rules, showing that this is a sign that nurtures and protects others as well as itself.

In ancient Egypt, Cancer was also represented by the scarab beetle, a symbol of regeneration and eternal life.

The Leo Glyph ♌

Notice that the Leo glyph seems to be an extension of Cancer's glyph, with a significant difference. In the Cancer glyph, the lines curve inward protectively. The Leo glyph expresses energy outwardly. And there is no duality in the symbol, the Lion, or in Leo, the sign.

Lions have belonged to the sign of Leo since earliest times. It is not difficult to imagine the king of beasts with his sweeping mane and curling tail from this glyph. The upward sweep of the glyph easily describes the positive energy of Leo: the flourishing tail, their flamboyant qualities. Another analogy, perhaps a stretch of the imagination, is that of a heart leaping up with joy and enthusiasm, also very typical of Leo, which also rules the heart. In early Christian imagery, the Leo Lion represented St. Mark.

The Virgo Glyph ♍

You can read much into this mysterious glyph. For instance, it could represent the initials of "Mary Virgin," or a young woman holding a staff of wheat, or stylized female genitalia, all common interpretations. The "M" shape might also remind you that Virgo is ruled by Mercury. The cross beneath the symbol reveals the grounded, practical nature of this earth sign.

The earliest zodiacs link Virgo with the Egyptian goddess Isis who gave birth to the god Horus, after her husband Osiris had been killed, in the archetype of a miraculous conception. There are many ancient statues of Isis nursing her baby son, which are reminiscent of medieval Virgin and Child motifs. This sign has also been associated with the image of the Holy Grail, when the Virgo symbol was substituted with a chalice.

The Libra Glyph ♎

It is not difficult to read the standard image for Libra, the Scales, into this glyph. There is another meaning, however, that is equally relevant: the setting sun as it descends over the horizon. Libra's natural position on the zodiac wheel is the descendant, or sunset position (as the Aries natural position is the ascendant, or rising sign). Both images relate to Libra's personality. Libra is always weighing pros and cons for a balanced decision. In the sunset image, the sun (male) hovers over the horizontal earth (female) before setting. Libra is the space between these lines, harmonizing yin and yang, spiritual and material, male and female, ideal and real worlds. The glyph has also been linked to the kidneys, which are ruled by Libra.

The Scorpio Glyph ♏

With its barbed tail, this glyph is easy to identify as the Scorpion for the sign of Scorpio. It also represents the male sexual parts, over which the sign rules. From the arrowhead, you can draw the conclusion that Mars was once its ruler. Some earlier Egyptian glyphs for Scorpio represent it as an erect serpent, so the Serpent is an alternate symbol.

Another symbol for Scorpio, which is not identifiable in this glyph, is the Eagle. Scorpios can go to extremes, either in soaring like the eagle or self-destructing like the scorpion. In early Christian imagery, which often used zodiacal symbols, the Scorpio Eagle was chosen to symbolize the intense apostle St. John the Evangelist.

The Sagittarius Glyph ♐

This is one of the easiest to spot and draw: an upward pointing arrow lifting up a cross. The arrow is pointing skyward, while the cross represents the four elements of the material world, which the arrow must convey. Elevating materiality into spirituality is an important Sagittarius quality, which explains why this sign is associated with higher learning, religion, philosophy, travel—the aspiring professions. Sagittarius can also send barbed arrows of frankness in the pursuit of truth, so the Archer symbol for Sagittarius is apt. (Sagittarius is also the sign of the supersalesman.)

Sagittarius is symbolically represented by the centaur, a mythological creature who is half man, half horse, aiming his arrow toward the skies. Though Sagittarius is motivated by spiritual aspiration, it also must balance the powerful appetites of the animal nature. The centaur Chiron, a figure in Greek mythology, became a wise teacher who, after many adventures and world travels, was killed by a poisoned arrow.

The Capricorn Glyph ♑

One of the most difficult symbols to draw, this glyph may take some practice. It is a representation of the sea goat: a mythical animal that is a goat with a curving fish's tail. The goat part of Capricorn wants to leave the waters of the emotions and climb to the elevated areas of life. But the fish tail is the unconscious, the deep chaotic psychic level that draws the goat back. Capricorn is often trying to escape the deep, feeling part of life by submerging himself in work, steadily ascending to the top. To some people, the glyph represents a seated figure with a bent knee, a reminder that Capricorn governs the knee area of the body.

An interesting aspect of this glyph is the contrast of the sharp pointed horns—which represent the penetrating, shrewd, conscious side of Capricorn—with the swishing tail—which represents its serpentine, unconscious, emotional force. One Capricorn legend, which dates from Roman times, tells of the earthy fertility god, Pan, who tried to save himself from uncontrollable sexual desires by jumping into the Nile. His upper body then turned into a goat, while the lower part became a fish. Later, Jupiter gave him a safe haven as a constellation in the skies.

The Aquarius Glyph ≈

This ancient water symbol can be traced back to an Egyptian hieroglyph representing streams of life force. Symbolized by the Water Bearer, Aquarius is distributor of the waters of life—the magic liquid of regeneration. The two waves can also be linked to the positive and negative charges of the electrical energy that Aquarius rules, a sort of universal wavelength. Aquarius is tuned in intuitively to higher forces via this electrical force. The duality of the glyph could also refer to the dual nature of Aquarius, a sign that runs hot and cold and that is friendly but also detached in the mental world of air signs.

In Greek legends, Aquarius is represented by Ganymede, who was carried to heaven by an eagle in order to become the cupbearer of Zeus and to supervise the annual flooding of the Nile. The sign later became associated with aviation and notions of flight.

The Pisces Glyph)(

Here is an abstraction of the familiar image of Pisces, two Fishes swimming in opposite directions yet bound together by a cord. The Fishes represent the spirit—which yearns for the freedom of heaven—and the soul—which remains attached to the desires of the temporal world. During life on earth, the spirit and the soul are bound together. When they complement each other, instead of pulling in opposite directions, they facilitate the Pisces creativity. The ancient version of this glyph, taken from the Egyptians, had no connecting line, which was added in the fourteenth century.

In another interpretation, it is said that the left fish indicates the direction of involution or the beginning of a cycle, while the right fish signifies the direction of evolution, the way to completion of a cycle. It's an appropriate grand finale for Pisces, the last sign of the zodiac.

CHAPTER 6

What Is Your Rising Sign?

Your rising sign, also called the *ascendant,* is the sign of the zodiac passing over the eastern horizon at the very moment you were born. The rising sign is one of the most important factors in your horoscope. The rising sign determines the way your chart is set up and the location of planets within the chart.

As the earth turns, a different sign rises over the horizon every two hours. This explains why other babies who were born in the same place, but later or earlier in the same day, would have a different chart. Even though the planets would be in the same signs, the rising sign would be earlier or later. Therefore, the planets would be in another place, or "house," in their horoscopes, emphasizing different areas of their lives.

If you have read the description of the "houses" in chapter 3 of this book, you'll know that the houses are twelve stationary divisions of the horoscope, which represent areas of life. The sign moving over the boundary (cusp) of each house describes that area of life.

The rising sign rules the first house, which is the physical body, your outward appearance, your style, tastes, health, and physical environment (where you are most comfortable working and living). After the rising sign is determined, then each of the next eleven houses in the chart will be influenced by the signs following in sequence.

When we know the rising sign of a chart, then we know where to put each planet. Without a valid rising sign, your collection of planets would have no "homes."

Once the rising sign is established, it becomes possible

to analyze a chart accurately because the astrologer knows in which house or area of life the planets will operate. For instance, if Mars is in Gemini and your rising sign is in Taurus, then Mars will most likely be active in the second house, the house of finances, of your chart. If you were born later in the day and your rising sign is Virgo, then Mars will be positioned at the top of your chart, energizing your tenth house, the house of career.

Many astrologers insist on knowing the exact time of a client's birth before they will analyze a chart. The more exact your birth time, the more accurately an astrologer can position the planets in your chart.

Your rising sign has an important relationship with your sun sign. Some will complement the sun sign; others hide it under a totally different mask, as if playing an entirely different role, making it difficult to guess the person's sun sign from outer appearances. This may be the reason why you might not look or act like your sun sign's archetype. For example, a Leo with a conservative Capricorn ascendant would come across as much more serious than a Leo with a fiery Aries or Sagittarius ascendant.

It is usually the rising sign that creates the first impression you make. However, if the sun sign is accompanied by other planets in the same sign, this might overpower the impression of the rising sign. For instance, a Leo sun plus a Leo Venus and Leo Jupiter would counteract the more conservative image that would otherwise be conveyed by the person's Capricorn ascendant.

Rising signs change every two hours with the earth's rotation. Those born early in the morning when the sun was on the horizon will be most likely to project the image of their sun sign. These people are often called a "double Aries" or a "double Virgo" because the same sun sign and ascendant reinforce each other.

Look up your rising sign from the chart at the end of this chapter. Since rising signs change every two hours, it is important to know your birth time as close to the minute as possible. Even a few minutes' difference could change the rising sign and therefore the setup of your chart. If you are unsure about the exact time, but know within a few hours, check the following descriptions to see which is most like the personality you project.

Aries Rising: High Energy

You are the most aggressive version of your sun sign, with boundless energy that can be used productively if it's channeled in the right direction. Watch a tendency to overreact emotionally and blow your top. You come across as openly competitive, a positive asset in business or sports. Be on guard against impatience, which could lead to head injuries. Your walk and bearing could have the telltale head-forward Aries posture. You may wear more bright colors, especially red, than others of your sign. You may also have a tendency to drive your car faster.

Taurus Rising: Earthbound

You're slow-moving, with a beautiful (or distinctive) speaking or singing voice that can be especially soothing or melodious. You probably surround yourself with comfort, good food, luxurious surroundings, and other sensual pleasures. You prefer welcoming others into your home to gadding about. You may have a talent for business, especially in trading, appraising, and real estate. A Taurus ascendant gives a well-padded physique that gains weight easily. This ascendant can also endow females with a curvaceous beauty.

Gemini Rising: The Communicator

You're naturally sociable, with lighter, more ethereal mannerisms than others of your sign, especially if you're female. You love to communicate with people, and express your ideas and feelings easily. You may have a talent for writing or public speaking. You thrive on variety, a constantly changing scene, and a lively social life. However, you may relate to others at a deeper level than might be suspected. And you will be far more sympathetic and caring than you project. You will probably travel widely, changing partners and jobs several times (or juggle two at once). Physically, your nerves are quite sensitive. Occasionally, you would benefit from a calm, tranquil atmosphere away from your usual social scene.

Cancer Rising: Nurturing

You are naturally acquisitive, possessive, private, a moneymaker. You easily pick up others' needs and feelings—a great gift in business, the arts, and personal relationships. But you must guard against overreacting or taking things too personally, especially during full moon periods. Find creative outlets for your natural nurturing gifts, such as helping the less fortunate, particularly children. Your insights would be helpful in psychology. Your desire to feed and care for others would be useful in the restaurant, hotel, or child-care industries. You may be especially fond of wearing romantic old clothes, collecting antiques, and, of course, dining on exquisite food. Since your body may retain fluids, pay attention to your diet. To relax, escape to places near water.

Leo Rising: Scene Player

You may come across as more poised than you really feel. However, you play it to the hilt, projecting a proud royal presence. A Leo ascendant gives you a natural flair for drama, and you might be accused of stealing the spotlight. You'll also project a much more outgoing, optimistic, sunny personality than others of your sign. You take care to please your public by always projecting your best star quality, probably tossing a luxuriant mane of hair, sporting a striking hairstyle, or dressing to impress. Females often dazzle with spectacular jewelry. Since you may have a strong parental nature, you could well be the regal family matriarch or patriarch.

Virgo Rising: Discriminating

Virgo rising masks your inner nature with a practical, analytical outer image. You seem neat, orderly, more particular than others of your sign. Others in your life may feel they must live up to your high standards. Though at times you may be openly critical, this masks a well-meaning desire to have only the best for loved ones. Your sharp eye for details could be used in the financial world, or your literary skills could draw you to teaching or publishing. The healing arts, health care, and service-oriented professions attract many with a Virgo ascendant. You're likely to take good care of yourself, with great attention to health, diet, and exercise. Physically, you may have a very sensitive digestive system.

Libra Rising: Charming and Social

Libra rising gives you a charming, social, public persona. You tend to avoid confrontations in relationships, preferring to smooth the way or negotiate diplomatically rather than give in to an emotional reaction. Because you are interested in all aspects of a situation, you may be slow to reach decisions. Physically, you'll have good proportions and physical symmetry. You will move with natural grace and balance. You're likely to have pleasing, if not beautiful, facial features, with a winning smile. You'll show natural good taste and harmony in your clothes and home decor. Legal, diplomatic, or public relations professions could draw your interest.

Scorpio Rising: Mysterious Charisma

You project an intriguing air of mystery with this ascendant, as the Scorpio secretiveness and sense of underlying power combines with your sun sign. There's more to you than meets the eye. You seem like someone who is always in control and who can move comfortably in the world of power. Your physical look comes across as intense. Many of you have remarkable eyes, with a direct, penetrating gaze. But you'll never reveal your private agenda, and you tend to keep your true feelings under wraps (watch a tendency toward paranoia). You may have an interesting romantic history with secret love affairs. Many of you heighten your air of mystery by wearing black. You're happiest near water and should provide yourself with a seaside retreat.

Sagittarius Rising: The Wanderer

You travel with this ascendant. You may also be a more outdoor, sportive type, with an athletic, casual, outgoing air. Your moods are camouflaged with cheerful optimism or a philosophical attitude. Though you don't hesitate to speak your mind, you can also laugh at your troubles or crack a joke more easily than others of your sign. A Sagittarius ascendant can also draw you to the field of higher education or to spiritual life. You'll seem to have less attachment to things and people, and may travel widely. Your strong, fast legs are a physical bonus.

Capricorn Rising: Serious Business

This rising sign makes you come across as serious, goal-oriented, disciplined, and careful with cash. You are not one of the zodiac's big spenders, though you might splurge occasionally on items with good investment value. You're the traditional, conservative type in dress and environment, and you might come across as quite formal and businesslike. You'll function well in a structured or corporate environment where you can climb to the top. (You are always aware of who's the boss.) In your personal life, you could be a loner or a single parent who is "father and mother" to your children.

Aquarius Rising: One of a Kind

You come across as less concerned about what others think and could even be a bit eccentric. Your appearance is sure to be unique and memorable. You're more at ease with groups of people than others in your sign, and you may be attracted to public life. Your appearance may be unique, either unconventional or unimportant to you. Those of you whose sun is in a water sign (Cancer, Scorpio, Pisces) may exercise your nurturing qualities with a large group, an extended family, or a day-care or community center.

Pisces Rising: Romantic Roles

Your creative, nurturing talents are heightened and so is your ability to project emotional drama. And your dreamy eyes and poetic air bring out the protective instinct in others. You could be attracted to the arts, especially theater, dance, film, and photography, or to psychology, spiritual practice, and charity work. You are happiest when you are using your creative ability to help others. Since you are vulnerable to mood swings, it is especially important for you to find interesting, creative work where you can express your talents and heighten your self-esteem. Accentuate the positive. Be wary of escapist tendencies, particularly involving alcohol or drugs to which you are supersensitive.

RISING SIGNS—A.M. BIRTHS

	1 AM	2 AM	3 AM	4 AM	5 AM	6 AM	7 AM	8 AM	9 AM	10 AM	11 AM	12 NOON
Jan 1	Lib	Sc	Sc	Sc	Sag	Sag	Cap	Cap	Aq	Aq	Pis	Ar
Jan 9	Lib	Sc	Sc	Sag	Sag	Sag	Cap	Cap	Aq	Pis	Ar	Tau
Jan 17	Sc	Sc	Sc	Sag	Sag	Cap	Cap	Aq	Aq	Pis	Ar	Tau
Jan 25	Sc	Sc	Sag	Sag	Sag	Cap	Cap	Aq	Pis	Ar	Tau	Tau
Feb 2	Sc	Sc	Sag	Sag	Cap	Cap	Aq	Pis	Pis	Ar	Tau	Gem
Feb 10	Sc	Sag	Sag	Sag	Cap	Cap	Aq	Pis	Ar	Tau	Tau	Gem
Feb 18	Sc	Sag	Sag	Cap	Cap	Aq	Pis	Pis	Ar	Tau	Gem	Gem
Feb 26	Sag	Sag	Sag	Cap	Aq	Aq	Pis	Ar	Tau	Tau	Gem	Gem
Mar 6	Sag	Sag	Cap	Cap	Aq	Pis	Pis	Ar	Tau	Gem	Gem	Can
Mar 14	Sag	Cap	Cap	Aq	Aq	Pis	Ar	Tau	Tau	Gem	Gem	Can
Mar 22	Sag	Cap	Cap	Aq	Pis	Ar	Ar	Tau	Gem	Gem	Can	Can
Mar 30	Cap	Cap	Aq	Pis	Pis	Ar	Tau	Tau	Gem	Can	Can	Can
Apr 7	Cap	Cap	Aq	Pis	Ar	Ar	Tau	Gem	Gem	Can	Can	Leo
Apr 14	Cap	Aq	Aq	Pis	Ar	Tau	Tau	Gem	Gem	Can	Can	Leo
Apr 22	Cap	Aq	Pis	Ar	Ar	Tau	Gem	Gem	Gem	Can	Leo	Leo
Apr 30	Aq	Aq	Pis	Ar	Tau	Tau	Gem	Can	Can	Can	Leo	Leo
May 8	Aq	Pis	Ar	Ar	Tau	Gem	Gem	Can	Can	Leo	Leo	Leo
May 16	Aq	Pis	Ar	Tau	Gem	Gem	Can	Can	Can	Leo	Leo	Vir
May 24	Pis	Ar	Ar	Tau	Gem	Gem	Can	Can	Leo	Leo	Leo	Vir
June 1	Pis	Ar	Tau	Gem	Gem	Can	Can	Can	Leo	Leo	Vir	Vir
June 9	Ar	Ar	Tau	Gem	Gem	Can	Can	Leo	Leo	Leo	Vir	Vir
June 17	Ar	Tau	Gem	Gem	Can	Can	Can	Leo	Leo	Vir	Vir	Vir
June 25	Tau	Tau	Gem	Gem	Can	Can	Leo	Leo	Leo	Vir	Vir	Lib
July 3	Tau	Gem	Gem	Can	Can	Can	Leo	Leo	Vir	Vir	Vir	Lib
July 11	Tau	Gem	Gem	Can	Can	Leo	Leo	Leo	Vir	Vir	Lib	Lib
July 18	Gem	Gem	Can	Can	Can	Leo	Leo	Vir	Vir	Vir	Lib	Lib
July 26	Gem	Gem	Can	Can	Leo	Leo	Vir	Vir	Vir	Lib	Lib	Lib
Aug 3	Gem	Can	Can	Can	Leo	Leo	Vir	Vir	Vir	Lib	Lib	Sc
Aug 11	Gem	Can	Can	Leo	Leo	Leo	Vir	Vir	Lib	Lib	Lib	Sc
Aug 18	Can	Can	Can	Leo	Leo	Vir	Vir	Vir	Lib	Lib	Sc	Sc
Aug 27	Can	Can	Leo	Leo	Leo	Vir	Vir	Lib	Lib	Lib	Sc	Sc
Sept 4	Can	Can	Leo	Leo	Leo	Vir	Vir	Vir	Lib	Lib	Sc	Sc
Sept 12	Can	Leo	Leo	Leo	Vir	Vir	Lib	Lib	Lib	Sc	Sc	Sag
Sept 20	Leo	Leo	Leo	Vir	Vir	Vir	Lib	Lib	Lib	Sc	Sc	Sag
Sept 28	Leo	Leo	Leo	Vir	Vir	Lib	Lib	Lib	Sc	Sc	Sag	Sag
Oct 6	Leo	Leo	Vir	Vir	Vir	Lib	Lib	Sc	Sc	Sc	Sag	Sag
Oct 14	Leo	Vir	Vir	Vir	Lib	Lib	Lib	Sc	Sc	Sag	Sag	Cap
Oct 22	Leo	Vir	Vir	Lib	Lib	Lib	Sc	Sc	Sc	Sag	Sag	Cap
Oct 30	Vir	Vir	Vir	Lib	Lib	Sc	Sc	Sc	Sag	Sag	Cap	Cap
Nov 7	Vir	Vir	Lib	Lib	Lib	Sc	Sc	Sc	Sag	Sag	Cap	Cap
Nov 15	Vir	Vir	Lib	Lib	Sc	Sc	Sc	Sag	Sag	Cap	Cap	Aq
Nov 23	Vir	Lib	Lib	Lib	Sc	Sc	Sag	Sag	Sag	Cap	Cap	Aq
Dec 1	Vir	Lib	Lib	Sc	Sc	Sc	Sag	Sag	Cap	Cap	Aq	Aq
Dec 9	Lib	Lib	Lib	Sc	Sc	Sag	Sag	Sag	Cap	Cap	Aq	Pis
Dec 18	Lib	Lib	Sc	Sc	Sc	Sag	Sag	Cap	Cap	Aq	Aq	Pis
Dec 28	Lib	Lib	Sc	Sc	Sag	Sag	Sag	Cap	Aq	Aq	Pis	Ar

RISING SIGNS—P.M. BIRTHS

	1 PM	2 PM	3 PM	4 PM	5 PM	6 PM	7 PM	8 PM	9 PM	10 PM	11 PM	12 MIDNIGHT
Jan 1	Tau	Gem	Gem	Can	Can	Can	Leo	Leo	Vir	Vir	Vir	Lib
Jan 9	Tau	Gem	Gem	Can	Can	Leo	Leo	Leo	Vir	Vir	Vir	Lib
Jan 17	Gem	Gem	Can	Can	Can	Leo	Leo	Vir	Vir	Vir	Lib	Lib
Jan 25	Gem	Gem	Can	Can	Leo	Leo	Leo	Vir	Vir	Lib	Lib	Lib
Feb 2	Gem	Can	Can	Can	Leo	Leo	Vir	Vir	Vir	Lib	Lib	Sc
Feb 10	Gem	Can	Can	Leo	Leo	Leo	Vir	Vir	Lib	Lib	Lib	Sc
Feb 18	Can	Can	Can	Leo	Leo	Vir	Vir	Vir	Lib	Lib	Sc	Sc
Feb 26	Can	Can	Leo	Leo	Leo	Vir	Vir	Lib	Lib	Lib	Sc	Sc
Mar 6	Can	Can	Leo	Leo	Vir	Vir	Vir	Lib	Lib	Sc	Sc	Sc
Mar 14	Can	Leo	Leo	Vir	Vir	Vir	Lib	Lib	Lib	Sc	Sc	Sag
Mar 22	Leo	Leo	Leo	Vir	Vir	Lib	Lib	Lib	Sc	Sc	Sc	Sag
Mar 30	Leo	Leo	Vir	Vir	Vir	Lib	Lib	Sc	Sc	Sc	Sag	Sag
Apr 7	Leo	Leo	Vir	Vir	Lib	Lib	Lib	Sc	Sc	Sc	Sag	Sag
Apr 14	Leo	Vir	Vir	Vir	Lib	Lib	Sc	Sc	Sc	Sag	Sag	Cap
Apr 22	Leo	Vir	Vir	Lib	Lib	Lib	Sc	Sc	Sc	Sag	Sag	Cap
Apr 30	Vir	Vir	Vir	Lib	Lib	Sc	Sc	Sc	Sag	Sag	Cap	Cap
May 8	Vir	Vir	Lib	Lib	Lib	Sc	Sc	Sag	Sag	Sag	Cap	Cap
May 16	Vir	Vir	Lib	Lib	Sc	Sc	Sc	Sag	Sag	Cap	Cap	Aq
May 24	Vir	Lib	Lib	Lib	Sc	Sc	Sag	Sag	Sag	Cap	Cap	Aq
June 1	Vir	Lib	Lib	Sc	Sc	Sc	Sag	Sag	Cap	Cap	Aq	Aq
June 9	Lib	Lib	Lib	Sc	Sc	Sag	Sag	Sag	Cap	Cap	Aq	Pis
June 17	Lib	Lib	Sc	Sc	Sc	Sag	Sag	Cap	Cap	Aq	Aq	Pis
June 25	Lib	Lib	Sc	Sc	Sag	Sag	Sag	Cap	Cap	Aq	Pis	Ar
July 3	Lib	Sc	Sc	Sc	Sag	Sag	Cap	Cap	Aq	Aq	Pis	Ar
July 11	Lib	Sc	Sc	Sag	Sag	Sag	Cap	Cap	Aq	Pis	Ar	Tau
July 18	Sc	Sc	Sc	Sag	Sag	Cap	Cap	Aq	Aq	Pis	Ar	Tau
July 26	Sc	Sc	Sag	Sag	Sag	Cap	Cap	Aq	Pis	Ar	Tau	Tau
Aug 3	Sc	Sc	Sag	Sag	Cap	Cap	Aq	Aq	Pis	Ar	Tau	Gem
Aug 11	Sc	Sag	Sag	Sag	Cap	Cap	Aq	Pis	Ar	Tau	Tau	Gem
Aug 18	Sc	Sag	Sag	Cap	Cap	Aq	Pis	Pis	Ar	Tau	Gem	Gem
Aug 27	Sag	Sag	Sag	Cap	Cap	Aq	Pis	Ar	Tau	Tau	Gem	Gem
Sept 4	Sag	Sag	Cap	Cap	Aq	Pis	Pis	Ar	Tau	Gem	Gem	Can
Sept 12	Sag	Sag	Cap	Aq	Aq	Pis	Ar	Tau	Tau	Gem	Gem	Can
Sept 20	Sag	Cap	Cap	Aq	Pis	Pis	Ar	Tau	Gem	Gem	Can	Can
Sept 28	Cap	Cap	Aq	Aq	Pis	Ar	Tau	Tau	Gem	Gem	Can	Can
Oct 6	Cap	Cap	Aq	Pis	Ar	Ar	Tau	Gem	Gem	Can	Can	Leo
Oct 14	Cap	Aq	Aq	Pis	Ar	Tau	Tau	Gem	Gem	Can	Can	Leo
Oct 22	Cap	Aq	Pis	Ar	Ar	Tau	Gem	Gem	Can	Can	Leo	Leo
Oct 30	Aq	Aq	Pis	Ar	Tau	Tau	Gem	Can	Can	Can	Leo	Leo
Nov 7	Aq	Aq	Pis	Ar	Tau	Tau	Gem	Can	Can	Can	Leo	Leo
Nov 15	Aq	Pis	Ar	Tau	Gem	Gem	Can	Can	Can	Leo	Leo	Vir
Nov 23	Pis	Ar	Ar	Tau	Gem	Gem	Can	Can	Leo	Leo	Leo	Vir
Dec 1	Pis	Ar	Tau	Gem	Gem	Can	Can	Can	Leo	Leo	Vir	Vir
Dec 9	Ar	Tau	Tau	Gem	Gem	Can	Can	Leo	Leo	Leo	Vir	Vir
Dec 18	Ar	Tau	Gem	Gem	Can	Can	Can	Leo	Leo	Vir	Vir	Vir
Dec 28	Tau	Tau	Gem	Gem	Can	Can	Leo	Leo	Vir	Vir	Vir	Lib

CHAPTER 7

Astrology Around the Worldwide Web

If you're connected to the Internet, you've got the gateway to a world of information about astrology. Thousands of astrological sites offer you everything from chart services to chat rooms to individual readings. Even better are the freebies! You'll find *free* software, *free* charts, *free* articles to download. You can get an education in astrology from your computer screen, share your insights with new astrology-minded pals in a chat room or on a mailing list, then later meet them in person at one of the hundreds of conferences around the world. You can even see how your face compares to others of your sign. Is there a "family resemblance" among Virgos?

If you're curious to see a copy of your chart (or someone else's), want to study astrology in depth, or chat with another astrology fan, please take our guided tour. The following sites were chosen for general interest and are ideal places to start your "surfing" adventures. Many are hubs of information with their own selection of links to other sites. One caveat: Though these sites were selected with longevity in mind, the Internet is a volatile place where sites can disappear or change without notice. Therefore, some of our sites may have changed addresses, names, or content by the time this book is published.

Free Charts

Astrolabe Software at *www.alabe.com* distributes some of the most creative and user-friendly programs now available; Solar Fire is a favorite of top astrologers. Visitors to the site are greeted with a chart of the time you log on. You can get your chart calculated, with a free mini-interpretation e-mailed to you.

Don't miss this fabulous site, one of our favorites. Go to *www.astro.com* and check into Astrodienst, an international site that has long been one of the best astrology sites on the Internet. Its world atlas will give you the accurate longitude and latitude of your birthplace for setting up your horoscope. Then you can print out your chart in a range of easy-to-read formats. One handy feature for beginners: The planetary placement is listed in words alongside the chart (a real help for those who haven't yet learned to read the astrology glyphs).

There are many other attractions at this site, such as a list of your astro-twins (famous people born on your birth date). The site even sorts the "twins" to feature those who also have your identical rising sign. You can then click on their names and get an instant chart of your famous signmates.

How about some astrological vacation planning? Let Astrodienst help you choose where on earth you'll be happiest, where you'll fall in love, or where you're in for a "heavy" time. First pull up an astro-map at Astro-click Travel, another clever feature on the Astrodienst site. On the interactive chart that appears, you can view your astrological chart projected on a map of the earth. The lines on the chart that track each of the planets indicate what type of experience you might expect at that location. Click on a line, and up pops an explanation. So click before you travel!

Free Software

Try before you buy. Software manufacturers on the Web are generous with free downloads of demo versions of their software. You may then calculate charts using their data. Before you invest serious money in astrology software, you can see how the program works for your needs. You can preview Astrolabe Software programs favored by many professional astrologers at *www.alabe. com.* Check out the latest demo of Solar Fire, one of the most user-friendly astrology programs available—you'll be impressed.

Matrix Software, another source of terrific astrology software, also offers free demo disks. Address: *www.astrologysoftware.com*

A Free Fully Functional Astrology Program

If you're computer-savvy, you can't go wrong with Walter Pullen's amazingly complete Astrolog program, which is offered absolutely free at the site. Address: *www.magitech.com/~cruiser1/astrolog.htm*

Astrolog is an ultrasophisticated program with all the features of much more expensive programs. It comes in versions for all formats—DOS, Windows, MAC, UNIX—and has some cool features such as a revolving globe and a constellation map. A "must" for those who want to get involved with astrology without paying big bucks for a professional-caliber program. Or for those who want to add Astrolog's unique features to their astrology software library. This program has it all!

Another Free Program!

Surf to *www.astroscan.ca* for a free program called Astroscan. Stunning graphics and ease of use make this basic program a winner. Astroscan has a fun list of celebrity charts you can call up with a few clicks.

A Super Shareware Program

Check out Halloran Software's site at *www.halloran.com.* There are several levels of Windows astrology software from which to choose. Of interest to beginners is the Astrology for Windows shareware program, which is available in unregistered demo form as a free download and in registered form for $26.50 (at this writing). The calculations in this program may be all that an astrology hobbyist needs. The price for the full-service program is certainly reasonable.

Free Oracle Readings

Got a decision to make? Get a cosmic consensus at the Matrix site; you may consult the stars, the I Ching, the runes, the tarot, even fortune cookies. Here's where to connect with news groups and on-line discussions. Their almanac helps you schedule the best day to sign on the dotted line, ask for a raise, or plant your rosebush. Address: *www.thenewage.com*

On-line Astrology Course

Schedule a long visit to *www.panplanet.com* where you will find the Canopus Academy of Astrology, a site loaded with goodies. For the experienced astrologer, there is a collection of articles from top astrologers. They've done the work for you when it comes to picking the best astrology links on the Web, so be sure to check out those bestowed with the Canopus Award of Excellence.

Astrologer Linda Reid, an accomplished astrology teacher and author, offers a complete on-line curriculum for all levels of astrology study plus individual tutoring. To get your feet wet, Linda is offering an excellent beginners' course at this site, a terrific way to get off and running in astrology.

Top Astrologers Comment on Current Events

Find out how top astrologers view the latest headlines at the "must-see" StarIQ site. Many of the best minds in astrology comment on the latest news, stock market ups and downs, political contenders. You can sign up to receive e-mail forecasts at the most important times keyed to your individual chart. This is one of the best of the on-line forecasts. Address: *www.stariq.com*

Astrology Lite

For lighter entertainment, go to Astronet, *www.astrology.com/astronet*, for the Internet's equivalent of an astrology mall. Astronet offers interactive fun for everyone. At this writing, there's a special area for teenage astrology fans, advice to the lovelorn, plus a grab bag of horoscopes, a shopping area for books, reports, and software as well as links to all the popular fashion magazine astrology columns.

Swoon.com is another mall-like site aimed at dating, mating, and relating. It has fun features to spark up your love life and plenty of advice for lovers. Address: *www.swoon.com*

Find an Astrologer Here

The A.F.A. Web site

This is the interesting Web site of the prestigious American Federation of Astrologers. The A.F.A. has a directory of astrologers restricted to those who meet their stringent requirements. Check out their correspondence course if you would like to study astrology in depth. Address: *www.astrologers.com*

The NCGR Web site

The Web site of the National Council for Geocosmic Research (NCGR), a leading astrology organization that places great emphasis on education, has a list of accredited astrologers nationwide on their site. Address: *www.geocosmic.org*

Tools Every Astrologer Needs Are On-line

Internet Atlas

Find the geographic longitude and latitude and the correct time zone for any city worldwide. You'll need this information to calculate a chart. Address: *www.astro. com/atlas*

The Exact Time Anywhere in the World

A fun site with fascinating graphics that give you the exact time anywhere in the world. Click on the world map, and the correct time and zone for that place light up. Address: *www.timeticker.com*

Check the Weather Forecast

More accurate than your local TV forecast is the Weathersage, who uses astrology to predict snowstorms and hurricanes. Get your long-range forecast at this super site. Other attractions here are charts and interpretations of people in the news as well as techniques of business forecasting to help us understand these changing times. Address: *www.weathersage.com*

Celebrate the Queen's Birthday

A great jumping off place for an astrology tour of the Internet, this site has a veritable Burke's Peerage of royal birthdays. There's a good selection of articles, tools such as a U.S. and World Atlas, information on conferences, software, tapes, and groups. The links at this site will send you off in the right direction. Information about the latest Palm Pilot astrology software is also available here. Address: *www.zodiacal.com*

Astrology Worldwide

Interested in astrology in Europe? Deborah Houlding, one of the U.K.'s top astrologers, has gathered some of the finest European talent on this super Web site, as well as a comprehensive list of links and conferences. Tour the world of astrology here. Address: *www.astrology-world.com*

Astrology Alive

Barbara Schermer has one of the most innovative and holistic approaches to astrology. She was one of the first astrologers to go on-line, so there's always a "cutting edge" to this site and a great list of links. Barbara is always on top of what's happening now in astrology. Address: *www.astrologyalive.com*

National Council for Geocosmic Research (NCGR)

A key stop on any astrological tour of the Net. Here's where you can find local chapters in your area, get information on the NCGR testing and certification programs, get a conference schedule. There is a list of certified astrologers for those who want readings. Order lecture tapes from their nationwide conferences, or get complete lists of conference topics to study at home. Good links to resources. Address: *www.geocosmic.org*

Where to Find Charts of the Famous

When the news is breaking, you can bet Lois Rodden will be the first to get accurate birthdays of the headline-makers, and put up their charts on her Web site: *www.astrodatabank.com*. Rodden's meticulous research is astrology's most reliable source for data of the famous and infamous. Her Web site specializes in birthdays and charts of current newsmakers, political figures, and international celebrities. You can also participate in an analysis of the charts and see what other astrologers have to say about them. The AstroDatabank program, which you can purchase at the site, provides thousands of birthdays sorted into categories. It's an excellent research tool.

Go to *www.imdb.com* for a comprehensive list of film celebrities including bios, plus lists of famous couples from today and yesteryear. Look under "biographies."

The Matrix software site maintains a list of 30,000 celebrities at: *www.astrologysoftware.com/resources*

Yet another good source for celebrity birth dates is the humorous Metamaze site: *www.metamaze.com/bdays*. You can find some interesting offbeat newsmakers here.

For Astrology Books

National Clearinghouse for Astrology Books

A wide selection of books on all aspects of astrology, from the basics to advanced, is available at this on-line bookstore. Also, many hard-to-find and recycled books. Address: *www.astroamerica.com*

The Heart Center Library site is an excellent resource if you are searching for a particular book or researching a specific aspect of astrology. Address: *www.thenew age.com*

The following addresses also have a good selection of astrology books for sale, some of which are unique to the site.

www.panplanet.com
www.astrocom.com

Browse the huge astrology list of on-line bookstore Amazon.com at *www.amazon.com.*

Astrology Tapes for At-Home Study

You can study at home with world-famous astrologers via audiocassette recordings from Pegasus Tapes. There's an extensive selection taped from conferences, classes, lectures, and seminars. An especially good source for astrologers who emphasize psychological and mythological themes. Address: *www.pegasustape.com*

For History and Mythology Buffs

Be sure to visit the astrology section of this gorgeous site, dedicated to the history and mythology of many traditions. One of the most beautifully designed sites we've seen. Address: *www.elore.com*

The leading authority on the history of astrology, Robert Hand, has an excellent site that features his cutting-edge research. See what one of astrology's great teachers has to offer. Address: *www.robhand.com*

The Project Hindsight group of scholarly astrologers is devoted to restoring the astrology of the Hellenistic period, the primary source for all later Western astrology. There are fascinating articles for astrology fans on this site. Address: *www.projecthindsight.com*

Readers interested in mythology should also check out *www.pantheon.org* for stories of gods and goddesses.

Astrology Magazine

The Mountain Astrologer

A favorite magazine of astrology fans, *The Mountain Astrologer* has an interesting Web site featuring the latest news from an astrological point of view, plus feature articles from the magazine. Address: *www.mountain astrologer.com*

Financial Astrology

Curious about how astrologers play the market? Financial astrology is a hot specialty, with many tipsters, players, and theorists. There are on-line columns, newsletters, specialized financial astrology software, and mutual funds run by astrology seers. One of the most respected financial astrologers is Ray Merriman, whose column on *www.stariq.com* is a "must read" for those following the bulls and bears.

Go to *www.afund.com* or *www.alphee.com* for tips and forecasts from two other top financial astrologers.

See an Image of the Newest Planet: Qua Wha?

As if we didn't have enough planets to interpret, NASA's Hubble Space Telescope has found a new one. Astronomers have measured the largest object in the solar system ever since the discovery of Pluto 72 years ago. Approximately half the size of Pluto, the new baby has been christened "Quaoar" (pronounced *kwa-whar*). Like Pluto, Quaoar dwells in the Kuiper belt, an icy belt of cometlike bodies extending 7 billion miles beyond Neptune's orbit.

View the new baby at the Hubble Web site address: *oposite.stsci.edu/pubinfo/pr/2002/17/index.html*

Do You Look Like Others of Your Sign?

Is there a "family resemblance" among Leos? Among Virgos? Find out at this fascinating site, which compares faces of people with the same sun, moon, and ascendant signs. Great fun! Then you can add a picture of your own face to the show. Address: *www.habarbadi.com/astrofaces*

CHAPTER 8

Astrology Resources

Would you like to delve deeper into astrology and meet other astrology fans? The astrology community welcomes you! You'll soon discover that there's no end to the fascinating techniques and aspects of our age-old art. What's more, you can connect with local astrologers at club meetings and conferences. There's always something new to learn, a lively debate to join, some information to share.

Here are the resources you need to find the right astrology software for your computer, to attend meetings and conferences, to study advanced techniques, or to buy books and tapes.

Whether you'd like to know more about such specialties as financial astrology or techniques for timing events, or if you'd prefer the psychological or mythological approach, you'll meet the top astrologers at conferences sponsored by the National Council for Geocosmic Research. NCGR is dedicated to providing quality education, bringing astrologers and astrology fans together at conferences, and promoting fellowship. Their course structure provides a systematized study of the many facets of astrology.

You can explore astrology via your computer no matter what your level of expertise. Even if you are using an older model, there are still calculation and interpretation programs available. They may not have all the bells and whistles or the exciting graphics, but they'll get the job done!

Newcomers to astrology should learn some of the basics, including the glyphs, before you invest in a computer program. Use chapter 5 in this book to help you learn the symbols easily; then you'll be able to read the charts without consulting the "help" section of your software every time. Several programs such as Astrolabe's Solar Fire have pop-up definitions to help you decipher the meanings of planets and aspects. Just click your mouse on a glyph or an icon on the screen, and a window with an instant definition appears.

You don't have to spend a fortune to get a perfectly adequate astrology program. In fact, if you are connected to the Internet, you can download one free. Astrology software is available at all price levels, from a sophisticated free application like Astrolog, which you can download from the Web site, to inexpensive programs for under $100 such as Winstar Express, to the more expensive astrology programs such as Winstar Plus, Solar Fire, or Io (for the Mac), which are used by serious students and professionals. Before you make an investment, it's a good idea to download a sample, which is usually available on the company's Web site, or to order a demo disk.

If you're baffled by the variety of software available, most of the companies on our list will be happy to help you find the right application for your needs.

Students of astrology who live in out-of-the-way places or are unable to fit classes into your schedule have several options. There are online courses offered at astrology Web sites, such as *www.panplanet.com*, the NCGR and A.F.A. Web sites. Some astrology teachers will send you a series of audiotapes, or you can order audiotaped seminars of recent conferences. Other teachers offer correspondence courses that use their workbooks or computer printouts.

Nationwide Astrology Organizations and Conferences

Contact these organizations for information on conferences, workshops, local meetings, conference tapes, referrals.

National Council for Geocosmic Research (NCGR)

Educational workshops, tapes, conferences, and a directory of professional astrologers are available from this nationwide organization devoted to promoting astrological education. For a $35 annual membership fee, you get their excellent publications and newsletters, plus the opportunity to network with other astrology buffs at local chapter events (there are chapters in 20 states).

To join NCGR, contact the current membership director (as of this writing):

Linda Fei, Membership Director
NCGR
1359 Sargent Ave.
St. Paul, MN 55105

For the latest information about NCGR, consult their Web site: *www.geocosmic.org*.

American Federation of Astrologers (A.F.A.)

This is one of the oldest astrological organizations in the United States, established 1938. They offer conferences, conventions, and a thorough correspondence course. If you are looking for a reading, the Web site will refer you to an accredited A.F.A. astrologer.

A.F.A.
P.O. Box 22040
Tempe, AZ 85285-2040
Phone: (888) 301-7630 or (480) 838-1751
Fax: (480) 838-8293
Web site: *www.astrologers.com*

Association for Astrological Networking (A.F.A.N.)

Did you know that astrologers are still being harassed for practicing astrology? A.F.A.N. provides support and legal information, and works toward improving the public image of astrology. A.F.A.N.'s network of local astrologers links with the international astrological community. Here are the people who will go to bat for astrology when it is attacked in the media. Everyone who cares about astrology should join!

A.F.A.N.
8306 Wilshire Blvd.
PMB 537
Beverly Hills, CA 90211
Phone: (800) 578-2326
E-mail: *info@afan.org*
Web site: *www.afan.org*

Astrology Conferences on Tape

Would you like to hear top astrology lectures on tape? Pegasus has a wonderful selection of tapes from conferences, featuring world-famous astrologers.

Pegasus Tapes
P.O. Box 419
Santa Ysabel, CA 92070
Phone: (800) 288-PEGASUS

International Society for Astrology Research (ISAR)

An international organization of professional astrologers dedicated to encouraging the highest standards of quality in the field of astrology with an emphasis on research. Among ISAR's benefits are a quarterly journal, a weekly e-mail newsletter, and a free biennial membership directory.

ISAR
P.O. Box 38613
Los Angeles, CA 90038

Web site: *www.isarastrology.com*
Fax: (800) 933-0301

Astrology Software

Astrolabe

One of the top astrology software resources. Check out
the latest version of their powerful Solar Fire software
for Windows. It's a breeze to use and will grow with
your increasing knowledge of astrology to the most sophisticated levels. This company also markets a variety
of programs for all levels of expertise and a wide selection of computer-generated astrology readings. A good
resource for innovative software as well as applications
for older computers.

Astrolabe
Box 1750-R
Brewster, MA 02631
Phone: (800) 843-6682
Web site: *www.alabe.com*

Matrix Software

A wide variety of software in all price ranges, demo
disks, student and advanced levels, lots of interesting
readings. Check out Winstar Express, a powerful but rea-
sonably priced program suitable for all skill levels.

Matrix Software
407 N. State Street
Big Rapids, MI 49307
Phone: (800) 416-3924
Web site: *www.astrologysoftware.com*

Astro Communications Services (ACS)

Books, software for MAC and IBM compatibles, individual charts, and telephone readings are offered by this California company. Find technical astrology materials here such as The American Ephemeris and PC atlases. ACS will calculate and send charts to you, a valuable service if you do not have a computer.

ACS Publications
5521 Ruffin Road
San Diego, CA 92123
Phone: (800) 888-9983
Fax: (858) 492-9917
Web site: *www.astrocom.com*

Air Software

Here you'll find powerful, creative astrology software, like Star Trax 2000. For beginners, check out Father Time, which finds your best days. Check out Nostradamus, which answers all your questions. Financial astrology programs for stock market traders are a specialty.

Air Software
115 Caya Avenue
West Hartford, CT 06110
Phone: (800) 659-1247
Web site: *www.alphee.com*

Time Cycles Research: For MAC Users

Here's where MAC users can find astrology software that's as sophisticated as it gets. If you have a MAC, you'll love their beautiful graphic IO Series programs.

Time Cycles Research
375 Willets Avenue
Waterford, CT 06385

Fax: (860) 442-0625
Web site: *www.timecycles.com*

Astrology Magazines

In addition to articles by top astrologers, most have listings of astrology conferences, events, and local happenings.

American Astrology
Dept. 4
P.O. Box 2021
Marion, OH 43306-8121

Dell Horoscope
P.O. Box 54097
Boulder, CO 80322-4097

The Mountain Astrologer
P.O. Box 970
Cedar Ridge, CA 95924
Web site: *www.mountainastrologer.com*

Astrology College

An accredited college dedicated to astrology is here at last! Check out the Kepler College listed below.

Kepler College of Astrological Arts and Sciences

A degree-granting college, which is also a center of astrology, has long been the dream of the astrological community and is a giant step forward in providing credibility to the profession.

Therefore, the opening of Kepler College in 2000 was a historical event for astrology. It is the only college in

the western hemisphere authorized to issue B.A. and
M.A. degrees in Astrological Studies. The entire curriculum is based on astrology.

For more information, contact:

Kepler College of Astrological Arts and Sciences
4630 200th Street SW
Suite P
Lynnwood, WA 98036
Voice: (425) 673-4292
Fax: (425) 673-4983
Web site: *www.kepler.edu*

CHAPTER 9

How About a Personal Reading?

If you are interested in astrology, at some point you'll consider having a personal reading. For instance, an important date is coming up, perhaps a wedding or the start of a new business, and you're wondering if an astrologically picked date could influence the outcome. You've fallen in love and must know if it will last forever. Your partnership is not going well, and you're not sure if you can continue to work together. You're in a downslide when problems seem insurmountable. Or you simply want to have your chart interpreted by an expert.

But what kind of reading should you have? There are so many options for readings that sorting through them can be a daunting task. Besides individual one-on-one readings with a professional astrologer, there are telephone readings, Internet readings, tapes, computer-generated reports, and celebrity-sponsored readings. Here's what to look for and some cautionary notes.

Done by a qualified astrologer, the personal reading can be an empowering experience if you want to reach your full potential, size up a lover or business situation, or find out what the future has in store. There are astrologers who are specialists in certain areas such as finance or medical astrology. And, unfortunately, there are many questionable practitioners who range from streetwise gypsy fortune-tellers to unscrupulous scam artists.

The following basic guidelines can help you sort out your options to find the reading that's right for you.

One-on-One Consultations with a Professional Astrologer

Nothing compares to a one-on-one consultation with a professional astrologer who has analyzed thousands of charts and can pinpoint the potential in yours. During your reading, you can get your specific questions answered. For instance, how to get along better with your mate or coworker. There are many astrologers who now combine their skills with training in psychology and are well-suited to help you examine your alternatives.

To give you an accurate reading, an astrologer needs certain information from you: the date, time, and place where you were born. (A horoscope can be cast about anyone or anything that has a specific time and place.) Most astrologers will then enter this information into a computer, which will calculate a chart in seconds. From the resulting chart, the astrologer will do an interpretation.

If you don't know your exact birth time, you can usually locate it at the Bureau of Vital Statistics at the city hall or county seat of the state where you were born. If you still have no success in getting your time of birth, some astrologers can estimate an approximate birth time by using past events in your life to determine the chart. This technique is called *rectification*.

How to Find an Astrologer

Choose your astrologer with the same care as any trusted adviser such as a doctor, lawyer, or banker. Unfortunately, anyone can claim to be an astrologer—to date, there is no licensing of astrologers or universally established professional criteria. However, there are nationwide organizations of serious, committed astrologers that can help you in your search.

Good places to start your investigation are o

tions such as the American Federation of Astrologers (A.F.A.) or the National Council for Geocosmic Research (NCGR), which offer a program of study and certification. If you live near a major city, there is sure to be an active NCGR chapter or astrology club in your area; many are listed in astrology magazines available at your local newsstand. In response to many requests for referrals, both the A.F.A. and the NCGR have directories of professional astrologers listed on their Web sites; these directories include a glossary of terms and an explanation of specialties within the astrological field. Contact the NCGR and A.F.A. headquarters (see also chapter 7 and chapter 8 in this book) for information.

Warning Signals

As a potentially lucrative freelance business, astrology has always attracted self-styled experts who may not have the knowledge or the counseling experience to give a helpful reading. These astrologers can range from the well-meaning amateur to the charlatan or street-corner gypsy who has for many years given astrology a bad name. Be very wary of astrologers who claim to have occult powers or who make pretentious claims of celebrated clients or miraculous achievements. You can often tell from the initial phone conversation if the astrologer is legitimate. He or she should ask for your birthday time and place, then conduct the conversation in a professional manner. Any astrologer who gives a reading based only on your sun sign is highly suspect.

When you arrive at the reading, the astrologer should be prepared. The consultation should be conducted in a private, quiet place. The astrologer should be interested in your problems of the moment. A good reading involves feedback on your part. So if the reading is not relating to your concerns, you should let the astrologer know. You should feel free to ask questions and get clarifications of technical terms. The more you actively participate, rather than expecting the astrologer to carry the reading or come forth with oracular predictions, the more meaningful your experience will be. An astrologer should help you validate your current experience and be frank about possible negative happenings, but also suggest a positive course of action.

In their approach to a reading, some astrologers may be more literal, others more intuitive. Those who have had counseling training may take a more psychological approach. Though some astrologers may seem to have an almost psychic ability, extrasensory perception or any other parapsychological talent is not essential. A very accurate picture can be drawn from the data in your horoscope chart.

An astrologer may do several charts for each client, including one for the time of birth and a "progressed chart," showing the evolution from birth to the present time. According to your individual needs, there are many other possibilities, such as a chart for a different location if you are contemplating a change of place. Relationships between any two people, things, or events can be interpreted with a chart that compares one partner's horoscope with the other's. A composite chart, which uses the midpoint between planets in two individual charts to describe the relationship, is another commonly used device.

An astrologer will be particularly interested in transits, those times when cycling planets activate the planets or sensitive points in your birth chart. These indicate important events in your life.

Many astrologers offer tape-recorded readings, another option to consider, especially if the astrologer you choose lives at a distance. In this case, you'll be mailed a taped reading based on your birth chart. This type of reading is more personal than a computer printout and can give you valuable insights, though it is not equivalent to a live dialogue with the astrologer when you can discuss your specific interests and issues of the moment.

The Telephone Reading

Telephone readings come in two varieties: a dial-in taped reading, usually recorded in advance by an astrologer, or a live consultation with an "astrologer" on the other end of the line. The taped readings are general daily or weekly forecasts, applied to all members of your sign and charged by the minute. The quality depends on the astrologer. One caution: Be aware that these readings can run up quite a telephone bill, especially if you get into the habit of calling every day. Be sure that you are aware of the per-minute cost of each call beforehand.

Live telephone readings also vary with the expertise of the astrologer. Ideally, the astrologer at the other end of the line enters your birth data into a computer, which then quickly calculates your chart. This chart will be referred to during the consultation. The advantage of a live telephone reading is that your individual chart is used and you can ask about a specific problem. However, before you invest in any reading, be sure that your astrologer is qualified and that you fully understand in advance how much you will be charged. There should be no unpleasant financial surprises later.

Computer-Generated Reports

Companies that offer computer programs (such as ACS, Matrix, Astrolabe) also offer a variety of computer-generated horoscope readings. These can be quite comprehensive, offering a beautiful printout of the chart plus many pages of detailed information about each planet and aspect of the chart. You can then study it at your convenience. Of course, the interpretations will be general, since there is no personal input from you, and may not cover your immediate concerns. Since computer-generated horoscopes are much lower in cost than live consultations, you might consider them as either a supplement or a preparation for an eventual live reading. You'll then be more familiar with your chart and able to plan specific questions in advance. They also make a terrific gift for astrology fans. There are several companies, listed in chapters 7 and 8, that offer computerized readings prepared by reputable astrologers.

Whichever option you decide to pursue, may your reading be an empowering one!

CHAPTER 10

Are You Having a Midlife Crisis? Signposts from the Stars

The stereotype is all too familiar. A middle-aged man divorces his wife and marries a younger woman, buys a red convertible and a snazzy new wardrobe, begins to diet and work out, and updates his hairstyle. Women are less dramatic. Perhaps she'll start a new career or take up activities outside the home, have plastic surgery, join a gym, and stock up on antiaging creams. She might break out of her normal routine by having an affair with a younger man or someone unlike her husband. Confirmed singles may finally marry or settle down with a partner. These signs all point to a midlife crisis.

As a milestone birthday or high school reunion approaches, we start to evaluate our lives. We look at our declining physical shape. We assess our accomplishments, or lack of them. And often we must face the fact that we're not the success we expected to be back then. (And we're certainly not the hot young thing we were in our twenties and thirties!)

To astrologers, the midlife crisis period is predictable and understandable. It's part of a natural process that affects individuals between the approximate ages of 37 to 47. This process involves major transits of the slow-moving outer planets, Neptune, Uranus, and Pluto, and also a phase in the transit of Saturn.

Neptune, Uranus, Pluto, and Saturn are the planets that cause profound and dramatic changes in our lives. These planets challenge the status quo, forcing us to evaluate where we've been and where we're going. If we are unhappy, then we will be strongly pushed to make changes, some of which will happen suddenly and dramatically. In the long view, this process is preparing us for the latter part of our lives, for accepting maturity.

Who's Likely to Have a Midlife Crisis This Year?

The Pluto Phase

This year, the Pluto phase of the midlife crisis will affect those born from 1967 to 1969 (those who would be age 37 to 39). During 2004, Pluto in Sagittarius will form a 90 degree ("square") angle to the Pluto in Virgo position in the individual's chart. This is considered a tense aspect, because the square angle falls in signs of the same quality (way of operating) but of different elements. This year, it will be the mutable (changeable) sign of the fire element Sagittarius and the mutable (changeable) sign of the earth element Virgo. Fire igniting earth can produce a volcanic eruption—or transform clay into beautiful ceramics!

Pluto is the planet of transformation, causing unconscious feelings to surface from deep inside us. It is a time when we face issues of power, control, and sexuality—when we ask ourselves who we really are. "Are you expressing your real self or one that has been programmed by parents and society?" This process could lead to great uncertainty. The challenge is to get past our fears, to eventually come to terms with ourselves, developing a better understanding of our true persona. Needless to say, this is a great time to do deep inner psychological work.

The Neptune Phase

During the Neptune phase this year, transiting Neptune in Aquarius will square the natal Neptune in Scorpio of those born from 1962 to 1964 (now age 42 to 44). At this phase of midlife, we are asked to go with the flow. But you may experience a lack of direction as you navigate this foggy Neptune transit. The past no longer provides security, yet the future is not clear.

This Neptune phase can be a very frustrating, confusing time when all is not as it seems. A tendency to escape, especially via Neptune-ruled drugs or alcohol, may be a strong temptation—a temptation to be avoided. Although nothing is certain, this transit can be used positively for inner development, for spiritual work, for projects that stretch the imagination.

The Uranus Phase

The Uranus phase is often the most dramatic, rattling the structure of your life. Uranus is the planet that shakes you up with a bolt from out of the blue. This year, Uranus in Pisces opposes Uranus in Virgo in the charts of those born from 1962 to 1964 (age 42 to 44). It's a double whammy for these midlifers, as they are going through the Neptune phase at the same time.

Uranus can prompt very sudden changes, breaking up patterns that are no longer working for you. It can make you feel as rebellious as an adolescent, if you've felt tied down for too long. The desire is intense to do something that will change your life, to break away from restrictions of any kind. Perhaps a divorce, adopting or having a child, changing your career, moving to another country will be options. There may be a feeling that this is your last chance, so you must do it now.

With Uranus opposite Uranus, you can act very radically and impulsively. So it might serve you well to ask beforehand what part of life is holding you back. Where do you need a chance to breathe? It may be possible to add some excitement to your life and to make changes without shaking up everyone else.

The Saturn Phase

The Saturn phase of this cycle happens when Saturn opposes an individual's natal Saturn. This year, Saturn in Cancer opposes the natal Saturn in Capricorn of those born from December 1959 to March 1961 (those now age 43 to 45).

Saturn is the testing planet that gives you a reality check. If you have been out of sync and need to rethink your situation, Saturn will make you do it. However, if you have cleared away outworn patterns during the previous transits, you may accept your newfound maturity and move on. Saturn will help you build for a fulfilling future.

Astrological Tips for Utilizing the Transits

The midlife crisis transits can be very uncomfortable. You may experience a wide range of feelings and often deep insecurity while you go through changes. You may baffle others. You may no longer feel satisfied with a lifestyle that seemed so stable for so long, which often happens during the Uranus phase. You may question the meaning of life, then develop your spiritual side during the Neptune phase. The Saturn and Pluto phases sometimes bring significant loss or change, such as the death of a parent, a divorce, or the loss of a job.

It is important to remember that these transits signal a natural process we all go through. Understanding the process from an astrological point of view can help you see ahead more clearly and avoid making impulsive decisions that you may later regret.

One way to utilize these transits is to ask what the experiences are revealing about your inner needs. If you haven't accomplished what you would like to do, you may be inspired to create a life that is more satisfying. Once you get over the bumpy parts of these transits, you may find that your midlife years are the most fulfilling ever.

CHAPTER 11

Sex and the Stars: A Leap Year Guide to Heating Up Your Love Life

Want to charm a Capricorn? Hook a Pisces? Corral a Taurus? Here are sun sign seduction tips guaranteed to keep your lover begging for more.

How to Love Every Sign

Aries: Daredevil Lover

This highly physical sign is walking dynamite with a brief attention span. Don't be too easy to get, ladies. A little challenge, a lively debate, a merry chase only heats them up. They want to see what you're made of. Once you've lured them into your lair, be a challenge, a bit of a daredevil, pull out your X-rated tricks. Don't give your all—let them know there's more where that came from.

Make it exciting, show you're up for adventure. Wear bright red somewhere interesting. Since Aries rules the head and face, be sure to focus on these areas in your lovemaking. Use your lips, tongue, breath (even your eyelashes) to the max. Practice scalp massages, deep kissing techniques.

Aries won't wait. So when you make your move, be sure you're ready to follow through. No head games or teasing!

To keep *you* happy: You've got to voice your own

needs. This lover will be focused on his. Teach him how to please, or this could be a one-sided adventure.

Taurus: Sweet Treats

Taurus wins as the most sensual sign, with the most sexual stamina. Taurus is earthy and lusty in bed, can go on all night. This is not a sign to tease. Like the Bull, they'll see red—not bed. So make them comfortable. Then bombard all their senses.

Good food gets Taurus in the mood. The right music (learn their preferences), fragrance, touchy-feely clothes and bed linens turn them on. Give them a massage with delicious smelling and tasting oils; focus on the neck area. Once that's relaxed, work downward.

Taurus is associated with the throat and neck area. They tend to favor oral techniques and are the best kissers! They hate interruptions, so turn off the phone. Since they can be very vocal lovers, choose a setting where you won't be disturbed. And don't ever rush them. Enjoy a long, slow, delicious encounter.

Gemini: Playtime

Playful Gemini loves games, so make your seduction fun and playful. Be their lost twin soul, their confidante. Share deep secrets, live out fantasies. This sign adores variety. Nothing bores Gemini more than making love the same way all the time, or bringing on the heavy emotions. So trot out all the roles you've been longing to play—here's the perfect partner. But remember to keep it light and fun.

Gemini's turn-on zone is the hands, and this sign gives the best massages. Let Gemini wrap you around their little fingers—literally. Gadgets that can be turned on with a touch are Gemini amusers. Gemini is great at doing two things at once, like making love while watching an erotic film. Do turn the cell phone off, however, unless you want company. On the other hand, Gemini is your sign for superhot phone sex.

Gemini loves a change of scene. So experiment on the floor, in the shower, on the kitchen table. Borrow a friend's apartment or rent a room in a hotel for variety.

Cancer: In the Mood

The key to Cancer is to get this Moon Child in the mood. Consult the moon—full moon is best. Wining, dining, old-fashioned courtship, breakfast in bed are turn-ons. Whatever makes your Cancer feel secure will promote shedding inhibitions in the sack. (Don't try any of your Aries daredevil techniques here!) Cancer prefers familiar, comfortable, homey surroundings.

Cancer's turn-on zone is the breasts. Cancer women often have naturally inflated chests. Cancer men may fantasize about a well-endowed playmate. If your breasts are enhanced, show them off. Cancer will want to know all your deepest secrets, so invent a few good ones. But lots of luck delving into their innermost thoughts!

A sure thing: Take your Cancer near water. The sight and sound of the sea can be their aphrodisiac. A moonlit beach, deserted swimming pool, Jacuzzi, or a bubble bath are good seduction spots. Listen to the rain patter on the roof in a mountain cabin.

Leo: The Royal Treatment

Leo must be The Best and hear it from you often. In return, they'll perform for you, telling you just what you want to hear (true or not). They like a lover with style and endurance, to be swept off their feet and into bed.

Leos like to go first-class all the way, so build them up with lots of attention, wining and dining, special gifts. Never mention other lovers or make them feel like second best. A sure signal for Leo to look elsewhere is a competitive spouse.

Leos take great pride in their body, so you should pour

on the admiration. A few well placed mirrors could inspire them. So would a striptease of beautiful lingerie, expensive fragrance on the sheets, and, if female, an occasional luxury hotel room, with champagne and caviar delivered by room service. Leo's erogenous zone is the lower back, so a massage with expensive oils would make your lion purr with pleasure.

Virgo: Pedestal Perfect

Virgo's standards are so sky-high that you may feel intimidated at first. The key to pleasing fussy Virgo lovers is to look for the hot fantasy beneath their cool surface. Secret tip: They're really looking for someone to makeover. So let Virgo play teacher and you play willing student; the doctor–patient routine works as well. Be Eliza Doolittle to his Henry Higgins.

Let Virgo help you improve your life, quit smoking, learn French, diet. Read an erotic book together, then practice the techniques. Or study the esoteric, erotic exercises from the Far East.

The Virgo erogenous zone is the tummy area, which should be your base of operations. Virgo likes things pristine and clean. Fall into crisp, immaculate white sheets. Wear a sheer, virginal white nightie. Smell shower-fresh with no heavy perfume. Be sure your surroundings pass the hospital test. A shower together afterward (with great-smelling soap) could get the ball rolling again.

Libra: The Beauty Lover

Libra must be turned on aesthetically. Make sure you look as beautiful as possible, and are wearing something stylishly seductive but never vulgar. Have a mental affair first, as you flirt and flatter this sign. Then proceed to the physical. Approach Libra like a dance partner, ready to waltz or tango.

Libra must be in the mood for love; otherwise, forget

it. Any kind of ugliness is a turnoff. Provide the right atmosphere, elegant and harmonious. No loud noise, clashing colors, or uncomfortable beds.

Libra is not an especially spontaneous lover, so it is best to spend time warming them up. Libra's back is his erogenous zone, your cue to provide backrubs with scented potions. Once in bed, you can be a bit aggressive sexually. Libra loves strong, decisive moves. Set the scene, know what you want, and let Libra be happy to provide it.

Scorpio: Sex in the Raw

Scorpio is legendary in bed, often called the "sex sign of the zodiac." But seducing them is often a power game. Scorpio likes to be in control—even the quiet, unassuming ones. Scorpio loves a mystery, so don't tell all. Keep them guessing about you, offering tantalizing hints along the way. The hint of danger often turns Scorpio on, so you'll find members of this sign experimenting with the exotic and highly erotic forms of sex. Sadomasochism, bondage, anything that tests the limits of power could be a turn-on for Scorpio.

Invest in some sexy black leather, some powerful music (depending on your tastes). Clothes that lace, buckle, or zip tempt Scorpio to untie you. Present yourself as a mysterious package just waiting to be unwrapped.

Once in bed, there are no holds barred with Scorpio. They'll find your most pleasurable pressure points, touch you as you've never been touched before. They are quickly aroused (the genital area belongs to this sign) and willing to try anything. But they can be possessive. Don't expect your Scorpio to share you with anyone. It's all or nothing for them.

Sagittarius: The Sexual Athletes

Sagittarius men are the Don Juans of the zodiac, love 'em and leave 'em types who are difficult to pin down.

Your seduction strategy is to join them in their many pursuits, then hook them with love on the road.

Sagittarius enjoys sex in venues that suggest movement—planes, SUVs, boats. But a favorite turn-on place is outdoors, in nature. A deserted hiking path, a field of tall grass, a remote woodland glade all give the Centaur sexy ideas. Athletic Sagittarius might go for some personal training in an empty gym. Join your Sagittarius for amorous aerobics, meditate together, explore the tantric forms of sex. Lovemaking after hiking and skiing would be healthy fun.

Sagittarius enjoys lovers from exotic ethnic backgrounds, lovers met in spiritual pursuits or on college campuses. Sagittarius are great cheerleaders and motivators, and will enjoy feeling that they have inspired you to "be all that you can be."

There may be a canine or feline companion sharing your Sagittarius lover's bed with you, so check your allergies. And bring Fido or Felix a toy to keep them occupied.

Capricorn: Animal Instincts

The great news about Capricorn lovers is that they improve with age. They are probably the sexiest seniors. So stick around, if you have a young one. They're lusty in bed (it's not the sign of the Goat for nothing), and can be quite raunchy and turned on by X-rated words and deeds. If this is not your thing, let them know. The Capricorn erogenous zone is the knees. Some discreet fondling in public places could be your opener.

Capricorn tends to think of sex as part of a game plan for the future. They are well-organized, and might regard lovemaking as relaxation after a long day's work. This sign often combines business with pleasure. So look for a Capricorn where there's a convention, trade show, or work-related conference.

Getting Capricorn's mind off his agenda and onto yours could take some doing. Separate him from his buddies by whispering sexy secrets in his ear. Then convince him you're an asset to his image and a boon to his health. Though he may seem uptight at first, you'll soon discover he's a love animal who makes a wonderful and permanent pet.

Aquarius: Far-out Lover

This sign really does not want an all-consuming passion or an all-or-nothing relationship. Aquarius need space. But once they feel free to experiment with a spontaneous and exciting partner, Aquarius can give you a far-out sexual adventure.

Passion begins in the mind, so a good mental buildup is key. Aquarius is an inventive sign who believes love is a playground without rules. Plan surprise, unpredictable encounters in unusual places. Find ways to make love transcendental, an extraordinary and unique experience. Be ready to try anything Aquarius suggests—if only once. Calves and ankles are the special Aquarius erogenous zone, so perfect your legwork.

Be careful not to be too possessive. Your Aquarius needs lots of space, tolerance for friends (including old lovers), and their many outside interests.

Pisces: Fantasy Time

Pisces is the sign of fantasy and imagination. This sign has great theatrical talent. Pisces looks for lovers who will take care of them. Pisces will return the favor! Here is someone who can psych out your deepest desires without mentioning them.

Pisces falls for sob stories and is always ready to empathize. It wouldn't hurt to have a small problem for Pisces to help you overcome. It might help if you cry on his shoulder, for this sign needs to be needed.

Use your imagination when setting the scene for love. A dramatic setting brings out Pisces theatrical talents. Or creatively use the element of water. Rain on the roof, waterfalls, showers, beach houses, waterbeds, and Jacuzzis could turn up the heat. Experiment with pulsating jets of water. Take midnight skinny dips in deserted pools.

The Pisces erogenous zone is the feet. This is your cue to play footsie. Learn to give a sensuous foot massage using scented lotions. Let him paint your toes. Beautiful toenails in sexy sandals are a special turn-on.

Your Hot Planets: Mars and Venus Tango Together

Here's a tip for finding your hottest love match. If your lover's Mars sign makes favorable aspects to your Venus—is in the same element (earth, air, fire, water) or is in the same sign—your lover will do what you want done! Mars influences how we act when we make love, while Venus shows what we like done to us.

Sometimes fighting and making up is the sexiest fun of all. If you're the type who needs a spark to keep lust alive (you know who you are!), then look for Mars and Venus in different signs of the same quality (fixed or cardinal or mutable). For instance, a fixed sign (Taurus, Leo, Scorpio, Aquarius) paired with another fixed sign can have a sexy standoff, a hot tug of war before you finally surrender. Two cardinal signs (Aries, Cancer, Libra, Capricorn) set off passionate fireworks when they clash. Mutable signs (Gemini, Virgo, Sagittarius, Pisces) play a fascinating game of cat and mouse, never quite catching each other.

The Best Time for Love

The best time for love is when Venus is in your sign, making you the most desirable sign in the zodiac. This only lasts about three weeks (unless Venus is retrograde), so don't waste time! And find out the time this year when Venus is in your sign by consulting the Venus chart at the end of chapter 4.

Who's the Sexiest Sign of the Zodiac?

It depends on what sign *you* are. Astrology has traditionally given this honor to Scorpio, the sign associated with the sex organs. However, we are all a combination of different signs (and turn-ons). Gemini's communicating ability and manual dexterity could deliver the magic touch. Cancer's tenderness and understanding could bring out your passion more than regal Leo.

Who'll Be Faithful?

The earth signs of Capricorn, Taurus, and Virgo are usually the most faithful. They tend to be more home-oriented and family-oriented, and they are usually choosy about their mates. It's impractical, inconvenient, and probably expensive to play around—so they think.

Who's Most Likely to Cheat?

The mutable signs of Gemini, Pisces, and Sagittarius win the playboy or playgirl sweepstakes. These signs tend to be changeable, fickle, and easily bored. But they're so much fun!

CHAPTER 12

Can Astrology Help You Get Rich? Financial Portents in the Stars

What financial portents are in the stars? What can you do about them? And what do solar flares signal about market investments?

Like many tyrants, kings, and tycoons you, too, can benefit from astrology's insights in predicting current growth trends. (The financial tycoon J. P. Morgan is rumored to have consulted an astrologer.) So find out where your best opportunities lie and what stage of the wheel of success you're on, then make savvy decisions to play the market or stay on the sidelines.

Using the trends in this chapter, you can formulate your strategy for building wealth in 2004.

Solar Flares Bring out the Bears

Some business astrologers swear by the solar flare. Whenever there is a dramatic fiery ejection from the sun, there seems to be a drop in the stock market. Unfortunately, there seems to be no reliable advance notice to enable us to time major solar flares. However, you can see some cool photos of the latest ones on-line at *www.spacewatcher.com*.

Pisces Issues Come Forward

The movements of the planet Uranus are big factors in the stability of the financial picture. After Uranus moved into Pisces last year, all things relating to Pisces are major issues for the next seven years. While in Aquarius, the sign of high technology, Uranus sent the stock of dotcoms and Internet startups soaring. Now watch what it does for Pisces businesses. Scientific medicine should have spectacular success. Look for new advances in pharmaceuticals, especially antibiotics (inspired by bioterrorism), in embryonic research, and in genetics. Hospitals should become more focused on treating each person as an individual, perhaps based on a personal genetic profile. There should be terrific investment opportunities in these areas.

Petroleum is associated with Pisces, so it's no surprise that oil issues will remain in the headlines. Our huge appetite for oil may remain one of America's most vulnerable points. This year, expect major changes in our energy policy and consumption. Redesigned fuel-efficient or electrical cars are possibilities. So are nonfossil sources of energy.

Offshore oil exploration and development of oceanic energy reserves may be accelerated, as well as development of hydroelectric power companies, as we tap oceans and rivers for power sources. Look for investment opportunities in power-saving devices of all kinds.

Pisces is associated with all things aquatic, of course. Fish farms, water purifying systems, swimming pools, ocean studies, shipping, sea plants as food, ocean exploration, submarine travel, and naval supplies are investment possibilities.

Creative areas have historically done well, as Uranus in Pisces stimulates avant-garde artists. New music, computer-generated art and entertainment, and the dance world (especially ballet) should thrive. Other Pisces areas include film, footwear, cosmetics, podiatry, fountains, gases, dance, alcohol and other intoxicants, any business involving fantasy and creativity, religion-oriented businesses, yoga and other spiritual practices, retreats, charities, and any institutions that help the underdog.

The Jupiter Factor

Good fortune and big money are always associated with Jupiter, which embodies the principle of expansion. Jupiter has a twelve-year cycle, staying in each sign for approximately one year. When Jupiter enters a sign, the fields influenced by that sign seem new and profitable, and they usually provide excellent investment opportunities. Areas of speculation governed by the sign Jupiter is passing through will have the hottest market potential—they're the ones that currently arouse excitement and enthusiasm.

This year Jupiter finishes its transit of Virgo, then moves into Libra in late September. The areas these signs influence should have expansive opportunities. Those born in earth signs (Virgo, Capricorn, Taurus) should take advantage of Jupiter's beneficial rays during the first half of the year. Those born in air signs (Libra, Aquarius, Gemini) should look for growth opportunities from October on.

Jupiter-Favored Growth Areas

All that is health-promoting, detail-oriented, and educational should get a big boost from Jupiter in Virgo. Watch efficient Virgo-related areas for growth opportunities: organizers, accountants, administrators, haute cuisine, public health, the medical and health industries, medicinal herbs, grain production, education, the service business, sanitation, sewing and tailoring, personal trainers, health clubs.

In Libra, Jupiter will promote harmony, justice, the arts, the legal profession, diplomacy, social life, and all the peripheral businesses associated with social events. With Jupiter in the "marriage sign," this should be a boom time for weddings and the wedding business. It should be an excellent time for the fashion business, interior design, and all the design-related fields. Perhaps we'll be wearing more pink, a Libra color. Look for opportunities in health fields that stress balance: diet, yoga, aerobics, dancing, skating.

In Your Personal Life

Find the house where Jupiter in Virgo and Jupiter in Libra will fall in your chart to indicate where you'll have the most expansive potential this year. Just look up your rising sign from the chart in this book (pp. 118–119) and check the following list. (Those who know their exact birth time and place, and who have access to the Internet, can get an accurate chart on-line from one of the sources recommended in the Internet chapter in this book.)

ARIES RISING: DETAILS, DETAILS

This is the time when you may seem bogged down in details, in learning the operation of the company from the ground up, or in taking care of the mundane aspects that make a business operate efficiently. But remember, it is only through creating a smooth working operation that fortunes can be made in the long haul. You have only to read the financial section of your newspaper to see how many promising companies get swept away by poor management. This is also an excellent time to take care of yourself. Set up a diet and exercise regime. Get your body in good shape. In the latter months of the year, consider joining a partner to get ahead faster.

TAURUS RISING: A CREATIVE BONANZA

For creative Taurus, this is bonanza time—the inspiration flows! Put some fun into your life and help others to do so for profit. Your best ideas will come when you play at your job (don't they always?), finding more creative ways to get the work done. The only danger here is too much fun—you may be more interested in pleasure than profit. Love affairs, fun times, and recreation can impose on work time. You may find it difficult to stick to any routines. Since this placement also rules children, you may find yourself involved with them in some way—or you may become a parent.

GEMINI RISING: LUCK BEGINS AT HOME
Your success potential is tied to your domestic life. This is often a time of moving or relocating, as you try to arrange your personal lifestyle for the next twelve years. This is the time to establish your personal space, strengthen family ties, and give yourself a solid base of operations. You can now create the much-needed balance between your private life and the outside world that will shore you up for the next twelve years. Aim for greater family harmony and inner strength. Opportunities to invest in real estate could be winners.

CANCER RISING: COMMUNICATIONS
You will overflow with ideas, so record them for future reference. Write up a storm! Sign up for a course that interests you—it could pay off in the future. Your social life is buzzing, as the phone rings off the hook. Make new business contacts in your local area. You may also find a lucky financial venture that involves your friends or siblings. In the fall, home life takes priority. This is the time to redecorate, renovate, expand, or buy a new home.

LEO RISING: INCREASE YOUR SECURITY
Be a saver, not a spender, this year. Now is the time to use those contacts you made last year to consolidate your financial security. You may find that your cash flow increases, as there is generally more money available for big splurges. Watch this tendency! It might be a better idea to use this time of opportunity to protect yourself

with backup funds for a more secure future. This is a time to develop good money management habits!

VIRGO RISING: THE IMAGE THAT SELLS
For most of the year, you hold the luckiest cards. With Jupiter energizing your ascendant, you look like a winner without even trying. Use this time to kick off the next twelve-year cycle in the most advantageous way. Circulate among influential people, make personal contacts, sell yourself. Push yourself out in the public eye, even if you're the shy type. This is the time to be your most social self! One cautionary note: Jupiter means expansion, and this position rules your physical body—so watch your diet. You'll tend to put on weight easily. The latter half of the year, focus on making a budget and savings plan that you can live with. If you've been caught up in an extravagant lifestyle, do a reality check.

LIBRA RISING: WARM-UP FOR THE BIG TIME
You've come to the end of a twelve-year Jupiter cycle, and late September will start another cycle when Jupiter enters your sign of Libra. Use the first half of the year to review what you've learned in the last twelve years, to experiment with new ventures. Proceed slowly, as you will be bringing many matters that have occupied you over the past dozen years to a close. It's also a good time to get centered spiritually, to line up your ducks in a row, so you'll be ready to seize the moment when opportunities arise late September with Jupiter entering Libra. Then go for it in October when you'll hold the best cards in the deck.

SCORPIO RISING: THE BIG LEAGUE
Jupiter brings you group connections this year. Others will be looking to you for inspiration. Since you can now win the support of the movers and shakers in your field and are ready to lead the pack, put some of the ideas formulated in previous cycles into action. This is the time when you make the team, come to the aid of your party,

or find a new audience for your talents. In the fall, you may be ready for some solitude! This is a good time to rest, regroup, do some solitary creative work, or fundraise for your favorite hospital or charity.

SAGITTARIUS RISING: BUILD YOUR PRESTIGE
It's a great time to promote yourself, be highly visible, and build up your professional image. This cycle favors public activities rather than domestic life. It's a great time to deal with VIPs and top brass. You should be feeling superconfident, and it will show. You may be starting a new career or making a stronger commitment to the one you're in. Follow up with social contacts, and exercise your leadership skill in the fall.

CAPRICORN RISING: AIM HIGH
This is the ideal time to get higher education, develop your philosophy of life, and formulate new directions for the future. Aim high, look at the big overall picture. Publish your book, get a college or graduate degree, travel abroad. Expand your mind and horizons. Take a calculated risk. You may feel like changing your life around and trying something completely new. The ideas you get early in the year and the interesting people you meet will enhance your reputation and career.

AQUARIUS RISING: WATCH THE CASH FLOW
You'll have opportunities to use credit and to deal with banks, loan companies, and the IRS. Be very careful with your credit cards during this period. There could be a strong temptation to overextend. You may find others more than willing to lend you money at high interest. If you're a risk taker, you may have to keep a strict eye on expenditures—Jupiter encourages gambling! You might also find yourself managing money for others and getting involved in joint ventures.

PISCES RISING: MAKING COMMITMENTS
Commitments can be fortunate for you this year. Many

people marry at this time. However, this is not a good time for solo ventures. You are best off working in tandem and letting your partner share the spotlight. You may have to submerge your own agenda for a while in order to take full advantage of this period. So think "togetherness." You can use others to your advantage, but don't try to take over. Since this is the area of open enemies, you could learn much about your adversaries and gain the advantage in the future. In the latter months, the focus shifts to joint finances.

CHAPTER 13

The Generation of 2004: Astrological Portraits of Children Born This Year

Children born this year belong to one of the most spiritual generations in history. The three outer planets, Uranus, Neptune, and Pluto, which stay in a sign for at least seven years, are the ones that most affect each generation. Now moving through Pisces, Aquarius, and Sagittarius respectively, the three most visionary signs, these planets are sure to imprint the children of 2004.

As Uranus moved into Pisces last year, it ushered in a new atmosphere. In the past century, Uranus in Pisces coincided with enormous creativity, which should impact this year's children. Neptune in Aquarius and Pluto in Sagittarius are continuing their transits, bringing a time of dissolving barriers, of globalization, of interest in religion and spirituality—breaking away from the materialism of the last century. In contrast, this generation will truly be "children of the world," searching for deeper meanings to existence.

Astrology can be an especially helpful tool. It can be used to design an environment that will enhance and encourage each child's positive qualities. Some parents start from before conception, planning the birth of their child in order to harmonize with the signs of other family members. However, each baby has its own schedule. If yours arrives a week early or late, or elects a different sign from the one you planned, recognize that the "new" sign may be more in line with the mission your child is meant to accomplish. In other words, if you were hoping for a Libra child and he or she arrives during Virgo, that Virgo energy may be just what is needed to stimulate or complement your family.

Remember, there are many astrological elements besides the sun sign that indicate strong family ties. Usually each child will share a particular planetary placement, an emphasis on a particular sign or house, or a certain chart configuration with the parents and other family members. Often there is a significant planetary angle that will define the parent-child relationship, such as family sun signs that form a T-square or a triangle.

One important thing you can do is to be sure the exact moment of birth is recorded. This will be essential in calculating an accurate astrological chart, if you should wish to have one drawn up in the future.

The following descriptions can be applied to the sun sign or to the moon sign (if known) of a child. The sun sign will describe basic personality, and the moon sign will indicate the child's emotional needs.

The Aries Child

Baby Aries is quite a handful! This energetic child will walk—and run—as soon as possible, and will perform daring feats of exploration. Caregivers should be vigilant. Little Aries seems to know no fear, and is especially vulnerable to head injuries. Many Aries children, in their rush to get on with life, seem hyperactive; they are easily frustrated when they can't get their own way. Violent temper tantrums and dramatic physical displays are par for the course with this child.

The very young Aries should be monitored carefully, since they are prone to take risks and may injure themselves. Aries love to take things apart and may break toys easily. But with encouragement, the child will develop formidable coordination. Aries bossy tendencies should be molded into leadership qualities rather than bullying techniques. Otherwise, the "me-first" Aries will have many clashes with other strong-willed youngsters.

Encourage this child to take out aggressions and frustrations in active, competitive sports, where they usually excel. When young Aries learns to focus energies long enough to master a subject and learns consideration for others, the indomitable Aries spirit will rise to the head of the class.

Aries born in 2004 will have both the sun and Saturn in active cardinal signs. This child will be a do-er, a real achiever. Look out, world!

The Taurus Child

Taurus is a cuddly, affectionate child who eagerly explores the world of the senses, especially the sense of taste and touch. The Taurus child can be a big eater and will put on weight easily if not encouraged to exercise. Since this child likes comfort and gravitates to beauty, try coaxing little Taurus to exercise to music. Or take him or her outdoors on hikes or long walks in a local park or woodland. Though Taurus may be a slow learner, this sign has an excellent retentive memory and generally masters a subject thoroughly. Taurus is interested in results and will see each project patiently through to completion, continuing long after others have given up.

Choose Taurus toys carefully to help develop innate talents. Construction toys, such as blocks or erector sets, appeal to their love of building. Paints or crayons develop their sense of color. Many Taurus have musical talent and love to sing, which is apparent at a young age.

Taurus will usually want a pet or two, and a few plants of his or her own. Give little Taurus a mini-garden and watch the natural green thumb develop. This child has a strong sense of acquisition and an early grasp of material value. After filling a piggy bank, Taurus graduates to a savings account—before other children have even started to learn the value of money.

This year's Taurus baby will benefit from lucky Jupiter in Virgo and sensible Saturn in Cancer. These placements give the little Bull super financial savvy. Start that savings account early!

The Gemini Child

Little Gemini will talk as soon as possible, filling the air with questions and chatter. This is a friendly child who enjoys social contact, seems to require company, and adapts quickly to different surroundings. Geminis have quick minds that easily grasp the use of words, books, and telephones, and will probably learn to talk and read at an earlier age than most.

Though they are fast learners, Gemini may have a short attention span, darting from subject to subject. Projects and games that help focus the mind could be used to help them concentrate. Musical instruments, typewriters, and computers help older Gemini children combine mental with manual dexterity.

Geminis should be encouraged to finish what they start before they go on to another project. Otherwise, they can become jack-of-all-trades types who have trouble completing anything they do. Their disposition is usually cheerful and witty, making these children popular with their peers and delightful company at home.

This year's Gemini baby should go to the head of the class! Jupiter in Virgo endows an extra dose of mental smarts. Uranus in Pisces could inspire Gemini to make an unusual career choice, perhaps in a high-tech field.

The Cancer Child

The emotional, sensitive Cancer child is especially influenced by patterns set in early life. Young Cancers cling to their first memories as well as their childhood possessions. They thrive in calm emotional waters, with a loving, protective mother, and usually remain close to her (even if their relationship with her was difficult) throughout their lives.

Divorce, death—anything that disturbs the safe family unit—is devastating to Cancers, who may need extra support and reassurance during a family crisis.

Cancers sometimes need a firm hand to push the positive, creative side of their personality and to discourage them from getting swept away by emotional moods or resorting to emotional manipulation to get their way. If this child is praised and encouraged to find creative expression, Cancers will be able to express their positive side consistently on a firm, secure foundation.

Saturn in Cancer makes the little Moon Child born in 2004 become a serious and responsible citizen who can accomplish much. Jupiter in Virgo will provide supportive friends and loving relatives.

The Leo Child

Leo children love the limelight and will plot to get the lion's share of attention. These children assert themselves with flair and drama, and can behave like tiny tyrants to get their way. But in general they have a sunny, positive disposition, and are rarely subject to blue moods.

At school, Leo is the type voted most popular, head cheerleader, homecoming queen. Leo is sure to be noticed for personality, if not for stunning looks or academic work; the homely Leo will be a class clown; the unhappy Leo can be the class bully.

Above all, a Leo child cannot tolerate being ignored for long. Drama or performing arts classes, sports, and school politics are healthy ways for Leo to be a star. But Leos must learn to take lesser roles occasionally, or they will have some painful put-downs in store. Usually, Leo popularity is well earned; they are hard workers who try to measure up to their own high standards—and usually succeed.

The Leo born in 2004 balances star quality with caring concern for others, thanks to Saturn in nurturing Cancer. Mercury in Virgo and Jupiter in Virgo give the Leo child practical smarts and tycoon potential.

The Virgo Child

The young Virgo can be a quiet, serious child, with a quick, intelligent mind. Early on, little Virgo shows far more attention to detail and concern with small things than other children. Little Virgo has a built-in sense of order and a fascination of how things work. It is important for these children to have a place of their own, which they can order as they wish and where they can read or busy themselves with crafts and hobbies.

This child's personality can be very sensitive. Little Virgo may get "hyper" and overreact to seemingly small irritations, which can take the form of stomach upsets or delicate digestive systems. But this child will flourish where there is mental stimulation and a sense of order.

Virgos thrive in school, especially in writing or language skills, and seem truly happy when buried in books. Chances are, young Virgo will learn to read ahead of classmates. Hobbies that involve detail work or that develop fine craftsmanship are especially suited to young Virgos.

This is the best year to be a Virgo! A planetary bonanza of Mars in Virgo and Jupiter in Virgo will give the Virgo-born child a double dose of luck. With benevolent rays from Saturn in Cancer, this child has a winning hand.

The Libra Child

The Libra child learns early about the power of charm and good looks. Libra is often a very physically appealing child with an enchanting dimpled smile, who is naturally sociable and enjoys the company of both children and adults. It is a rare Libra child who is a discipline problem. But when their behavior is unacceptable, they respond better to calm discussion than displays of emotion, especially if the discussion revolves around fairness.

Because young Libras without a strong direction tend to drift with the mood of the group, these children should be encouraged to develop their unique talents and powers of discrimination so they can later stand on their own.

In school, this child is usually popular and will often have to choose between social invitations and studies. In the teen years, social pressures mount as the young Libra begins to look for a partner. This is the sign of "best friends," so Libra's choice of companions can have a strong effect on his or her future direction. Beautiful Libra girls may be tempted to go steady or have an unwise early marriage. Chances are, both sexes will fall in and out of love several times in their search for the ideal partner.

Lucky Libra! Jupiter moves into Libra in 2004, making this year one of the sign's luckiest years. Mars in Libra endows the child with energy. And if the child is born between September 28 and October 16, Mercury in Libra will give a lively intelligence. Here is another winner in the zodiac sweepstakes!

The Scorpio Child

The Scorpio child may seem quiet and shy on the surface, but will surprise others with intensity of feelings and force of willpower. Scorpio children are single-minded when they want something and intensely passionate about whatever they do. One of a caregiver's tasks is to teach this child to balance activities and emotions, yet at the same time to make the most of their great concentration and intense commitment.

Since young Scorpios do not show their depth of feel-

...easily, parents will have to learn to read almost imperceptible signs that troubles are brewing beneath the surface. Both Scorpio boys and girls enjoy games of power and control on or off the playground. She may take an early interest in the opposite sex, masquerading as a tomboy, while he may be intensely competitive and something of a loner.

When their powerful energies are directed into work, sports, or challenging studies, Scorpio is a superachiever thoroughly focused on a goal. With trusted friends, young Scorpio is devoted and caring—the proverbial friend "through thick and thin," loyal for life.

This year's Scorpio child could be quieter than others, with a lot going on beneath the surface. There's plenty of imagination and creativity to be developed in this visionary child.

The Sagittarius Child

The restless, athletic Sagittarius child will be out of the playpen and off on explorative adventures as soon as possible. Little Sagittarius is remarkably well coordinated, attempting daredevil feats on any wheeled vehicle from scooters to skateboards. These natural athletes need little encouragement to channel their energies into sports. The cheerful, friendly dispositions of Sagittarius youngsters earn them popularity in school. Once they have found a subject where their talent and imagination can soar, they will do well academically. They love animals, especially horses, and will be sure to have a pet or two, if not a home zoo. When they are old enough to take care of themselves, they'll clamor to be off on adventures of their own, away from home if possible.

This is a child who loves to travel, will not get homesick at summer camp, and may sign up to be a foreign exchange student or spend summers abroad. Outdoor adventure appeals to little Sagittarius, especially if it involves an active sport, such as skiing, cycling, or mountain climbing. Give them enough space and encouragement, and their fiery spirit will propel them to achieve high goals.

The Sagittarius born in 2004 has charisma and power, thanks to potent Pluto in Sagittarius. Jupiter in Libra endows a sense of fairness and love of beauty. What a beautiful mind!

The Capricorn Child

The purposeful, goal-oriented Capricorn child will work to capacity if he or she feels this will bring results. They're not ones who enjoy work for its own sake—there must be an end in sight. Authority figures can do much to motivate this child. But once set on an upward path, young Capricorn will mobilize his or her energy and talent and will work harder, and with more perseverance, than any other sign. Capricorn has built-in self-discipline that can achieve remarkable results, even if lacking the flashy personality, quick brainpower, or penetrating insight of others. Once involved, young Capricorn will stick to a task until it is mastered. This child also knows how to use others to advantage, and may well become the team captain or class president.

A wise parent will set realistic goals for the Capricorn child, paving the way for the early thrill of achievement. Youngsters should be encouraged to express their caring, feeling side to others, as well as their natural aptitude for leadership.

Capricorn children may be especially fond of grandparents and older relatives, and will enjoy spending time with them and learning from them. It is not uncommon for young Capricorns to have an older mentor or teacher who guides them. With their great respect for authority, Capricorn children will take this influence very much to heart.

The Capricorn born in 2004 will have serious and responsible partnerships, thanks to Saturn in the opposite sign of Cancer. Jupiter promises a stellar career, with high earning power.

The Aquarius Child

The Aquarius child has an innovative, well-focused mind that often streaks so far ahead of peers that this child seems like an "oddball." Routine studies never hold the restless youngster for long; he or she will look for another, more experimental place to try out their ideas and to develop their inventions. Life is a laboratory to the inquiring Aquarius mind.

School politics, sports, science, and the arts offer scope for this child's talents. But if there is no room for expression within approved social limits, Aquarius is sure to rebel.

Questioning institutions and religions comes naturally, so these children may find an outlet elsewhere, becoming "rebels with a cause." It is better not to force this child to conform. Instead, channel forward-thinking young minds into constructive group activities.

Aquarius children born this year will have far-out glamour as well as charisma, thanks to their planetary ruler, Uranus, in a friendly bond with planet Neptune. This child could become a rock star, a statesman, a scientist. It's the most creative Aquarius ever!

The Pisces Child

Give young Pisces praise, applause, and a gentle but firm push in the right direction. Lovable Pisces children may be abundantly talented. But they may be hesitant to express themselves because they are quite sensitive and easily hurt. It is a parent's challenge to help them gain self-esteem and self-confidence. However, this same sensitivity makes them trusted friends who'll have many confidants as they develop socially. It also endows many Pisces with spectacular creative talent.

Pisces adores drama and theatrics of all sorts. Encourage them to channel their creativity into art forms rather than indulging in emotional dramas. As they develop their creative ideas, they may need more solitude than other children. But though daydreaming can be creative, it is important that these natural dreamers not dwell too long in the world of fantasy. Teach them practical coping skills for the real world.

Since Pisces are sensitive physically, parents should help them build strong bodies with proper diet and regular exercise. Young Pisces may gravitate to individual sports, such as swimming, sailing, and skiing, rather than to team sports. Or they may prefer artistic physical activities like dance or ice skating.

Born "givers," these children are often drawn to the underdog (they fall quickly for sob stories) and attract those who might take advantage of their empathic nature. Teach them to choose friends wisely and to set boundaries in relationships, to protect their emotional vulnerability—invaluable lessons in later life.

With the planet Uranus now in Pisces, this generation of Pisces will be movers and shakers. This child may have a rebellious streak that rattles the status quo. Saturn in Cancer is a stabilizing force, while Jupiter in Virgo could bring luck in love.

CHAPTER 14

The Leo Personality

In the northern hemisphere, Leo occurs when nature is in full bloom under the hot summer sun. Like its ruling planet, the sun, Leo wants to shine, to stand out. Leo is the sign of creativity, self-consciousness, self-expression. The Leo Lion and Lioness demand to be "King and Queen of the Jungle." Besides its position as fifth sign of the zodiac, Leo is further defined by the element of fire, which is hot and impulsive; by its ruling planet, the sun; by its masculine, positive, yang polarity; and by its fixed modality (the way it operates), a steady beam of light.

Your personal blend of planets and rising sign, based on your moment of birth, adds another set of colors to your horoscope. Otherwise, all Leos would be alike. Key planets in solid, practical earth signs could quiet your Leo personality down. An emphasis on water signs might make you more empathic than the usual Leo. However, the more planets in Leo you have, the more you'll recognize yourself in the following descriptions.

The Leo Man: The Sun King

The Leo man behaves like a king, regardless of bank statement or position in life. Everything you do has a larger-than-life oversized quality, as if it is to be viewed on a giant movie screen. You're a scene-stealer, whether you're naturally impressive physically, like Arnold

Schwarzenegger or Antonio Banderas, or by sheer force of personality, like Dustin Hoffman or Mick Jagger. However, your greatest pleasure is sharing your wealth and prestige with loyal followers, treating them to a first-class trip, then picking up the check.

Your confidence and natural dignity seem to attract wealth and fame, even when your ascendant (rising sign) makes you seem a bit shy and retiring. Once there is a chance to step into the spotlight, you will do so with natural flair.

If you can't perform in front of an audience of some sort, you'll grab the headlines as an impresario or entrepreneur. Your love of applause might lead you to cultivate those who admire you and ignore those who could offer constructive criticism. But the Leo who feels he is not getting his fair share of attention is an unhappy Lion who can hide in his lair, suffering from wounded pride.

When you do achieve life's riches, you truly enjoy your wealth and all the perks of your position. You live life to the maximum in a royal style, rather than hoarding money for a rainy day. Never losing a childlike love of play, many wealthy Leos have a collection of adult toys (yachts, motorcycles, balloons, estates), which they love to show off and share with others.

In a Relationship

The king of the zodiac naturally wants a royal queen as a consort. Many Leos marry "princess" types, glamorous women of prestigious pedigree. You want a mate you can show off, yet she must always remember to put you first in her life. You'll revel in her successes, as long as she doesn't become a rival. You'll make sure she has the best of everything (even if you can't afford the tab). In return, you expect to be treated as lord of the manor, awarded the loyalty, respect, and loud applause you deserve.

Many famous Leos have wives who are equally famous: Arnold Schwarzenegger (Maria Shriver), Frank Gifford (Kathie Lee Gifford), Gerald McRaney (Delta Burke), former President Bill Clinton (Hillary Rodham Clinton). The secret of a successful Leo relationship, though each has separate territory, is that the Leo male gets his Lion's share of the limelight. When a Leo man's love life runs into trouble, it is usually because he is not getting enough attention from his wife and craves an ego boost from an attractive admirer. The charismatic Leo man usually has plenty of female fans to choose from. But he is likely to run into trouble if he plays the heartbreaker, because he is not the type to live a secretive double life.

The Leo Woman: A Royal Romantic

The Leo woman gets her energy from the sun, the giver of personality. You are special, and you feel this divine right from birth, which gives you natural optimism and radiant self-confidence. Under the best of circumstances, you are able to take your natural talents and play them to the max. The celebrity roster is studded with brilliant Leo stars, all of whom stand out from the crowd with unique, unforgettable personalities. Domestic divas like Julia Child and Martha Stewart and show business beauties like Madonna, Jennifer Lopez, Melanie Griffith, and Charlize Theron all rise above the crowd for their unique qualities.

The proud Leo woman is rarely a loner. Like a playful, exuberant child, you have a show-off quality that basks in the attention and admiration of others. You need an audience to receive your special energy, and you know how to get their attention, keeping them entertained and fascinated. You'll keep your fans' attention by keeping them guessing, like Madonna, whose changes in personal style keep her far ahead of the pack. Or laughing, like

Lucille Ball. Under intense pressure, your dignity and poise can move the world, as Jacqueline Kennedy Onassis demonstrated. And you'll project your own unique personality, regardless of the scene you're required to play.

Your career is the stage where your talent can shine. You thrive in fields such as politics, where you are constantly in the public eye, like Elizabeth Dole and Tipper Gore. You make excellent teachers and excel in any kind of sales work, both requiring you to perform for an audience. Your desire to give love and to set others' lives on a more positive course often draws you to healing and counseling work. You surround yourself with creative people and admirers who support you and help you look your best. (It is a rare Leo who doesn't have a hairdresser on call!) While using your team to best advantage, you'll return favors by boosting their confidence and sometimes rewarding them with sumptuous gifts. You Leos understand how to promote yourself and those you care for. Instantly recognizable, some Leos are first-name celebrities, such as J-Lo, Madonna, and Iman.

Your stellar qualities are nowhere more evident than in difficult times. You have the strength to surmount impossible odds, thanks to the power of your positive mental outlook. Circumstances that could devastate anyone else are often conquered by the powerful solar energy of Leo. A Leo woman holds her head high no matter what life offers her.

Your career provides a way to shine on your own merits. Two of your best professional assets are your stamina and confidence. Your radiant, positive energy is sure to get you noticed. Though you can be very demanding at times, your warmhearted nature usually wins defectors back to your side.

In a Relationship

It's natural for you to want to share your life with a loving companion. Ideally, this would be a man as powerful, loyal, and devoted as you are, one who will not stint on lavishing you with adoration and attention. You love nothing more than to have a strong, handsome, and attentive escort on your arm. You know how to make your husband look and feel his best by building up his status and position in the world.

Unfortunately, as a Leo you often pick men who are not up to your level and who disappoint you in the long run. You often attract flatterers and hangers-on who are drawn to your radiant self-confidence and positive energy. Many Leo women end up as heads of their own families, because their marriage could not take the strain of two stars, or because Leo's husband felt eclipsed by her strong personality.

When you find the right partner, however, you'll remain loyal, even in difficult times. Your positive outlook can help you both turn things around for the better. Ultimately, you may attain the relationship you've always longed for, one based on mutual respect and friendship.

Leo in the Family

The Leo Parent

The strong, positive sign of Leo is considered one of the natural parenting signs of the zodiac. Children can blossom under Leo's radiant energy—no one can promote self-confidence and self esteem like you. You let them know how wonderful they are. You praise them to the limit, encourage them to express their talents, and then proudly show them off. You want only the best for your children, and will give them the finest education you can afford. Though you are naturally protective, you raise your children to be strong and independent, to meet your super-high standards. Sometimes you can be quite demanding, but your children will be inspired to reach royal heights and often attain them.

The Leo Stepparent

Your natural generosity is your greatest asset as a stepparent. You'll reach out warmly to your extended family—you enjoy having even more cubs around. But there will be no doubt who's the boss! You make it very clear who rules the roost. Your strong, confident personality can provide direction and stability, while your poise and confidence rub off on socially insecure youngsters. You'll plan gala occasions to bring the whole family together, and be equally generous with presents and praise. Stepchildren respond to your warmth at a difficult transition in their lives and often become as close to you as your own children are, retaining this closeness long after they've left the nest.

The Leo Grandparent

You command royal respect as a grandparent, holding court at family gatherings. You'll burst with pride over the youngest generation, especially when you see them well dressed and well mannered. Though you delegate child-rearing responsibilities to parents, you'll generously offer help with education, buy them the smartest party outfits, and coach them in social poise and grooming. A visit with a Leo grandparent is a special occasion, whether Leo is the honored guest at sports outings or the superlative host, treating your grandchildren to the best restaurant in town. You'll happily preside at weddings, bar mitzvahs, and anniversaries, looking every inch the family matriarch or patriarch.

CHAPTER 15

Leo Style: Fashion, Home, and Healthy Living Tips Especially for You!

Finding the lifestyle that suits you best couldn't be easier. Just follow your Leo solar muse! Since each sun sign resonates to certain colors, styles, places, music, you can't miss. In the following pages are cosmic tips for selecting the clothes, home environment, colors, sounds, and places that enhance your personality.

Leo Home Decor

The perfect Leo home is also your castle and a dramatic setting for your life. Those of you who are celebrity fans should find decorating inspiration in the luxurious homes of Madonna, Antonio Banderas, and Melanie Griffith—all Leos, of course. The more conservative Leo might prefer the naturalistic ideas of Martha Stewart.

You decorate with the Midas touch, using a bit of glitter and a lot of glamour. There should be a great room for lavishly entertaining friends, family, and business associates. Mirrored walls and antique furniture (or good reproductions) make you feel like royalty. Photos and portraits (of guess who!) and trophies of your achievements should be on display. You love touches of fur and feline-print rugs or bedspreads. An impressive bedroom, with oversized mirrors, a dramatic bed, and high-thread-count linens, is the perfect resting place for lazy Lions. You should have a well-equipped entertainment center to bring the theater to you. Since sun-ruled Leo needs bright light, plenty of windows and a spotlight here and there keep your mood upbeat.

Leo Music

Dramatic Leos need the right sound track. Collect the scores of Broadway hits and movie musicals to keep the party going. Big band sounds, opera, hundreds of serenading strings, and sweeping symphonies appeal to Leo's big-time tastes. The music of Leo superstars Jennifer Lopez, Madonna, Whitney Houston, Mick Jagger, and Tony Bennett delights Leo fans. Plan your music menu to complement the many moods of your life by making a special tape of your favorite songs to use as background music for brunch and dinner parties, or to set the scene for seduction. Leos with video equipment might like to add personal slides or films to make their own multimedia shows.

Leo Colors

When you color your rooms or plan your wardrobe, be sure to add a touch of gold, the special color and metal of your sign. Yours are the colors of the sun, from sunrise to sunset, from deep gold to brilliant yellow to the corals and mauves of the last rays of the day. Or, like Mae West, you could shine in all white, lit up with lots of gold trim.

The Leo Fasionista

You are destined for the spotlight wherever you go, so dress for it! Make that entrance with flair and style. Your hair is a focal point. (Many are the Leo women who become a hairdresser's best advertisement.) A bouffant, immaculately groomed, looks best. Try sunny shades of blonde or red, like Charlize Theron or Melanie Griffith. Or wear a dark shining mane, like Sandra Bullock. Or streak your hair with gold, like Jennifer Lopez. Whatever you do, go for drama in your coiffure—it's Leo's crown.

You are sure to be a jewelry fan. Dramatic glitter looks right on you! Some Leo women start collecting gold jewelry as a teenager and never stop. Have a signature gold piece that you always wear, like the beautiful earrings of Elizabeth Dole or J-Lo's big gold hoops.

With your strong personality, you can get away with superstar colors. (Remember Jacqueline Kennedy's simple elegant clothes in brilliant colors.) The trick is to keep the star player in your outfit in the spotlight. If you're wearing fabulous jewelry, keep your clothes simple. If your dress is the star, then don't pile on competing accessories. And don't forget your best fashion asset—your radiant smile!

Leo fashion designers have always led the pack. For inspiration, look to the retro designs of Chanel and Yves St. Laurent, who understood how to be glamorous, comfortable, and practical at all times.

Leo models and actresses have always been fashion favorites. Stephanie Seymour, Iman, Jennifer Flavin, Halle Berry combine style with sex appeal.

The Healthy Leo

Leo is associated with the spine and heart, two important areas to guard throughout your life. Be sure you have a good mattress to support the vulnerable Leo spine. Learn some therapeutic exercises to strengthen and protect your spine. Aerobic exercises that benefit the heart and lungs are also "musts" for Leo.

Ruled by the sun, you're one sign that usually loves to tan. However, considering the permanent damage sun exposure can cause, you may elect to remain porcelain white, like Madonna or the ever-beautiful Arlene Dahl. So don't leave for the beach without a big hat, umbrella, and sunblock formulated for your skin type. Many makeup foundations now come with a sunblock added, a good idea for Leo ladies.

As a Leo you are proud of your body and usually take excellent care of it. To maintain your public image, you'll summon up great discipline and determination, including sticking to a healthful diet. Your downfall could be your preference for the finer things in life, which might include dining on gourmet food at the best restaurants. Indulge yourself now and then, but balance this with regular exercise. And a Lion that is not getting the love and attention you need can easily turn to food for consolation. Learn to give yourself the royal treatment in nonfood ways, such as an extra trip to the beauty salon for some pampering or a massage.

Like bodacious film stars Jennifer Lopez and Charlize Theron, Leos love showing off a beautiful body. To make your body worthy of the spotlight, consider a body-building regime where you're supervised by a personal trainer. Be sure any exercise routine you choose emphasizes good posture. The way you carry yourself can make the most of your figure type and dramatically affect your energy level. Get that regal bearing!

Leo Getaways

The three "s" words for Leo places are sun, service, and social life. Leo likes to shine in the sun. Like actor

George Hamilton, many of you sport all-year tans. Pampering places such as spas and superresorts that treat you royally are Leo favorites. Leo wants to go first-class all the way. Superspas in gorgeous settings, like the Golden Door, are the perfect places to retreat from your hectic life, get treated royally, and drop a few pounds while reviving your glorious looks and energy.

Glamorous cruises appeal to Leo explorers who like to see the world in style, without giving up any luxurious amenities. Evening entertainment on a big ship gives you a chance to dress to the nines and sparkle with jewelry. Leos might choose their dream vacation destination from among these lion-favored places: the South Pacific, the Alps, Bombay, Rome, Sicily, Prague, and Zanzibar.

Leos should plan their packing carefully. Select luggage that organizes your wardrobe, so you can unpack quickly. Martha Stewart uses lots of tissue paper; plastic packs keep designer clothes looking their regal best. One well-traveled Leo star packs a bag for each city she'll visit, with the appropriate clothes and accessories in each bag. Locate a good hairdresser in the city (ask someone who travels there frequently), or book your hair appointments immediately after you board a cruise ship in order to keep your royal mane in shape. Since Leos rarely travel light, you should consider luggage with wheels or a sturdy folding luggage cart for those times when porters are not available.

CHAPTER 16

Leo at Work

You need a job that is up front and highly visible, rather than behind the scenes, since you are not one to stay in the background for long. You'll get noticed no matter what, but a strong push from a supportive mentor will send you soaring quickly. Office politics, senior executives locked into their positions, and a low-key atmosphere can dampen your spirits, so look for a company with room at the top.

Job perks are important to you. Because you work for glory as well as security, it is very important that you choose a company you can be proud of. Your position should have a title, the more impressive the better. Good choices are jobs in sales, management, public relations, advertising, politics, personnel training, or teaching. These areas bring you before the public. Show business in its many forms is a Leo natural. Choose a company that thinks big, with a generous expense account and impressive offices. Avoid companies with gloomy working conditions, spartan expense accounts, and discounted or low-status products.

The current Leo prototype in business is billionaire Larry Ellison, the founder of Oracle software. His enormous risks and daring moves made him one of the greatest success stories of the Internet era. In an industry dominated by poorly dressed geeks, Ellison truly looks the part of a Leo leader with his tailor-made Italian suits and shirts, flamboyant lifestyle, expensive yachts and jets. His drive, character, and success inspired a biography entitled *The Difference Between God and Larry Ellison*. In the Leo mogul tradition of Adnan Kashoggi and the late Malcolm Forbes, Ellison believes in living the royal lifestyle to the hilt—with all the perks.

The Leo Boss

You'll gravitate to the command position because nobody does it better! You're a natural leader for many reasons. You understand the art of delegating. You have a charismatic presence and phenomenal energy. You have a gift for inspiring others to do their best. You project an air of authority at all times. Your verbal skills enable you to make great speeches and presentations. You'll get the visuals right, too, with the perfect wardrobe, posture, and gestures. You are always visible—playing the role with style, conducting meetings with flair and a sense of drama. You'll demand loyalty from underlings, and you can be very generous to those you favor as long as they do not outshine you or threaten your territory. You enjoy doing things in a big way, which could put a strain on your expense account. But you'll find many ways to combine business with pleasure to the greater glory of both.

Leo on a Team

When working in a group, Leo will gravitate toward the spotlight—the most public position. You may leave lesser chores or behind-the-scenes activity to others. Your self-promotion could cause friction with less assertive members of the team. But you do take great pride in your work, and you deliver full value for your time. You are careful to fulfill job requirements, even when it means working long hours. The more recognition you get, the harder you will work, so it behooves your employer to dish out praise and perks. Sharing the spotlight can be a problem on the Leo team—particularly if there are two Leos in the group! This can be circumvented by a job that has well-defined territory, which gives you a chance to prove what you can do.

How to Succeed

Choose a job where you'll get attention and recognition. Play up these stellar Leo talents:

- Style and flair
- Poise and confidence
- Salesmanship
- Risk taking
- Stamina
- Optimism and sincerity
- Ability to manage others and delegate responsibility
- Big-time ideas

CHAPTER 17

Learn from the Leo Famous

There's no better way to learn about the pitfalls and prizes of your sign than to study the lives of your rich and famous sign-mates. For sure you'll find the Leo traits of leadership, personality, poise, and flair in Elizabeth Dole, Bill Clinton, Larry Ellison. You recognize the royal style of Madonna, Charlize Theron, Jennifer Lopez.

Astrology can tell you more about your sun sign heroes and heroines than tabloids or magazine articles. Like what really turns them on (check their Venus). Or what makes them rattled (scope their Saturn). Compare similarities and differences between the celebrities who embody the typical Leo sun sign traits and those who seem untypical. Then look up the influence of other planets in the horoscope of your favorites, using the charts in this book. It's a fun way to further your education in astrology.

Leo Celebrities

Terence Stamp (7/23/39)
Woody Harrelson (7/23/61)
Stephanie Seymour (7/23/68)
Michael Richards (7/24/49)
Lynda Carter (7/24/51)
Barry Bonds (7/24/64)
Jennifer Lopez (7/24/70)
Estelle Getty (7/25/23)

Iman (7/25/55)
Blake Edwards (7/26/22)
Stanley Kubrick (7/26/28)
Mick Jagger (7/26/43)
Susan George (7/26/50)
Dorothy Hamill (7/26/56)
Peggy Fleming (7/27/48)
Sally Struthers (7/28/48)
Peter Jennings (7/29/38)
Michael Spinks (7/29/56)
Kevin Spacey (7/29/59)
Henry Ford (7/30/1863)
Paul Anka (7/30/41)
Arnold Schwarzenegger (7/30/47)
Delta Burke (7/30/56)
Lisa Kudrow (7/30/63)
Hillary Swank (7/30/74)
Geraldine Chaplin (7/31/44)
Wesley Snipes (7/31/63)
Dean Cain (7/31/66)
Dom DeLuise (8/1/33)
Yves St. Laurent (8/1/36)
Jerry Garcia (8/1/42)
Giancarlo Giannini (8/1/42)
Carroll O'Connor (8/2/24)
Peter O'Toole (8/2/32)
Tony Bennett (8/3/36)
Martin Sheen (8/3/40)
Martha Stewart (8/3/41)
The Queen Mother Elizabeth (8/4/1896)
Billy Bob Thornton (8/4/55)
Neil Armstrong (8/5/30)
Loni Anderson (8/5/46)
Robert Mitchum (8/6/17)
Abbey Lincoln (8/6/30)
Alberto Salazar (8/7/58)
Charlize Theron (8/7/75)
Esther Williams (8/8/23)
Dustin Hoffman (8/8/37)

Sam Elliott (8/9/44)
Melanie Griffith (8/9/57)
Eddie Fisher (8/10/28)
Rosanna Arquette ((8/10/59)
Antonio Banderas (8/10/60)
Arlene Dahl (8/11/28)
Steve Wozniak (8/11/50)
John Derek (8/12/26)
George Hamilton (8/12/39)
Jane Wyatt (8/13/12)
Fidel Castro (8/13/26)
Don Ho (8/13/30)
Kathleen Battle (8/13/48)
Steve Martin (8/14/45)
Susan St. James (8/14/46)
Danielle Steel (8/14/47)
Jackee (8/14/56)
Magic Johnson (8/14/59)
Jennifer Flavin (8/14/68)
Napoleon (8/15/1769)
Ethel Barrymore (8/15/1879)
Lawrence of Arabia (8/15/1888)
Julia Child (8/15/12)
Wendy Hiller (8/15/12)
Abby Dalton (8/15/35)
Linda Ellerbee (8/15/45)
Princess Anne of England (8/15/50)
Ben Affleck (8/15/72)
Frank Gifford (8/16/30)
Lesley Ann Warren (8/16/46)
Kathie Lee Gifford (8/16/54)
Angela Bassett (8/16/58)
Madonna (8/16/58)
Timothy Hutton (8/16/60)
Mae West (8/17/1893)
Maureen O'Hara (8/17/21)
Robert De Niro (8/17/43)
Larry Ellison (8/17/44)
Belinda Carlisle (8/17/58)

Sean Penn (8/17/60)
Shelley Winters (8/18/22)
Rosalynn Carter (8/18/27)
Roman Polanski (8/18/33)
Robert Redford (8/18/36)
Patrick Swayze (8/18/54)
Christian Slater (8/18/69)
Malcolm Forbes (8/19/19)
Gerald McRaney (8/19/40)
Jill St. John (8/19/40)
Willie Shoemaker (8/19/41)
Bill Clinton (8/19/46)
Tipper Gore (8/19/48)
Ron Darling (8/19/60)
John Stamos (8/19/63)
Jacqueline Susann (8/20/21)
Carla Fracci (8/20/36)
Connie Chung (8/20/46)
Count Basie (8/21/1906)
Princess Margaret (8/21/30)
Wilt Chamberlain (8/21/36)
Kenny Rogers (8/21/58)
Jim McMahon (8/21/59)
Ray Bradbury (8/22/20)
Norman Schwarzkopf (8/22/34)
Valerie Harper (8/22/40)
Cindy Williams (8/22/47)

CHAPTER 18

Leo Relating: How You Get Along with Every Sign

Dynamic fire signs need supportive relationships, and the first step is to understand each other's needs. Whether you're looking for a business partner or a life companion, this compatibility "cheat sheet" will help you. Once you understand how your partner's sun sign is likely to view commitment and what each of you wants from a relationship, you'll be in a much better position to judge whether your cosmic combination has lasting potential.

Leo/Aries

THE PERKS:
The heat's on with this pair of romantics. You both share high hopes, high energy, and high ideals. You both can express your finest qualities. If you learn to feed each other's egos and costar, rather than take over center stage, this could be a long-run relationship.

THE CHALLENGES:
The problems appear when romance turns to reality. Both of you are delegators, and neither likes to do the nitty-gritty follow-through. If either sign gets overly bossy, this romance could explode. Leo may long to be fussed over, while Aries will want to feel like number

one once in a while. If these two self-centered signs learn to give and occasionally *give in* to each other, it could work.

Leo/Taurus

THE PERKS:
When Leo passion meets Taurus sensuality, there's a volcanic physical attraction as you test each other's strength. Both lovers of beauty and comfort, you have high ideals, mutual fidelity, love of good food, and music going for you. Taurus money management could provide Leo with a royal lifestyle.

THE CHALLENGES:
Tensions between these two fixed signs are inevitable, especially if Taurus clamps down on Leo spending. Leo plays dangerous games here, such as withholding affection or sex until your royal orders are fulfilled. Focus on building emotional security and avoiding no-win emotional showdowns. Your Leo extravagance and the Taurus possessiveness could be bones of contention.

Leo/Gemini

THE PERKS:
Gemini good humor, ready wit, and social skills delight and complement Leo. Here is someone who can share the spotlight without trying to steal the show from the regal Lion. It's one of the most entertaining combinations. Steady Leo provides the focus Gemini often lacks, and directs the Twins toward achieving goals and status.

THE CHALLENGES:
Gemini loves to flirt and flit among many interests, romantic and otherwise. This is sure to irritate the Lion, who does one thing at a time and does it well. Gemini might be a bit bored with Leo self-promotion, and might poke fun at this sign's notorious vanity. The resulting feline roar will be no laughing matter!

Leo/Cancer

THE PERKS:
These neighboring signs come through for each other like good buddies. Cancer gives Leo total attention, backup support, and the VIP treatment the Lion craves. Here is someone who won't fight for the spotlight. Leo gives Cancer confidence and injects a positive mental outlook, which is good medicine for Cancer moods.

THE CHALLENGES:
Cancer blue moods and tendency to cling tenaciously can weigh Leo down. But your high-handed Leo behavior may steamroll sensitive Cancer feelings.

Leo/Leo

THE PERKS:
This mirror-image couple can be a mutual admiration society. You'll love showing each other off, spotlighting each other's talents, and radiating confidence, warmth, optimism. If you can get the right working dynamics, you'll move ahead together socially and professionally.

THE CHALLENGES:
You may be too dazzled to deal with practical realities. Popularity won't take the place of long-range goals and clear priorities. You could burn out from high living or eclipse each other. You must learn to share the stage and take turns applauding each other.

Leo/Virgo

THE PERKS:
Leo confidence, sales power, optimism, and aristocratic presence is a big Virgo draw. Virgo will have a ready-made job efficiently running the mechanical parts of your Leo lifestyle, which you are only too happy to delegate. And your Leo social poise brings Virgo into the public eye, helping this shy sign bloom! Both are faithful and loyal signs who find much to admire in each other.

THE CHALLENGES:
You may not appreciate each other's point of view. Virgo is more likely to dole out well-meaning criticism and vita-mins than the admiration and applause Leo craves. Virgo might also object to your leonine high-handedness with the budget. Virgo makes house rules, but Leo is above them, a rule unto yourself. Leo always looks at the big picture, Virgo at the nitty-gritty details. You might dampen each other's spirits, unless you find a way to work this out early in the relationship.

Leo/Libra

THE PERKS:
Libra is the perfect audience for Leo theatrics. Libra knows how to package you for stardom. You both love

the best things in life: you both are intelligent, stylish, and social. Since you have similar priorities, and stroke each other the right way, you could have a long-lasting relationship.

THE CHALLENGES:
Getting the financial area of your life under control could be a problem for these two big spenders. Since you both love to make an elegant impression, you may find yourself perennially living beyond your means. You are both flirts, which is easier for Libra to tolerate than for Leo, so you could unleash your lethal Leo jealousy.

Leo/Scorpio

THE PERKS:
Scorpio innate power with your Leo confidence and authority can make a fascinating high-profile combination like Bill and Hillary Clinton. There is a great mutual respect and loyalty here, as well as sexual dynamite. You two magnetic, unconquerable heroes offer each other enough challenges to keep the sparks flying.

THE CHALLENGES:
Scorpio natural secretiveness and your Leo openness could conflict, especially if Scorpio reveals a powerful will and need for control underneath the deceptively quiet facade. And Leo is often surprised by the sheer intensity of Scorpio drive and willpower. Though Scorpio won't fight for the spotlight, they will often control behind the scenes. When these two intense, stubborn, demanding signs collide, it's a no-win situation.

Leo/Sagittarius

THE PERKS:
Under Sagittarius optimism and good humor, your Leo luck soars. You both inspire each other and boost each other's creativity. If you like the outdoor life, have a spirit of adventure, and love to travel, you're a winning combination that could feel destined to be together.

THE CHALLENGES:
Sagittarius is not one to pour on the flattery you Leos love. Nor is this sign known for monogamy! When both your fiery tempers explode, Leo roars and Sagittarius heads for the door. Leo must tone down bossiness and give Sagittarius a very long leash. Sagittarius must learn to coddle your Leo ego and keep your blazing temper on hold.

Leo/Capricorn

THE PERKS:
Here's the perfect mix of business and pleasure. Dignified, refined Capricorn has energy and discipline to match your Leo passion. And Leo comes to the rescue of this ambitious workaholic, adding confidence, poise, and joie de vivre. Capricorn reciprocates with the royal treatment.

THE CHALLENGES:
Capricorn prefers underplayed elegance to glitz and glamour, so you may have to tone down your show-off style. Capricorn cuts off the cash flow when Leo becomes extravagant, and may not pour out the megadoses of affection that you as a Leo require. Leo can't bear a partner who is stingy with love or money!

Leo/Aquarius

THE PERKS:
Love at first sight often happens between these magnetic zodiac opposites. You both flourish in the public eye and enjoy sharing your life with admiring fans. You enjoy taking on big projects and helping humanity together. Your Leo warmth is a social plus for Aquarius. And Aquarius vision tunes in to your spiritual side.

THE CHALLENGES:
Cool, detached Aquarius may not give Leos the devotion they demand. Aquarius may need to devote more time and attention to stroking the Leo ego. Aquarius likes an open relationship, with lots of freedom to roam—though not necessarily to stray. You will need to put this sign on a very long leash.

Leo/Pisces

THE PERKS:
Highly sensitive Pisces admires the Leo radiant confidence, and will gain stability under your warm, encouraging, royal protection. Leo will gain a charming, adoring admirer. Pisces easily shows affection, satisfying your constant craving for romance and glamour. This is a noncompetitive mutual admiration society where you promote each other enthusiastically.

THE CHALLENGES:
Pisces also loves to flirt, but is not basically monogamous. A stickler for loyalty, Leo may try to keep Pisces dancing attendance by strong-arm tactics. Pisces operates best in free-flowing waters, and will swim off when he or she senses a "hook."

CHAPTER 19

Astrological Outlook for Leo in 2004

You rediscover your "direction in life" this year. The emphasis is on partnership and marriage. You realize once and for all that you are not alone.

The year gets off to a fast start. Your popularity will be on the rise in January. You will be consulted about diet and fashion. If you maintain your sense of humor and showmanship, you could succeed beyond your original expectations.

Saturn will be back and forth in your twelfth house all year long. People will want to hear what you say about mystery. They want to read what you write about "forbidden territory."

During March, you will do more writing. This could be a period of self-revelation. You could be vexed concerning taxes, so keep records straight and realize you get nothing for nothing. You learn the difference between generosity and extravagance.

June will be your most challenging, romantic, and profitable month. During April, you could change your residence or marital status. It will be important during May to see people and relationships as they are, not merely as you wish they could be. In May, you will be involved in a real estate transaction; get commitments in writing, and learn once again that all that glitters is not gold.

Your most fortunate numbers: 3, 6, 9.

Capricorn and Cancer will play important roles in activities. Some could have these letters or initials in their names: B, K, T.

With the Cancer person, you learn secrets. You also learn how to "exploit the unknown." There is much joy in this relationship—it will be mingled with mystery and intrigue.

With Capricorn, you discover innovative ways to get the job done. What at first appeared impossible to repair will be "fixed" in a remarkable way. With Capricorn, you learn more about general health, including exercise, diet, and knowledge of nutrition.

On the following pages, you will find your diary in advance. Each day will be analyzed. You will learn when to play the waiting game and when to forge ahead. You will be given hints about how to win at the racetrack. You will learn more about your love, money, and health.

You will be taking a cold plunge into the adventure of your future! Start now by reading on.

CHAPTER 20

Eighteen Months of Day-by-Day Predictions—July 2003 to December 2004

Moon sign times are calculated for Eastern Standard Time and Eastern Daylight Time. Please adjust for your local time zone.

JULY 2003

Tuesday, July 1 (Moon in Cancer to Leo 9:11 a.m.) On the first day of the month, you will be pulled in two directions. A decision will be made whether or not to remain close to home or to embark upon a journey. Consider one phase of your life finished—another is about to begin.

Wednesday, July 2 (Moon in Leo) Your cycle is high; therefore, your judgment and intuition are on target. Make a fresh start. Exercise independence of thought and action. Be original; don't follow others. A new kind of love provides stimulation, stirring creative juices. Lucky lottery: 1, 12, 18, 22, 8, 5.

Thursday, July 3 (Moon in Leo to Virgo 4:15 p.m.) At the track: post position special—number 3 p.p. in the fifth race. Hot daily doubles: 3 and 5, 2 and 1, 1 and 6.

203

Away from the track, the question of your marital status looms large. Focus on direction, motivation, and meditation. There will be a decision affecting your reputation or public image.

Friday, July 4 (Moon in Virgo)   On this holiday, share anecdotes about the history of the country. People will be informed and entertained by your words. Take special care if handling fireworks. Gemini and Sagittarius play important roles. Your lucky number is 3.

Saturday, July 5 (Moon in Virgo to Libra 9:19 p.m.) Be willing to revise and rewrite. You are on the brink of publication and recognition. The message of this cycle is: "Don't quit now!" What you had given up as a lost cause will prove to be alive and kicking. A Scorpio figures prominently.

Sunday, July 6 (Moon in Libra)   You are in the rhythm of the day, so you will be at the right place at the right time. A Virgo relative could be involved. Teach and learn. Share knowledge, disseminate pertinent information. A flirtation gets more serious than you originally anticipated. Be careful!

Monday, July 7 (Moon in Libra)   Pay attention to a family member who of late has complained of being neglected. A Libra could hold the key to your future success. Know it, and act accordingly. Focus on decorating and remodeling—making your home beautiful. Your lucky number is 6.

Tuesday, July 8 (Moon in Libra to Scorpio 12:42 a.m.) Play the waiting game. Define terms. Outline a project that could put you "over the top." You will be flattered, and most of it is sincere. Maintain your emotional equilibrium. Pisces and Virgo will claim roles in today's scenario. Avoid self-deception!

Wednesday, July 9 (Moon in Scorpio) Your opinion will be sought concerning the value of a building or home. Don't attempt to move the "immovable." A tough competitor will make a gesture of consideration. Take it seriously, without abandoning your principles. A Capricorn figures prominently.

Thursday, July 10 (Moon in Scorpio to Sagittarius 2:47 a.m.) Let go of a situation that drains you emotionally and financially. You have made important progress. Competitors respect you. So now is the time to change your pace, to let go of "tension worries." Aries and Libra will surprise with their roles.

Friday, July 11 (Moon in Sagittarius) Give full play to your intuitive intellect. Find an outlet for your creativity. Working with words proves fruitful. A relationship is exciting, but protect yourself in emotional clinches. An Aquarius and another Leo will play outstanding roles.

Saturday, July 12 (Moon in Sagittarius to Capricorn 4:20 a.m.) Questions about children and marriage demand attention. A relative wants you to join in a short trip. Be sure it is short; don't get involved in a wild-goose chase. Legal papers could be involved. A Cancer will supply the "missing link."

Sunday, July 13 (Moon in Capricorn) The full moon in Capricorn, your sixth house, relates to general health and employment. Get together with a coworker or person who shares your basic interests. Protect your valuables, however. Refuse to give up something for nothing. A Gemini is in this picture.

Monday, July 14 (Moon in Capricorn to Aquarius 6:37 a.m.) Hold back on major decisions. You do not at present have the complete story. Information is being withheld because of red tape. Do not, however, equate delay with defeat. Tear down in order to begin the rebuilding process. Taurus and Scorpio are represented.

Tuesday, July 15 (Moon in Aquarius)   The lunar position accents legal matters, your marital status, and proposals of partnership. Get your thoughts on paper. Be sure the "right people" are aware of your intentions and talents. There is no need to trust "middlemen." Do it yourself, which assures it will be done.

Wednesday, July 16 (Moon in Aquarius to Pisces 11:14 a.m.)   Focus on family relationships, your home, making your living quarters attractive, even fixing the plumbing. Be diplomatic. Make concessions, without abandoning your principles. The spotlight is on where you live, your marital status, and earning power. Your lucky number is 6.

Thursday, July 17 (Moon in Pisces)   Be sure of the correct interest rates. There are possible complications relating to lending or borrowing. See people and situations as they exist. Avoid self-deception. Someone may not be giving pertinent information. Make inquiries; insist on facts, not evasions.

Friday, July 18 (Moon in Pisces to Aries 7:19 p.m.)   Focus on organization, priorities, and added responsibility. The pressure is on, but you will be up to it. A relationship is serious. Be aware of it, and act accordingly. Time is on your side, if you don't wait too long. A Cancer is involved.

Saturday, July 19 (Moon in Aries)   This could be a Saturday of "decisions." Today's scenario features distance, communication, and the end or beginning of a romance. Maintain a universal outlook. Whatever your decision, it will be long lasting. Take charge of your destiny. Be creatively selfish—do what is best for you.

Sunday, July 20 (Moon in Aries)   Make contact with someone in a distant city or foreign land. Make known your views. Emphasize independence of thought and of action. You will be giving and receiving love—don't "give" to one who is not worthy.

Monday, July 21 (Moon in Aries to Taurus 6:47 a.m.) Within 24 hours, you will know for sure that your plan or promotion has been accepted. Discern the correct direction; be sure of your motivation. Capricorn and Cancer play major roles. The moon moves from your ninth to tenth house, so people await further information.

Tuesday, July 22 (Moon in Taurus)   Highlight versatility. Focus on the fine arts. Show appreciation for special skills. In turn, you will be applauded for what you give and for your encouragement to others. Be up-to-date in connection with fashion news. Keep resolutions about diet and nutrition.

Wednesday, July 23 (Moon in Taurus to Gemini 7:41 p.m.)   The Taurus moon relates to your tenth house, which spotlights your career or business as well as your ability to hobnob with higher-ups. Turn on your Leo charm; emphasize humor and versatility. Taurus, Scorpio, and another Leo play instrumental roles.

Thursday, July 24 (Moon in Gemini)   You will experience more freedom of thought and of action. You could excel at fund-raising. Blend humor with your sales talk. Some of your fondest hopes and wishes will be fulfilled. In matters of speculation, stick with number 5.

Friday, July 25 (Moon in Gemini)   Attention revolves around where you live and with whom. The Gemini moon is in your eleventh house, which means your popularity increases, and you win friends and influence people. A romance that had "suffocated" could be revived, if you so permit.

Saturday, July 26 (Moon in Gemini to Cancer 7:22 a.m.)
Secrets could be the order of the day. You learn you did the right thing following a tense period. Deception was involved—you knew what was going on, but did not do anything about it. Pisces and Virgo play memorable roles.

Sunday, July 27 (Moon in Cancer)   The moon will be in its own sign, Cancer, which is your twelfth house. Secret information will be released to you. Keep it secret; maintain an aura of exclusivity. Terms are being worked out in your favor. A Capricorn will play an "amazing" role.

Monday, July 28 (Moon in Cancer to Leo 4:15 p.m.)   Let go of a situation that is embarrassing and that could lead to financial loss. Somehow, you got yourself into something, and it would serve you well to get out of it quickly. Aries and Libra will play creative roles. Do plenty of listening, but in the long run, you must make your own decision.

Tuesday, July 29 (Moon in Leo)   With the new moon in your sign and number 1 numerical cycle, this is the day if there ever was one to take the initiative, to make contacts, to take a chance on romance. Do your own thing; don't follow others. Let people know you are alive and kicking.

Wednesday, July 30 (Moon in Leo to Virgo 10:25 p.m.)   At the track: post position special—number 1 p.p. in the first race. Hot daily doubles: 1 and 1, 3 and 7, 3 and 4. Away from the track, the accent is on your domestic situation, including your home environment. Focus on partnership, marriage, and local politics.

Thursday, July 31 (Moon in Virgo) On this Thursday, the last day of July, you could reap rewards for recent efforts. Your popularity is on the rise. People actually vie to wine and dine you. What was lost will be recovered. Your earning capacity improves. Guard your personal possessions. Don't give up something of value for nothing.

AUGUST 2003

Friday, August 1 (Moon in Virgo) The sun in your sign, number 1 numerical cycle, equates to a dramatic comeback of energy. Your creative juices are activated. Show what you can do—be creatively selfish! Don't follow others, no matter how well-meaning they might be. This day is strictly your show!

Saturday, August 2 (Moon in Virgo to Libra 2:46 a.m.) A Cancer edges into your life. Focus on direction, motivation, and meditation. Emphasize cooperative efforts. Participate in local politics. Major questions relate to where you live and with whom.

Sunday, August 3 (Moon in Libra) What was lost will be recovered. Timing and luck ride with you. A discussion of social mores and religious services could dominate. Debate ensues: Should it be good works or a blend of actions that count? Some insist, "If I accept in my heart the dictums of the church, I will be saved." Others maintain the opposite.

Monday, August 4 (Moon in Libra to Scorpio 6:11 a.m.) By turning on your Leo charm, you could win over someone who once opposed you. Highlight humor, diversity, and intellectual curiosity. Laugh at your own foibles. Rebuild! This can be your "makeover" day. Check details and measurements.

Tuesday, August 5 (Moon in Scorpio)   Building material should be tested for solidity and quality. This is not the day for secondhand bargains. Insist on and obtain first-rate goods for best results. The written word is important, so get your thoughts and ideas on paper. Perhaps start a diary!

Wednesday, August 6 (Moon in Scorpio to Sagittarius 9:10 a.m.)   The emphasis is on decorating and remodeling—making your home beautiful. A passionate Scorpio comes into your life, bringing excitement and creativity. Luxury items help make your living quarters attractive. Music is involved; your voice is melodious.

Thursday, August 7 (Moon in Sagittarius)   You will be involved in a drama of truth versus falsehood. See people and relationships as they are, not merely as you wish they could be. Maintain an aura of mystery, of intrigue. Don't tell all; don't confide or confess.

Friday, August 8 (Moon in Sagittarius to Capricorn 12:02 p.m.)   The spotlight is on organization. Find out where you stand in the "arena of romance." Focus on style, fashion, and your ability to adapt to changing conditions. Capricorn and Cancer play fascinating roles. Have luck with number 8.

Saturday, August 9 (Moon in Capricorn)   Finish what you start. Remember recent resolutions about exercise, diet, and nutrition. Look beyond the immediate. Get ready for a possible journey overseas. There's a dramatic reunion tonight, which could involve someone you once loved.

Sunday, August 10 (Moon in Capricorn to Aquarius 3:23 p.m.)   Stress independence. Separate yourself from one who encourages superstition, fear, or doubt. Highlight original thinking. Don't follow others. Speak from your heart. Avoid heavy lifting. Deal gingerly with an Aquarius who is having a spell of temperament.

Monday, August 11 (Moon in Aquarius) Questions of a partnership and your marital status will loom large. You will be with unorthodox people who think nothing of delving into your personal life. Let it be known: "Enough is enough!" Capricorn and Cancer attempt to grab the spotlight.

Tuesday, August 12 (Moon in Aquarius to Pisces 8:18 p.m.) The full moon in Aquarius around midnight last night accents your seventh house. This means the emphasis is on legal rights and permissions as well as marriage and partnership. People check references; they will find yours in good order, possibly with excellent credit. If not, do something about it!

Wednesday, August 13 (Moon in Pisces) Focus on hidden matters. Others might accuse you of being in the "playground of the occult." Money changes hands, so protect yourself in the emotional clinches. Be sure you are on the right side of the law. Permit your books to be examined.

Thursday, August 14 (Moon in Pisces) Keep your options open. Get ready for change, travel, and variety. You receive surprising news concerning someone close to you. The emphasis is on reading and writing, learning through the process of teaching others. A Virgo is involved.

Friday, August 15 (Moon in Pisces to Aries 3:59 a.m.) Family strife is over. A diplomatic "surrender" takes place, to the advantage of all. This domestic adjustment could include a change of residence or marital status. Taurus, Libra, and Scorpio play major roles and have these letters in their names: F, O, X.

Saturday, August 16 (Moon in Aries)   An adventure-filled Saturday night! You learn more about languages and foreign nations. You will be fascinated by someone who speaks and acts in a "different" way. During a romantic interlude, know when to say, "Enough!" A Pisces is featured.

Sunday, August 17 (Moon in Aries to Taurus 2:52 a.m.) Come down to earth! Don't confuse fascination with love. Focus on setting priorities. Be aware of your own worth. Capricorn helps elevate your spirits. More recognition is featured, along with a possible promotion. Have luck with number 8.

Monday, August 18 (Moon in Taurus)   What was stubborn opposition will melt. You will win a heated contest. Stress universal appeal. Create your own tradition. Toss aside preconceived notions. A love relationship reignites. Protect yourself in emotional clinches.

Tuesday, August 19 (Moon in Taurus)   Make a fresh start. A Taurus will no longer block your way. A superior tells you, "Don't think I haven't noticed your good work, because I have!" This raises your morale and becomes the highlight of the day. An Aquarius and another Leo figure prominently.

Wednesday, August 20 (Moon in Taurus to Gemini 3:40 a.m.)   Many hopes and wishes are fulfilled. Be careful what you ask for because you are likely to get it. In matters of speculation, stick with number 2. Elements of timing and luck ride with you. A decision is reached concerning your partnership or marriage.

Thursday, August 21 (Moon in Gemini)   You will have something to celebrate! Ask for what you need, as well as for luxury items. Your hopes and wishes are fulfilled. Know it, and act accordingly. Careful! Don't ask for too much too soon. Gemini and Sagittarius play outstanding roles.

Friday, August 22 (Moon in Gemini to Cancer 3:43 a.m.) Take advantage today of a "rare opportunity." A restless Gemini helps you make a decision, which could work to your advantage. Check details, including plumbing facilities. Be willing to revise, to rewrite, to rebuild. A Scorpio plays a featured role.

Saturday, August 23 (Moon in Cancer) Face the unknown without fear, doubt, or suspicion. Write your impressions, perhaps start a diary. Also, take note of your dreams. Properly interpreted, they provide the doorway to your future. Lucky lottery: 5, 18, 15, 12, 24, 33.

Sunday, August 24 (Moon in Cancer) Stay close to home, if possible. Don't attempt to impress by taking a dangerous route. Strive for harmony, sound, and music. Your voice is melodious; you will be told so. A domestic adjustment is necessary; strive to make your home beautiful.

Monday, August 25 (Moon in Cancer to Leo 12:46 a.m.) Your cycle is high, so define your objectives. By so doing, you will be at the right place at a special moment. Focus on personality, confidence, sex appeal. Pisces and Virgo play unique roles. Don't believe everything you hear; deception could be involved.

Tuesday, August 26 (Moon in Leo) You get results! You will be at the right place at a special moment. A relationship seems torrid one day, cool the next. There are secrets, and you will learn them—to your advantage. Capricorn and Cancer will play outstanding roles.

Wednesday, August 27 (Moon in Leo to Virgo 6:25 a.m.) The new moon is in Virgo, your second

213

house—the money house. You get another chance to straighten out finances. Good news: A lost valuable will be retrieved. Show gratitude without being obsequious. Aries and Libra play behind-the-scenes roles.

Thursday, August 28 (Moon in Virgo)   It is time for a "new deal." Emphasize a fresh start in a different direction. Highlight original thinking and your pioneering spirit. People are attracted to you, especially members of the opposite sex. An Aquarius and another Leo figure in this scenario.

Friday, August 29 (Moon in Virgo to Libra 9:40 a.m.)   Get ready for a short journey in connection with a relative who is trying to find a lost legal document. This is fine, but don't get caught up in a wild-goose chase. Proposals concerning career or marriage could be part of today's scenario. A Capricorn is involved.

Saturday, August 30 (Moon in Libra)   With the moon in Libra, your third house, this could be a joyous day if you so permit. Elements of timing and luck ride with you. In matters of speculation, stick with number 3. Keep resolutions about your diet, exercise, and nutrition.

Sunday, August 31 (Moon in Libra to Scorpio 11:59 a.m.)   Thank your lucky stars! You have been in and out of some tight spots. Spiritual values surface. Emphasize intellectual curiosity. Keep up-to-date with fashion news. Fill out forms, thereby getting rid of red tape. A Scorpio is involved.

SEPTEMBER 2003

Monday, September 1 (Moon in Scorpio)   Attention revolves around your property or home—where you want to settle. Cancer and Capricorn figure in today's scenario. Both may be well-meaning, but follow your heart as well as first impressions. Keep resolutions about exercise, diet, and nutrition.

Tuesday, September 2 (Moon in Scorpio to Sagittarius 2:31 p.m.)   You'll be saying, "What a Tuesday!" The Scorpio moon in your fourth house could make you feel restricted. A passionate outburst from Scorpio should not be taken too seriously. Maintain your emotional equilibrium. Your popularity is on the rise.

Wednesday, September 3 (Moon in Sagittarius)   The Sagittarius moon in your fifth house includes children, variety, sex appeal. Be ready for change and travel, especially for beginning a creative project. News from a distance makes you feel good. A Taurus plays a role.

Thursday, September 4 (Moon in Sagittarius to Capricorn 5:50 p.m.)   Restrictions are removed. You experience more freedom of thought and of action. Communicate with someone in a distant city or foreign land. You need someone to represent your talent or product. The written word is important, so get ideas on paper. A Virgo figures in this scenario.

Friday, September 5 (Moon in Capricorn)   A domestic adjustment could include an actual change of residence or marital status. Take care of your general health. Be sympathetic to a coworker who seeks your opinion on what turns out to be a half-baked scheme. A Libra is in this picture.

Saturday, September 6 (Moon in Capricorn to Aquarius 10:14 p.m.)   Define terms. Get commitments in writing. A project talked about is not yet ready to be produced. Overcome a tendency toward self-deception. A family member wants to tell you something, but does not have the nerve. Be open-minded.

Sunday, September 7 (Moon in Aquarius)   Let your "inner feelings" surge forward. Lie low; don't be too available. Let others know you refuse to be taken for granted or to be at their beck and call. Capricorn and Cancer figure in today's "complicated" scenario.

Monday, September 8 (Moon in Aquarius)   Finish what you start. Get legal clearance on a project that you will undertake in the near future. A relationship is tested; know when to let go. Aries and Libra play memorable roles. News is received from someone in a distant land.

Tuesday, September 9 (Moon in Aquarius to Pisces 4:06 a.m.)   What seems far away is closer than might be anticipated. Focus on style. Emphasize initiative and the courage of your convictions. Don't follow others; let them follow you. Aquarius and another Leo figure in this colorful scenario. Your lucky number is 1.

Wednesday, September 10 (Moon in Pisces)   You will be asking yourself, "Is this déjà vu?" Today's scenario features familiar places and faces. You will be saying, "I've done this before!" Cooperative efforts, partnership, and marriage figure prominently. A Cancer is involved.

Thursday, September 11 (Moon in Pisces to Aries 12:09 p.m.)   During a social affair, you meet a mysterious person who apparently can "read your mind." Focus on engaging in political activities. An Aquarius and a Sagittarius will play key roles. Keep up with the fashion news; you might be asked to track down a story in this area.

Friday, September 12 (Moon in Aries)   Focus on distance, glamour, mystery. Be aware of details and the mechanical wherewithal needed to "fix things." You are going places, so be prepared. Instructions could come at a moment's notice. Taurus, Scorpio, and another Leo play significant roles.

Saturday, September 13 (Moon in Aries to Taurus 10:49 p.m.)   Settle in your mind where you are going and why. A long-distance communication resolves this dispute, making you feel easy and confident. Gemini, Virgo, and Sagittarius play significant roles. Lucky lottery: 5, 9, 14, 22, 18, 23.

Sunday, September 14 (Moon in Taurus)   On this Sunday, be with your family, if possible. Keep "in touch" with a loved one at a distance. Maintain a universal outlook. Participate in charitable political activities. Aries and Libra will play significant roles. Your lucky number is 6.

Monday, September 15 (Moon in Taurus)   Overcome a tendency to brood. Meditate instead. Get familiar with who you are and why you are here. The Taurus moon relates to your tenth house, which represents business, career, and possible dealings with the government.

Tuesday, September 16 (Moon in Taurus to Gemini 11:31 a.m.)   You wondered whether you did the right thing in taking the initiative for a new project. By tonight, you learn you not only did the right thing but also what you did results in profit. Capricorn and Cancer play key roles. Have luck with number 8.

Wednesday, September 17 (Moon in Gemini)   At the track: post position special—number 1 p.p. in the seventh race. Hot daily doubles: 1 and 5, 3 and 7, 4 and 6. Away from the track, finish what was started two months ago. Take charge of your own fate. The emphasis is on popularity.

Thursday, September 18 (Moon in Gemini)   Many of your hopes and wishes can now be fulfilled. The Gemini moon is in your eleventh house, bringing you luck in matters of speculation, especially by sticking with number 1. People are drawn to you and some admit, "I can hardly keep my hands off you!"

Friday, September 19 (Moon in Gemini to Cancer 12:06 a.m.)   A family member has a streak of luck. This is no time to lecture! Join in the frivolity of victory. Cancer and Capricorn will play major roles. The emphasis is on family and home. A domestic adjustment could include a change of residence or marital status.

Saturday, September 20 (Moon in Cancer)   You'll have something to celebrate this lively Saturday night. The moon in your twelfth house relates to fear, doubt, and suspicion. Plunge ahead. Take a cold dive into the future. Gemini and Sagittarius figure into this scenario. Your lucky number is 3.

Sunday, September 21 (Moon in Cancer to Leo 10:00 a.m.)   On this Sunday, attend to details; check the plumbing. A family member who withheld a secret will now confide and confess. Express pleasure. Let it be known: "I appreciate your confidence." A Scorpio is involved.

Monday, September 22 (Moon in Leo)   Break free from the prison of mediocrity. Your cycle is high, so take an unusual approach to achieve your objective. Focus on reading, writing, teaching, and learning. A relationship is exciting, and will prove worthwhile. Gemini, Virgo, and Sagittarius play stimulating roles.

Tuesday, September 23 (Moon in Leo to Virgo 4:03 p.m.)   Your cycle continues high. Take charge of decorating and remodeling. Focus on making your home beautiful. To get things done, be diplomatic. That way you win; you'll lose if you force issues. Taurus and Libra play significant roles.

Wednesday, September 24 (Moon in Virgo)   Protect yourself in emotional clinches. Someone truly is "after your money." Refuse to give up something of value for nothing. Possessions are worth more than you originally anticipated. You might be getting rich! A Pisces figures prominently. ·

Thursday, September 25 (Moon in Virgo to Libra 6:48 p.m.)   Financial backing is almost assured, if you show off your talent or product. People express a desire to be with you, even to pay for the privilege. Capricorn and Cancer play fascinating roles. An engineering project requires consideration and serious study.

Friday, September 26 (Moon in Libra)   The new moon in your third house last night warns: Be especially careful in traffic. Some people, usually steady, will be temperamental and difficult to please. Express humor, but let it be known you will not hold on to a losing proposition.

Saturday, September 27 (Moon in Libra to Scorpio 7:51 p.m.)   On this Saturday, you make vital, dynamic contacts. An Aquarius and another Leo will play sensational roles. Don't follow others; let them follow you. Wear bright colors, including yellow and gold. Lucky lottery: 1, 11, 22, 18, 5, 40.

Sunday, September 28 (Moon in Scorpio)   Spend this Sunday close to home. Renew family contacts. Straighten out a financial puzzle. Cancer and Capricorn will play "passionate" roles. Check the structure of your building or home; be sure your pool is roped off. Safety measures save time and money.

Monday, September 29 (Moon in Scorpio to Sagittarius 8:56 p.m.)   Expand your horizons. You will have more room in your living quarters. Enjoy without asking too many questions. People want to please you today, so let them do just that. Gemini and Sagittarius play essential roles. Have luck with number 3.

Tuesday, September 30 (Moon in Sagittarius)   On this last day of September, find a creative outlet for your talents. You exude personality, sensuality, and sex appeal. A relationship might go too far unless you say, "Enough is enough!" Taurus, Scorpio, and another Leo will figure prominently.

OCTOBER 2003

Wednesday, October 1 (Moon in Sagittarius to Capricorn 11:21 p.m.)   You could be debating the Einstein dictum: "Intuition is more important than knowledge." Participate in a social political gathering. Let others know you do have a sense of humor. A Sagittarius figures prominently. Your lucky number is 3.

Thursday, October 2 (Moon in Capricorn)   Your creative juices stir. Express yourself freely, mainly in writing. Communicate your ideas, and let the chips fall where they may. On this Thursday, let freedom ring. You could be acclaimed for what you say or write. Scorpio is represented.

Friday, October 3 (Moon in Capricorn)   Focus on your ability to look into areas previously dark. Give full play to your intellectual curiosity. Demand answers, not evasions. Within 24 hours, a favorite theory will be put to the test. Appreciate the adventure that accompanies a clash of ideas.

Saturday, October 4 (Moon in Capricorn to Aquarius 3:45 a.m.)   Stay close to home. Lie low, play the waiting game. An artistic endeavor that may involve music is destined to succeed. Attention revolves around show-manship and color coordination. A change of residence or marital status is possible.

Sunday, October 5 (Moon in Aquarius)   Spiritual values surface. You will be greatly aided through meditation. Be sure you have "private moments." Maintain an aura of mystery, of intrigue. Separate yourself from those who take you for granted. A Pisces plays an amazing role.

Monday, October 6 (Moon in Aquarius to Pisces 10:20 a.m.)   Focus on organization and priorities. Be willing to invest in your own capabilities. An engineering project is brought to your attention. Accept the challenge of added responsibility. Protect your legal rights and permissions. A Cancer is involved.

Tuesday, October 7 (Moon in Pisces)   Finish what you start. Look beyond the immediate. Travel to a foreign nation is a distinct possibility. Within 24 hours, you'll be granted permission to experiment, to write, to report. For now, a love relationship is getting hot and heavy.

Wednesday, October 8 (Moon in Pisces to Aries 7:07 p.m.)   Let go of previous notions. Make a fresh start. Emphasize original thinking. You could be on the brink of fame and fortune. Aquarius and another Leo figure in today's scenario. Make a personal appearance; wear bright colors. Stick with number 1.

Thursday, October 9 (Moon in Aries)   You have the feeling: "At last I have come home!" Focus on your marital status, choosing a place to live and with whom. The emphasis is on direction, motivation, and the need for meditation. Keep health resolutions. This includes exercise, diet, and nutrition. A Capricorn is involved.

Friday, October 10 (Moon in Aries)   The full moon in Aries in your ninth house means communication from one at a distance. Let idealism rule! Attend a social affair where different languages are spoken. Your popularity zooms, and people want to wine and dine you.

Saturday, October 11 (Moon in Aries to Taurus 6:04 a.m.)   Be willing to rebuild. Dress in a different style. Let others know you are not "one-dimensional." Taurus, Scorpio, and another Leo will play memorable roles. Don't attempt to please everyone. If you please yourself, most people will also be pleased.

Sunday, October 12 (Moon in Taurus)   Your career gets a boost. A Taurus will be involved. The pressure is on, but you will be up to it. The written word is especially important. What you write will be read to a "congregation." Utilize showmanship. Advertise and publicize your talent or product.

Monday, October 13 (Moon in Taurus to Gemini 6:44 p.m.)   The spotlight is on art, music, and culture. The emphasis is also on a possible change of residence or marital status. In any dispute, be diplomatic. You are due to win, but avoid enmity. Make intelligent concessions, but don't abandon your basic beliefs.

Tuesday, October 14 (Moon in Gemini)   Maintain an aura of mystery, of privacy. Don't confide, don't confess. Keep some secrets sacred. Discretion is the best course to follow. This message becomes crystal clear tonight. Pisces and Virgo will play memorable roles.

Wednesday, October 15 (Moon in Gemini)   Your hopes and desires could be fulfilled. Stress versatility. Read, teach, learn. Your financial structure is strengthened. Lively people will show appreciation for your showmanship and intelligence. You might say, "I never had it so good!"

Thursday, October 16 (Moon in Gemini to Cancer 7:39 a.m.)   More recognition is due. A relationship that went asunder could be repaired. Focus on idealism and romance. Participate in a humanitarian project. People will be drawn to you with their problems. Do what you can, but know when to say, "Enough!"

Friday, October 17 (Moon in Cancer)   Within 24 hours, a light will shine. Right now, however, make your own light by stressing independence and original thinking. Don't follow others; let them follow you. Wear bright colors, including yellow and gold. An Aquarius plays a fascinating role.

Saturday, October 18 (Moon in Cancer to Leo 6:40 p.m.)   The emphasis is on your domestic environment, including the sale or purchase of property. You'll be told, "You have what you wanted—now appreciate it!" There is much truth in that, so think about it and respond to it. Capricorn and Cancer play important roles.

Sunday, October 19 (Moon in Leo)   As your cycle moves up, circumstances take a dramatic turn in your favor. Your popularity is on the rise. Many want to wine and dine you. Your great asset today is your sense of humor. When you laugh at your own foibles, others will learn to laugh at their own.

Monday, October 20 (Moon in Leo)   Revise, review, rewrite. What had been rejected will now be accepted. Stand tall for your principles, but be willing to make intelligent concessions. Taurus, Scorpio, and another Leo will play prominent roles.

223

Tuesday, October 21 (Moon in Leo to Virgo 1:59 a.m.) Research proves that you had the correct answers. Your views are verified. A relationship that was murky will become crystal clear. You will know where you stand in the "romantic arena." A flirtation is exciting, but could prove expensive.

Wednesday, October 22 (Moon in Virgo) You get what you pay for. A genuine bargain is available. Stress kindness and diplomacy. You could be the center of a celebration. Decorating or remodeling works out just fine. You look good; your home is beautiful! Have luck with number 6.

Thursday, October 23 (Moon in Virgo to Libra 5:26 a.m.) An aura of confusion exists. Play the waiting game until clouds clear. Maintain an aura of mystery. Define terms. Outline boundaries. Written material is important; instructions are due for a sudden change. Pisces and Virgo play outstanding roles.

Friday, October 24 (Moon in Libra) A relative with financial "power" wants to be on your side. Focus on priorities, organization, and distribution. You discover where you are going and why. Since answers come from within, meditate. Cancer and Capricorn are involved.

Saturday, October 25 (Moon in Libra to Scorpio 6:07 a.m.) The new moon in Scorpio represents your fourth house. You'll be dealing with property and basic values. Look beyond the immediate. Toss aside preconceived notions. Communication from a foreign land is significant, and could lead to an overseas journey.

Sunday, October 26—Daylight Saving Time Ends (Moon in Scorpio) On this Sunday, your spiritual values surface. You will provide enlightenment. Many who were cynics will change their minds. Imprint your own style; don't follow others. Create your own tradition. A different kind of romance is on the horizon. Aquarius is involved.

Monday, October 27 (Moon in Scorpio to Sagittarius 4:54 a.m.)   The question of your marital status looms large. Creative juices stir. Find an outlet for your talent, then move ahead. The spotlight is on children, challenge, change, and a variety of experiences. Capricorn and Cancer will play outstanding roles.

Tuesday, October 28 (Moon in Sagittarius)   You will have plenty to celebrate, so maintain your emotional equilibrium and sense of humor. What happened 24 hours ago could repeat. Don't close the door to suggestions that tap your creative abilities. Gemini and Sagittarius will play featured roles.

Wednesday, October 29 (Moon in Sagittarius to Capricorn 5:36 a.m.)   Keep resolutions about your work, basic issues, and general health. Be aware of details; check the commodity market. On this day you make discoveries perhaps too subtle for others to understand. Taurus, Scorpio, and another Leo play fantastic roles.

Thursday, October 30 (Moon in Capricorn)   The emphasis is on your ability to get ideas across through the written word. Someone of the opposite sex, much attracted, implies, "At times I can hardly keep my hands off you!" An excellent day for your morale, but be skeptical. Virgo and Sagittarius figure in this scenario.

Friday, October 31 (Moon in Capricorn to Aquarius 8:41 a.m.)   Many people will be celebrating Halloween. However, magicians around the world will be taking note of National Magic Day in honor of the memory of Houdini. Stay close to home. Taurus, Libra, and Scorpio will play fascinating roles.

Saturday, November 1 (Moon in Aquarius)   Go slow, lie low. You require legal clearance. You find out who means most to you. Also, you discover "open enemies." Taurus, Scorpio, and another Leo play significant roles. Some could have these letters or initials in their names: D, M, V.

Sunday, November 2 (Moon in Aquarius to Pisces 2:52 p.m.)   On this Sunday, read and write; share knowledge; think seriously about starting a diary. Focus on cooperative efforts, partnership, legal rights, and marital status. A flirtation starts innocently, but could get hot and heavy.

Monday, November 3 (Moon in Pisces)   Stay close to home, if possible. Delve into subjects considered by most people as "the occult." Money belonging to another will be a major subject. You could be attracted to someone who is not worthy of you. A Libra is involved.

Tuesday, November 4 (Moon in Pisces)   Go slow, play the waiting game. All facts are not yet in. If you dig deep enough, you could strike pay dirt. On a personal level, protect yourself at close quarters. You are not hearing the whole truth. A Pisces is involved.

Wednesday, November 5 (Moon in Pisces to Aries 12:02 a.m.)   You'll be saying, "Things are getting better!" You get recognition long overdue. Focus on design, architecture, promotion, and distribution. In a love relationship, defer a decision. Give the other person and yourself a chance to reflect, to review.

Thursday, November 6 (Moon in Aries)   These lyrics will be repeated in your head: "Long ago and far away!" Obtain a universal view. Toss aside preconceived notions.

A dramatic affair of the heart will be part of today's exciting scenario. Aries and another Leo play sensational roles.

Friday, November 7 (Moon in Aries to Taurus 11:28 a.m.)   Take the initiative. Shake off any hint of emotional lethargy. Don't follow others. Imprint your own style! Wear bright colors, including yellow and gold. You could confront someone who will play a major role in your life.

Saturday, November 8 (Moon in Taurus)   The question of marriage looms large. The Taurus moon in your tenth house spotlights business and career, with added prestige for you. Steer clear of those who take you for granted. You are a very important person. Others should know it and act accordingly.

Sunday, November 9 (Moon in Taurus)   Last night there was a full moon and lunar eclipse in Taurus, your tenth house. This brings a shake-up in your organization, business, or career. Despite what happens, you will land on your feet. The number 3 numerical cycle brings good luck. You will more than weather the storm.

Monday, November 10 (Moon in Taurus to Gemini 12:13 a.m.)   This is your "makeover day." Dress differently; change your appearance. Some will comment, "You are wearing your hair in a different style." Answer bluntly, "This is my makeover day—I should look different!" A Scorpio is involved.

Tuesday, November 11 (Moon in Gemini)   Elements of timing and luck ride with you. A surprise visit from a Gemini relative is featured. Soon there will be laughter. Show appreciation for the visit, but say, "I would like to have at least a little advance notice!"

Wednesday, November 12 (Moon in Gemini to Cancer 1:09 p.m.)   On this Wednesday, you could change your residence or marital status. Whatever you do, do so with diplomacy and humor. Music is involved; your voice is melodious; dance to your own tune. Focus on versatility, especially key dealings with another Leo and a Virgo. Your lucky number is 6.

Thursday, November 13 (Moon in Cancer)   Accent sensitivity, but keep plans flexible. Don't make yourself too available. Secrets are being passed, which you could learn about tonight. Incidentally, a Cancer may be preparing a surprise dinner for you this evening.

Friday, November 14 (Moon in Cancer)   A relationship heats up. You will enjoy dinner and seriously wonder, "How far can this go?" You get more responsibility, a promotion, and more money. Capricorn will be in the middle of these negotiations. You will be fascinated by an engineering project.

Saturday, November 15 (Moon in Cancer to Leo 12:46 a.m.)   Your cycle moves up, and you are due for a "lucky streak." For today, stick with number 9. Stress universal appeal. Participate in a political charitable project. Someone who had been "standoffish" will now show admiration, even affection. An Aries figures prominently.

Sunday, November 16 (Moon in Leo)   Even as you read these words, circumstances turn in your favor. Highlight original thinking and your pioneering spirit. Take the initiative. Make an appointment to see a higher-up. The focus is on your personality, sensuality, sex appeal. Have luck with number 1.

Monday, November 17 (Moon in Leo to Virgo 9:34 a.m.) Focus on direction, motivation, and the need for meditation. You get the answers to questions. While your cycle is high, test the waters. Imprint your personal style; do not follow others. You are going places—do it your way. Cancer and Capricorn will play amazing roles.

Tuesday, November 18 (Moon in Virgo)   Elements of luck and timing are with you. You could win a contest or money. In matters of speculation, stick with number 3. Keep up-to-date on fashion news. Your opinions will be sought. A Sagittarius plays an instrumental role.

Wednesday, November 19 (Moon in Virgo to Libra 2:40 p.m.)   Lucky lottery: 9, 19, 5, 6, 26, 18. Handle details early. You have money coming to you, and will probably receive it tonight. Your property value is estimated; you will get your fair share. Taurus, Scorpio, and another Leo figure in this scenario.

Thursday, November 20 (Moon in Libra)   Get ready for change, travel, variety. The Libra moon represents your third house, which means activity in connection with relatives, perhaps a short trip. Write a report. Submit material that is creative and original. A Virgo is involved.

Friday, November 21 (Moon in Libra to Scorpio 4:22 p.m.)   Be gentle and diplomatic yet dance to your own tune. An important domestic adjustment could include a change of residence or marital status. You could obtain a real bargain in connection with a luxury item. The sound of your voice is different, compelling, attractive.

Saturday, November 22 (Moon in Scorpio)   On this Saturday, protect yourself at close quarters. Promises are made, but nothing has been signed. Deception is involved, deliberate or otherwise. Someone attempts to make something appear more valuable than it is. A Scorpio figures prominently.

Sunday, November 23 (Moon in Scorpio to Sagittarius 4:02 p.m.)   There is a new moon and a solar eclipse in Scorpio, your fourth house. What appears to be a defeat will boomerang in your favor. Your vitality makes a comeback—you exude personal magnetism and sex appeal. Capricorn and Cancer figure in this fascinating scenario.

Monday, November 24 (Moon in Sagittarius)   Toss aside preconceived notions. The moon in your fifth house stirs your creative juices. Look beyond the immediate. Make visions become realities. Focus on psychology, philosophy, and theology. Aries and Libra are destined to play important roles.

Tuesday, November 25 (Moon in Sagittarius to Capricorn 3:31 p.m.)   This is your day for self-expression and creative projects. Focus on children, challenge, change, variety. Use showmanship and color coordination to put across your talents or products. This is rare emotional weather—take advantage of it.

Wednesday, November 26 (Moon in Capricorn)   Keep a promise concerning exercise, diet, and nutrition. You receive proposals involving your career or marriage. The realization hits home that you can do anything if you don't get in your own way. A Cancer will display amazing talent.

Thursday, November 27 (Moon in Capricorn to Aquarius 4:48 p.m.)   You'll enjoy this Thanksgiving. Set up a game that provides information about the holiday. There is much history to be discussed while enjoying a great Thanksgiving dinner. Gemini and Sagittarius play meaningful roles. Your lucky number is 3.

Friday, November 28 (Moon in Aquarius)   Don't equate delay with defeat. Time is on your side! You can afford to play the waiting game. Legal obstruction must be removed. Cooperation needs to be given from Aquarius. What appears to be in disarray will fall into place. You will say, "I am very lucky!"

Saturday, November 29 (Moon in Aquarius to Pisces 9:26 p.m.)   Requests will be fulfilled, especially if put in writing. Someone of the opposite sex tells you, "Frankly, you are more attractive than you imagine!" Start imagining yourself as attractive, then act accordingly. Your lucky number is 5.

Sunday, November 30 (Moon in Pisces)   On this last day of November, you get good news: A debt will be paid; you will be held in high regard. Focus on your income potential as well as where you live and with whom. You'll sum it up: "This has been a very good month for me!"

DECEMBER 2003

Monday, December 1 (Moon in Pisces)   Read and write, teach and learn. Enter waters you previously feared. You will find that your mate or partner has more money than you imagined. It's important to use words carefully. Gemini, Virgo, and Sagittarius will play dynamic roles.

Tuesday, December 2 (Moon in Pisces to Aries 5:55 a.m.)   At the track: post position special—number 2 p.p. in the fourth race. Pick six: 2, 4, 6, 5, 3, 1. Hot daily doubles: 2 and 4, 3 and 5, 4 and 2. Away from the track, brighten your home. Utilize color coordination. Taurus and Libra play top roles.

Wednesday, December 3 (Moon in Aries)   Protect yourself in emotional clinches. Someone in a distant city or foreign land entices you to "do something foolish." The element of deception exists. Pisces and Virgo will play memorable roles. A real estate "bargain" requires further examination.

Thursday, December 4 (Moon in Aries to Taurus 5:29 p.m.)   Powerful emotional urges should be transformed into creative activity. Whatever you do, you will do all the way, including romance. Don't give up something of value for nothing. You'll be flattered to the hilt. Capricorn and Cancer play fascinating roles.

Friday, December 5 (Moon in Taurus)   Toss aside preconceived notions. You have a rare opportunity to hit the financial jackpot. Take a cold plunge into your future. Let go of what has been draining you emotionally and financially. Aries and Libra figure in today's dramatic scenario.

Saturday, December 6 (Moon in Taurus)   New ways to improve your income will be much in evidence. Good news: What was lost will be recovered. On top of this, you receive the gift of a valuable "stone." Be on the lookout for persons with nefarious motives. Have luck with number 1.

Sunday, December 7 (Moon in Taurus to Gemini 6:25 a.m.)   People remember and talk about Pearl Harbor. No matter what your age, people seek your opinions and predictions. Focus on cooperative efforts, local politics, partnership, and your marital status. Cancer and Capricorn play domineering roles.

Monday, December 8 (Moon in Gemini)   The full moon in Gemini, your eleventh house, means you have luck in contests and also via the written word. People tend to make promises they cannot fulfill. Be careful!

Put commitments in writing. Gemini and Sagittarius will play outstanding roles.

Tuesday, December 9 (Moon in Gemini to Cancer 7:10 p.m.)   Revise, review, rewrite, rebuild. Much of what you need or request will be given. You win friends and influence people. Where personal happiness is concerned, it can be yours if you so permit. This message becomes crystal clear tonight.

Wednesday, December 10 (Moon in Cancer)   Now is the time to be "creatively selfish." Maintain control of your life. Realize that some people, perhaps well-meaning, want your love and respect for greedy reasons. Gemini, Virgo, and Sagittarius play puzzling roles. Your lucky number is 5.

Thursday, December 11 (Moon in Cancer)   Someone who once "snubbed" you will now plead for forgiveness. Be lenient, not weak. Insist on your rights. Don't make yourself too available. A degree of exclusivity is necessary. Know it, and act accordingly. A Libra is involved.

Friday, December 12 (Moon in Cancer to Leo 6:39 a.m.)   You make discoveries, mainly about yourself. Focus on where you live and with whom. A domestic adjustment restores family harmony. Make an intelligent concession. Avoid self-deception. Pisces and Virgo play exciting roles.

Saturday, December 13 (Moon in Leo)   Your cycle is high, so this could be a "lively Saturday night." In a power play, you hold the trump card. Trust your judgment and intuitive intellect. Even as you read these words, circumstances are turning in your favor. A Capricorn figures prominently.

Sunday, December 14 (Moon in Leo to Virgo 4:05 p.m.) The moon in your sign accents your personality and sex appeal. Separation from someone you care about is temporary. Plan ahead for travel, perhaps to a foreign land. Finish what you start. Let go of fears, doubts, suspicions. An Aries is represented.

Monday, December 15 (Moon in Virgo) Changes in your employment schedule are indicated. Find innovative ways to achieve your goals, including distribution. Don't follow others; let them follow you. Wear bright colors, make personal appearances. The answer to your question: Affirmative! This is the time for a new project.

Tuesday, December 16 (Moon in Virgo to Libra 10:44 p.m.) Settle down in connection with where you live. Assess the value of your property. People want answers where no answers are immediately available. Rather than hem and haw, state the case as it exists. No answers are yet available. A Cancer is involved.

Wednesday, December 17 (Moon in Libra) Lucky lottery: 3, 10, 7, 18, 22, 44. A relative surprises you, pleasantly! A previous promise that was broken will be repaired. Be gracious and express gratitude without being obsequious. People want to do things for you, to wine and dine you.

Thursday, December 18 (Moon in Libra) A short trip involves music as well as a special relationship. Be ready to revise material. Avoid temperamental outbursts. Taurus, Scorpio, and another Leo figure prominently. In matters of speculation, stick with number 4.

Friday, December 19 (Moon in Libra to Scorpio 2:18 a.m.) You experience more freedom of thought and of action. The sale or purchase of property is involved. A passionate Scorpio encourages you. It could be fun, this relationship, but know when to say, "No!" The written word is very important, so put your thoughts and feelings on paper.

Saturday, December 20 (Moon in Scorpio)   A domestic adjustment could include a change of residence or marital status. When property is evaluated, you will be pleasantly surprised by its true worth. Gemini, Virgo, and Sagittarius play important roles. Please check the plumbing facilities.

Sunday, December 21 (Moon in Scorpio to Sagittarius 3:14 a.m.)   Spiritual values surface. Reading material elevates your morale. Define terms. Get promises in writing. Avoid self-deception. See people and relationships in a realistic light. Look behind the scenes for answers. A Pisces plays a dramatic role.

Monday, December 22 (Moon in Sagittarius)   Make holiday preparations for Christmas and New Year's Eve. Focus on organization and recognition of priorities. The powers that be express a desire for you to join them. Welcome a chance for promotion; delineate ways of distribution. A Capricorn is involved.

Tuesday, December 23 (Moon in Sagittarius to Capricorn 2:55 a.m.)   The new moon in Capricorn represents your sixth house. In turn, this relates to your general health, employment, and basic issues. A business venture is destined to succeed, so move ahead with confidence. Aries and Libra will play intriguing roles.

Wednesday, December 24 (Moon in Capricorn)   Relatives get together at a family gathering. Your original, innovative thoughts will be much appreciated. Don't copy or follow others. Aquarius and another Leo will make this Christmas Eve memorable. Be gracious, not obsequious. Moderation is required regarding adult beverages.

Thursday, December 25 (Moon in Capricorn to Aquarius 3:13 a.m.)   On this Christmas Day, make a gesture of friendship to a family member who, for one reason or another, has been "hurt." The emphasis is on your home, family, and marital status. When you talk about the theme of the holiday, remember it is the "greatest story ever told."

Friday, December 26 (Moon in Aquarius)   Christmas gifts received had much to do with home and family. Utilize them. Explain with humor about some of the presents. You really can bring joy to those you care about. Explore the possibility of a cruise.

Saturday, December 27 (Moon in Aquarius to Pisces 6:09 a.m.)   Prepare lists of activities and commitments for New Year's Eve. Do not wait until the last minute! Be sure people who drink too much are not on the list. Be aware of details, directions, and promises made. Revise, review, rewrite. An apparent defeat will be transformed into a rousing victory.

Sunday, December 28 (Moon in Pisces)   Find out where you are going and with whom. Questions will arise concerning your budget and expenditures. Tonight, a flirtation is fun, but could go too far. Gemini, Virgo, and Sagittarius are in this picture. Have luck with number 5.

Monday, December 29 (Moon in Pisces to Aries 1:09 p.m.)   Stay close to home, if possible. Avoid heavy lifting. Find out from yourself who you really care about. Original thinking is necessary along with a spirit of adventure. Taurus, Libra, and Scorpio play memorable roles and have these letters in their names: F, O, X.

Tuesday, December 30 (Moon in Aries)   Overcome a tendency to brood. The Aries moon in your ninth house promotes meditation. You somehow get insights into the future. The spotlight is on psychology, philosophy, and theology. Pisces and Virgo will play mysterious roles.

Wednesday, December 31 (Moon in Aries)   On this New Year's Eve, you play a powerful role. At least one person will confide, "At times I can hardly keep my hands off you!" Consumption of adult beverages is heavy, so accent moderation for yourself. Capricorn and Cancer will play amazing roles.

HAPPY NEW YEAR!

JANUARY 2004

Thursday, January 1 (Moon in Aries to Taurus 12:03 a.m.)   On this first day of the year, the moon will be in your ninth house. You could advertise and publish. You could also be on the verge of becoming a "national figure." Rewrite, rebuild. Wear your hair and clothing in a different style. Scorpio will be represented.

Friday, January 2 (Moon in Taurus)   You will be rewarded for a creative endeavor. A flirtation is serious and will provide sparks. But know when to say, "Enough is enough!" Be ready for directions that change. The accent will be on a variety of experiences. Nothing will remain the same!

Saturday, January 3 (Moon in Taurus to Gemini 12:57 p.m.)   The search has ended in connection with comfortable living quarters. You receive cooperation, even on foreign territory. You learn that to get a smile, you must give a smile. Diplomacy is featured. If you are dip-

237

lomatic, nothing can stop your progress. Have luck with number 6.

Sunday, January 4 (Moon in Gemini)   Spiritual values surface. Many of your hopes and wishes will become realities. Elements of timing and of luck ride with you; don't get in your own way! Define terms, perfect techniques, and streamline procedures. Pisces and Virgo will play major roles.

Monday, January 5 (Moon in Gemini)   You get more than a proverbial "pat on the back." You receive the authority to do what must be done, according to your standards. The pressure will be on; you will be up to it. Many will rely on you for their emotional and financial welfare. A relationship intensifies, and will get hot and heavy.

Tuesday, January 6 (Moon in Gemini to Cancer 1:39 a.m.)   You might be asking, "Is this déjà vu?" Today's scenario features familiar places and faces. Your lucky streak has not ended! Know it, and proceed with confidence. In matters of speculation, stick with number 9. You could meet the love of your life during a sea journey.

Wednesday, January 7 (Moon in Cancer)   The full moon in Cancer is in your twelfth house. Interpreted literally, this could mean a "hot romance" behind the scenes. Are you engaging in a secret love affair? Focus on romance, on emotions that "take charge" of logic. Make a fresh start. Stress independence and self-reliance.

Thursday, January 8 (Moon in Cancer to Leo 12:38 p.m.)   The emphasis continues on a close relationship that relates to partnership or marriage. The focus is on direction, meditation, and a clear indication of where you are going and your motives. Capricorn and Cancer figure in today's dramatic scenario and have these letters in their names: B, K, T.

Friday, January 9 (Moon in Leo) Before the day is over, you will be hugged and kissed many times. Your lunar cycle is high, so you will exude an aura of sensuality and sex appeal. You will be at the right place at a crucial moment almost effortlessly. Your powers of persuasion are overwhelming—you could be popular and rich!

Saturday, January 10 (Moon in Leo to Virgo 9:38 p.m.) Revise and review. You are capable of transforming an apparent defeat into a "rousing victory." The moon is in your sign; you get what you want. The key is to know what you really need. Taurus, Scorpio, and another Leo will play diligent roles and have these letters in their names: D, M, V.

Sunday, January 11 (Moon in Virgo) On this Sunday, it will be an "old story." You learn who is your real friend and who is merely a hanger-on. You will enjoy this day. It will be filled with surprises, change, travel, and a variety of "sensations." A Gemini will play an active role.

Monday, January 12 (Moon in Virgo) The more you read and write, the more you will teach and learn. The Virgo moon is in your second house. An opportunity exists to increase your earnings. Good news: The item you lost had sentimental value and will be returned tonight. A Libra figures prominently.

Tuesday, January 13 (Moon in Virgo to Libra 4:38 a.m.) A slow pace. Be analytical. Also be discriminating about a companionship that is "threatening" to become romantic. Don't be taken for granted. Someone

239

wants something for nothing, and you could be the prime target: Know it, and take protective measures.

Wednesday, January 14 (Moon in Libra)   A short trip may be necessary in connection with a relative who says, "I miss you so much. If you don't come to see me, I will truly be angry!" Capricorn and Cancer will play stimulating roles and could involve you in "big business." Lucky number is 8.

Thursday, January 15 (Moon in Libra to Scorpio 9:33 a.m.)   What you have been waiting for will arrive. If romance is part of your "waiting," that also will arrive. Finish what you start. Look beyond the immediate. Take charge of your own destiny. Aries and Libra will play sensational roles.

Friday, January 16 (Moon in Scorpio)   Move ahead! There will be threats. Some urge you to "stay put." However, it will be best if you walk away, then emphasize independence, creativity, and original thinking. Aquarius and another Leo will play mysterious roles.

Saturday, January 17 (Moon in Scorpio to Sagittarius 12:19 p.m.)   The Scorpio moon represents your fourth house. This means that some restrictions are for your own protection. Learn more about direction and what to do when you arrive at your destination. Capricorn and Cancer will play provocative roles. Your lucky number is 2.

Sunday, January 18 (Moon in Sagittarius)   People comment, "You appear to be brimming with vitality!" A contact you made 24 hours ago will prove important to your future. Entertain and be entertained. Keep up-to-date on fashion; you will be quizzed and challenged on that subject.

Monday, January 19 (Moon in Sagittarius to Capricorn 1:25 p.m.) The Sagittarius moon is in your fifth house. This equates to creativity, challenge, and sex appeal. You will be "on the move." It is possible you could be the "talk of the town!" Be willing to revise, to review, to rewrite. What appears to be a defeat will boomerang in your favor.

Tuesday, January 20 (Moon in Capricorn) On this Tuesday, you experience more freedom of thought and of action. The Capricorn moon is in your sixth house. This relates to general health and work that must be done. A serious approach to details is necessary. You are being observed; your marks are high.

Wednesday, January 21 (Moon in Capricorn to Aquarius 2:12 p.m.) On this Wednesday, you take a deep breath and resolve: "From now on, I am going to enjoy life!" People you respect return the compliment. Many will prove loyal, dedicated friends and fans. Taurus, Libra, and Scorpio figure in this scenario. Your lucky number is 6.

Thursday, January 22 (Moon in Aquarius) The moon in Aquarius is in your seventh house. This places emphasis on unusual events that result in publicity. The focus also will be on cooperative efforts and marital status. Pisces and Virgo will play admirable roles.

Friday, January 23 (Moon in Aquarius to Pisces 4:30 p.m.) Work behind the scenes. Become familiar with your organization. Line up priorities. Refuse to be distracted by one who complains and gossips. A relationship is hot and heavy; you will not escape responsibility. Capricorn and Cancer play fascinating roles.

Saturday, January 24 (Moon in Pisces) The Pisces moon is in your eighth house. You could hear disturbing news about the health of one you adore. The numerical cycle is number 9; it marks the beginning or end of a relationship. Do what you can in a humanitarian way, but know when to say, "Enough!"

Sunday, January 25 (Moon in Pisces to Aries 10:07 p.m.) On this Sunday, take the initiative in making friends and influencing people. Speak up; express your feelings. Let people know you are alive and kicking. The Pisces moon tells of internal pressure, your intuitive intellect, and the need to follow a hunch.

Monday, January 26 (Moon in Aries) What you feared most could turn out to be a proverbial "paper tiger." Within 24 hours, you will be relieved of a burden that was not your own to carry in the first place. Express gratitude to someone who helped without even being asked. A Cancer is involved.

Tuesday, January 27 (Moon in Aries) The Aries moon is in your ninth house. Open the lines of communication. Someone in a distant land has something of importance to tell you. The focus is also on idealism, romance, and a willingness to take yet another chance. This time your heart will not be broken.

Wednesday, January 28 (Moon in Aries to Taurus 7:47 a.m.) You come down to earth. It will be pleasant, because you obtain material needed to complete a mission. What was missing will be located. You will find that Taurus and Scorpio prove to be true allies. Lucky lottery: 22, 18, 33, 15, 16, 1.

Thursday, January 29 (Moon in Taurus) At the track, choose number 5 post position in the fifth race. The Taurus moon is in your tenth house. This relates to added recognition and prestige. A flirtation is serious, and if you so permit, it could lead to a "permanent relationship." Virgo is represented.

Friday, January 30 (Moon in Taurus to Gemini 8:18 p.m.) A domestic adjustment could include an actual change of residence or marital status. You will be in a leadership position, whether or not you asked for it. Here is the good news: You will be lucky where money is concerned! You could receive an inside tip on the stock market.

Saturday, January 31 (Moon in Gemini) On this last day of January, you will win if careful. Number 7 numerical cycle relates to Neptune. That means glamour, popularity, and the danger of self-deception. Someone intrigued by you wants also to exploit you. A Pisces figures prominently.

FEBRUARY 2004

Sunday, February 1 (Moon in Gemini) A burden is lifted. A friendship that has gone "sour" will be restored. Give a smile to get a smile. Communicate ideas and opinions. Gemini, Virgo, and Sagittarius play leading roles and could have these letters in their names: E, N, W. Your lucky number is 5.

Monday, February 2 (Moon in Gemini to Cancer 9:03 a.m.) Attention revolves around making your home beautiful. The question of your marital status will loom large. What was lost will be recovered. Ways will be found to increase your income. Circumstances are turning in your favor. Don't go hat in hand. You have plenty to offer, so act accordingly.

Tuesday, February 3 (Moon in Cancer) You receive lots of information, not all of it valid. Get the story. See

243

people and relationships in a realistic light. Define terms and outline boundaries. A flirtation could be transformed into love. A Pisces figures prominently.

Wednesday, February 4 (Moon in Cancer to Leo 7:50 p.m.) You receive privileged information. Be discreet. Don't tell all; do not confide or confess. A relationship that had been mild could turn hot and heavy. If single, you meet your future mate. If you are married, an addition to your family is "on the way."

Thursday, February 5 (Moon in Leo) Events are transpiring to bring you closer to your goal. Ride with tide, and do not get in your own way. Emphasize universal appeal. Reach beyond the immediate. Spiritual values surface. This could be a day of self-discovery!

Friday, February 6 (Moon in Leo) The full moon in your sign plus number 1 numerical cycle adds up to "nothing can stop you now!" You will be regarded as a romantic figure and a natural leader. Don't follow others. Take the initiative in creating your own tradition. Have luck with number 1.

Saturday, February 7 (Moon in Leo to Virgo 4:03 a.m.) Decide on your direction. Be aware of motivation. If you meditate tonight, the answers will come from within and problems will be resolved. Cancer and Capricorn will play fascinating roles and have these letters in their names: B, K, T.

Sunday, February 8 (Moon in Virgo) "Everything is going my way!" That could be your theme for today. You will successfully blend spirituality with materialism. You meet a fascinating Capricorn, who helps you fulfill your goal. Gemini and Sagittarius will also play key roles.

Monday, February 9 (Moon in Virgo to Libra 10:13 a.m.)   Rewrite and rebuild. Get rid of safety hazards. What you lost 48 hours ago had great sentimental value. Good news: It will be recovered tonight. Taurus, Scorpio, and another Leo pay major roles and could have these letters or initials in their names: D, M, V.

Tuesday, February 10 (Moon in Libra)   Be ready for a change of itinerary. A Libra relative expresses gratitude for past favors and will wine and dine you. Be careful! Give logic equal time with emotional responses. Gemini, Virgo, and Sagittarius will play outstanding roles.

Wednesday, February 11 (Moon in Libra to Scorpio 2:58 p.m.)   Attention revolves around the ability to beautify your surroundings, including the home. The Libra moon represents your third house. Stress humor and intellectual curiosity. Gardening could play a role; read and write about the "good earth." Your lucky number is 6.

Thursday, February 12 (Moon in Scorpio)   Attend to details. Be ready for a pleasant development in connection with a Scorpio. Someone who once blocked your way could now become a valuable ally. Taurus and another Leo will also figure in today's scenario and have these letters in their names: G, P, Y.

Friday, February 13 (Moon in Scorpio to Sagittarius 6:36 p.m.)   This will not be an unlucky day! Your lucky number will be 8. You will be on "talking terms" with "big shots." The emphasis is on responsibility and a relationship that grows intense. If you are married, the spark that brought you together in the first place will reignite.

Saturday, February 14 (Moon in Sagittarius)   On this Valentine's Day, you receive cards from distant lands. You will be assured that you have not been forgotten. The moon in your fifth house and number 9 numerical cycle combine to make you a very attractive individual who exudes an aura of sensuality and sex appeal.

Sunday, February 15 (Moon in Sagittarius to Capricorn 9:15 p.m.)   Take a chance on romance. Move ahead; don't wait for others. Accent original thinking, confidence, and independence of thought and action. The answer to your question: Yes, it is time to start your own business and to take charge of your own destiny.

Monday, February 16 (Moon in Capricorn)   Go slow. Events will unfold to throw light on a possible deal involving the sale or purchase of property. Be aware of direction and motivation. Keep health resolutions. Deal gingerly with Cancer and Capricorn. Number 2 is lucky!

Tuesday, February 17 (Moon in Capricorn to Aquarius 11:28 p.m.)   Accent diversity. Refuse to be intimidated by one who lacks imagination and spiritual awareness. You possess the gift of making people laugh, even through their grief. Be up-to-date regarding fashion news; you could be tested and interviewed on that subject.

Wednesday, February 18 (Moon in Aquarius)   Go slow, attend to details; get repair work done early. If you rewrite, review, and modernize concepts, you will have good fortune. What had been turned down could now be accepted. Taurus, Scorpio, and another Leo will play dramatic roles.

Thursday, February 19 (Moon in Aquarius)   What had been a "stalemate" will be ended, and you will be declared "The Winner!" Start a diary, read and write, teach and learn. A short trip will involve a relative. Taking a gift along would be an excellent idea. A Gemini figures prominently.

Friday, February 20 (Moon in Aquarius to Pisces 2:27 a.m.)   At the track, choose number 6 post position in the sixth race. The lunar position highlights a secret source of income. An associate might claim the lion's share. Don't give in—fight for your rights! Taurus, Libra, and Scorpio will play major roles.

Saturday, February 21 (Moon in Pisces)   Maintain an aura of mystery. Don't tell all; do not confide or confess. Keep some secrets "sacred." Work behind the scenes. Answers will come forth as a result of meditation. Pisces and Virgo will play mysterious roles and have these letters in their names: G, P, Y.

Sunday, February 22 (Moon in Pisces to Aries 7:45 a.m.)   On this Sunday, you solve a puzzle that has haunted you for months. Your confidence is restored. Be aware of it, and act accordingly. Someone of the opposite sex confides, "I can hardly keep my hands off you!" Capricorn and Cancer will play sensational roles.

Monday, February 23 (Moon in Aries)   The lunar position accents philosophy, theology, and communication to faraway places. Focus on getting your thoughts on paper, advertising, and publishing. Participate in a humanitarian project. You learn that your love is not unrequited. Aries is represented.

Tuesday, February 24 (Moon in Aries to Taurus 4:30 p.m.)   Highlight originality. Present your product in an innovative way. Wear bright colors and make personal appearances. The world will know you are alive and kicking. Imprint your own style; do not follow others. Your way is the best way for you, so act accordingly.

Wednesday, February 25 (Moon in Taurus) You might be asking, "Is this déjà vu?" Today's scenario features familiar places and faces. Focus on where you live, your marital status, and an ability to put across a real estate transaction. The accent is also on direction, motivation, and the need for meditation. A Capricorn is involved.

Thursday, February 26 (Moon in Taurus) You could meet someone destined to play an important role in your life. This "encounter" takes place during a social affair. Your popularity is on the rise. People who once rejected you can now become valuable allies. A Sagittarius plays a role.

Friday, February 27 (Moon in Taurus to Gemini 4:23 a.m.) Your powers of persuasion are heightened. Your sales ability could be considered "awesome." The moon in your eleventh house means that many of your hopes and wishes can be fulfilled. Luck rides with you. In matters of speculation, stick with number 4.

Saturday, February 28 (Moon in Gemini) At the track, choose number 5 post position in the fifth race. You will be very lucky in connection with the "written word." Take notes of ideas and opinions; do not neglect dreams. If properly interpreted, they could be the doorway to your future. Tonight's dream will be especially fascinating.

Sunday, February 29 (Moon in Gemini to Cancer 5:12 p.m.) Don't let tonight pass without stating your views and elucidating your hopes and wishes. What began as a flirtation is now serious, and could mean marriage. The key words are music, domestic harmony, and deference to the desires of your family. Dance or march to your own tune!

Monday, March 1 (Moon in Cancer)   The spotlight revolves around where you live, the sale or purchase of a home, and your marital status. A secret meeting takes place, which involves Capricorn and Cancer. Do not be offended because you are not invited; people who care about you feel you would be upset for no reason.

Tuesday, March 2 (Moon in Cancer)   Lie low, play the waiting game. Time is on your side. Perfect techniques and streamline procedures. You do not have the complete story. Be aware of it, and insist on additional information. Pisces and Virgo figure in this fascinating scenario.

Wednesday, March 3 (Moon in Cancer to Leo 4:18 a.m.)   Your lunar cycle is high, so events transpire to bring you closer to your ultimate goal. You get a lucky break as circumstances turn in your favor. You exude sex appeal. Be careful; don't choose below your station. Capricorn and Cancer figure in this scenario. Your lucky number is 8.

Thursday, March 4 (Moon in Leo)   Look beyond the immediate. Take a cold plunge into your own destiny. You are going to get recognition, perhaps on an international scale. Your powers of persuasion are heightened. You can convince people of almost anything. Aries is represented.

Friday, March 5 (Moon in Leo to Virgo 12:19 p.m.) A new idea will prove inspirational and profitable. Take the initiative. Don't wait to be told. Make a fresh start. Exercise independence of thought, of action. Avoid heavy lifting. Wear brighter colors. Another Leo is involved.

Saturday, March 6 (Moon in Virgo) The full moon in Virgo represents your second house. This relates to money, payments, collections, and invoices. A financial transaction will be completed, and could involve where you live and your marital status. Cancer and Capricorn will edge their way into this important scenario.

Sunday, March 7 (Moon in Virgo to Libra 5:32 p.m.) Entertain and be entertained. You could invent a game and might win a contest. The element of luck rides with you, especially if you stick with number 3. At the track, choose number 3 post position in the third race. Sagittarius makes a delightful companion.

Monday, March 8 (Moon in Libra) Take special care in traffic. You will be meeting with relatives for a special occasion, perhaps an engagement party. The emphasis is on diversity, versatility, and intellectual curiosity. Accept an invitation to a sociopolitical gathering.

Tuesday, March 9 (Moon in Libra to Scorpio 9:04 p.m.) An excellent day for getting your thoughts on paper. Be ready for change, travel, and a variety of sensations. Someone of the opposite sex confides, "I am very much drawn to you!" Gemini, Virgo, and Sagittarius play major roles and have these letters in their names: E, N, W.

Wednesday, March 10 (Moon in Scorpio) Attention revolves around your home and property. Focus on the necessity for a domestic adjustment. You will "hear music"—find your own rhythm and dance to your own tune. You receive a gift—a luxury item that will help brighten your home. Have luck with number 6.

Thursday, March 11 (Moon in Scorpio to Sagittarius 11:58 p.m.) A real estate transaction dominates. Avoid self-deception; see people and places as they actually exist. Look behind the scenes—someone wants to "tell you something." An idea might appear outlandish, but it is worth a follow-up. A Pisces is involved.

Friday, March 12 (Moon in Sagittarius) A favorable lunar aspect coincides with physical attraction and creativity. You get the green light to proceed with organization. Line up priorities, then make use of them. You win favor from associates, the public, and your superiors. Your lucky number is 8.

Saturday, March 13 (Moon in Sagittarius) Finish what you start. A relationship could be the start of something big. Participate in a humanitarian project. By helping others today, you eventually will help yourself. The "Golden Rule" is alive and kicking. A Libra figures prominently.

Sunday, March 14 (Moon in Sagittarius to Capricorn 2:52 a.m.) On this Sunday, spiritual values surface. Number 1 numerical cycle equates to the sun, which is your significator. By taking the initiative, you will be at the right place at a crucial moment. Your leadership will be praised. You'll be asked to assume responsibility and rewarded as a result.

Monday, March 15 (Moon in Capricorn) Keep health resolutions. This includes exercise, diet, and knowledge of nutrition. The focus is also on where you live and your marital status. You know the right way, and it is your way—refuse to be pushed aside. Capricorn and Cancer will play dramatic roles.

Tuesday, March 16 (Moon in Capricorn to Aquarius 6:11 a.m.) Leave "serious" work for another day. Tonight, accent social activity. Entertain and be entertained. People will know you are around, and many will want to wine and dine you. Be selective; maintain an aura of exclusivity. A Gemini figures prominently.

Wednesday, March 17 (Moon in Aquarius)   On this St. Patrick's Day, have fun without overindulging in adult beverages. You could be involved in a debate concerning St. Patrick: Did he really remove snakes from Ireland and were there snakes in the first place? A Taurus plays a creative role.

Thursday, March 18 (Moon in Aquarius to Pisces 10:26 a.m.)   Within 24 hours, many of your fears, doubts, and suspicions will be removed. Use the written word! Take notes; write your impressions and opinions. A flirtation lends spice. Protect yourself in emotional clinches. Don't give up something of value for a temporary thrill.

Friday, March 19 (Moon in Pisces)   You could be dealing with someone who claims to have "mystic powers." Be skeptical! Keep an open mind, without being naive. Do not lend money for a proposed enterprise. There could be a "con artist" at work here. A Libra figures prominently.

Saturday, March 20 (Moon in Pisces to Aries 4:29 p.m.)   The new moon in Pisces represents your eighth house. This equates to mystery, intrigue, and forbidden territory. Light will be shed on motives. The financial status of someone who would be your partner or mate will be revealed. Funding will come from an unorthodox source. Your lucky number is 7.

Sunday, March 21 (Moon in Aries)   Organize your priorities. Arrange a showing of your products and paintings. On a personal level, a relationship is hot and heavy. Don't break hearts—the heart you break could be your own. Capricorn and Cancer will figure prominently.

Monday, March 22 (Moon in Aries) Someone is "stringing you along." Be perceptive. Know when to say, "I have had enough of this!" A long-range project is featured. You profit by participating, especially if it involves a humanitarian activity. An Aries is in the picture.

Tuesday, March 23 (Moon in Aries to Taurus 1:10 a.m.) You will be chosen to initiate a creative project. Imprint your style. Insist on your policy being followed. A recalcitrant individual should be told, "Follow instructions or please leave!" Aquarius and another Leo will play dramatic roles.

Wednesday, March 24 (Moon in Taurus) Your partner or mate will cooperate as you lead the way to fame and fortune. You will be in the news, making news. Create your own tradition; don't follow others. Focus on civic activities and your marital status. Lucky lottery: 2, 22, 18, 5, 8, 12.

Thursday, March 25 (Moon in Taurus to Gemini 12:35 p.m.) Within 24 hours, you receive a unique honor. Tonight, get priorities in order and write down words you intend to speak. Highlight versatility, diversity, and intellectual curiosity. People desire to be with you, to entertain you, and to wine and dine you.

Friday, March 26 (Moon in Gemini) Despite the original delay or obstacle, your major wishes will be fulfilled. The Gemini moon is in your eleventh house, which equates to luck in matters of speculation. Stick with number 4! Some will attempt to steer you away from the "winning number." Follow your intuitive intellect.

Saturday, March 27 (Moon in Gemini) Exciting changes take place. Your confidence is restored, and you might be engaged in a serious flirtation. Protect yourself at close quarters. An excellent day for reading and writing, teaching and learning. You have the ability to make education a pleasure. Your lucky number is 5.

Sunday, March 28 (Moon in Gemini to Cancer 1:24 a.m.) Participate with your family in religious and social activities. Be diplomatic, but do not abandon your principles. You will learn more about the lives of composers. Your own interest in music will be sparked. Taurus, Libra, and Scorpio will play unusual roles.

Monday, March 29 (Moon in Cancer) Play the waiting game. Work behind the scenes. Make yourself "invisible." There are mysterious goings-on, so you need not become involved in something that flirts with the law. Just say, "No!" Define terms and outline boundaries. Deal gingerly with a Pisces.

Tuesday, March 30 (Moon in Cancer to Leo 1:08 p.m.) Within 24 hours, the moon will be in your sign, and your cycle will be high. Tonight, a family member tells you something you did not know. Be mature and respond wisely. Express gratitude to someone who took you into confidence. A Capricorn will figure prominently.

Wednesday, March 31 (Moon in Leo) On this last day of March, your ability to persuade is heightened. Your judgment and intuition will be on target. You will know what to do and when to do it. Express confidence. Do away with fear, doubt, and suspicion. Have luck with number 9.

APRIL 2004

Thursday, April 1 (Moon in Leo to Virgo 9:46 p.m.) You cannot be "fooled" by anyone except yourself. This means avoid self-deception. See people, places, and relationships in a realistic light. Define terms and get commitments in writing. A real estate offer requires another look; obtain answers, not evasions.

Friday, April 2 (Moon in Virgo)   Focus on organization, priorities, and acceptance of added responsibility. A chance exists that you will "turn a profit." People rely upon you for their economic and emotional welfare. The pressure is on, but you will be up to it. A Capricorn plays a role.

Saturday, April 3 (Moon in Virgo)   On this Saturday, you will be conferring with someone from a foreign land. The financial aspects of a proposal or project will be made clear. Romance could be involved with a business prospect. Look beyond the immediate. Realize your potential.

Sunday, April 4—Daylight Saving Time Begins (Moon in Virgo to Libra 3:53 a.m.)   Keep plans flexible. Make room for an additional person destined to play a role in your life. Emphasize independence, creativity, and inventiveness. Toss aside preconceived notions. Imprint your own style; do not wait for others.

Monday, April 5 (Moon in Libra)   The full moon in Libra represents your third house. This relates to neighbors, relatives, short trips, and ideas that can be developed into creative concepts. A romance is brewing! Take a chance, but protect yourself in emotional clinches.

Tuesday, April 6 (Moon in Libra to Scorpio 6:25 a.m.) Don't attempt to please everyone. Do your best to please yourself, and that will be quite enough. The Scorpio moon is in your fourth house. This relates to your property, residence, and marital status. A Sagittarius figures in today's scenario.

Wednesday, April 7 (Moon in Scorpio)   Check details, make home repairs. Revise and review. What had been rejected could now be accepted. Pay attention to the fine print. Be familiar with rules and regulations. You'll gain approval regarding zoning areas. Proceed with confidence.

Thursday, April 8 (Moon in Scorpio to Sagittarius 7:51 a.m.)   This Thursday will be your "creative day." Find an outlet for your talents and ideas. You will exude sex appeal. Be careful. Don't attract someone who wants to use you and who takes you for granted. Gemini, Virgo, and Sagittarius will play major roles.

Friday, April 9 (Moon in Sagittarius)   The emphasis is on where you live, your marital status, and the necessity for being diplomatic. Music could figure prominently; find your own rhythm. A gift is received; it will be a luxury item that helps beautify your surroundings. Be grateful, not obsequious.

Saturday, April 10 (Moon in Sagittarius to Capricorn 9:34 a.m.)   Keep resolutions concerning your work and health. Define terms and outline boundaries. See people and relationships as they are, not merely as you wish they could be. This message becomes crystal clear tonight. Your dreams, properly interpreted, could be a doorway to the future.

Sunday, April 11 (Moon in Capricorn)   The Capricorn moon is in your sixth house. This relates to the work you do, your health, and the ability to make a "selling presentation." Put priorities in order. You could be appointed head of an organization. A relationship intensifies and gets hot and heavy.

Monday, April 12 (Moon in Capricorn to Aquarius 12:33 p.m.)   Your work could take you to a distant land, but separation from a loved one is only temporary. Reach beyond the immediate. Take a cold plunge into your destiny. You need not be prisoner of the status quo or of mediocrity. You are fated for recognition, perhaps fame and fortune.

Tuesday, April 13 (Moon in Aquarius)   The moon in Aquarius is in your seventh house. The focus will be on legal affairs, your partnership, and your marital status. Number 1 numerical cycle relates to original thinking, independence, and a fresh start in a different direction. Avoid heavy lifting. Highlight the courage of your convictions.

Wednesday, April 14 (Moon in Aquarius to Pisces 5:24 p.m.)   You gain "public notice." A legal issue will be resolved. Unorthodox procedures are most likely to succeed. The spotlight is on your home, property, and marital status. One close to you needs help, but has too much pride to ask for it. A Cancer is involved.

Thursday, April 15 (Moon in Pisces)   Entertain and be entertained. Dig deep into areas regarded as "forbidden." Don't fear the unknown! You receive surprising news about the financial status of your partner or mate. Interest in the mantic arts is heightened. A Sagittarius is involved.

Friday, April 16 (Moon in Pisces)   The Pisces moon represents your eighth house. This involves mystery and intrigue, also an aura of exclusivity. Do not tell all; don't confide or confess. People are drawn to you, and you will be regarded as a "figure of mystery." That is all to the good for you!

Saturday, April 17 (Moon in Pisces to Aries 12:25 a.m.)   The Aries moon represents your ninth house. This relates to travel, publishing, and information about a foreign land. Excellent day for reading and writing, learning and teaching, perhaps starting a diary. A romantic involvement is highlighted. Give romance another chance.

Sunday, April 18 (Moon in Aries) Spiritual values surface. Participate in activities with your family. Stay close to home. You will be needed and appreciated. The grass is not greener somewhere else. If single, you meet your future mate. Married or single, you will enjoy the "comforts of home."

Monday, April 19 (Moon in Aries to Taurus 9:43 a.m.) The new moon and solar eclipse fall in the last degree of Aries. This places emphasis on your ability to make news and to be in the news. Protect the copyright of your material. Be lenient with a flirtation, but know when to say, "Enough is enough!" Pisces is represented.

Tuesday, April 20 (Moon in Taurus) This is your power pay day. The Taurus moon represents your tenth house. This means advancement in your career and recognition from those you admire. A relationship intensifies. If you are not serious, move on. A Cancer is involved.

Wednesday, April 21 (Moon in Taurus to Gemini 9:11 p.m.) Look beyond the immediate. A tempting offer could involve travel. Finances figure prominently. Ask yourself, "Is it worth it?" Shake off preconceived ideas. Take charge of your own destiny. The sky is the limit, if you so permit. Your lucky number is 9.

Thursday, April 22 (Moon in Gemini) The Gemini moon represents your eleventh house. This position is favorable for having your dreams, hopes, and wishes come true. In matters of speculation, stick with number

1. At the track, choose number 1 post position in the first race. You could be "madly in love."

Friday, April 23 (Moon in Gemini)   You get what you want in connection with your home, emotional security, and marital status. Elements of timing and of luck ride with you. Don't get in your own way. Accept good fortune, without asking too many questions. This is the "lucky break" you asked for.

Saturday, April 24 (Moon in Gemini to Cancer 9:57 a.m.)   On this Saturday, you will entertain and be entertained. Your sense of humor is "contagious." You can help people overcome grief, and many want to wine and dine you. Be selective. Know when to say, "Enough!" Gemini and Sagittarius play roles. Your lucky number is 3.

Sunday, April 25 (Moon in Cancer)   Visit someone temporarily confined to home or hospital; the more generous with your time, the better. By giving, you will also receive. The "Golden Rule" is alive and kicking. Favors you do for others on this Sunday will be returned twofold. A Taurus figures prominently.

Monday, April 26 (Moon in Cancer to Leo 10:15 p.m.)   The moon in Cancer represents your twelfth house. Focus on secrets. Accept the advice that discretion is the better part of honor. Be discreet; keep some secrets sacred. You will learn who really cares and who merely wants to "use you."

Tuesday, April 27 (Moon in Leo)   Your lunar cycle is high. You will read and write; your words will have tremendous impact. Events transpire to bring you closer to your goal. Focus on your home, financial security, and marital status. Your personality is overwhelming, and you exude instant sex appeal.

Wednesday, April 28 (Moon in Leo)   You get what you want, but be sure you do not ask for more than you can handle. Define terms, perfect techniques, and streamline procedures. A mysterious Pisces comes into your life. Enjoy, but protect yourself in emotional clinches.

Thursday, April 29 (Moon in Leo to Virgo 8:01 a.m.) Within 24 hours, you'll have a chance to "hit the financial jackpot." Follow a hunch. Organize priorities. Accept a promotion that entails added responsibility. A love relationship "sizzles." Don't break hearts; the heart you break could be your own.

Friday, April 30 (Moon in Virgo)   On this last day of April, you retrieve what had been lost, missing, or stolen. You could "find" love during a journey. Someone from a foreign land intrigues. You ask yourself: "Is this love or lust?" Aries and Libra will be involved.

MAY 2004

Saturday, May 1 (Moon in Virgo to Libra 2:03 p.m.)   This will be a meaningful day. What had been kept from you will be revealed. Written material is involved; your "power" will be enhanced as a result. Capricorn and Cancer will play fascinating roles. Have luck with number 8.

Sunday, May 2 (Moon in Libra)   Keep plans flexible. Let spiritual values surface. A close relative has something important to say. Be a good listener, but don't believe everything you hear. Finish what you start. Participate in a humanitarian project. A Libra figures prominently.

Monday, May 3 (Moon in Libra to Scorpio 4:37 p.m.)   Make a fresh start. Highlight independence and original thinking. Don't wait for others. Use your instinctive knowledge of publicity and showmanship. Attention will revolve around your product and talent. An Aquarius plays an important role.

Tuesday, May 4 (Moon in Scorpio)   The full moon in Scorpio represents your fourth house. This relates to a safe harbor, protection, land, and real estate. What had been settled and possibly dull will come to life. You could be involved in controversy as a result. A Taurus plays an outstanding role.

Wednesday, May 5 (Moon in Scorpio to Sagittarius 5:07 p.m.)   Expand your horizons. Entertain at home. You soon will be having some "very important guests." The emphasis is on social activities, versatility, and humor. People express the desire to be with you, and offer to wine and dine you. Have luck with number 3.

Thursday, May 6 (Moon in Sagittarius)   The Sagittarius moon is in your fifth house. This relates to creative activity, flirtation, surprise meetings, and sex appeal. You gain via the written word. What had been rejected could now be accepted. Taurus, Scorpio, and another Leo figure in this scenario.

Friday, May 7 (Moon in Sagittarius to Capricorn 5:16 p.m.)   What you forgot or lost 24 hours ago will be retrieved. You meet someone who is drawn to you. That is very nice, but remember to protect yourself in emotional clinches. Don't give up something of value for a temporary thrill. A Virgo figures prominently.

Saturday, May 8 (Moon in Capricorn)   Attention revolves around your home and marital status. Keep resolutions about your health; this includes exercise, diet, and more knowledge of nutrition. Events transpire to help you enjoy your work. Taurus, Libra, and Scorpio play major roles. Your lucky number is 6.

Sunday, May 9 (Moon in Capricorn to Aquarius 6:46 p.m.)   The Capricorn moon is in your sixth house. This relates to special services for others, your work routine, and general health. Avoid extremes; be diplomatic. Recognize the difference between generosity and extravagance. Pisces and Virgo play dramatic roles.

Monday, May 10 (Moon in Aquarius)   Blend lessons learned in the past with modern challenges. An older person recalls a favor you did and will exert influence on your behalf. Capricorn and Cancer will play extraordinary roles and could have these letters in their names: H, Q, Z.

Tuesday, May 11 (Moon in Aquarius to Pisces 10:52 p.m.)   Look beyond the immediate. Lie low, play the waiting game. You will obtain legal clearance. A zoning controversy works to your benefit. Aries and Libra play fascinating roles and have these letters in their names: I and R. Your fortunate number is 9.

Wednesday, May 12 (Moon in Pisces)   Dig deep for information that had been held "under cover." You might learn more than you care to know, but remember that knowledge is power. Investigate the occult; you will find the key to a dilemma in arcane literature. Aquarius and another Leo will play relevant roles.

Thursday, May 13 (Moon in Pisces)   You will change your mind more than once. You could even reflect on the possibility of a name change. Someone you admire will return the compliment. Your morale is elevated as a result. Capricorn and Cancer play major roles and are apt to have these letters in their names: B, K, T.

Friday, May 14 (Moon in Pisces to Aries 6:01 a.m.) Accent diversity, advertising, and publishing. Communicate with friends in a distant city or foreign land. Be current with fashion news; you could be tested and challenged. Wear your clothes and hair in "modern" styles. A Gemini figures prominently.

Saturday, May 15 (Moon in Aries) An excellent day for revising, reviewing, and rebuilding. By rewriting, you'll find that what had been rejected can now be accepted. The emphasis is on language and the ability to make meanings crystal clear. Someone of the opposite sex from a foreign land will intrigue you. A Scorpio is involved.

Sunday, May 16 (Moon in Aries to Taurus 3:56 p.m.) Within 24 hours, you receive news of a promotion; an assignment will add to your prestige. Keep plans flexible. Today's scenario features change, travel, and a variety of experiences. Words will be of special importance; read and write. A Virgo figures prominently.

Monday, May 17 (Moon in Taurus) Be benevolent and forgiving. A family member admits an error in finances. Highlight maturity and understanding. Being forceful will only complicate matters. Know where you stand and what to do about it. Taurus, Libra, and Scorpio play top roles.

Tuesday, May 18 (Moon in Taurus) Think twice before accepting an assignment that could cause a family rift. You are not being told the complete story; insist on answers, not evasions. Define terms. Avoid self-deception. Maintain an aura of exclusivity. Don't become too available. A Pisces is in the picture.

Wednesday, May 19 (Moon in Taurus to Gemini 3:46 a.m.) The new moon emphasizes that someone in authority can no longer hold that position. Within 24 hours, you will be celebrating. A major wish will be fulfilled. Tonight, be kind to a Taurus who becomes somewhat of a "lost soul." Your lucky number is 8.

Thursday, May 20 (Moon in Gemini)   You are on the precipice of recognition on a universal scale. The number 9 numerical cycle, plus the moon in your eleventh house, means that your influence will be widespread and perhaps will include foreign nations. You will be in the news and making news!

Friday, May 21 (Moon in Gemini to Cancer 4:34 p.m.)   Emphasize independence, creativity, and original thinking. Do not wait for others. Take the initiative in making dreams come true. Wear bright colors when you make personal appearances. Exercise showmanship and publicity. Let others know you can do "something different."

Saturday, May 22 (Moon in Cancer)   On this Saturday, stick close to home ground. Your family will be of great comfort to you. The focus is on partnership and marital status. You will enjoy dinner tonight; remember diet resolutions and knowledge of nutrition. A Capricorn is in the picture.

Sunday, May 23 (Moon in Cancer)   Social activities are highlighted, and could take place in a theater or church. Remember to elevate the morale of one confined to home or hospital. The emphasis is on diversity, versatility, and your intellectual curiosity. Gemini and Sagittarius will play important roles.

Monday, May 24 (Moon in Cancer to Leo 5:06 a.m.) What begins as a routine task could be transformed into an exciting, creative project. You will rewrite, revise, review, and rebuild. Your lunar cycle is high. Almost effortlessly, you will be at the right place at a crucial moment. A Scorpio figures prominently.

Tuesday, May 25 (Moon in Leo)   You experience more freedom of thought and of action. The lunar position highlights your personality, which can be "overwhelming." You'll exude sex appeal. Enjoy the spice in your life, but don't go "overboard." Virgo and Sagittarius play mysterious roles.

Wednesday, May 26 (Moon in Leo to Virgo 3:50 p.m.)   Attention revolves around your ability to beautify the surroundings, including your home. Focus on romance, flowers, and music; find your own rhythm and dance to your own tune. Taurus and Libra figure in this exciting scenario. Lucky lottery: 6, 12, 16, 5, 18, 33.

Thursday, May 27 (Moon in Virgo)   The Virgo moon relates to your second house. This emphasizes money, payments, collections, and the ability to increase your income potential. A lost article will be retrieved; express gratitude without being obsequious. Pisces and Virgo will play sensational roles.

Friday, May 28 (Moon in Virgo to Libra 11:20 p.m.)   Let people know you mean business! You have the responsibility of "pointing in the right direction." Many depend on you for their emotional and financial welfare. Accept the challenge of added duties. The pressure will be on, but you will be up to it. A Capricorn is involved.

Saturday, May 29 (Moon in Libra)   On this Saturday, reach beyond the immediate. A short trip could involve a relative and music. Entertain and be entertained. A Libra relative expresses gratitude for a past favor, and will repay you tonight. An Aries is in the picture. Your lucky number is 9.

Sunday, May 30 (Moon in Libra)   The answer to your question: Positive! Start a business. Make a fresh start. Emphasize independence and creativity. Dare to dream. Avoid heavy lifting. Speak from the heart. Realize that the one you admire could be in love with you. Another Leo will play a dramatic role.

Monday, May 31 (Moon in Libra to Scorpio 3:06 a.m.)   On this last day of May, you will be concerned with your home, property, real estate, sales, and purchases. Focus also on partnership and marriage. Reflect on direction and motivation. Please do meditate. Capricorn and Cancer will play fascinating roles.

JUNE 2004

Tuesday, June 1 (Moon in Scorpio)   Finish what you start. Don't give up the ship. A long-distance communication verifies your views and builds your morale. You could encounter the "love of your life" during a journey. Dare to dream! Your vision of the future will prove accurate. A Libra is represented.

Wednesday, June 2 (Moon in Scorpio to Sagittarius 3:51 a.m.)   Make a fresh start. Be sure your working tools are in order. Don't wait for others; create your own tradition. Speak from the heart; avoid heavy lifting. A former "lover" will make a surprise appearance. Maintain your emotional equilibrium. Lucky lottery: 1, 11, 8, 5, 22, 13.

Thursday, June 3 (Moon in Sagittarius)   The full moon in Sagittarius is in your fifth house. This equates to creativity and a variety of sensations. Attention revolves around direction and motivation. Please do not forget to meditate! Capricorn and Cancer will pay surprising roles and have these letters in their names: B, K, T.

Friday, June 4 (Moon in Sagittarius to Capricorn 3:12 a.m.)   Attend to basic issues that include home repairs. Revise, review, tear down for the purpose of rebuilding. Highlight versatility, humor, and intellectual curiosity. Deal gingerly with a temperamental Scorpio. Gemini and Sagittarius will be involved.

Saturday, June 5 (Moon in Capricorn)   A day of changes! There could be a serious discussion concerning the possibility of changing your name. You will locate a diary you started some months ago. Elaborate, taking note of your opinions and feelings. A Taurus figures in this scenario.

Sunday, June 6 (Moon in Capricorn to Aquarius 3:10 a.m.)   Give full rein to your intellectual curiosity. Make inquiries; obtain answers, not evasions. A family member will make a major concession, which will help bring about domestic tranquillity. Purchase a gift to show your appreciation. Gemini is represented.

Monday, June 7 (Moon in Aquarius)   Lie low and go slow. Time is on your side. Look behind the scenes for answers. If you meditate, the answers will come from within. Define terms. Outline boundaries. Decide on where you are going and why. Your question should be: "Is this trip necessary?"

Tuesday, June 8 (Moon in Aquarius to Pisces 5:38 a.m.)   The Pisces moon represents your eighth house. This has to do with mystery as well as money belonging to another. One close to you will discuss the manner of demise. Do not fear the occult. You will make a stunning discovery while reading literature dealing with the mantic arts and sciences.

Wednesday, June 9 (Moon in Pisces)   You come down to earth and could be directing a business of your own. A relationship progresses and could get too hot not to cool down. Focus on business arrangements and your marital status. Capricorn and Cancer will play amazing roles. Your lucky number is 8.

Thursday, June 10 (Moon in Pisces to Aries 11:50 a.m.)
Subtle changes happen in your life. What had been a mystery will become crystal clear. Prepare for a journey. You are going to travel; you will meet exciting, creative people. You need not be a prisoner of mediocrity. An Aries plays a major role.

Friday, June 11 (Moon in Aries)   Let go of preconceived ideas. Look beyond the immediate. Dare to dream. More people take note of your character and talent; you will be wined and dined. Imprint your own style; do not wait for others. Have luck with number 1.

Saturday, June 12 (Moon in Aries to Taurus 9:36 p.m.)   The Aries moon relates to your ninth house. This places emphasis on communication that includes publicity, advertising, and publishing. Tonight, you will be engaged in a metaphysical discussion. Your knowledge of philosophy will be enhanced as a result.

Sunday, June 13 (Moon in Taurus)   The Taurus moon relates to your tenth house. This means additional funds or income in connection with your business or career. On this Sunday, enjoy yourself and let your spiritual values surface. A Sagittarius plays an important role.

Monday, June 14 (Moon in Taurus)   Be meticulous in checking the details. What begins as a boring routine will be transformed into an exciting creative endeavor. Revise, review, and rewrite. What had been rejected will now be accepted. Know it, and respond accordingly. Scorpio is represented.

Tuesday, June 15 (Moon in Taurus to Gemini 9:43 a.m.)
Within 24 hours, some of your major wishes could be fulfilled. Money is involved; don't ask for more than you can handle. Tonight, express yourself via the written word. A flirtation lends spice, and could become serious. A Gemini is in the picture.

Wednesday, June 16 (Moon in Gemini)   Many of your desires will be fulfilled in the domestic area. If you are married, a family member makes an important concession. You learn that an addition to the family is "on the way." If single, you are likely to meet your future mate. Your popularity will be on the rise.

Thursday, June 17 (Moon in Gemini to Cancer 10:36 p.m.)   The new moon in Gemini in your eleventh house means that life will be brighter. You will replace gloom with optimism. Your powers of persuasion are heightened. What appeared a loss could be transformed into a rousing victory. Pisces and Virgo figure in this scenario.

Friday, June 18 (Moon in Cancer)   You learn more than you care to know. You have more responsibility. People will rely upon you for their emotional and financial welfare. The key is organization and getting your priorities in order. The pressure is on, and you will be up to it. Your lucky number is 8.

Saturday, June 19 (Moon in Cancer)   A Cancer will help you with a major project that could have international implications. Look beyond the immediate. Get off the bench and into the game—it could be the "game of your life!" Aries and Libra play stunning roles and have these letters in their names: I and R.

Sunday, June 20 (Moon in Cancer to Leo 11:03 a.m.)
Within 24 hours, the moon will be in your sign. Be pre-

pared for a fresh start in a new direction. What you want, you will receive. Blend practicality with imagination. Romance lends spice and could stir your creative juices!

Monday, June 21 (Moon in Leo) You are doing better than you give yourself credit for. Be confident; then proceed accordingly. The spotlight is on direction, motivation, and meditation. Major questions are likely to concern partnership and marriage. A Cancer is involved.

Tuesday, June 22 (Moon in Leo to Virgo 10:08 p.m.) Combine showmanship with entertainment and your power of persuasion. You will be at the right place at a crucial moment, almost effortlessly. Accent diversity and versatility. Don't be afraid to ask questions. People want to be with you and will wine and dine you.

Wednesday, June 23 (Moon in Virgo) The Virgo moon relates to your second house. This means you could locate a lost article and earn more money. Get formats, ideas, and plans in writing. Be capable of presenting written material to one who shows interest in your work. Scorpio is represented.

Thursday, June 24 (Moon in Virgo) Be ready for change and a variety of experiences. An excellent day for reading and writing, teaching and learning. A relationship is more serious than you expected. You could take a trip with a special member of the opposite sex. Gemini, Virgo, and Sagittarius play key roles.

Friday, June 25 (Moon in Virgo to Libra 6:49 a.m.) Attention revolves around your home, flowers, music, and appreciation of art. Someone who pays you a compliment means more than mere flattery. Show appreciation without being obsequious. You receive a gift, a luxury item that helps beautify your home.

Saturday, June 26 (Moon in Libra)   The Libra moon represents your third house. You will have plenty to do with relatives and short trips. Don't scatter your forces. Avoid self-deception. No one can fool you, but you could deceive yourself, if you so permit. A Pisces plays a sensational role.

Sunday, June 27 (Moon in Libra to Scorpio 12:10 p.m.)   You will resurrect your "fading" prestige. In a way, you are on the spot. People rely on you for their financial and emotional welfare. You will have more responsibility. The pressure will be on, but you will be up to it. Capricorn and Cancer play instrumental roles.

Monday, June 28 (Moon in Scorpio)   You will complete a major task. This will relate to home repairs and could include fixtures, roofing, and plumbing. Look beyond the immediate. Realize that a current relationship is growing hot and heavy. Do not play games with emotions; the heart you break could be your own.

Tuesday, June 29 (Moon in Scorpio to Sagittarius 2:14 p.m.)   Make a fresh start. Be sure your home is properly lit; take special care in walking down dark hallways. The key is light and enlightenment. If you are married, the spark that brought you together will reignite. An Aquarius and another Leo play roles today.

Wednesday, June 30 (Moon in Sagittarius)   On this last day of June, your creative juices stir. The focus will be on direction, motivation, and meditation. You are going places—you will learn where and why. Questions about partnership and marriage could loom large. A Cancer is in the picture.

Thursday, July 1 (Moon in Sagittarius to Capricorn 2:00 p.m.) On this first day of the month, you will be ambitious, creative, and successful. Open the lines of communication. Investigate a publishing opportunity. Avoid heavy lifting. Speak from the heart. Use color coordination in displaying your product. Your lucky number is 1.

Friday, July 2 (Moon in Capricorn) The full moon in Capricorn is in your sixth house. This relates to employment, service to others, and general health. The spotlight is on where you live and with whom; your marital status figures prominently. Be sure of your direction and motivation. A Cancer is involved.

Saturday, July 3 (Moon in Capricorn to Aquarius 1:22 p.m.) A lively Saturday night! You will entertain, and others will entertain you. Focus on diversity and versatility. Give full rein to your intellectual curiosity. Questions will be answered, but many in a superficial way. Gemini and Sagittarius play interesting roles. Your lucky number is 3.

Sunday, July 4 (Moon in Aquarius) On this holiday, have your guests or family members read aloud at least part of the Declaration of Independence. Be aware of details and safety measures. Steer clear of explosives; protect pets. Taurus, Scorpio, and another Leo will play fascinating roles.

Monday, July 5 (Moon in Aquarius to Pisces 2:27 p.m.) Work behind the scenes. Put thoughts, impressions, and opinions on paper. Words will be important, and could mean the difference between winning and losing. Gemini, Virgo, and Sagittarius play meaningful roles and could have these letters in their names: E, N, W.

Tuesday, July 6 (Moon in Pisces)   The Pisces moon relates to your eighth house. This could mean the "death" of a relationship, and could also spark new interest in the occult. Attention also revolves around your home, remodeling and beautifying your surroundings. If single, you could meet your future mate.

Wednesday, July 7 (Moon in Pisces to Aries 7:03 p.m.)   Get to the heart of matters. Someone is not telling the entire truth. Define terms; insist on answers, not evasions. Maintain an aura of mystery. Don't be too available. Emphasize exclusivity. Pisces and Virgo play "tantalizing" roles.

Thursday, July 8 (Moon in Aries)   Your words and actions will have an impact on people "far away." A personal relationship could get out of control. Don't play games; the heart you break could be your own. Capricorn and Cancer figure in this scenario. Your lucky number is 8.

Friday, July 9 (Moon in Aries)   A communication is received from someone in a distant land; your morale is elevated as a result. You get a combination of commendation and invitation. Think things over. Don't rush headlong into something that could have multidimensional qualities. An Aries figures prominently.

Saturday, July 10 (Moon in Aries to Taurus 3:50 a.m.)   You have been waiting for this day! Your views will be vindicated. You could be promoted as a result. Money is involved. You will be rewarded and perhaps obtain a raise in pay. Those who overlooked you will be apologetic. Let them rest assured you hold no grudge. Your lucky number is 1.

Sunday, July 11 (Moon in Taurus)   Let spiritual values surface. Remain close to home; you will have much to discuss

273

with your family. Questions arise in connection with where to reside. Capricorn and Cancer figure in today's dynamic scenario and have these letters in their names: B, K, T.

Monday, July 12 (Moon in Taurus to Gemini 3:44 p.m.)   Accent humor. Keep plans flexible. Answer correspondence and make necessary telephone calls. Be up-to-date on the fashion news; you will be tested and challenged. Luck rides with you. You could win a contest. Gemini and Sagittarius will play featured roles.

Tuesday, July 13 (Moon in Gemini)   Revise, review, and rebuild. The Gemini moon is in your eleventh house. This means that many of your fondest hopes and wishes could become realities. Your power of persuasion is heightened. You win your way, and this could include romance. Taurus and Scorpio will play major roles.

Wednesday, July 14 (Moon in Gemini)   Read and write, learn by teaching. The moon in your eleventh house means that you will continue to be lucky, especially by sticking with number 5. A flirtation lends spice; do not fear romance. Someone who cares about you will make known those feelings—it could be the "real thing."

Thursday, July 15 (Moon in Gemini to Cancer 4:40 a.m.)   A family member talks about a "hiding place." Be a good listener, heap no ridicule. Exercise diplomacy. Make it crystal clear that you are interested, even though skeptical. You will learn more about what this hiding place is and where it is. A Libra is involved.

Friday, July 16 (Moon in Cancer)   You could be engaged in a "secret mission." See relationships in a realistic light. Avoid self-deception. People will be drawn to you due to your aura of mystery and intrigue. Do not tell all; don't confide or confess. Pisces and Virgo will play romantic roles.

Saturday, July 17 (Moon in Cancer to Leo 4:55 p.m.) The new moon in Cancer represents your twelfth house. This is the sector of your horoscope relating to mystery, magic, and romantic illusions. In business matters, you win via the practical approach; funding will be obtained for a unique project. Your lucky number is 8.

Sunday, July 18 (Moon in Leo) Your lunar cycle is high, so your personality will be overwhelming. You exude sex appeal. Be discriminating. Do not get involved with one "below your station." Take the initiative. Participate in an organization that could operate overseas. An Aries plays a significant role.

Monday, July 19 (Moon in Leo) Take the initiative in making a fresh start. Be independent in thought and in action. You will be regarded as a "glamorous figure." Avoid heavy lifting. Wear bright colors. Use your instinctive knowledge of showmanship. Another Leo could be involved.

Tuesday, July 20 (Moon in Leo to Virgo 3:43 a.m.) Be analytical, especially in connection with the sale or purchase of property. You receive proposals that include business, career, and marriage. Your services are valuable. Know it, and act as if aware of it. Capricorn and Cancer play distinctive and entertaining roles.

Wednesday, July 21 (Moon in Virgo) Lucky lottery: 3, 21, 9, 18, 38, 12. At the track, choose number 3 post position in the third race. The element of luck rides with you; test your skills. During a social affair, you could meet someone destined to pay an important role in your life. Gemini is represented.

Thursday, July 22 (Moon in Virgo to Libra 12:37 p.m.) By tonight, you receive good news about an investment. Be aware of details and subtle points. You will not obtain something for nothing, but you will receive valuable information about a specific stock. Do some investigating, then respond accordingly.

Friday, July 23 (Moon in Libra)   A relative takes an active interest in your creative hobbies or pursuits. If you need help in any way, this is the time to ask for it. You exude an aura of excitement, adventure, sensuality, and sex appeal. You can get almost anything you want. Toss aside your pride and ask for it!

Saturday, July 24 (Moon in Libra to Scorpio 7:07 p.m.)   You will hear the sound of music. Find your own rhythm; dance or march to your own tune. Your voice gathers attention; people want to hear you talk and sing. Your powers of persuasion are strong; you could sell a unique program to one who appeared uninterested.

Sunday, July 25 (Moon in Scorpio)   The Scorpio moon relates to your fourth house. This means you will be concerned with home, shelter, rules, and regulations. Be especially aware of "zoning laws." You have not been told the entire truth. Pisces and Virgo will figure in this unusual scenario.

Monday, July 26 (Moon in Scorpio to Sagittarius 10:46 p.m.)   Practical issues dominate. Let people know you mean business. You will have the authority to put policies into effect. Many will rely upon you for their emotional and financial welfare. A personal relationship is heated, and something must give eventually. A Capricorn is involved.

Tuesday, July 27 (Moon in Sagittarius)   What you started two months ago can be completed. The lunar position accents creativity, style, challenge, and sex appeal. Reach beyond the immediate; deal with Aries and Libra. At the track, choose number 8 post position in the ninth race.

Wednesday, July 28 (Moon in Sagittarius to Capricorn 11:56 p.m.)   You get the proverbial "second chance." Make a strong impression. Imprint your style. Make personal appearances and appeals. Attract attention with bright colors. Assert your views in a positive way. Don't wait for others. Refuse to play "second fiddle." Have luck with number 1.

Thursday, July 29 (Moon in Capricorn)   A family member talks about a possible "name change." Interest will be displayed in the mantic arts, including numerology and astrology. You will learn much and could be the life of the party. A Cancer will display skill as a gourmet chef.

Friday, July 30 (Moon in Capricorn to Aquarius 11:54 p.m.)   The moon in Capricorn represents your sixth house. This means keep resolutions about your general health and work. The number 3 numerical cycle coincides with entertainment and perhaps a night of love and laughter. Gemini and Sagittarius will pay leading roles.

Saturday, July 31 (Moon in Aquarius)   On this last day of July, there will be a blue moon in Aquarius, your seventh house. Emphasis is placed on public relations and legal affairs. Focus on the ability to revise, to review, and to rebuild. Someone behind the scenes wants to "get to know you." A Scorpio figures prominently.

AUGUST 2004

Sunday, August 1 (Moon in Aquarius)   Spiritual values surface. You learn where you stand and what to do about it. You will be in the company of one who "understands the law." Capricorn and Cancer will play outstanding roles. You decide upon which direction to go and why. Follow a hunch!

Monday, August 2 (Moon in Aquarius to Pisces 12:35 a.m.) The Pisces moon relates to your eighth house. Delve deep into subjects such as astrology and number mysticism. The answer to a problem will be found in literature covering the mantic arts and sciences. Gemini and Sagittarius will play fascinating roles.

Tuesday, August 3 (Moon in Pisces) On this Tuesday, you resolve a dilemma and feel more secure as a result. You will be dealing with a sensitive Pisces who cares about you, but might be too shy to admit it. Rewrite and rebuild; wear your hair and clothes in different styles. Have an exciting time!

Wednesday, August 4 (Moon in Pisces to Aries 3:59 a.m.) You make a discovery that heightens your interest in metaphysical subjects. The emphasis is on reading and writing, learning and teaching. Be careful in connection with flirtation—some of your subtle nuances could be misinterpreted! Virgo is represented.

Thursday, August 5 (Moon in Aries) Look beyond the immediate. Conditions at home will improve, if you make an intelligent concession to your family. Don't force issues; accent diplomacy. Art and music will play roles. You will be complimented on your knowledge of these subjects.

Friday, August 6 (Moon in Aries to Taurus 11:26 a.m.) Within 24 hours, you will receive news of a promotion that elevates your prestige. Today, avoid self-deception; see people and places as they are, not merely as you wish they could be. Maintain an aura of exclusivity. A Pisces figures in this scenario.

Saturday, August 7 (Moon in Taurus) Focus on added responsibility, promotion, and direction. Realize that you are "playing for keeps." Someone who takes you for granted should be told, "No more of it!" This is your power play day—make the most of it. Have luck with number 8.

Sunday, August 8 (Moon in Taurus to Gemini 10:32 p.m.)   A communication is received from a distant city or foreign land. Your words will be quoted; take care in what you say or write. Romance on the high seas is a distinct possibility. Aries and Libra play fascinating roles and have these letters in their names: I and R.

Monday, August 9 (Moon in Gemini)   The answer to your question: Positive! Make a fresh start in a new direction. You will win friends and influence people. Gemini and Sagittarius will play key roles. Avoid heavy lifting. Get to the heart of matters. You'll have luck in speculating by sticking with number 1.

Tuesday, August 10 (Moon in Gemini)   The Gemini moon represents your eleventh house. This is very lucky and coincides with wishes and dreams that come true. In matters of speculation, your timing will be "exquisite." Capricorn and Cancer will play interesting roles.

Wednesday, August 11 (Moon in Gemini to Cancer 11:19 a.m.)   You might be asking, "Is this déjà vu?" The scenario features familiar places and faces. You'll be saying to yourself, "I am sure I have been here before—perhaps there is something to reincarnation!" Gemini and Sagittarius will play memorable roles. Your lucky number is 3.

Thursday, August 12 (Moon in Cancer)   Fix things at home. As far as your product is concerned, obtain a colorful display. A broken article will be mended, and so will a relationship. Taurus, Scorpio, and another Leo figure in today's dynamic scenario. The Cancer moon is in your twelfth house, so visit someone confined to home or hospital.

Friday, August 13 (Moon in Cancer to Leo 11:28 p.m.) What appeared to be "out of reach" will be made available. Luck changes in your favor. Events will transpire to bring you closer to your ultimate goal. Read and write, teach and learn. This day will not be unlucky. As a matter of fact, this will be one of your "lucky days."

Saturday, August 14 (Moon in Leo) Stick close to familiar ground. A family member has a financial surprise—it will be of the pleasant variety. What you recently lost had sentimental value; it could be returned tonight. Taurus, Libra, and Scorpio play outstanding roles. Your lucky number is 6.

Sunday, August 15 (Moon in Leo) Your lunar cycle is high. You get what you want, and you will know when to ask for it. Your personality is overwhelming. You exude an aura of glamour and sex appeal. Be discriminating. Choose with care when it comes to admitting people into your "inner circle."

Monday, August 16 (Moon in Leo to Virgo 9:48 a.m.) The new moon in your sign last night highlights an opportunity for romance and creative projects. You will be saying: "This is not a usual Monday—it is a day I won't soon forget!" Focus on inventiveness and the ability to organize your priorities. Capricorn is on your side.

Tuesday, August 17 (Moon in Virgo) You get rid of a losing proposition and begin a profitable enterprise. On a personal level, you will love and be loved. You might call for "unconditional love," but that might not be possible. You could be traveling with one with whom you are emotionally involved.

Wednesday, August 18 (Moon in Virgo to Libra 6:08 p.m.)   Invent and create. Nothing for you is impossible. Don't wait for others. Do your own thing and make a fresh start. Another Leo is in a romantic mood and could confide, "I can hardly keep my hands off you!" You'll become more familiar with subtle legal nuances. Aquarius helps in this area.

Thursday, August 19 (Moon in Libra)   A family member talks about many things, but finds it difficult to achieve a "central theme." Don't take others or yourself too seriously. The emphasis is on social activity, entertaining, and being entertained. You will be tested and challenged regarding fashion.

Friday, August 20 (Moon in Libra)   Just 24 hours ago, questions concerning your marriage loomed large. Today, you find answers and laugh at your own foibles. Gemini and Sagittarius will be featured, and so will the number 3. Elements of luck ride with you. Trust your hunch and intuitive intellect.

Saturday, August 21 (Moon in Libra to Scorpio 12:35 a.m.)   On this Saturday, complications arise concerning who owns what and what to do about it. The sale or purchase of land or a building is featured. You will be dealing with temperamental people. Know it, and be extremely delicate and diplomatic. A Scorpio plays a featured role.

Sunday, August 22 (Moon in Scorpio)   On this Sunday, you will feel: "At last I belong!" You will be popular and flirtatious. Gemini, Virgo, and Scorpio will figure prominently. The emphasis is on the written word. Take notes of your impressions and opinions; don't neglect your dreams.

Monday, August 23 (Moon in Scorpio to Sagittarius 5:07 a.m.)   You could open the "door to your future." Accent creativity. Accept challenges. Move forward in a confident way. Taurus and Libra play "amazing" roles. Music sounds; dance or march to your own tune. You have permission to sing in or out of the shower!

Tuesday, August 24 (Moon in Sagittarius)   Today will feature a blend of creativity and appreciation of the fine arts. People will ask, "What do you think of this painting or story?" Don't hold back. Express yourself in a frank and fascinating manner. A Pisces is in the picture.

Wednesday, August 25 (Moon in Sagittarius to Capricorn 7:45 a.m.)   This will be one of your most memorable days. Attention revolves around your business, career, and possible promotion. On a personal level, a relationship "sizzles." Don't play games with your emotions; the heart you break could be your own. Your fortunate number is 8.

Thursday, August 26 (Moon in Capricorn)   On this Thursday, keep resolutions about health, including exercise, diet, and better knowledge of nutrition. People who once ignored you could now be at your doorstep. Don't hold a grudge. Welcome this opportunity to make a favorable impression on people ready to become your allies.

Friday, August 27 (Moon in Capricorn to Aquarius 9:07 a.m.)   Within 24 hours, questions concerning legal rights and permissions and marriage will loom large. Today, emphasize independence of thought and of action. Highlight your pioneering spirit and original thinking. A romantic relationship lends spice. It can be exciting and make life worth living.

Saturday, August 28 (Moon in Aquarius) In matters of speculation, stick with number 2. The Aquarius moon represents your seventh house. Be aware of your legal rights and permissions. Focus on your home, marital status, and the ability to make life more exciting and comfortable. A Cancer is involved.

Sunday, August 29 (Moon in Aquarius to Pisces 10:33 a.m.) During a social gathering, you will meet people whose interests are considered "borderline." This means there will be serious discussions of such subjects as reincarnation, numerology, and astrology. You will prove that you understand and that you are no slouch when it comes to occult knowledge.

Monday, August 30 (Moon in Pisces) Last night's full moon fell in Pisces, your eighth house. Focus on mystery and intrigue. Learn more about the assets of your partner or mate. There will be an abundance of creative or sex drive. Protect yourself in emotional clinches. Don't tell all; do not confide or confess.

Tuesday, August 31 (Moon in Pisces to Aries 1:46 p.m.) On this last day of August, you will say, "Life is worth living. I am going to read and write and learn by teaching." In matters of speculation, stick with number 5. A flirtation is serious. Don't go too far, unless you mean to go all the way. A Gemini figures prominently.

SEPTEMBER 2004

Wednesday, September 1 (Moon in Aries) On this first day of the month, you will receive "pleasant news." The Aries moon represents your ninth house. Your popularity increases due to published work. An element of luck rides with you. At the track, choose number 3 post position in the third race.

Thursday, September 2 (Moon in Aries to Taurus 8:16 p.m.)   A secret that had been "locked away" will be in the open. Look behind the scenes. Defend yourself in emotional clinches. Communicate with someone you care about who could be confined to home or hospital. Taurus, Scorpio, and another Leo figure in this scenario.

Friday, September 3 (Moon in Taurus)   You will be promoted. It will be requested that you write your views and opinions. Focus on the learning process, a flirtation, and a possible trip out of town. Gemini, Virgo, and Sagittarius will figure in this scenario. Have luck with number 5.

Saturday, September 4 (Moon in Taurus)   Attention revolves around the cost of remodeling your home. Focus also on your income potential and marital status. You will hear the sound of music; dance or march to your own tune. Get into the rhythm of your life. If diplomatic, you get your way in connection with a family dispute.

Sunday, September 5 (Moon in Taurus to Gemini 6:24 a.m.)   See people the way they are, not merely as you want them to be. The Gemini moon is in your eleventh house. Many of your hopes and wishes will be fulfilled. Not since the first of the month have you been under such auspicious aspects. A Pisces is involved.

Monday, September 6 (Moon in Gemini)   Power play! You will be in a position of authority. Your way is the right way. Be sure your policy is followed. A personal relationship is dotted with controversy, romance, and "true love." Capricorn and Cancer will play outstanding roles.

Tuesday, September 7 (Moon in Gemini to Cancer 6:49 p.m.)   Your wishes come true in an "amazing" way. Use showmanship and publicity to put across your product and ideas. Someone who once scorned you will now beg forgiveness. Be generous, but not naive. Aries and Libra will play major roles.

Wednesday, September 8 (Moon in Cancer)   Highlight inventiveness and the courage of your convictions. Do not wait for others. Take the initiative in making a fresh start, perhaps even starting your own business. Persons who care about you will cooperate and encourage. Lucky lottery: 1, 11, 12, 13, 33, 24.

Thursday, September 9 (Moon in Cancer)   A family secret will be revealed. This will be to your advantage. The emphasis is on building, property, sales, and purchases. What you own represents more value than you expected. You experience good fortune during an auction. A Capricorn is involved.

Friday, September 10 (Moon in Cancer to Leo 7:05 a.m.)   Your cycle is high. Almost effortlessly, you will be at the right place at the "right time." Your personality is strong, almost overwhelming. The emphasis is on humor, versatility, and intellectual curiosity. You will exude an aura of sensuality and sex appeal. Your lucky number is 3.

Saturday, September 11 (Moon in Leo)   On this Saturday, you overcome obstacles, you win friends, and your "love life" will prove exciting. Wear bright colors and make personal appearances. Let the whole world know you are alive and kicking. Taurus and Scorpio will play meaningful roles.

Sunday, September 12 (Moon in Leo to Virgo 5:15 p.m.)   A big money deal is in the offing—don't get in your own way! Discern your fair share, then be sure you obtain it. Not many will oppose you. This is your winning day, and you display winning ways. Gemini, Virgo, and Sagittarius figure in this scenario.

Monday, September 13 (Moon in Virgo)   In matters of speculation, stick with number 6. At the track, choose number 6 post position in the sixth race. Get into your own rhythm. The spotlight will be on your home, beauty, music, and art. Taurus, Libra, and Scorpio will play memorable roles.

Tuesday, September 14 (Moon in Virgo)   A financial transaction takes place in your favor, if you are willing to wait. An element of deception exists. Get the facts and figures. Define terms, perfect techniques, and streamline procedures. A lost article will be retrieved tonight.

Wednesday, September 15 (Moon in Virgo to Libra 12:52 a.m.)   The pressure is on. You will be up to it. Many will rely on you for their emotional and financial welfare. A short trip will involve a Libra who is on your side. The key is to get organized and to recognize priorities. Lucky lottery: 8, 33, 44, 12, 18, 7.

Thursday, September 16 (Moon in Libra)   Complete a mission. Don't stop. Refuse to give up the ship! Your popularity continues. Highlight your versatility and humor. Give full play to your intellectual curiosity. Ask questions of authorities; they will be flattered, not displeased. Know it, and act accordingly.

Friday, September 17 (Moon in Libra to Scorpio 6:24 a.m.)   Make a fresh start. Take the initiative. Do not wait for others. You will be comfortable on home ground, and could make exciting contacts as a result. A love relationship simmers. Whether you like it or not, you are "involved." An Aquarius is represented.

Saturday, September 18 (Moon in Scorpio)   Focus on land, real estate, and locating a home in which you want to settle. Questions about partnership and marriage will dominate. The emphasis is on direction, motivation, and the need for meditation. Capricorn and Cancer will play spectacular roles.

Sunday, September 19 (Moon in Scorpio to Sagittarius 10:28 a.m.)   Good news tonight! Within 24 hours, circumstances take a dramatic turn in your favor. Events will transpire to bring you closer to your ultimate goal. People want to wine and dine you. Many want to be with you because of your ability to make them laugh.

Monday, September 20 (Moon in Sagittarius)   The Sagittarius moon is in your fifth house. This relates to creativity and sex appeal. Focus on change, travel, and a variety of sensations. A young person admires you and says so. No excess modesty, please! A Scorpio is in this picture.

Tuesday, September 21 (Moon in Sagittarius to Capricorn 1:34 p.m.)   Keep plans flexible. Your itinerary will change and so will your instructions. A flirtation gets serious. You will be asking yourself, "Is this love or lust?" Hope that it is a combination of both! You are attracted and will be attractive. A Virgo is involved.

Wednesday, September 22 (Moon in Capricorn)   The focus will be on basic issues that include security and where you live. Questions about marriage will loom large. Your voice will be especially melodious; you have permission to sing in or out of the shower! Your lucky number is 6.

Thursday, September 23 (Moon in Capricorn to Aquarius 4:09 p.m.)   What you need is not too far away. Do not force issues. A surprise presentation tonight will make you happy; be courteous and somewhat modest. Pisces and Virgo will play astonishing roles and have these letters in their names: G, P, Y.

Friday, September 24 (Moon in Aquarius) The spotlight is on public relations as well as legal rights and permissions. The moon in your seventh house represents cooperative efforts, partnership, and marriage. Capricorn and Cancer will figure in today's dynamic scenario and could have these letters in their names: H, Q, Z.

Saturday, September 25 (Moon in Aquarius to Pisces 6:55 p.m.) Idealism rules. You receive inspiration to complete a project that could elevate your prestige. The temptation will be to drop it and to go on to something less difficult or idealistic. Do not let go—don't give up the ship! Have luck with number 9.

Sunday, September 26 (Moon in Pisces) Maintain an aura of mystery. Don't be too available. Make a fresh start. Imprint your style, wear bright colors, and make personal appearances. This day will not be devoid of romance. Keep health resolutions that include exercise, diet, and knowledge of nutrition.

Monday, September 27 (Moon in Pisces to Aries 10:57 p.m.) What had been kept in the background will move forward. You will know what to do. You'll know what you are dealing with, and you'll realize you are very capable. Be "in touch" with one confined to home or hospital. A Cancer is involved.

Tuesday, September 28 (Moon in Aries) The full moon in Aries represents your ninth house. Romance will blossom. The spotlight will also be on travel and publishing. Gemini and Sagittarius play roles in this scenario and could have these letters in their names: C, L, U. Your fortunate number is 3.

Wednesday, September 29 (Moon in Aries) Someone from a foreign land could intrigue and tantalize you. Broaden your horizons; be open-minded. Taurus, Scorpio, and another Leo play exciting roles, and have these letters in their names: D, M, V. It will be necessary to review, to revise, and to rebuild. You will be successful in doing it!

Thursday, September 30 (Moon in Aries to Taurus 5:23 a.m.) On this last day of September, you have more freedom of thought and of action. The Taurus moon represents your tenth house. This equates to production, promotion, and having the authority to do things your way. Gemini, Virgo, and Sagittarius will play unique roles.

OCTOBER 2004

Friday, October 1 (Moon in Taurus) On this first day of October, some of your ambitions will become crystal clear. You will know where you want to go and how to obtain your objective. Taurus, Scorpio, and another Leo will play fascinating roles. Don't back down from a challenge.

Saturday, October 2 (Moon in Taurus to Gemini 2:55 p.m.) Focus on reading and writing, teaching and learning. You will be dealing with stubborn, temperamental, creative people. Make intelligent concessions without abandoning your principles. A flirtation lends spice, but know when to say, "Enough is enough!"

Sunday, October 3 (Moon in Gemini) Stick close to home, if possible. A surprise awaits. You have been asking for a "lucky break," and tonight you get it. Dare to dream! You will have luck in matters of speculation, especially by sticking with number 6. A Libra plays a fascinating role.

Monday, October 4 (Moon in Gemini)   Everything is going your way, if you avoid self-deception. Tonight, you have an aura of glamour, of intrigue. There will be romance. Be sure to see people and relationships in a realistic light. A secret will be revealed, making you happy. Pisces is represented.

Tuesday, October 5 (Moon in Gemini to Cancer 2:53 a.m.)   The pressure is on due to added responsibility; you will be up to any challenge. A romantic relationship "sizzles." You can run, but you cannot hide. You gain confidential information that could be transformed into a profitable enterprise. A Capricorn is involved.

Wednesday, October 6 (Moon in Cancer)   Let go of a situation that finds you being taken for granted. Visit someone temporarily confined to home or hospital. You will be repaid for past endeavors. You will learn again that the "Golden Rule" is alive and kicking. An Aries plays a sensational role.

Thursday, October 7 (Moon in Cancer to Leo 3:22 p.m.)   Within 24 hours, circumstances will take a dramatic turn in your favor. Find out what it is you desire, then take direct action. Don't wait for others. Imprint your own style. Make a fresh start in a new direction. Speak from the heart; avoid heavy lifting.

Friday, October 8 (Moon in Leo)   Focus on direction, motivation, and the need for meditation. Even as you read these lines, circumstances are moving in your favor. Events transpire to bring you closer to your ultimate goal. You will be at the right place at a crucial moment, almost without half trying.

Saturday, October 9 (Moon in Leo)   What a Saturday night! It could be a night of love and laughter. The emphasis is on versatility, diversity, and added popularity. Gemini and Sagittarius will play meaningful roles. What you had been doing merely for fun could turn out to be a paying proposition. Your lucky number is 3.

Sunday, October 10 (Moon in Leo to Virgo 1:58 a.m.)   The element of luck rides with you, especially if you stick with number 4. At the track, choose number 4 post position in the fourth race. What had been rejected could now be accepted. Your spirits will be elevated as a result. A Scorpio figures prominently.

Monday, October 11 (Moon in Virgo)   Do not reject the need for change. You will experience the "adventure of romance." A lost article will be retrieved. Express gratitude, without being obsequious. You gain via the written word. Open the lines of communication. A Virgo is in the picture.

Tuesday, October 12 (Moon in Virgo to Libra 9:30 a.m.)   A relative who had been "out of sight" could make a surprise appearance. Keep plans flexible. A short trip will be part of your scenario. Don't try to figure everything out, and do not attempt to please everyone. Taurus and Libra are involved and have these letters in their names: F, O, X.

Wednesday, October 13 (Moon in Libra)   Emphasize versatility and interest in "mysticism." Someone you admire will confide: "At times, I can hardly keep my hands off you!" Your extrasensory perception is on target; follow your inner feelings. A Pisces plays a major role.

Thursday, October 14 (Moon in Libra to Scorpio 2:09 p.m.)   The new moon and solar eclipse last night occurred in Libra, your third house. This warns you to be extra careful today in traffic and to steer clear of explosives. A disagreement with a relative should not be blown out of proportion. Capricorn and Cancer will play instrumental roles.

Friday, October 15 (Moon in Scorpio) Look beyond the immediate. Your property value will be assessed. Your position is strong, so do not enter negotiations with hat in hand. You have plenty to offer, and others will realize it. Aries and Libra will play "sensational" roles.

Saturday, October 16 (Moon in Scorpio to Sagittarius 4:57 p.m.) Make a fresh start. Hold off on a final decision—you do not possess all the information. A passionate Scorpio could attempt to intimidate you. Regard this with humor; that will be your "best weapon." Aquarius and another Leo also figure in this scenario. Your lucky number is 1.

Sunday, October 17 (Moon in Sagittarius) Focus on creativity, style, and sex appeal. Someone with "young ideas" could become your valuable ally. Questions relate to partnership and marriage. Find out what you really believe via meditation. Capricorn and Cancer will play astounding roles.

Monday, October 18 (Moon in Sagittarius to Capricorn 7:06 p.m.) During a social affair, you could meet someone who physically and mentally attracts you. The experience will be mutual. Bring forth humor and intellectual curiosity. Obtain the answers to questions, not evasions. Gemini and Sagittarius play "mysterious" roles.

Tuesday, October 19 (Moon in Capricorn) Be willing to review and to revise. If you rewrite, you will have success with something that had originally been rejected. Taurus, Scorpio, and another Leo figure prominently and could have these letters in their names: D, M, V.

Wednesday, October 20 (Moon in Capricorn to Aquarius 9:37 p.m.)   A platform that had been weak will be rebuilt. Keep health resolutions that include exercise, diet, and knowledge of nutrition. A relationship that had been broken will be mended by tonight. Gemini, Virgo, and Sagittarius play meaningful roles.

Thursday, October 21 (Moon in Aquarius)   Lie low, play the waiting game. You gain most through diplomacy. You lose most if you attempt to force issues. You find ways to beautify your surroundings and to make your living quarters more comfortable. Taurus, Libra, and Scorpio figure in this scenario.

Friday, October 22 (Moon in Aquarius)   Backstage work would be suitable. You will have access to classified information. Keep secrets sacred. Don't tell all. Do not confide or confess. A secret meeting could relate to a romantic situation. Don't give up something of value for a temporary thrill.

Saturday, October 23 (Moon in Aquarius to Pisces 1:13 a.m.)   The Pisces moon relates to your eighth house. Maintain an aura of mystery, of intrigue. Nothing today will be halfway. Realize it, and don't start something you cannot finish. The key is organization and recognition of priorities. Your lucky number is 8.

Sunday, October 24 (Moon in Pisces)   You finally get credit for your work. Separate yourself from those who take you for granted. Finish what you started two months ago—you could be on the precipice of fame and fortune. An argument with a loved one should not be blown out of proportion. You are due to take a "romantic journey."

Monday, October 25 (Moon in Pisces to Aries 6:24 a.m.)   In answer to your question: Yes, a new outlook will be to your advantage and could lead to prosperity.

Do not underestimate your "invention" or your value. A different kind of romance is on the horizon. Put aside fear, doubt, and suspicion. Another Leo is involved.

Tuesday, October 26 (Moon in Aries)   A long-distance communication will verify your views. This is your day of vindication! Accent original thinking. Imprint your style. Take the initiative in creating your own tradition. Focus on cooperative efforts, civic activity, and your marital status. A Cancer is involved.

Wednesday, October 27 (Moon in Aries to Taurus 1:37 p.m.)   What had been regarded as a "lost cause" will be revived. Within 24 hours, you receive notice of a promotion and a raise in pay. Maintain your emotional equilibrium. What you receive is not a gift—you have earned it! Lucky lottery: 2, 12, 33, 14, 22, 18.

Thursday, October 28 (Moon in Taurus)   Last night's full moon and lunar eclipse fell in Taurus, your tenth house. This relates to your career and to an unusual business opportunity. Previous plans and concepts could be blown out of the water. Don't be discouraged; begin a rebuilding program. Taurus, Scorpio, and another Leo figure in this scenario.

Friday, October 29 (Moon in Taurus to Gemini 11:11 p.m.)   Written words become your great "allies." Take note of impressions, opinions, and dreams. What happens to you will be largely up to you. A Virgo confides an attraction. Be sure this person is free before you reciprocate.

Saturday, October 30 (Moon in Gemini)   Your wishes in connection with your home will be fulfilled; you will beautify your surroundings. A domestic adjustment works out just fine, if you so permit. Make concessions.

You do not have to win every argument. You receive a gift as a peace offering. A Libra is involved.

Sunday, October 31—Daylight Saving Time Ends (Moon in Gemini)   Someone wants to fool you. Protect yourself in emotional clinches. Define terms and get promises in writing. Use your reasoning power. Don't believe everything you hear. It is Halloween to some, but to magicians it is National Magic Day in memory of Houdini. A Virgo plays a "scary" role.

NOVEMBER 2004

Monday, November 1 (Moon in Gemini to Cancer 9:53 a.m.)   You should be happy this Monday. What seemed to be long ago and far away will be available. Many of your hopes and wishes could become realities. Your popularity is on the rise; you will win friends and gain allies. Have luck with number 5.

Tuesday, November 2 (Moon in Cancer)   Your living quarters will be made more comfortable. A Cancer communicates information that will prove valuable. Your powers of persuasion are heightened. You get your way, and your way will be the right way. Taurus and Libra also figure in this scenario.

Wednesday, November 3 (Moon in Cancer to Leo 10:32 p.m.)   You play your best role backstage. Be discreet. Don't tell all; do not confide or confess. Maintain an aura of mystery, of intrigue. Pisces and Virgo will play dynamic roles and could have these letters in their names: G, P, Y. Your fortunate number is 7.

Thursday, November 4 (Moon in Leo)   Your lunar cycle is high, so you will be at the right place at a crucial moment. Deal gingerly with Capricorn and Cancer. Your personality is overwhelming; you exude an aura of sensuality and sex appeal. Protect yourself in emotional clinches. Be selective and discriminating.

Friday, November 5 (Moon in Leo)   Accent universal appeal. You are due for recognition and could be invited to visit a distant city or foreign nation. Steer clear of those who take you for granted. Aries and Libra play fascinating roles and have these letters in their names: I and R.

Saturday, November 6 (Moon in Leo to Virgo 10:00 a.m.)   The answer to your question: This is the time to initiate a project. Highlight independence of thought, of action. Don't wait for others. Make a fresh start. Create your own tradition. Aquarius and another Leo play dramatic roles. Your lucky number is 1.

Sunday, November 7 (Moon in Virgo)   Attention revolves around where you live and your marital status. A genuine bargain is available in connection with beautifying your surroundings. Home repairs are necessary, including plumbing. What was lost 24 hours ago will be retrieved. A Cancer is involved.

Monday, November 8 (Moon in Virgo to Libra 6:23 p.m.)   Good news is received concerning your income potential. Money will come from a surprise source. Display your talent and product. Use your natural instincts for publicity and showmanship. Gemini and Sagittarius figure prominently and have these letters in their names: C, L, U.

Tuesday, November 9 (Moon in Libra)   A short trip could involve a relative who is a musician. Take special care in traffic. Avoid scattering your forces. Keep recent resolutions about exercise and nutrition. Taurus, Scorpio, and another Leo play fascinating roles. Stick with number 4.

Wednesday, November 10 (Moon in Libra to Scorpio 11:06 p.m.)   Read and learn. Give full play to your intellectual curiosity. Excitement exists due to change, travel, and a variety of experiences. Written material will be of great importance. Get your thoughts and ideas on paper. A member of the opposite sex has romance in mind.

Thursday, November 11 (Moon in Scorpio)   You will meet some opposition, but at the same time you gain allies. Be ready to receive important guests at home. Deal gingerly with a Scorpio who is subject to temperamental outbursts. You receive a gift, a luxury item that helps beautify your home.

Friday, November 12 (Moon in Scorpio)   The new moon in Scorpio represents your fourth house. Stick close to familiar ground. There will be plenty of activity at home. Define terms. Obtain answers, not evasions. Pisces and Virgo will edge their way into your scenario.

Saturday, November 13 (Moon in Scorpio to Sagittarius 12:57 a.m.)   Creative juices are stimulated. Accent original thinking. Realize that you exude sex appeal. Protect yourself in emotional clinches. Don't give up something of value for a temporary thrill. You will be "promoted," and the pressure will be on as a result.

Sunday, November 14 (Moon in Sagittarius)   Look beyond the immediate. Steer clear of an avaricious individual who takes you for granted. Your presence will be required during a unique ceremony. Show gratitude without being obsequious. Aries and Libra will play valuable roles.

Monday, November 15 (Moon in Sagittarius to Capricorn 1:34 a.m.)   Shake off lethargy. Make a fresh start in a new direction. Wear brighter colors; make personal appearances. You might be asking, "Is this love or lust?" An Aquarius and another Leo will figure prominently and could have these letters in their names: A, S, J.

Tuesday, November 16 (Moon in Capricorn)   You will be reunited with a relative who declares, "Home sweet home!" Focus on direction, motivation, and the need for meditation. Answers will come from within, if you so permit. The question of marital status will loom large. A Capricorn plays a role.

Wednesday, November 17 (Moon in Capricorn to Aquarius 2:40 a.m.)   Lie low; leave the details for another time. Social activities accelerate. Steer clear of a Sagittarius who wants to argue. Questions will arise about legal rights and permissions. Keep records and books up-to-date. Have luck with number 3.

Thursday, November 18 (Moon in Aquarius)   Join forces with Taurus, Scorpio, and another Leo. Attention will revolve around partnership, legal affairs, and marriage. Maintain your emotional equilibrium. This could be a memorable, successful day if you so permit. You pass the "test" with flying colors.

Friday, November 19 (Moon in Aquarius to Pisces 5:38 a.m.)   The Pisces moon represents your eighth house. You will delve into mysteries and be fascinated by metaphysical subjects. Read and write, teach and learn. A flirtation is serious, and could get hot and heavy. Don't break hearts; the heart you break could be your own.

Saturday, November 20 (Moon in Pisces)   This is one Saturday night you won't soon forget! Personal subjects

298

will be discussed with someone who is practically a stranger. Proposals are received that involve your business, career, and marriage. Lucky lottery: 6, 33, 22, 8, 5, 14.

Sunday, November 21 (Moon in Pisces to Aries 11:12 a.m.) Within 24 hours, you receive a long-distance communication that verifies your views. This is your day of vindication! Avoid self-deception. See people and relationships in a realistic light. Keep some secrets sacred. Don't tell all; do not confide or confess.

Monday, November 22 (Moon in Aries) This is your "power play" day! Take the initiative. Contact someone who could represent your talent or product in a foreign land. Focus on promotion and added responsibility. Look to a love relationship that intensifies. A Cancer is involved.

Tuesday, November 23 (Moon in Aries to Taurus 7:16 p.m.) Finish what you start. Don't quit now. Do not give up the ship. Dare to dream. Some of your "fantasies" could become realities. Ignore someone who has little talent or faith. Aries and Libra will figure in this scenario.

Wednesday, November 24 (Moon in Taurus) You will be engaged in getting a creative project "off the ground." Take the initiative. Don't wait to be told. Imprint your own style; make personal appearances. A flirtation that begins mildly could get too hot not to cool down. Another Leo is involved.

Thursday, November 25 (Moon in Taurus) You will handle Thanksgiving activities with great aplomb. Someone you admire will pay a meaningful compliment. Be close to your family; discuss the "true meaning" of the holiday. In romance, the spark that brought you together in the first place will reignite.

Friday, November 26 (Moon in Taurus to Gemini 5:25 a.m.)   The full moon in Gemini is in your eleventh house. Elements of timing and of luck ride with you. Your powers of persuasion are strong; you will convince others that your point of view is the correct one. At the track, choose number 3 post position in the third race.

Saturday, November 27 (Moon in Gemini)   A hyperactive relative will say things that should be kept off the record. Be a good listener, but don't believe everything you hear. Keep recent diet resolutions. Taurus, Scorpio, and another Leo will play sensational roles.

Sunday, November 28 (Moon in Gemini to Cancer 5:11 p.m.)   Within 24 hours, your prestige moves upward. You finish a creative project and successfully meet a challenge. A flirtation lends spice, but know when to say, "Enough is enough!" Gemini, Virgo, and Sagittarius will figure in this scenario.

Monday, November 29 (Moon in Cancer)   Attention revolves around your home, family, and major domestic issues. You could change your residence or marital status. Be diplomatic; realize it is not necessary to win every argument. Broken chinaware can be replaced; there is no need to brood. Libra is represented.

Tuesday, November 30 (Moon in Cancer)   On this last day of November, be understanding of a loved one who confesses an "indiscretion." Secrets will be revealed; you will be trusted to be discreet. Realize the past is gone, and you should look forward to the future. Pisces and Virgo will play helpful roles.

Wednesday, December 1 (Moon in Cancer to Leo 5:50 a.m.)   Reach an agreement with your family about holiday festivities. Prepare your invitation list; review which presents are needed for each person. A domestic adjustment that has been long overdue takes place. Taurus, Libra, and Scorpio play major roles. Your lucky number is 6.

Thursday, December 2 (Moon in Leo)   Your lunar cycle is high. Hopes, dreams, and wishes can come true, if you so permit. Avoid self-deception; see people and relationships as they are, not merely as you wish they could be. Your personality is overwhelming; you exude an aura of sensuality and sex appeal.

Friday, December 3 (Moon in Leo to Virgo 6:01 p.m.)   Within 24 hours, a financial transaction will be completed. You have much to offer. Others are aware of it. Proceed accordingly. Exude an aura of confidence. Capricorn and Cancer will play fascinating roles. Have luck with number 8.

Saturday, December 4 (Moon in Virgo)   A lively Saturday night! A special relationship could begin or end. The good news is that a money dispute will be settled. Follow your heart, be idealistic. Aries and Libra will play major roles and have these letters in their names: I and R.

Sunday, December 5 (Moon in Virgo)   Put aside previous notions. Be inventive. Realize that nothing is impossible. Spiritual values surface. Take the initiative. Make a fresh start in a new direction. Special note: Protect your right eye from danger. Another Leo figures in this scenario.

Monday, December 6 (Moon in Virgo to Libra 3:47 a.m.) Attention will revolve around your home, family, and a decision whether to "go or stay." Stick to familiar ground; the grass may appear greener across the way, but appearances can be deceiving. Capricorn and Cancer will play "amazing" roles.

Tuesday, December 7 (Moon in Libra) Be free to ask questions about this historic date. Find out about your own and the nation's security. Social life accelerates. Your popularity is on the rise. Gemini and Sagittarius play fascinating roles. Your fortunate number is 3.

Wednesday, December 8 (Moon in Libra to Scorpio 9:45 a.m.) Attend to basics that include home repairs. Revise, review, and rebuild; make this your makeover day. What had been turned down could now be accepted, if you so permit. Taurus, Scorpio, and another Leo will play major roles.

Thursday, December 9 (Moon in Scorpio) Keep plans flexible. A surprise trip could be on the agenda. A family member presents a peace offering, perhaps a luxury item. Be gracious; extend the hand of friendship. What had been lost and had sentimental value will be retrieved. Express gratitude, without being obsequious.

Friday, December 10 (Moon in Scorpio to Sagittarius 11:55 a.m.) The emphasis is on your ability to beautify your surroundings. Make your home more interesting; hang pictures and posters. In dealings with others, be diplomatic without abandoning your principles. You win a major concession, but don't attempt to win every argument.

Saturday, December 11 (Moon in Sagittarius) A romantic Saturday night! Give free rein to your emotions, but do make room for logic. Refuse to fall victim to self-deception. The focus is also on creative endeavors; finding a profitable outlet for your talent. Lucky lottery: 7, 12, 22, 18, 5, 40.

Sunday, December 12 (Moon in Sagittarius to Capricorn 11:42 a.m.) The new moon in Sagittarius last night accents your fifth house. This could mean a new love or a relighting of the spark that brought the two of you together. Focus on children, challenge, change, and a variety of sensations. A Capricorn is in the picture.

Monday, December 13 (Moon in Capricorn) Let go of a losing proposition. Don't let others take you for granted. Keep recent health resolutions that include exercise, diet, and nutrition. A long-distance communication is necessary to verify your views. An Aries plays a major role.

Tuesday, December 14 (Moon in Capricorn to Aquarius 11:10 a.m.) Make a fresh start. Emphasize independence of thought and of action. Avoid heavy lifting. Be the leader; don't wait for others. Let go of preconceived notions. Be inventive, creative, and, if necessary, dramatic. Another Leo is involved.

Wednesday, December 15 (Moon in Aquarius) Lie low, play the waiting game. Check legal rights and permissions. Avoid self-deception. See people and relationships as they exist, not merely as you wish they could be. Your marital status will be a question that looms large. A Cancer is involved.

Thursday, December 16 (Moon in Aquarius to Pisces 12:24 p.m.) Be sure you're on the "right side of the law." Overcome a tendency to play games with emotions. Don't break hearts; the heart you break could be your own. Proposals received could involve business, career, and marriage.

Friday, December 17 (Moon in Pisces)   Keep some secrets sacred. Don't tell all; do not confide or confess. Someone close to you might attempt to "borrow" your signature. It might not be easy to say, "No," but you should do it. Money is involved—if you are not wise, you will pay a dear price.

Saturday, December 18 (Moon in Pisces to Aries 4:52 p.m.)   In answer to your question: This is the time to make a change. A trip out of town could be necessary. Read and write, teach and learn. A flirtation lends spice, but know when to say, "Enough is enough!" A Gemini plays a major role.

Sunday, December 19 (Moon in Aries)   Spiritual values surge forth. Share your experience with a family member. You receive a surprise gift, a luxury item that helps beautify your home. Tonight, you reunite with a friend who has been absent from your life. Libra is represented.

Monday, December 20 (Moon in Aries)   Keep your feet on the ground today. Be sure plans are realistic. There will be much illusion, so don't proceed until you get promises and commitments in writing. Don't be too available; maintain an aura of mystery and exclusivity.

Tuesday, December 21 (Moon in Aries to Taurus 12:52 a.m.)   A broken promise will be mended. Your views will be vindicated, and as a result, you will be handsomely rewarded. A relationship grows hot and heavy. If you are not serious, it is best to move on. Capricorn and Cancer will play outstanding roles.

Wednesday, December 22 (Moon in Taurus)   Finish what you start. You are on the right track and your way today is the right way. Someone you helped in the past will return the favor. What begins as friendship could be turned into a "hot romance." Lucky lottery: 45, 13, 18, 22, 11, 9.

Thursday, December 23 (Moon in Taurus to Gemini 11:33 a.m.)   Within 24 hours, many of your fondest hopes and wishes could become realities. Find out what it is you really need, then make a list. Elements of timing and of luck will ride with you. Emphasize originality; do not copy others.

Friday, December 24 (Moon in Gemini)   Be with your family, if possible. You will remember this Christmas Eve with pleasure; gifts received far exceed expectations. You will be reassured that your love is not unrequited. The true spirit of the holiday will become crystal clear. An Aquarius figures in this scenario.

Saturday, December 25 (Moon in Gemini to Cancer 11:39 p.m.)   On this Christmas Day, the realization hits home that many of your fondest hopes and wishes are being fulfilled. Relax from holiday tensions. Ask questions; obtain answers, not evasions. Go over your plan for New Year's Eve. A Sagittarius plays a key role.

Sunday, December 26 (Moon in Cancer)   The full moon in Cancer represents your twelfth house. A family secret is featured and will dominate today's scenario. You have long learned that no person is perfect; don't expect one close to you to reach that impossible level. A Scorpio plays the top role.

Monday, December 27 (Moon in Cancer)   You wake up with an idea that can be transformed into a profitable enterprise. Get your thoughts on paper; make note of your dreams. If a dream is properly interpreted, it could be the door to your future. Gemini, Virgo, and Sagittarius play instrumental roles.

Tuesday, December 28 (Moon in Cancer to Leo 12:15 p.m.)   Your cycle moves up. Circumstances will turn in your favor. Wear bright colors; make personal appearances. New Year's Eve arrangements are being made; be an active participant. Taurus and Libra will play significant roles. Your lucky number is 6.

Wednesday, December 29 (Moon in Leo)   Define terms; outline boundaries. Events will transpire to bring you closer to your ultimate goal. Almost effortlessly, you will be at the right place at a special moment. Someone behind the scenes wants to "tell you something." A Pisces plays a dynamic role.

Thursday, December 30 (Moon in Leo)   A power play day. You will have the authority to do things your way. Let it be known: "It is my way or the highway!" A relationship is strong, but carries with it responsibility. Many will rely upon you for their emotional and financial welfare. Although the pressure is on, you will be up to it.

Friday, December 31 (Moon in Leo to Virgo 12:34 a.m.) Steer clear of people who drink too much. This can be one of your most pleasant New Year's Eves, if you so permit. You will hear words of love and romance; don't believe everything you hear. An Aries figures prominently.

HAPPY NEW YEAR!

ABOUT THE AUTHOR

Born on August 5, 1926, in Philadelphia, Sydney Omarr was the only person ever given full-time duty in the U.S. Army as an astrologer. He also is regarded as the most erudite astrologer of our time and the best known, through his syndicated column (300 newspapers) and his radio and television programs (he was Merv Griffin's "resident astrologer"). Omarr has been called the most "knowledgeable astrologer since Evangeline Adams." His forecasts of Nixon's downfall, the end of World War II in mid-August of 1945, the assassination of John F. Kennedy, Roosevelt's election to the fourth term and his death in office . . . these and many others are on the record and quoted enough to be considered "legendary."

ABOUT THE SERIES

This is one of a series of twelve
Day-by-Day Astrological Guides
for the signs of 2004
by Sydney Omarr.

AMERICA'S #1
ASTROLOGER
LIFTS SPIRITS

SYDNEY OMARR'S®
SPIRIT GUIDES

Nationally syndicated astrologist Sydney Omarr® shows
how you can contact your guardian spirit to awaken your
spirituality and actualize your potential.

• Learn what your sun sign reveals about your identity—
and how to make it work for you
• Tap the energy and unique advice of your sun sign's polarity
• Embrace your abilities and allow them to develop fully
• Gain personal growth and meaning
• Enrich your life and loves

209656

Available September 2003

Available wherever books are sold, or
to order call: 1-800-788-6262

SYDNEY OMARR'S®
ASTROLOGICAL GUIDE
FOR YOU IN 2004

SYDNEY OMARR®

Brimming with tantalizing projections, this
amazing single-volume guide contains advice
on romantic matters, career moves, travel,
even finance, trends and world events. Find
year overviews and detailed month-by-month
predictions for every sign. Omarr reveals
everything new under the stars, including:

- Attraction and romance
- New career opportunities for success in the future
- Lucky numbers and memorable days for every month of
  the year
- Global shifts and world forecasts

...and much more! Don't face the future
blindly—let the Zodiac be your guide.

209214

Available July 2003